SEKTOR 47

SEKTOR 47

N.N. JEHANGIR

The Book Guild Ltd

First published in Great Britain in 2024 by
The Book Guild Ltd
Unit E2 Airfield Business Park,
Harrison Road, Market Harborough,
Leicestershire. LE16 7UL
Tel: 0116 2792299
www.bookguild.co.uk
Email: info@bookguild.co.uk
X: @bookguild

Typeset in 11pt Minion Pro

Printed on FSC accredited paper
Printed and bound in Great Britain by 4edge

ISBN 978 1916668 676

British Library Cataloguing in Publication Data.
A catalogue record for this book is available from the British Library.

To my Mother:
Everything I am, everything I have achieved, began with you.
I love you more than anything.
Thank you for being my mentor, my reader, my first editor and my mother.

CHAPTER ONE

Sektor 47

Saída ran across the red earth, as fast as her little legs would carry her. She saw the long line leading to the town square. She clutched her bucket tight and took a deep breath. She had barely made it in time for the water ration this week. Young children, like her, held bottles and buckets and waited silently in a line. Redcloaks lounged around the square. Some guarded the water pump, others glared at the kids who came up to fill their ration of water. Some Redcloaks strutted about, waving their batons, searching for the slightest provocation. The children watched the batons, their eyes glued to the brutal shock-sticks as they pulsed and crackled.

Saída joined the other children in the line, trying to look unobtrusive. They were supposed to be quiet. Some of the younger children up ahead snickered, playing a game. Saída's gaze flicked towards the Redcloaks. She tightened her grip on the bucket handle. She held her breath. A Redcloak yanked one of the boys out of the line. The other boy shrank in silence. He turned his back on his friend, his shoulders hunched, his head bowed. The other boy was already on the ground and when he tried to rise to his feet, a swift kick from the Redcloak threw him back to the ground. The boy whimpered as the Redcloak cracked his knuckles with a sneer. Saída focused on her task, struggling to block out the noise of the boy's punishment, his wails of pain. The Redcloak had decided to be merciful. After all, he hadn't used his baton. Saída watched the water steadily pour into her bucket, concentrating on the noise made by the trickle of water. She caught a glimpse of the wounded boy. She bit her tongue to keep from crying out. His face was... broken. Bloody. Disfigured. The Redcloak wasn't done. Saída blinked away tears. The boy's cries had stopped but the Redcloak still wasn't done. He made sure everybody knew he was not done. Saída kept her head down and walked away as fast as she could.

Miles away from the town square, Saída ripped off the cloth face mask that Uncle Abbas had given her and hurled. The smog that came from the factories in the outer city travelled all the way into their little town, squeezing their lungs and stinging their eyes raw. She retched again, keeping the bucket well out of the way. She couldn't get the image of the boy out of her head. The way his face looked. Saída fought the bile that rose in her throat and grabbed the bucket, continuing home towards Uncle Abbas's bar. The water sloshed in the bucket, collecting flecks of ash that fell in due to the smog. Saída looked up at the grey, cloudy mass that obscured the morning sky and wept.

At the end of the dusty road stood Uncle Abbas's bar, a

rickety shack far above the mines. Redcloak guards posted nearby would usually come and demand drinks during or after their shifts. Uncle Abbas had to comply, lest they were subjected to more punishment. This was all she knew. A life ruled by the Redcloaks. *Colonisers*, Uncle Abbas had called them. Invaders who had stolen their world long before even Uncle himself had been born.

As she approached the bar, Saída heard loud voices and the chatter of excited Redcloaks. She peered through the old windows and saw Uncle Abbas pouring drinks for a group of them. He spotted Saída and she saw fear in his brown eyes. She nodded to indicate that she understood. She snuck around to the back of the bar, toward the thin ledge that protruded behind the building.

Saída took a deep breath and secured herself onto the narrow ledge, trying not to look down at the deep drop below. She held onto her bucket, careful not to spill the precious water, and skirted around to the window at the back of the bar. She had to be careful of her footing. One wrong move and she would fall into the mining pit below. The window was open, as always. Saída inched towards it, one careful step at a time.

She put her hand on the windowsill, then one leg after the other, climbed inside. She tried pulling her bucket in after her, but it was stuck; caught under the jutting windowsill on the outside. Saída clasped the handle with both hands and tried shifting the bucket, but it was difficult to get it unjammed. Saída tried to unhook the bucket, but the sight of the drop below hit her with vertigo. She shut her eyes and pulled at the bucket once more, sending drops of water everywhere. She had pulled harder than she had meant to and fell backwards with a thud, still clutching something. The bucket handle. She rushed to the window with a cry, but the bucket had already fallen into the pit below.

There would be no more water rations that week.

Uncle Abbas found Saída crying softly in the corner of the small room, the bucket handle at her feet. She didn't look at him, but she felt his hand on her head, reassuring her.

"It's alright, beti," he said. "We will make do."

She had heard those words many times, but it was getting harder to believe them. She looked up at Uncle Abbas with teary eyes and hugged him, wailing into his soft, comforting belly. He held her in his arms, shielding her from the world. Saída knew how difficult she had made things, but he would never hold it against her. After all, it was just the two of them, together in an unforgiving world.

CHAPTER TWO

Sektor 31-B

Saída awoke with her mouth tasting of regret. An unwelcome residue from the dreams her memory had conjured. She was twenty-three that year, but no matter how much time had passed, she couldn't forget those early years of her life. Her helplessness. Her fears. Raindrops landed on her skin. She had still not gotten used to the coolness of rain, its wetness and the delicious petrichor that accompanied it. How could she, after living on Sektor 47, with its perpetual pollution and dead, red earth? She lay there unmoving, under her favourite tree, feeling the miracle of gentle raindrops on her face, calming her. Sektor 31-B, or Little Hal as the locals had nicknamed it, was one of her favourite places in the galaxy. Here, on a tiny hill overlooking a city on a tiny moon, she had found a comfortable spot in the galaxy. It rained often, and the grass was always lush, smelling rich and green. It was *green*. It was *life*.

A familiar mechanical whirring prompted Saída to lazily open an eye. She spotted her android partner, Rodok sitting a few feet away, near some wildflowers.

"*Our* target *is* on *the* move," he buzzed. Saída closed her eye when a rogue ray of sunlight bounced off Rodok's extensively polished, but aged, black chassis. The rain was letting up.

"Let him sweat a bit. We've got five more minutes in us," she said.

"*Let* us *not* waste *the* shards *we* spent *on* that *informant* and *his* overpriced *scans*," said Rodok, clicking a few buttons on his human-like mechanical arm, sending Saída a holofeed directly to her prosthetic eye.

Saída groaned. She hated when he did that. Her left eye, a crimson prosthetic, displayed the holofeed to her in full colour. A man in his mid-twenties, lean build, and brown hair, lumbered around a street full of vendors and not so subtle dealers. He wore an ugly grey jacket with a faded print. He was looking to purchase a contraband shipment in the city below the hill.

"Should we let him get in on some deals?" asked Saída. "Rack up a higher bounty?"

Rodok buzzed a monotone chuckle, though it was more akin to the grinding of gears than any human expression.

"Better *not*. *The* Guild *will* not *pay* us *extra*."

Saída frowned. Yeah. Probably not.

"Can you keep the drone fixed on our guy? We don't wanna lose him on our way back down to the city."

"We *will* not *lose* him."

"Well, don't make me root for him." Saída smirked.

6

Rodok rotated his head one-eighty degrees then snapped it back. His version of a grin. While the rest of his body was clearly designed to mimic a human-like appearance, his head was the exception. A sharp, pointed, featureless face, and a single red eye that flitted around his head, using the myriad grooves carved into his metallic face.

Saída got up, patted off the grass from her coat and hair. She scowled. Lying in the grass always came at the disadvantage of finding very noticeable green intermingled with the curly black mess of her hair. Very unprofessional. What would their target think?

"The flowers will be here when you get back, Rodok," said Saída.

"*Indeed. They are growing well.*"

"We can still get a terrarium for the *Lancer* you know," said Saída as they walked down the hill, back into the city below. "We could grow some herbs. Maybe get some well-seasoned food for a change. I'm tired of eating bland food like the assholes on Sektor Prime. No seasoning at all. And don't get me started on the crusty ration bars…"

"*Hmm. No, I think not. Suffer more.*"

Saída grinned.

The city was loud as always. Droves of people walking through the busy streets. The sounds of distant barking and vehicles gliding across roads filled the air. Smoke rose out of food stalls on the side of the roads and people chatted their days away. It was no surprise to Saída though. The whole moon was akin to an extremely dense, multi-layered agora, where goods were bought and sold en masse; people mingled and networked and only a small handful really managed to profit off of the commercial chaos. Little Hal was one of those Sektors where people got connecting space flights or waited to have their ships refuelled, before heading out to other, more business- or luxury-oriented worlds. It also made great cover for smugglers. If there was any reason for their target to be here today, it was because he already had a shipment of contraband he was going after. At least according to their informant. Of course, the bounty wasn't the real reason Saída had come for him.

"Weapons or drugs?" whispered Saída, as they walked through the crowds. Rodok always attracted strange looks. So did she. Not many people looked like her around this part of the galaxy.

"*What?*"

"Weapons or drugs. What's the guy dealing in, do you think?"

"*Going* off *the* files *sent* to *us* by *the* Guild, *I* would *think* drugs. *Easy* to *hide*. Also, *he* has *been* incarcerated *for* drug-trafficking *before*."

Saída nodded along, pretending she already knew all that information.

"You *should* have *read* the *files*," he chided.

Saída scoffed. "I did."

"You *skimmed*."

"Pfft. That's good enough. Besides, all that really matters is that he's a Voidstrider."

Saída nearly spat the word out. The Voidstriders were an up-and-coming pirate gang. Nothing special in the criminal underworld, but they had a knack for being elusive. Especially their leader.

Rodok's eye moved across the grooves on his blank, expressionless face towards the back of his head, so he could look Saída in the eye.

Up ahead, their target was sipping a green beverage in front of a restaurant, loitering near a visibly agitated vendor's stall. He was trying to look inconspicuous, while the old man selling juice tried to get him to move on and make way for new customers. The holofeed in her eye showed Saída a top-down angle of the street, thanks to Rodok's miniature drone, which flew overhead. There were two ways out, no way to box him in if both she and Rodok approached from the centre.

"Rodok," she said, pointing with her head.

Rodok whirred in understanding. The two of them split up, Rodok took a side road to flank from the left, while Saída continued from the main road.

Saída tried to stay incognito, but her brown complexion stood out amongst the sea of white faces. It wasn't hard to figure out she was a bounty hunter from her get-up either. She wore a worn leather coat over blast-resistant armour. The target noticed her the moment she got too close.

"Shit. He's seen us," Saída grumbled into the comms in her silver earring. Rodok chortled in response.

The target tossed his drink away and turned to run but stopped when he noticed Rodok stalking towards him from the left. Blocked off on both ends, he slammed through the door of the restaurant and bolted. Saída followed in after him, following the glances of shocked customers towards an exit at the back of the shop. It led her to a set of stairs which took her up to the roof.

The target was waiting for her and attacked as soon

as she walked through the roof exit, but Saída had been expecting the strike. She ducked and swept the man's legs, dropping him to the floor. Then she punched him in the face, knocking his head against the hard surface. Rodok followed in shortly after, and lifted the man up, allowing Saída to cuff him.

"You're coming with us, buddy," Saída said, searching his pockets and confiscating the contraband he had on him, a pack of red powder called Firedust.

"His *name* is *Mac*," said Rodok.

"Rodok, I don't care about his name. I only care that he's a Voidstrider."

Mac was reeling from the blow but still lucid enough to spit at the ground, swearing at her. She punched him in the gut, causing him to keel over.

Mac was getting ready to yell another slur but stopped when Saída shoved her pistol under his chin.

"Go on," she goaded. "*Say it.*"

Mac raised his bound arms in surrender. "P-please..." he managed.

Saída smacked the butt of her pistol against his face, knocking him to the ground. She squatted beside him as Rodok placed one of his metallic feet firmly on Mac's chest.

Mac howled in pain, but Saída had no patience for pitiful theatrics, and gave him another smack.

"Digby Hickston. I know you're one of his pirates. Where is he, Mac?"

"Who? I've got no idea what you mea—"

"Don't bullshit me, Mac. I've seen scans of you with a package bearing the Hickston crest. I know you're his man."

This was it. This is what all the shards, all the leads

had been leading up to. Saída's informant had been right on the money. Here he was, a Voidstrider, one of Digby's pirate goons, and he would lead her straight to him.

Mac's eyes betrayed his thoughts. Uncertainty. She could push him.

"You lead me to Digby, and I'll let you live."

"I swear, I don't—" Mac squirmed under Rodok's foot.

Rodok applied pressure to Mac's chest, causing him to yell out in pain.

"Talk and maybe my friend won't turn your ribs to dust," threatened Saída, gesturing with her pistol.

"Screw you," spat Mac.

"Rodok, two or three ribs."

"Just *two* or *three*?" Rodok asked.

"Alright, alright! I'll talk. I'll talk," yelped Mac.

Saída laughed. "Every time."

"*Matthias* will *not* find *this* as *humorous* as *you*," muttered Rodok.

"Yeah, well, Matthias is an asshole."

Saída turned back to Mac, watching him writhe like a maggot under Rodok's foot.

"Digby, I don't know where he is, *but…* but I can tell you where I dropped the package off," pleaded Mac.

Saída shook her head. "I don't care about pirate contraband, Mac. I want to find Digby."

Mac raised his arms. "It ain't contraband, it's worth way more shards. It's a medallion. I checked. Gotta be worth more than the bounty on my head, right?"

Saída's eyes widened. "A medallion? He gave you his *medallion*?" She looked at Rodok. "The Hickston medallion, Rodok," she whispered.

"*We* may *not* need *Digby* after *all,*" buzzed Rodok.

Saída closed her eyes and took a deep breath. With the medallion she would finally have her ticket back home. She thought of Uncle Abbas and smiled.

"That's g-good, right? I'll give you the signal ID so you can track it. S-so you'll let me go now, right?" Mac said.

Saída opened her eyes. "I said I wouldn't kill you, Mac. Never said I'd let you go."

*

In the darkness of space hovered a massive space station, home to the Bounty Hunters Guild. The space station was suspended by a single ring that rotated in its centre, funnelling artificial gravity into it, keeping it anchored in the void. A beacon to bounty hunters everywhere, the Needle was a silver obelisk that shone like the stars around it. One of the last remnants of the pre-colonial era, the names of its architects and the nature of its purpose had been lost forever. It hovered in Augustine Territory, near one of the commercial colonies of the Grand Design. Every established bounty hunter in the galaxy was affiliated with the Guild in some way. That was partly why Saída was able to find steady work there as a bounty hunter. Enough that it helped her and Rodok survive.

Saída's ship docked inside the hangar of the Needle. Walking down the ramp and across the ship, Saída brushed her hand against the length of its hull. The word "*LanceR*" was painted across the hull in faded maroon. The 'R' at the end was a lighter shade of red and was an obviously late addition. She and Rodok walked through the hangar depressurisation chamber and into the lobby of the Needle and Saída squinted. The interior was still an eyesore. Bright white lights lit the Needle. The walls in the lobby looked like they were made of marble and red carpeted floors replaced the metallic floor of the hangar. In the lower levels were the prison cells. The lights were always bright, in order to keep the prisoners awake. Tired. Manic. Until they were ready to be transferred to a Prison Sektor. There was no rest to be found here, not for the prisoners, not for the guards and not for the Warden of the Needle, and head of the Guild, Matthias. Most of the Guild's bounty hunters never stayed longer than they had to. Saída was no different.

She took the main elevator up to the very top of the Needle, passing the floors near the top where the bureaucratic pen-pushers had their offices and sorted out the day-to-day minutiae of the Needle's operations. What bounties were worth, what bounty hunters were supposed to earn, the ever-evolving database of criminal scum and traitors of the Kaiser's will. That was at least how Saída assumed they maintained a balance between their vigilante justice and the Grand Design's own military forces. The elevator slid open at the top and Saída walked forward, Rodok and Mac in tow. At the other end of the hallway, Saída saw another elevator. Both led down to the lobby. In the centre, the hallway converged towards the right, leading to the head of the Guild, the Warden's office. The walls in the hallway at the top were made of synthmetal glass, which made it look like they were walking on the stars. Saída looked out to see the vast expanse of space before them. The only thing separating it from her was the glass.

The Warden and Guildmaster, tall and lanky with pale

skin, was waiting for them in his office. Behind his desk, the wall was all made of the same glass as the hallway. The rest of the office was designed to emulate the marble aesthetic of the lobby, but through her prosthetic eye, Saída could see it wasn't real, but a thin layer of synthetic marble-like material over the mechanical walls of the Needle, full of panels and wiring and circuits flowing into each other like an ever-growing web. Matthias had hung up various paintings and framed scanographs of him meeting with important officials from around the galaxy. Saída resisted the urge to roll her eyes when she spotted Matthias grinning like an idiot while meeting Archbishop Augustine in one of them.

"Matthias," said Saída. "Got another dreg for you."

Rodok stayed quiet, but gripped Mac's shoulder firmly, keeping him centred.

Matthias grumbled and scowled behind his spectacles.

"Thirty shards," he said.

"Eat shit," said Saída.

Rodok rolled his eye. Saída knew he hated the haggling between her and Matthias.

Matthias ignored the insult and added a note to the document he was working on at his terminal and then he repeated:

"Thirty shards."

"Matthias, I wouldn't kick your ass for thirty shards," said Saída.

"Hm. How much were you expecting for a low-level thug like him?"

"He's a Voidstrider."

Matthias sneered. "The Voidstriders are a joke. Low-level pirate trash isn't worth more than thirty."

Saída clenched her fists. Digby's man had to be worth more than fifty shards at least, but Matthias had a nasty habit of undercutting her every time. Still, the last thing she wanted was to let Matthias catch on to why she was after Mac in the first place.

"Low-level or not, I don't see any of your boys cleaning up the trash around those Sektors," said Saída, keeping Mac's connection to Digby to herself.

"So *upset*," said Matthias with a chuckle. "You need to calm down. I'm giving you what your work is worth."

Saída bristled at that. She'd made the right decision to leave her gun on the *Lancer*.

"I'll take fifty shards, no less."

Matthias rose from his seat and walked around his desk. Hands placed behind his back, he stepped toward her, close enough to whisper to Saída.

"Do you really think you're in any position to be making demands? Don't forget, you're employed as a contractor. You have no real status here. Besides," he said, leaning in closer. "We both know you don't want any Redcloaks on your tail."

Saída glared at Matthias, who walked back to his desk smiling.

"Thirty-five," he said. "I'm not completely heartless."

Saída turned around and walked out of his office, still seething. Rodok and Mac followed. They went to the detention level of the station and got their new prisoner ready for processing.

"For what it's worth, I also think I'm worth at least fifty shards," Mac said.

"Shut the hell up, Mac," snapped Saída.

"But—"

"We *do* not *care*, Mac," said Rodok.

Mac sulked, and the detention guards scanned his retinas and took him into processing. Once the guards took Mac away, she and Rodok made their way back to the *Lancer*.

"Gonna kill him one of these days," Saída growled as she tossed her coat on her pilot seat and fell into it. A quick beep prompted Saída to grab a tiny device from her belt, her Shard Counter, just in time to see that thirty-five shards had been credited to her ID. She scowled and snapped the Shard Counter back to her belt.

"*Are* you *considering* an *assassination*?" asked Rodok, plugging into the *Lancer's* main terminal and transferring his consciousness to the ship. The lights fluctuated as he took control, his smooth voice moving from his mechanical body into the ship's internal systems.

"Yeah, maybe his terminal blows up in his face. Maybe his food gets poisoned. Who knows?"

"*How* tragic. *No* one *saw* it *coming*," continued Rodok.

The lights in the cockpit reacted to the rhythm of his voice. Saída shut her eyes and put her feet up on the dash. The *Lancer* exited the Needle and flew off towards one of the connecting Rings that floated in space. Giant mechanical Rings controlled by the Grand Design, floated in suspension all across the charted galaxy, enabling ships to utilise lightspeed travel to get from one end of the galaxy to the other. The *Lancer* came up to one of the Rings and Saída felt the ship vibrate, as the Ringway System sent out a pulse wave that acknowledged the *Lancer's* ID. The darkness of space and the countless twinkling stars were at once inverted. The darkness gave way to a ghostly whiteness and the countless stars turned to black flecks of ash that reminded Saída too much of home. The *Lancer* was now travelling faster than the speed of light, with the help of the Rings, onward to their goal, the location of the medallion.

The interior lights of the *Lancer* dimmed as Rodok began to hum one of his favourite tunes, a classic called 'Beneath the Flower Patch'. It was quite upbeat despite its disturbing lyrics. That's why he liked it so much. There was some time before they would arrive. Saída already missed the grass on the hill. She was tired. She missed the rain on her face. Thoughts of home flooded her mind's eye. After years of cold leads, the medallion was finally within her grasp.

CHAPTER THREE

Sektor 47

The scalding red earth burned her back through the thin fabric of the rags Saída wore. Her hair was slick with perspiration and the sun glared with intensity, burning her eyes. She squinted and could just about make out the silhouettes of her friends huddling around her. Someone yelled for the others to fetch water, but she tried to tell them not to. They were not allowed to share. They could not take more than what was given. Her throat was dry, and her lips cracked. She struggled to stand up but couldn't move. The other children gave her room, they asked her if she was okay, in their native tongue. The way they used to when the Redcloaks weren't around to hear.

One of the kids came running back and splashed some water on her face. The coolness was a welcome shock and her eyes opened wide. She coughed, but already relief was seeping into her hot skin. Saída whispered her thanks, and the kids helped her up. Once she was up, everyone went back to their tasks, picking up rocks and dirt, and cleaning up after the miners who had been working there just a few hours earlier. Saída joined in slowly.

She gathered rocks and stones, placing them in her basket, cleaning up whatever she found, when something shiny caught her eye. She blinked twice, still recovering from fainting. A tiny stone, hidden beneath a larger rock. She picked it up, feeling its weightlessness in her tiny palm. It was so light. Not something she would have expected from a stone, however small. The stone was pure black, but shiny enough to reflect Saída's little face back at her. She called the others over to come and see. They gasped.

"*Roshun*," one of them whispered excitedly. He tapped it in Saída's palm, causing the black stone to change colour, becoming a few shades lighter. The children's excitement became louder. Saída tapped the stone against a rock, one-two-three times, causing it to become several shades lighter still. Another, sharp tap, and the little stone blazed a brilliant white, growing warmer. It was like a little sun resting in the palm of her hand, but just as soon as it came, the light and warmth faded away.

"What's going on over there?" a gruff-sounding man called out.

The children turned to see a Redcloak with a fancy moustache walk over to them.

"Get back to work," he snapped.

Saída went back to collecting rocks when he spoke again.

"Not you. Show me what you have in your hand."

Saída walked over to him. She was afraid. She didn't

want another beating. She didn't want to lose her little sun either. She handed it over to him.

He wordlessly tapped it with his finger a few times, watching it grow brighter in the palm of his hand.

"Good work," he said. He nodded to another Redcloak, who produced a pair of tin coins from his hip pouch and handed them to Saída.

"You can go home now," said the Redcloak with the fancy moustache.

Saída was relieved she wasn't being punished. She ran home, back to Uncle Abbas's bar, ecstatic about her two coins, and to tell him about the nice Redcloak.

She walked through the front door when she noticed the lights were off inside. She was expecting Uncle Abbas to be in the back, or to be resting. Instead, she found him passed out in the corner, slumped against the wall. His face was bruised, and his lip was bloody. There were broken bottles littered around the room. Saída stifled her tears and did what she could to lay Uncle Abbas down on the floor, placing one of their pillows under his head. She put her two coins next to him, and set to work, cleaning the bar.

CHAPTER FOUR

Sektor 23

Rodok's voice buzzed through the intercoms, alerting Saída. She looked up from the dashboard terminal.

"We *are* in *Samson* Territory. *We* are *nearing* Sektor *23*."

"How's it looking?"

"*We* had *a* close *call* earlier."

Saída furrowed her brows. "How many?"

"*The* radar *shows* three *Scouts* patrolling *the* area. *Hammer*-class *cruisers*."

Saída looked out the window and watched the misty green orb of Sektor 23 come into view as the *Lancer* exited lightspeed and flew out of the Ringway system. Various blinking lights beeped around the cockpit as Saída watched their approach into the system. Trails of space dust lingered around Sektor 23 like a sash around the planet.

"Why the hell is the Grand Design still patrolling around this system? That Sektor looks abandoned," she said.

"*My* records *are* incomplete. *I* do *not* know."

"Scav," muttered Saída, rubbing her forehead. "How soon can we land?"

"*Soon*. You *will* need *your* helmet."

Saída looked at the swirling green miasma of Sektor 23 as the *Lancer* drew closer. The atmosphere seemed clouded by the strange storm of gas. It was a small Sektor, but that didn't explain the anomaly before them.

"Why is it like that?"

"*The* only *data* I *have* on *it* suggests *that* it *is* now *off-limits*," buzzed Rodok.

Saída half-nodded.

"Well, that's where the signal points us," said Saída. She didn't want to harbour false hope. "We need that medallion if we're going to rescue Uncle Abbas."

"*Faith*, Saída. *We* will *succeed*."

Saída placed a hand on Rodok's inanimate body, then left the cockpit. She went through the atrium which was designed in a circular fashion, with entrances to every part of the *Lancer*. Saída's tiny sleeping quarters, spare rooms that never saw any use, the bath, the engine room, the depressurisation chamber that led outside, the storage closet and finally the armoury. The *Lancer* was a Spear-class cruiser, designed to act as a balance between a battle-ready ship and a temporary living space. For Saída and Rodok, it was permanent. Once in the armoury, she put on her spacesuit, a charcoal-grey Complex-Carbonweave armoured jumpsuit with green highlights. She pushed a button on the suit, and it tightened around her body. She holstered her pistol, which magnetically attached to her belt, and tucked her dagger away next to it. The last thing she pulled out of the armoury was a metallic mask which she put on. The weathered grey mask transformed, expanding over her head, becoming a helmet. It had glowing, thin red slits for eyes, and a small rebreathing apparatus affixed at the mouth.

"We *are* landing *now*," said Rodok.

The engine of the *Lancer* grew louder as the ship began its descent onto Sektor 23.

Saída grabbed her coat back off the chair and put it on over her spacesuit, while Rodok transferred his consciousness back into his physical body and landed the ship. Saída pulled out two small delicate cylinders – oxygen tubes – from a pouch on her belt and slid them into the rebreather on her helmet. That would allow her to recycle her own oxygen for a few hours as they searched for the medallion.

The two of them exited the *Lancer* and were immediately met with the noxious fumes of Sektor 23. The atmosphere was thick with a green gas that would have melted away Saída's skin, had she not been wearing her spacesuit.

"*We* cannot *stay* too *long*," buzzed Rodok. With a clink, his miniature pen-sized drone popped out of a compartment in his shoulder and flew off to scan their surroundings.

Saída could hear her own breathing through the rebreather on her helmet. It was louder and heavier. Even with all this protection, she felt like the gas was grasping at her lungs. Like Sektor 47.

Saída scanned the landscape before them. Her prosthetic eye allowed her to make out the old landing pad where they stood next to the *Lancer*, then from the pits and the rocks to the broken walkways that led up to a dilapidated old factory that stood, derelict, casting a shadow over all who beheld it.

"We have six hours before my oxygen runs out. Keep the *Lancer* deactivated. We don't want to risk the Redcloaks catching our signal."

Rodok extended his arm, pointing his long mechanical fingers toward the dilapidated processing plant, the factory, in the distance. Various platforms and walkways dotted the way towards the main building, but many had been worn down with age and by the corrosive elements of the gas that permeated the tiny green world of Sektor 23. In the distance, Saída could see that a gigantic industrial chimney had collapsed over one of the walkways around the old building.

"*There. My drone has detected something,*" said Rodok.

"What've you got?"

"*Seems to be empty. No heat signatures detected, but the stash is in there.*"

"The whole place looks like it could fall over."

"*Indeed. I expect there to be heavy structural damage.*"

"But that's where Mac's coordinates point us. That's where we'll find our ticket back to Sektor 47."

Rodok leaped onto another platform, landing effortlessly. He tapped the railing, checking to make sure it was stable.

"*Sektor 23 was an old processing colony. Clearly abandoned now. We might as well find something worth salvaging, while we are here.*"

Saída took a running start and leapt over from the

landing pad, towards Rodok. It wasn't as easy for her, but she was agile enough to make the jump.

"Did your drone pick up anything useful? What could we salvage from here?" Saída asked, mindful of her footing.

"The *drone* has *already* marked *scrap* which *I* can *put* to *good* use *for* the *Lancer*. Beyond *that*, this *was* a *processing* plant *for* a *specific* type *of* ore. *One* that *is* only *found* on *one* world. *Sektor* 47."

Saída stopped. "The Redcloaks brought the Roshun here?"

"It *seems* that *way*. This *was* one *of* their *many* processing *colonies*."

"Before whatever the hell happened here, happened."

"*It* seems *they* did *not* leave *here* unharmed."

Rodok let out an amused chortle, the gears in what stood for his throat, turned, and ground against each other. Whatever happened here, it was bad enough that the Redcloaks never came back. Saída figured the gas had something to do with it. It must have been something they had not anticipated.

Saída hopped onto the giant industrial chimney that had fallen through the walkway, splitting it in two. She was careful not to slide down, then jumped to the other side. Rodok leapt from one side of the walkway to the other without needing to use the chimney. Saída rolled her eyes then continued onwards. They were almost at the factory.

"I doubt even the Grand Design would let irradiated Redcloaks back onto Sektor Prime. What do you think happened here? Where did the gas come from?"

"My *records* on *this* place *are...* incomplete," Rodok reaffirmed, a hint of annoyance in his tone.

"It's alright, Rodok. We can't all be perfect," said Saída smugly.

"*Indeed. I suppose I will just have to settle for being like you.*"

Saída gave Rodok a light punch on the shoulder, then vaulted over some debris.

Rodok stopped to check his drone. Saída leaned against the railing on the side of the platform. They were just outside the main building now. Saída could see some industrial chimneys were still attached to the building. Why had the Redcloaks brought all the illuminite here? Several ideas ran through Saída's head. But she already knew the truth. They hoarded it because they could. The simplest answer was always the worst. And the worst answer was always the right one.

She peered over the edge, staring into an abyss of thick green gases, going far enough below that even her prosthetic eye could no longer see what was beyond it. She heard a clack. Rodok had turned around.

"Saída. *Turn* around. *Back* to *the* ship."

"Why? What's happening?"

"*We* have *miscalculated.*"

"We can't exactly go back u—" Saída stopped. A deep, bellowing rumble reverberated through the very platform they were standing on.

Rodok reacted instantaneously, tackling Saída forward and leaping off the metal platform just in time as it crumbled beneath them. They didn't have time to waste. She could feel the steel breaking apart under them. They jumped from platform to platform, making their way around the factory building, but before they could get to safety, the platform under them gave way. Saída latched onto a chunk of rock jutting out of the terrain and reached for Rodok's hand, but he refused to grab it, trying instead to grab onto the deteriorating rails of the platform.

There was another quake that echoed throughout the landscape and the ground collapsed once more. Rodok was tossed aside by a falling beam and Saída was unable to jump far enough away, getting struck by more falling debris which tossed her back onto the metal platform. She struggled, through disorientation, to get back up to her feet, but it was impossible. The platform broke apart beneath her and she was swallowed by the green abyss below.

CHAPTER FIVE

Sektor 47

Uncle Abbas was never this late. Saída paced near the bar counter, taking stock of all the bottles and glasses in the cabinet behind it. She had already cleaned the bar twice and made sure to set their plates for dinner, but Uncle Abbas was a no-show. She was worried that he had been stopped by a Redcloak patrol or worse, that they'd found a reason to detain him again.

Then she heard the familiar jingle of the bell that meant someone had come into the bar. She ran to the front and saw Uncle Abbas closing the door behind him. He was grinning ear to ear, as he stepped forward and wrapped her up in a big hug, taking special care not to let her see the surprise he had in his bag.

"Sorry for making you wait, Saída, but I told you, it would be worth it," he said.

He set his bag on the counter, setting up a pair of cups then getting some water ready. Saída wanted to check the bag while he wasn't looking but she resisted. A smile broke out on her little face. She enjoyed watching Uncle Abbas walk in and out of the back room, fiddling around with appliances. Eventually, he brought out a small kettle.

He poured water into the kettle, filling it to the brim. Then, from the bag, Uncle Abbas brought out a small pouch, showing its contents to Saída.

"You see this, Saída? Do you know what this is?"

Dry dirt, she had guessed. Uncle Abbas enjoyed that.

"These are tea leaves. Today I am going to make you Chai, our people's favourite drink."

Uncle Abbas let Saída smell the dried tea leaves. The richness of the smell caught her off guard and she coughed. She had never experienced anything like that. The scent of the tea leaves and cardamom tickled her nose.

Uncle Abbas emptied the pouch into a pestle and mixed in contents from another, smaller pouch he pulled from the bag, then began mashing the leaves and spices together. Once he was satisfied that they had been mixed, he scraped them into the kettle. The kettle beeped and began to glow, bringing the water to a steady boil.

Saída's eyes widened when Uncle Abbas poured a small flask of pure white liquid into the kettle, mixing it into the water and spices. She had thought it was a different colour of water, which meant that there were surely other colours of water that she had not yet seen. It was milk, Uncle Abbas told her when she asked.

Finally, he poured the light-brown liquid into the two cups and placed them in front of Saída and himself, then took a seat on the stool next to her.

29

He brought it up to his nose and inhaled deeply, closing his eyes. He let out a satisfied sigh. Saída emulated him, and he laughed. The two of them took a sip. The taste was nothing like Saída had been imagining. It was like a sharp kick, but the mingle of the sweet spices in the hot liquid soothed her aching throat. It was like medicine that tasted good.

"You know, a long time ago my dada-abu told me that when he was a boy, there were entire farms full of plants which would produce these leaves and spices. They would boil them and drink every day. He owned a teahouse, right here. In this city. People would come from all across the continent to taste his famous Chai, to take part in the merriment of community, to sing and dance and enjoy one another's company. Chai and music every evening. Can you imagine?"

Saída could see the pain of reminiscence in his eyes, she didn't really understand what he was talking about. She just couldn't imagine it. She would have liked to see what he was imagining.

Saída and Uncle Abbas continued to drink their Chai in silence. They didn't get days like that often. She didn't want to ruin their peace with her questions.

*

Saída ran after the other children, trying to catch them. They cheered as she failed to grab one of them, and she grinned when one of them tripped, closing in, and tagging them. They groaned, but Saída was already off, joining the other children as they collectively tried to escape their new pursuer. They often played in the little courtyard near Uncle Abbas's bar, it was an old plot of land where an old burned-down building stood. Long ago, it had been the home of the head of their community. That was even before Uncle Abbas's time. Before the Redcloaks came. Saída narrowly avoided being caught by her friend but jumped right as he got close. The other kids laughed as they renewed their game, running around the plot, it was a kind of chaos they all relished. Saída darted in and out of what remained of the burned building, surprising the other kids whenever it was her turn to catch them. Before long, evening descended, and her friends had to leave for their homes. Despite the darkening sky, Saída elected to remain at the ruins for a while longer. She knew there would still be customers at the bar, and she didn't want to go around the back if she could help it.

She played around for a while longer, collecting rocks and organising them into different piles, one with jagged edges, one with smoother, oval-shaped stones. She liked the sound they made when she tossed another smooth stone into its pile. It was a satisfying click. She looked up and noticed the sky had gone black like charcoal, thick with smog and the darkness of night. She had been here too long, but the Redcloaks were probably all gone by now.

She dusted off her hands and snuck out of the old plot, making her way back to Uncle's bar. It wasn't too far, so she decided to make a run for it. The faster she got back, the less of a risk there was in her getting spotted out after curfew. At least that's the logic she came up with at the time. The bar came into sight, and she ran towards it.

Saída looked forward to having dinner with Uncle Abbas. She hoped they weren't having daal again. She hated daal.

In her excitement, Saída didn't notice the voices that were coming from the bar. The door to the bar opened and a massive Redcloak walked out. She didn't slow down in time. It happened faster than she could process. Cold, sharp metal struck her in the face. The Redcloak had hit her with his big, gauntleted fist. Saída hit the ground with a loud cry. Then she could no longer scream. Searing hot pain surged in her left eye. She felt something warm dripping down her face like sweat. Not sweat. Blood. A steady flow, as cold numbness spread from her eye and crept across the left side of her face. Her vision blurred through tears and blood. She wanted to cry out, but no sound escaped her lips.

"Holy shit, you knocked her eye out," she heard a voice say. Two figures approached her, looking down on her. A skinny twig next to a massive tree.

"It surprised me," the bigger one said. His voice was like gravel.

Saída whimpered, unable to process the pain she was feeling.

"Captain's gonna be pissed at you. League's gonna be crawling up his ass cos of what you've just gone and done," the smaller one said, matter-of-factly.

The big one sneered. "Not the first time. They can't do shit."

"Whatever. Just leave her."

"If we leave it, then we'll definitely have a problem. Might as well finish the job."

"Your devotion to the Grand Design is inspiring," the small one said sarcastically.

"Shut up," snarled the big one, preparing to stomp Saída. She could barely make out the shape of his boot.

Then she heard an enraged bellow, she didn't know what he was saying, but Uncle Abbas was swearing at them in fury. She saw his shape collide with theirs, the sounds of fighting, of fists making contact, of pained cries. She couldn't see anymore. Everything was fading. Saída wanted to cry out for them to leave Uncle Abbas alone. She wanted him to be okay. She was scared. She didn't want to be alone.

CHAPTER SIX

Sektor 23

Saída heard a faint beeping as she came to, surrounded in pitch black. It was coming from her helmet. She got up with a groan. Where the hell had she ended up?

Her helmet's HUD indicated that she only had three hours of oxygen left. Saída removed one of the empty oxygen tubes from her rebreather. Each tube was only good for three hours of clean air filtration and one of them had already run out. She tossed it, and the empty tube clinked against the porcelain floor. She tried to contact Rodok.

"Don't you dare," she muttered as she brought a finger to her helmet's temple. The comm was dead. "*Scav,*" she cursed.

Saída looked around. She thought she had fallen into one of the pits, but where she had ended up was more like an old storage room. Shelves, weird-looking machinery with pistons and pumps and other mechanical parts strewn about the floor along with debris. She looked up, just about making out a cracked opening in the ceiling above her. How far had she fallen?

Her vision adjusted to the darkness, and she tiptoed around the room, putting her hands on whatever she could, getting a better sense of the layout. She crossed a half-broken table and noticed pillars supporting the ceiling. She could hear a faint buzzing, accompanied by a distorted cry. *Hmm-hm.* Saída shuddered. She had a feeling she knew what made the sound. She tried to connect remotely to Rodok's drone but had no luck. The connection was dead. She hoped Rodok had made it somewhere safe. She was angry at him for not grabbing her hand. They both knew he was far too heavy for her to have been able to lift him up, but she wished she could have still tried.

"Dammit, Rodok," she mumbled.

The sound of the low buzzing and the distorted, staggered cry mingled with the raspy sound of her own breathing, passed through her rebreather. With no other options, she decided to follow the buzzing to its source, carefully feeling her way in the darkness.

As the distorted cry grew louder, Saída moved faster. *La-lalaa.* Saída was right. She *did* know what was making the noise. She found her way out of the spacious room and into a hallway. The noise was coming from there. The closer she got to the source, the better she was able to see. There was a tiny source of light coming from the end of the hall. Very faint, like it was dying, but it was still noticeable through the thick green gas and the darkness. She reached the end of the hallway and came upon the light source, a broken drone that still hummed. The source

35

of the buzzing, of the infernal clicking, and the distorted song she had been hearing. *Hm-hmm-hm. La. La. La.* The light was coming from its eye. Saída placed her hands on the drone's central eye, gently digging her fingers into it and gripping it tight. She ripped it out, severing the wires that connected it to the orb-like core. Saída frowned. It was a Redcloak drone. A tiny central orb protected by several interlocking spiral rings that housed multiple tiny cameras, eyes that watched everything. A Watcher. Saída had dark memories of the Watchers from her time on Sektor 47. They would watch and they would sing. And they would destroy. Entire streets, houses, neighbourhoods, engulfed in explosions and flames, reduced to rubble with ease, if prompted by their Redcloak operators. Vile machines. Saída's grip tightened around the Watcher's eye.

She moved the eye around, using the small light source to find a way forward. There was a narrow passageway ahead. She went through the open door at the end of the passageway. The light from the drone's eye shone through the darkness like a torch. There was less gas in this room, it was thinner somehow.

"Please let this be a way out."

The indicator in her helmet showed that she was moving further away from Mac's coordinates, but she ignored it. She had to find a way out and link up with Rodok first. The stash would have to wait.

Her foot hit a hard chunk of… something. She turned her light downwards and squinted under her helmet. The remains of a partially melted skeleton lay at her feet. Waving the light across the rest of the room revealed more skeletons. She took a sharp breath, creating an awfully loud, distorted sound through her rebreather. She wasn't getting close to an exit, but rather, she was getting closer to the source of all this destruction.

Drip.

Saída looked around for the source of the sound.

Drip. Drip.

Again, she heard it. It sounded like water dripping out of a tap. She listened intently.

Drip.

It sounded like it was coming from within the room, but a thorough inspection showed her that there was nothing there. Saída pressed her hand against the walls, tracing the location of the noise across the room. This time it was clearer. Right behind the wall. She started pushing her hands against it, hoping to find a switch or activate some mechanism to reveal a path forward. There was nothing.

She kicked the wall in frustration. The sound of her armoured boot was loud, clanging against the wall. Saída stopped for a moment. The sound was hollow. She took a deep breath, collecting herself. It used to be a doorway, but it had been covered up. Why?

Saída kicked the wall again, in the same spot. The noise was different this time. She could feel the wall beginning to give way. She shone the light on the spot where she had kicked. A crack had begun to form. Hasty patchwork was no match for the armoured boots of her spacesuit.

With each kick, the crack grew deeper. Saída stopped for a moment to rest. She thought about Rodok, and where he might have ended up. She thought about the surface. About Uncle Abbas. How many years he had been on

Sektor 47. Alone. But now she had a chance. With Digby's medallion she would finally have a way to return home. She could finally rescue him.

There was no time for indecisiveness. She took a running start, then slammed into the wall with a dropkick, shattering it, and creating a small opening. Saída exhaled and dusted herself off.

There was a path ahead, and Saída could now clearly hear liquid dripping. She saw a busted pipe, leaking a strange golden-white substance. Beyond that, stairs that led downwards into darkness. Saída closed her eyes and prayed. Just as Uncle Abbas had taught her.

With a deep breath, she descended, the red slits in her helmet glowing in the darkness. She used the light from the drone's eye to help her navigate the steps carefully. Saída followed into a long passageway, which twisted at the end. The signal in her helmet changed. She stopped. The distance to Mac's stash was no longer in the negatives. She was closer to it now. She swallowed in anticipation. Quickening her pace, she followed the signal ID into a gigantic basement at the end of the passageway. It was brilliantly lit; all over the walls, there were specks that glowed bright, and in the centre of the room, a massive hole with machinery and processing equipment having fallen part-way in. Saída took a closer look, peering inside. It led into a tunnel-like slope underground, far too deep for her comfort. Saída noticed that this was a source of the thick green gas. It wafted out of the hole upwards, out of the factory. The hole led deeper underground. Saída looked around, surveying the specks of light across the wall. They reminded her of Roshun, but she had never seen it like this before. It was like the illuminite had been splashed across the walls like a liquid. The signal for the stash was close by. Saída looked around the room at the remains of the processing machinery. Chunks of ore had spilled out.

Illuminite. Scores of it. And nestled amongst the ore, a small white box with a blinking gold light, held in the grasp of a disabled commercial drone. Mac's signal had pointed her here.

Saída walked over to the drone and pried it apart from the white box. It bore the symbol of the Hickston family, a seagull flying over an ocean. Saída held her breath. The box exhaled a wisp of steam as she unlocked it, pulling out a gold medallion. Around the rim, were strange etchings of symbols that Saída couldn't recognise. It was weighty and had some kind of mechanism in the centre, where it was clearly missing an emblem. The emblem with the Hickston crest. It wasn't there. The medallion was incomplete. Saída thought about Uncle Abbas. His smile. She squeezed the medallion in her hand, shaking with fury.

She screamed, kicking away the white box.

"*Scav it,*" she yelled, and threw the medallion onto the ground. All of this had been for *nothing!*

When all the anger was gone, Saída stifled the urge to cry. She would have to worry about it later. For now she had to find Rodok and get the hell off this gas ball. Saída picked up the medallion and placed it in her coat. She had thrown it into the pile of illuminite ore. She picked up the largest chunk and inspected it. Illuminite was extremely rare. Saída scowled. The wealth of her homeworld, stolen and wasted. Her own dagger was made of illuminite, but that had been the only piece of the precious metal she had ever owned, save for the tiny pebble she had given up to the moustached Redcloak so long ago. She was taking the illuminite. As far as she was concerned, it belonged to her.

"Uncle, wait for me," she whispered, half in prayer.

Saída placed the chunk of illuminite in her pack. Then she heard a familiar rumbling.

Another quake. Her eyes darted around the room, for a place to take cover, to hold onto. She glanced up at the ceiling, directly above the hole. There was a large hole in the ceiling beyond too, with processing machinery threatening to slip out. Saída theorised that the quakes must have caused the equipment to fall through the floors and make the craters she now saw.

The ground shook, illuminite fell through the hole above and Saída rolled out of the way, avoiding being crushed by accompanying debris. A pillar collapsed, blocking off the door she had come in from. Then the shaking stopped.

There was no way back up above. Nothing left but the gamble of the crater in the centre of the room, and where it could lead.

Saída steeled herself and climbed down into the hole, her fingers dug into the dirt, and she descended down the slope. The gas got thicker the deeper she went through, and at the end, she found a deep drop. Any faster and she would have fallen in. She muttered a prayer of thanks. Beyond the drop, she spotted another slope, which led upwards. To freedom, she hoped.

Saída swallowed her fear and jumped, grabbing onto the opposite slope with her gauntlets, clawing at the earth and climbing up, narrowly avoiding the gaseous abyss below. She was sweating inside her helmet. She crawled up the slope in a panic. The earth under her hands began to vibrate. She could feel it in her bones. Another quake. Saída got up onto her feet to run, but the ground under her quaked and she fell backwards.

"*Shit!*" Saída yelled, sliding down the slope, headfirst towards the abyss.

Then she felt a metallic hand grab onto her leg with a clunk. She looked up to see Rodok's familiar pointed face looking down at her from above.

"We *were* separated," he buzzed matter-of-factly, eye fixed on her. Saída relaxed her head against the slope. Relief washed over her like a wave of cool water.

"Yes. Yes, we were, Rodok."

CHAPTER SEVEN

Sektor 47

Saída felt something soft under her head, a pillow. She was on the floor, under a blanket. Her vision was blurry, but she could see again. Though it was different. It was less. A dull pain throbbed in the left side of her face, concentrating in the hollow socket that used to contain her eye. Life would never be the same. Half her face was covered in bandages, but she was in Uncle's bar. Safe in the room that was free of the smell of booze, free of Redcloak invaders. The sound of shuffling came from the front and Uncle Abbas came into the room. He had bruises on his face, a black eye and there was a limp in his step. He brought a tray with a rag and a bowl of water. He knelt next to Saída, placing a hand on her head.

Was he crying? She couldn't tell. It was hard to understand what was going on. Saída put her hand on his and gingerly squeezed it.

"Saída," he whimpered. He shut his eyes a moment,

then took the rag and doused it in what little water there was in the bowl. He squeezed the rag and water trickled into the tin basin. Uncle Abbas placed the rag on Saída's forehead. She felt instant relief from the heat and fell asleep to the cool sensation of the damp rag on her skin.

Days turned into weeks, as Uncle Abbas took care of Saída. He brought her food and water, far more often than they used to be able to afford. It was more than the usual daal or plain bread. Now she would be treated to white rice, Chai and even mutton bones for broth. She wondered if her friends' parents had been helping. Had they all known what happened to her? Had they all been pitching in for these luxuries? Whatever it was, it had helped her recover faster. Uncle Abbas had made sure of it.

Saída sat in the back room one day, eating a bowl of rice, peering out the window, watching the pit below, where the miners worked. They looked like little straw dolls from this height, but day in and day out, they worked, tiring themselves to the bone. Saída heard Uncle Abbas talking to some of them lately. Normally they stayed far away from the bar, at Uncle's insistence. He didn't want the Redcloaks hurting them, but there hadn't been any Redcloaks coming by recently.

"Abbas, this is a real chance. You need to get in touch with them," said a man. He sounded like he was the same age as Uncle Abbas. It must have been Jameel, the father of one of her friends.

"No. There is nothing to be gained from talking to them. They will use Saída as a prop. She deserves better than—"

43

"She deserves better than *this*, Abbas. All our children do. You have an opportunity here. All of us do. Maybe we can finally get out of this hell-hole."

Uncle Abbas laughed, his voice dripped with venom. She pulled away from the window. He spat, his voice low and threatening. "I won't let those Liberation League bastards use my *child.*"

There was silence and then the other man spoke. "Then the dream for Meraji independence is dead."

"Wake up you fool. It died with our forefathers. One child will not make a difference. It wasn't brutality when it happened to us as children, it isn't considered brutality now."

"The League has managed to change—"

"They haven't changed *anything*," yelled Uncle Abbas.

Saída gasped. He must have heard her because he immediately quietened his voice.

"I'm done. Please leave, dost. I cannot help you," muttered Uncle Abbas.

Saída heard the door open, and the other man spoke again.

"You know that they've been talking about your bar, yes? We hear them every day, down at the mines. They talk about burning this place down. About how they'll torture you. Both of you."

"Get out."

"Be careful. Dost."

Saída heard the door shut. Uncle Abbas came into the room, shortly after. Saída was looking out the window again, pretending that she had been doing so the whole time. Uncle Abbas knew better, however. He hugged her.

"Fear not, beti. No one will hurt you again. Not when I'm here," he whispered in their native tongue. Saída hugged him back. She trusted Uncle Abbas with all her heart, but her eye lingered on the door to the front of the bar. How simple it would be for any Redcloak with a weapon to break in and snuff them out for good. Her grip around Uncle Abbas tightened and Saída shut her eye. She could still hear the sound of the big Redcloak's fist as he crushed her eye. The sound of flesh breaking, the pop. The pain that coursed through her face like trails of fire. Saída began sobbing and Uncle Abbas caressed her hair as she wept. Neither of them would ever truly be safe.

Not while the Redcloaks still ruled.

CHAPTER EIGHT

Sektor 23

"*The* gas *is* much *thinner* here," lied Rodok. He helped Saída over to a pile of debris so she could rest. They were in another part of the factory, but here the gas was spilling in from the outside through several large openings.

"Rodok," panted Saída. "How did you find me?"

Rodok straightened up. "*I* almost *did* not. *I* was *following* the *signal* to *Mac's* stash. *Then* I *found* you."

Saída nodded and pulled out the medallion from her pocket.

"You *found* it?"

Saída nodded again. It was getting hard to breathe.

"*Then* what *is* wrong?" Rodok tilted his head.

Saída showed him the medallion. "The emblem in the centre, Rodok. It's missing. No emblem, no passage."

"*Then* we *just* have *to* interrogate *Mac* again."

Saída shut her eyes in frustration. "No, Rodok, it's not that simple. Mac didn't have the emblem on him when we processed him. That means Digby removed it from the medallion before he shipped it off to Mac for him to hide."

"*Then* we *will* resume *our* hunt *for* Digby. *This* is *a* minor *setback*. Nothing *more*."

It wasn't just some minor setback. This was supposed to be it. This was their way home. So they could finally rescue Uncle Abbas.

"These last four years, Rodok… All those leads, all the searching. To come this close and just…" Saída trailed off.

"*Saída*." Rodok paused, considering his next words.

"If this was how things were going to turn out then maybe we never should've left Silwanapur," Saída mumbled.

Rodok buzzed. "*Do* not *be* defeatist, *Saída*. Uncle *Abbas* has *waited* long *enough*. We *are* not *giving* up *now*."

Saída looked up at Rodok. Even through the thick gas, she could see Rodok's crimson gaze. Challenging her, inspiring her to keep moving. She nodded. Rodok twisted his head in response. They would keep going.

Saída's HUD beeped. Her oxygen tube was running out.

"The *Lancer*, Rodok. How far?"

"From *my* estimation, *it* will *take* us *another* two *hours*."

Saída placed a hand on her knee. Her breathing was growing ragged, coming out of her rebreather as obnoxiously loud static.

"I've got one hour," she managed.

Rodok held out his hand. "*Then* we *will* make *it* in *one* hour."

Taking his hand, Saída followed Rodok out of a large gap in the wall, shifting from the charred remains of the factory floor to the green air and rocky terrain of Sektor 23. They had a bit of a climb ahead of them, but Saída could see the tip of the *Lancer* from where they were, far in the distance.

"Did you happen to grab any spare parts?" Saída asked.

"As *a* matter *of* fact, *I* did *not.*"

"Seriously?" Saída's voice dropped.

"*Most* of *the* scrap *tagged* by *the* drone *has* been *lost.*"

Saída nodded. "Well, it wasn't a total waste. I got my hands on some Roshun."

Rodok twisted his head curiously. "*Illuminite? That is* a *good* haul."

The two of them made their way back up to the hills overlooking the factory, climbing up the rocks, jumping from platform to platform, and making their way back to the spot where the *Lancer* was docked. Saída was beginning to feel the pressure of the gas straining against her helmet. The oxygen tube was running out, and the rebreather wouldn't be able to function too long after that. She quickened her pace. There were still occasional rumblings, but nothing as major as before. Still, Saída couldn't shake the feeling of dread that hadn't left her since she found herself in the old processing plant. Saída vaulted over a rail that was sticking out of rock. She could see the *Lancer* in the distance.

"I found some messed-up processing equipment, where I found the medallion. I think it malfunctioned. Probably toppled over and fell through the floors of the factory. Illuminite got hot and melted through the floors…"

"So, *you* think *the* gas *is* a *result* of *the* heated *illuminite* reacting *to* chemicals *under* the *earth*?"

"It's certainly one explanation for what happened here. It's a small Sektor, but accidents like this must have happened in factories all over the world for so much gas to be up in the air now. The walls, the ceiling, everything in the bottom of the factory was plastered with this… liquid light."

"Say *what* you *are* thinking, *Saída*," said Rodok in monotone, fixing his crimson eye on her.

Saída maintained her pace, looking him in the eye. "I think there's something deep inside the world, under the earth and it reacted to the illuminite and exploded into this gas. That's why the Redcloaks abandoned this place, why the Grand Design didn't let the irradiated ones return. There's something here. Maybe something we can use."

Rodok stared at her, buzzing, "Ha. *Ha*. Ha," and continued to stride towards the ship.

Saída knew it was crazy, but she couldn't let go of the feeling that gnawed at the pit of her stomach. That green abyss that she had barely escaped, there was something down there. Some kind of chemical or substance. *Something*. There was a reason the quakes never stopped on this Sektor. Whatever it was, it didn't mix with the illuminite.

A hissing sound, accompanied by a sudden crack in the eye-slits of her helmet caused a loud blinking icon to appear on her heads-up display, a warning. The oxygen tube had run out.

Then again, perhaps that theory was better left alone for now, she thought, and ran, tossing the depleted tube from her rebreather. The *Lancer* was still a few steps away.

"Partial Activation: Decontamination. Saída Abbas," ordered Saída breathlessly as she and Rodok sprinted up

49

the ramp and back onto the ship. She had been holding her breath in the last few moments that they had been surrounded by the noxious fumes of Sektor 23.

The *Lancer's* decontamination chamber buzzed to life, spraying Rodok and Saída with jets of chemical-infused water, clearing away the dirt, grime, and foul residue of the gases outside. Then the chamber hit them with pressurised air that dried them back up and eliminated hostile bacteria that would threaten the inside of the ship, or Saída's own skin, before it opened into the rest of the ship. Saída headed back to the armoury to ditch her spacesuit then hit the shower. Rodok went back to the cockpit and transferred his consciousness into the *Lancer*, making a check to see if the Redcloaks were still out there. Once he was satisfied that they were clear to take off, he activated the shields of the *Lancer*, fired up the subluminal drive and blasted off into space, connecting with the Rings system and finding an appropriate path in the Ringway, shooting off into lightspeed.

It was as if the *Lancer* was completely still, unmoving in the void of negative space. They were safe from Redcloak patrols and far out of range for any radars to pick out their signal in particular. Rodok allowed them some peace before they decided their next move. Saída came into the cockpit, having swapped out her usual bounty-hunting attire for a maroon tank top and baggy pink pyjamas, and took a seat at the dashboard, next to Rodok's unmoving body. She had a can of fruit synthshake in her hand and relaxed her feet on the dashboard of the terminal.

"*Must* you *subject* me *to* that *mismatched* atrocity?" said Rodok in monotone.

"Your face is mismatched," retorted Saída, taking a sip of her synthshake. The sweetness of the mango-orange mixture always brought a tinge of satisfaction to Saída, synthetic fruit or not.

"We should start looking into leads on Digby," said Saída, taking another sip.

Rodok's voice vibrated throughout the *Lancer's* interiors. "I *have* put *the* call *out*. Our *man* on *Sektor* 12 *may* prove *to* be *of* use."

"Anyone else?" said Saída, finishing up her synthshake. "Colton isn't the only info-broker in the galaxy."

"*We* could *try* Isiah *Thomas* again? *Sektor* 15. *We* know *that* the *Hickstons* were *close* to *the* Viceroy *there*."

"Isiah? I don't know, Rodok. We've not been to Sektor 15 for ages."

"*He* came *through* for *us* with *that* Trevino's *bounty*. Why *not*? It *is* a *lead*."

"Alright. Well, let's see if there are any jobs available around Sektor 15. May as well get paid while we collect info."

"*Searching* the *Guild* Directory *now*," Rodok buzzed. "*Three* targets *in* Samson *Territory*. One *on* Sektor *15*... Hmm."

Rodok grew silent. Saída raised an eyebrow. "Well now I definitely wanna know."

"Perhaps, *we* should *refrain* from *returning* to *Sektor* 15."

"Rodok..." Saída warned.

"Very *well*. Aveline *Gardener*. Age: *Twenty*-four. *Wanted* for *disturbing* the *peace*, refusal *to* cooperate *with* authorities *and* conspiracy *to* commit *treason* against *the* Grand *Design*. There *are* more *charges*."

Saída whistled. "I like her already. Where have I heard that name before? Gardener? It sounds familiar."

"Apparently, *Aveline* Gardener *is a renowned* gunsmith *within* Samson *Territory*."

"A gunsmith? We could use a gunsmith, Rodok. Especially if we're gonna hunt Digby down."

"You *already* have *a* gun."

Saída swivelled her seat to face Rodok's motionless body. "Well I want *another* one. Let's take it."

"*There* is *a* problem."

"Always is," Saída whispered.

"The *Redcloaks* have *currently* blockaded *Sektor* 15 *due* to *riots* related *to* taxation. *The* Grand *Design* has *given* them *orders* to *cut* off *all* supplies. *Getting* in *will* be *next* to *impossible*."

Saída scratched her head. "Then why the hell would they even put in the request for Gardener to be apprehended? If the assholes have the whole world locked out, they hardly need a bounty hunter."

"*I* would *assume* finding *Gardener* is *more* important *to* them, *than* they *are* willing *to* let *on*."

"The true cause of the riots might not be taxes, then," Saída said.

"*Perhaps* it *is* too *risky* after *all.*"

"It is… But it's just like you said. Isiah may have a lead for us. We have to try."

They sat in silence for some time, both contemplating how best to approach the situation.

"*I* have *a* suggestion," Rodok offered.

"Let's hear it."

"*You* will *not* like *it.*"

Saída pinched her nose. "Shit."

"Yes."

"I'm not doing that, Rodok. No way."

"*Joining* the *Guild* in *an* official *capacity* will *give* us *far* more *legitimacy* than *as* contractors."

"I don't think Matthias would even go for it," complained Saída.

"Saída," Rodok's voice buzzed through the ship. "*He* has *been* trying *to* recruit *you* for *a* while *now.*"

"And I always refuse, because he's a piece of shit."

"*The* question *remains. Do you* want *to* learn *what* Isiah *knows*, or *do* you *want* to *move* on? *We* both *know* the *Guild* will *provide* resources *and* aid *we* did *not* have *access* to *before.*"

Saída stewed, going over various scenarios in her head. She needed her freedom, and joining the Guild in an official capacity would lock her in. She wouldn't be able to choose her own assignments anymore, she wouldn't be able to control where she went most of the time. Were better pay and resources really worth all that? She clenched her fists. Rodok's suggestion was certainly one way to get past the blockade, but things weren't so simple. One wrong move and she would be branded a criminal again. She had left that life behind, but now it was rearing its ugly head, encroaching back into her life like a disease with no cure. The fear of being pulled back into that abyss was too much.

Screw it.

"Rodok," said Saída. "Patch me through to Matthias."

CHAPTER NINE

Sektor 47

It had been a year since Saída had lost her eye. She sat outside Uncle's bar, watching her friends playing close by. Following the attack, the Redcloaks had stopped coming around the place, and the bar had become a haven for the children. Saída looked up at the sky with her one eye, feeling a light breeze upon her skin. Her friends played in front of the empty bar, yelling in excitement as they kicked a ball around, sending waves of red dirt flying. There was a sudden loud noise and Saída's arms instinctively went to her head. She curled up and whimpered, still shielding herself. The ball had smacked into the bar's door. Her friends came over to make sure she was okay. Saída managed a smile and hasty reassurances for her friends, and they returned to their game. Saída brought her fingers to her bandaged eye socket. The ringing in her ears, the sensation of the cold, metal fist colliding with her eye, the smell and taste of blood. It haunted her still.

Ash drifted towards her fingers, and all around her. The red earth was speckled with dark spots. The factories were running again. In the far distance, the sounds of machines churning and breaking down illuminite, the thunderclaps of the Redcloaks' industrial beasts began anew. Soon it would be time for the miners to end their shifts.

The sudden silence of her friends made her look up. She saw her friends cowering at the sight of approaching Redcloaks. Saída gasped. Shaking with adrenaline, she prepared herself. She clutched a fistful of dirt and waited.

The Redcloaks sneered, pleased to see how easily they frightened the children. They walked towards Uncle's bar. Saída's friends ran out of the yard, leaving their ball behind. They called for her to run, but Saída did not move. She wanted to run, her legs trembled, but she remained, standing with a fistful of Meraji dust.

The Redcloak stared at her. He opened his mouth to speak, but Saída glared back at him with her one eye. The Redcloak shut his mouth, and a puzzled expression replaced his smugness. They weren't used to this kind of defiance. He brought his hand up to slap Saída, but she was faster and tossed the fistful of dirt in his face. And then she ran. She heard him coughing and spluttering, but she was already springing towards the old plot with the burned manor.

The Redcloaks followed Saída, but she managed to evade them. She ducked into the house, taking cover inside a hollow fireplace. She was out of sight from the Redcloaks. She saw one of them turn a corner and step into what used to be the living room. Saída picked up a small, sharp-edged rock near the fireplace and flung it at his face.

The rock made contact. Blood spilled from the Redcloak's mouth as he clutched it in pain. The lip was torn, and his attention turned to Saída. In a frenzy, he lunged at her, but Saída was already crawling back into a smaller room. Another Redcloak grabbed her hair from behind and yanked at it, but it was too short to pull Saída back. She lurched forward and turned to chuck another rock. It missed, startling the Redcloak and gave Saída an opportunity to kick at him and get away.

Saída ran out into the largest room, intending to run out of the burned house, but two more Redcloaks walked in from the only exit. She turned around to see the two she had just avoided, also closing in behind her. She was trapped. She still had a few large stones in her pocket, and she was prepared to do as much damage as she could before she was beaten. She made ready to aim another stone at the Redcloak in front of her, but there was a creak in the floor. The floor was rotting. It was going to give way. One of the Redcloaks called out to the others to wait. The others ignored him and inched closer, eyes fixed on Saída. Another long creak. The floor under them was straining. The noise wasn't familiar to Saída.

The two Redcloaks in front jumped at Saída. The Redcloak behind them yelled, but his warning came too late. The floor gave way, splintering apart and swallowing all four of them.

Saída shut her eyes in anticipation for the hard crash, but instead she hit one of the Redcloaks, who unintentionally cushioned her fall. She recovered faster than them and looked around. She was in a dilapidated basement, by old mining machinery, some which had been used to drill tunnels. The Redcloak that cushioned her fall had hit his head, she couldn't tell whether he was knocked out or dead, but the other one was rising to his feet, his cold eyes fixed on Saída.

His lips frothed in rage as he screamed, "I'll *wring* your neck, *bitch.*"

Saída ran towards one of the tunnels, pursued by the Redcloak. She could tell that he was badly wounded by the way his voice sounded, but the violence of his words had clutched at her throat. Saída felt tears well up in her eye. She would die down here, never seeing Uncle Abbas again. This man was going to kill her.

The tunnel became smaller the deeper she went. She reached a dead end with a broken mining drill. There was a small opening ahead, a tight fit for her, but the Redcloak's fury grew louder as he caught up to her. Saída dove into the opening, painfully squeezing through, trying to get to the other side. A hand seized her foot and she screamed, thrashing in the tight space. The Redcloak shrieked, but she could no longer make out the words he hurled at her. She managed to push through to the other side. In the struggle, she felt the jagged insides of the hole cut into her feet and legs.

Squeezing out the other side, free of her pursuer, Saída fell. She smacked her forehead against a blunt rock jutting out of the shaft. She prayed all the prayers Uncle Abbas had taught her in secret. Prayers for safety. For security. For hope. She prayed that she would survive, that Uncle Abbas would be okay, that somehow, if she lived, she would find him again.

Saída braced for impact. For death.

She fell into a pile of stones, sending them flying in every direction. Pain shot through every part of her body. She didn't know how far she had fallen, but she knew one thing: she was alive. She opened her eyes, looking around to see where she had ended up. A dark cavern. Huge. Ancient. The miners hadn't found this place yet. In the silence, an echo resounded from the darkness. The sound of ore being chipped away, steadily, with precision. She faced the direction of the noise. Was it a miner after all? She called out for help, a weak whimper escaping her bruised lips.

The chipping stopped. A new sound. Heavy steps, like lumbering steel. A sound of mechanical whirring. She whimpered again. Two crimson eyes shone bright in the darkness as a giant, lanky figure shambled towards her, one heavy step at a time. The sound of whirring did not stop. Saída stared into the glare of those crimson eyes. Long arms reached out of the darkness. Bony fingers clacking as they reached for her. Saída tried to crawl away, but she felt the creature's fingers dig into her arm and she screamed.

CHAPTER TEN

Sektor 15

Saída had never liked Sektor 15. The Grand Design saw fit to garrison their military Crusaders here and so there were always Redcloaks around. This time though, things seemed worse. Swarms of armed Redcloaks were patrolling in groups. Far too reminiscent of home. Saída and Rodok walked out of the *Lancer* and off the landing pad, heading towards the Redcloak officers for documentation checks. This hangar was dotted with bright white lights similar to those at the Guild. The garish chromatic walls were only rarely treated to a different splash of colour with the insignia of the Grand Design. Golden scales in front of a blazing red sun. Saída sneered. The hypocrisy was sickening. *Their* justice was the *only* justice.

"Documents," said the Redcloak at the check-in station.

Saída removed a cartridge from her SETRA, a device known as a Sub-Etheric Transceiver, and handed it over, along with her newly acquired Guild badge. Rodok stood behind her, remaining silent. Every so often the Redcloak would sneak a glance at him. He took his sweet time connecting the cartridge to his terminal and looking through Saída's documents, mouthing the words he read and raising his eyebrows. He enjoyed his job too much.

"State your business," he finally said.

"Captain Abbas. Here for the Guild. You know this," Saída replied, already done with the conversation.

"Calm down, ma'am. Never can be too careful," said the Redcloak, handing her back her badge. "Your Origin Point is listed as Sektor 12, but you don't look like any Twelver I've ever seen. Your accent doesn't sound familiar."

Saída retrieved her cartridge and pinned her badge to the inside of her coat. "Then broaden your horizons," she said, walking away.

Rodok lumbered after her. Having him with her always drew eyes. Probably even more than she did on her own. The questions got annoying after some time, so she just had Rodok remain silent and pretend he was a new type of drone.

"*I* hate *demeaning* myself *like* that," he buzzed.

"Really? Cos I love demeaning you like that."

"I *am* touched."

Exiting Hangar Nine and walking out to the spaceport, Saída suppressed a scowl. The entire area was crawling with Redcloaks. Far more than she remembered from the last time she had been on Sektor 15. The barracks were situated in the spaceport, just like on Sektor 47, and heavy maglock anti-air cannons were set up across the length of the walls. The spaceport was a military outpost as much as a port for travel. Saída and Rodok walked out of the main gate and past the heavy fortifications and barricades that separated the spaceport from the rest of the city. They were watched by the Redcloaks the entire time. It made Saída's skin crawl.

The city had been completely ruined, the skyscrapers that Saída remembered had been reduced to rubble. The roads had been torn apart. Destroyed vehicles, grav-buses, the remains of solar-powered hover-cars. Pillars that were once part of surrounding structures, Tetrasteel beams and other debris was strewn about. They walked through the ruined city and found no signs of life but the mechanical *rat-tat-tat* clicking and low-pitched sing-song whispers of Redcloak Watcher drones flitting in and around the city blocks. Saída clenched her fists.

"The *state* of *this* Sektor *has* been *obscured* by *the* hyperwave *networks*."

Saída shot him a look of worry. They had to be more cautious. No wonder the Grand Design had ordered a blockade. They were going to turn this place into another Sektor 47.

"Find us a lead on Gardener and the resistance fighters."

"*But* what *of* Isiah?" Rodok asked.

Saída gestured to the carnage around them. "Look around, Rodok. If Isiah's even still alive, the only place he could be is with a resistance cell. The Redcloaks are gonna turn this city to dust before long."

Rodok buzzed and rotated his head in agreement, remotely piloting his drone and seeking out anything besides the military presence in the checkpoints they had passed through. Saída tapped into the holofeed as Rodok spied heat signatures coming from inside a network of tunnels that were laid out under the ruined city. An elaborate sewer system, but something more too. Rodok carefully navigated the drone through the grime and walls of muck, coming upon armed soldiers. They weren't military. They looked like civilians.

Saída turned to Rodok.

"The spaceport, the city? Armed civilians? I'm beginning to think we were right. This blockade definitely isn't just because of taxes."

"*The* Grand *Design* lied? *I* cannot *believe* it," Rodok replied flatly.

They found an entryway into the sewers close by. Rodok dug his mechanical fingers into the steel reinforcement that guarded the manhole cover on the ground, ripping it off with ease.

"No one outside Sektor 15 is gonna know what the Redcloaks are doing here. Not until they find a way to spin it in their favour, like they did with Sektor 47. Like they do everywhere," said Saída, climbing down the manhole, into the sewers.

Rodok followed in after her, signalling for his drone to return.

Saída covered her nose and groaned. "I should've brought the rebreather."

"*There* is *no* need. *Sektor* 15 *has* enough *oxygen* for *humans*," said Rodok.

Saída rolled her eyes and instinctively tapped her belt to make sure her handgun was still magnetically attached to it. Rodok's drone returned to him, depositing itself back into a small opening on his shoulder. It blended in well as part of his body. It never failed to impress Saída how advanced the technology he possessed was.

Saída and Rodok walked through the labyrinth under the city, hours went by, and it was like they were walking in circles, though Rodok assured her that they weren't. As they turned a corner, they heard guns clicking behind them and froze.

"We *are* here," buzzed Rodok.

"Hands above your heads," said a man from behind them. They complied.

Two men came around and faced them, still aiming their rifles on Saída and Rodok. One was older, his hair a dull grey and he wore a black flak jacket with a red undershirt. He looked to be in his forties. The other wore a simple grey shirt and black trousers. He was still just a teenager, his long hair was tied back in a dreadlock ponytail. The two of them were roughed up, covered in dirt and soot. It was no surprise, given the state of the city.

"You two with the Redcloaks?" the older one asked. Both had dark skin, they were natives of Sektor 15.

Saída raised an eyebrow. "Do I look like I'm with the Redcloaks?"

The older man shook his head. "I ain't taking the risk."

"I'm looking for Isiah Thomas. He's an info-broker."

The men looked at each other and then back at Saída. "Who's asking?"

"Saída Abbas," she said.

"And why exactly are you looking for an info-broker, Saída Abbas?"

"My reasons are my own. I don't mean you or your resistance any harm. I just need to talk to Isiah."

Rodok stared down the boy.

"What are—" the boy began, but Rodok shut the question down fast.

"*Please* do *not* ask."

"We can't help you," snapped the older man.

"They've seen us," murmured the younger one.

The older man studied them for a moment and weighed his options. Saída was ready to fight. Then the older man spoke.

"You need to go back where you came from and forget you ever saw us."

He was letting them go. Saída wouldn't have risked that.

"Wait, then what about Gardener? Aveline Gardener?" blurted Saída. "Let me talk to her then?"

The older man's eyes widened. "What do you want with Aveline?"

He raised his rifle just an inch. It was uncomfortably close.

"I heard that she's a very talented gunsmith. I want her to make me a gun."

"She doesn't exactly have the time," he snapped.

"I think she'll make an exception once she sees what I brought her."

The men lowered their weapons slightly.

"I don't think so. We'll let you leave, but don't think we're just gonna walk you into our—"

"Illuminite," interrupted Saída. "Tell her, I've got illuminite. If she still says no, then we'll leave."

"Illuminite?" the older man murmured.

The men were silent for a while. Saída hoped it would work. If she couldn't get word on Isiah from them, then maybe Gardener would have the answers. The older man activated his SETRA device, a clunky piece of hardware just like hers, and relayed Saída's request back to their hideout. After some back and forth, the man turned to Saída.

"You're in luck. She wants to see you too. Both of you have to wear blindfolds."

Saída agreed and both she and Rodok put on the blindfolds. Unbeknownst to the men leading them, Rodok's drone was still active within his shoulder. Even blindfolded, the holofeed was directly transmitted to his and Saída's mechanical eyes.

The way to their hideout was quite confusing, even when they could see where they were going. A labyrinthine series of tunnels, passageways, and little paths that most would have overlooked. Saída couldn't help but respect their efforts. There was no wonder why the Redcloaks were so hesitant to push forward. They would be utterly lost in the maze down here.

Following winding, twisting paths, Saída was convinced the sewer water became darker. The mould on the walls grew larger. Until finally the malodorous air seemed to change, and they came upon a dead end. An unmarked wall. The older man gave it five loud knocks and whistled. The sound of heavy, sliding stone filled the air, as the wall was pushed open by a pair of lookouts who let them in. Saída and Rodok were led into a bunker, where they were finally allowed to remove their blindfolds.

The bunker was quite big, spacious, green, and much too hot. The inside seemed to be built directly into the maze-like sewer system, running under the city itself. This was how the resistance had managed to stay hidden. The bunker housed several rooms all connected by a large hallway. Saída and Rodok followed the men towards the end of the hall, noticing how one room was designated the sickbay, where medics catered to the sick and injured, among them a man with a savage cut on his arm. Saída winced at the sight. Another room was turned into an armoury, where Saída saw some women taking stock of their inventory. She heard the familiar clicks of weapons being loaded with ammunition, and the sound the magazines made as they were firmly slotted back into their weapon chambers. Then there was a kitchen with the spicy-sweet smells of meat rations and an old woman who poured more water into a pot of broth. Saída felt a pang of hunger. The bunker was bustling with activity, and Saída wondered just how many bunkers like this were across the city, or even across Sektor 15 as a whole.

"Through there," said the older man, pointing towards a room at the end, which glowed with the distinct orange light of fire.

Saída and Rodok walked into the room which housed Gardener's forge. The difference in temperature was immediately apparent, with the hot steam already starting to make her sweat. Oil-stained, ash-covered mechanised anvils with piston-hammers, and ore-dispensaries were scattered about the room, an auto-smelter was perilously close to the entrance, while on each wall there was an array of tools, such as sparkhammers, vibro-tongs and stuff Saída didn't even know what to call. In the centre was a grand mechanical forge. Swirls of red-hot flame danced behind a glass pane inside the forge and steam poured out of the exhaust ports on the side.

A dark-skinned woman dressed in blue overalls and protective gear stopped her work and came over to Saída, removing the bulky safety goggles that went atop her short, curly black hair.

"Gardener, I presume," said Saída.

"Abbas. You're looking for a gunsmith, I hear. The one on your Sektor not good enough?" Gardener asked.

"Guessing you don't know much about Sektor 47?"

"Should I?"

"Probably," said Saída. "But then, you've got your own battles to fight, don't you? What happened here? I know it's not about taxes or whatever other bullshit the Grand Design is spinning."

"I'm sure that's the story they'll be going for, until they can prove they've got a good reason to revert to the old governmental system without too much backlash from opposing lobbies on Sektor Prime."

"As if they give a shit," Saída said.

"Of course they don't." Gardener waved her hand. "They're more pissed about things changing than anything else."

"So, it's that simple, huh?"

"Isn't it always? What kind of gun are you looking for?"

"A gun isn't the only thing I'm looking for, Gardener. Do you know where I can find Isiah Thomas?"

Gardener deflated at the mention of the name.

"Isiah's dead, Abbas. Has been for months."

Saída clenched her fists. And just like that, the lead had run cold. Again.

"What happened?" Saída asked.

Gardener said bitterly, "Seen the city on your way down? Redcloaks dropped bombs on us. Watchers burned it all down. Isiah and his family were some of the first to go."

Saída lowered her gaze. Just like Sektor 47.

"What were you gonna ask him?" Gardener asked.

Saída paused. This wasn't something she wanted to discuss with anyone, but without Isiah she had nothing. She was desperate. Maybe Gardener had something. Could Saída risk it?

"I was going to ask him if he had any info on Digby Hickston. Long shot, but you wouldn't happen to know—"

"Sorry, but no. I don't know anything about Hickston. What I do know is how to make a damn fine gun. So what've you got?" Gardener held out her hand expectantly.

Scav.

Saída produced the chunk of illuminite ore that she had found on Sektor 23, and a spec sheet that she had made and handed them over to Gardener.

Gardener's face dropped as she studied the specs of Saída's weapon.

"This looks like it was drawn up by a kid."

Rodok chortled in monotone and Saída scowled.

"Can it be made or not?" she asked, trying to hide her embarrassment.

"I'll need to make some adjustments, but yes. It can. I'll need some time."

"That's what I'd expect from a renowned gunsmith. How many shards?"

Gardener studied the chunk of ore that Saída had given her. "We'll talk about what you owe me once I'm done. Oh, and try *legendary*, Abbas." She smirked.

Saída folded her arms. "You pull this off and you just might be."

Gardener set the spec sheet to the side and placed the illuminite in a vice on the mechanised anvil, getting it ready for processing. She set the piston-hammer to work on the illuminite and Saída felt just a tinge of pride as she saw the hammer fail to crack the ore. Gardener wore special gloves and deactivated the piston-hammer, grabbing the now-glowing illuminite ore with a pair of vibro-tongs, and placed it into a central node under the glass pane of the forge. She entered some calibrations into the forge terminal and then shifted over to a special fabricator in the corner. Saída could tell that it had been modified for smithing work. Almost in a trance, Saída didn't notice Gardener was speaking.

"On your specs you said you want a word engraved on the barrel, but I don't recognise the language. What is it?" Gardener asked.

Saída's eyes were fixed on the flames that were melting the illuminite ore, processing it into a finer material.

"It's Meraji," said Saída. "It says *Scimitar*."

CHAPTER ELEVEN

Sektor 47

In the darkness of the cave, Saída felt cold, metallic hands grip her body as the red-eyed mechanical monster lifted her out of the rubble. She thrashed around, trying to get free, but she was too weak. She screamed for help, but she knew no one would come. The colossus came to a stop and with Saída in one hand, it used the other to start drilling into a cave wall. Little by little, the wall gave way and with a final thrust of its drill, the monster broke it apart. It tossed Saída outside the cave and she felt the heat of the sun on her face once again as she hit the ground. She risked another peek at the monster and saw its crimson eyes staring back at her, inhuman, but shifting and moving around in its sharp, pointed face. The machine's black chassis blended into the darkness of the cave and then, with a grinding, mechanical buzz it spoke.

"*Leave*, little *one*. You *are* disrupting *my* work."

It rotated its head and walked backwards, or forwards,

into the cave. She was alive. Saída couldn't believe it. The mechanical monster hadn't hurt her. She got up and limped away from the cave, trying to make sense of her whereabouts. The scorching sun bore down on her. Her injuries stung across her body. Saída panted, struggling across the dirty red earth.

Before long, she heard metal hacking away at rock, and followed the sound to an open area, where several men worked, mining ore deposits with dark metal pickaxes. Saída hobbled towards them, then suddenly noticed a pair of Redcloaks standing guard. She tried to hide, but it was too late. She had been spotted. One of the Redcloaks sighed and nudged the other one, who promptly walked over to Saída.

"How the hell did you end up here, kid?" she demanded.

Saída mumbled that it had been an accident and she had fallen. She said she was sorry. The Redcloak rolled her eyes.

"Come with me," she said, and led Saída away.

Saída followed her, trying to avoid the gaze of the other Redcloak. He wasn't paying much attention, so Saída steadied her breathing. They came to a path that sloped upwards, leading back up the mountain.

The Redcloak pointed to it and said, "Can you make your way back from here? Don't let me catch you down here again. Accident or not."

With that she walked away, muttering something about *sandskins.* Saída began walking up the path, making a silent prayer of thanks that she had been spared so far.

By nightfall, she returned to Uncle's bar, to open

arms. Uncle Abbas patched up her wounds and gave her a scolding, but she knew he held back because of how bad she looked. What worried Saída was that there had seemingly been no retaliation for what she had started with the Redcloaks. She was afraid.

"Beti," said Uncle Abbas, holding Saída close. "What happened?"

Tears welled in her eye as she remembered the horror she felt as the Redcloaks pursued her. Uncle Abbas dropped the question.

"It is okay, beti. I am here now. I am here."

Uncle Abbas hugged her tight, soothing her until she was ready to sleep.

Saída buried her face into the thin pillow she had, letting the temporary peacefulness of sleep take over. The last thoughts she had were of the monster in the cave. She had to go back.

*

As she spent the days recovering from her injuries, hidden in the bar, Saída would study the miners and the Redcloaks. She would watch them go down into the mines in the morning and come back up every night. Without exception, they would vacate the area. Saída considered how long it would take her to go all the way down, find the cave and the monster, then come back up to Uncle's bar, but there was no way she would make it back in time, not before Redcloaks on their way down would see her. If she took food with her and remained in the cave for a day, then Uncle Abbas would be worried. Then it hit her.

She ran out of the bar, heading towards the old plot. She was apprehensive the closer she got, but snuck closer to it, watching out for any Redcloaks. Fortunately, it was empty. Walking into the plot, Saída saw just how much damage had been done to it. Some of the walls that had even survived the burning, were now shattered, and a new opening had been uncovered. It had stairs that led down to the basement that Saída and the Redcloaks had fallen into. The hole that they had fallen from was patched up with a sheet of synthmetal. Saída followed the stairs down, hoping the Redcloaks would have no further reason to return here.

The basement was dark, and still cluttered with a lot of old machinery and mining equipment, but Saída did notice that there was some equipment that was missing. The Redcloaks must have returned here later and taken some of it back. As to their intention, Saída didn't know or care. She rooted around in the old mining equipment, tossing away old, rusted pickaxes made of much older, weaker metals. She found old gloves and goggles and other useless items. Then she came upon an old harness with a long cable attached to it. Miners still used similar, albeit more advanced, harnesses to get to ore that was out of reach, and this would help Saída get back down to the cave. Saída had found what she was looking for.

She dusted off the harness and the cable and fastened it around her waist, the belt-like contraption snapping into place easily with a mechanical lock. She then tied the cable around to the biggest piece of machinery in the basement, securing it around tightly, and connecting the cable hook to a clasp and making sure it was set properly, just as she had seen the miners do. The equipment was old, but simple enough to use. Modern cables went far longer and were even retractable, but Saída had to handle this one manually.

Once she was satisfied that the cable was secure, she found the same opening which she had used to escape, and crawled in. She managed to squeeze through carefully, avoiding any injury. Without the danger of being captured, she was able to carefully navigate the rocks with her climbing gloves, using the cable to help ease her back down to the bottom of the cave.

As she descended, she recognised some of the jutting formations that had broken her fall on the way down. The shaft became tighter, more claustrophobic the further she spelunked, but she kept her breathing steady and continued. Before long, her legs hovered a few feet above solid ground. Saída unclasped her harness and dropped to the ground, leaving the harness swinging side to side, like a dangling claw.

It was inconvenient, but Saída was sure she could grab onto the cable and reattach the harness.

She recognised the sound of mechanical drilling, deeper in the cave. Taking a deep breath, she began to sneak towards it, noticing bright lights appearing around the walls and ceiling, the deeper she went in. Eventually she found herself in a cavern that was illuminated by glowing ore all around it, on the walls, the ceiling, even embedded into stalactites and stalagmites. At the far end was the mechanical colossus. It bore into the illuminite deposits that littered the cavern. Its back was turned to her, but as she approached, she heard its voice buzz throughout the cave, so loud that she felt it vibrate through her ribcage.

"*I* told *you* to *leave.*"

Saída ignored it and pressed onwards, studying its body more closely. The chassis was badly rusted and caked in dust, but beneath the age, she could tell that it had once been black like obsidian. It had legs and arms like a human's, but completely mechanical in nature. The strangest thing about it was how tall it was, and the way its crimson eyes rotated and shifted around its head. Those same eyes moved to the back of its head, looking directly at Saída. It didn't even have to turn around or stop drilling.

"What are you?" Saída asked.

"What *indeed*?"

"Are you a person?" Saída inched closer.

A sound akin to the grinding of gears came from inside the machine. Was it… was *he* chuckling?

"I *am* an *android*. Designation *1-1-2-1-3-4-7.* Priority *target:* Confidential. *Serial:* Unlisted. *Manufacturer:* Redacted," buzzed the android, causing Saída's head to spin.

"You are an… and…" attempted Saída, trying to repeat the Android's words.

He stopped drilling and his lower body turned to match the direction of his face. He looked at Saída for a moment.

"Hm. *I* am *a* robot," he said.

Saída tilted her head. "A… rodok?"

"You *are* quite *a* stupid *child*, aren't *you*?" he buzzed.

Saída frowned. "I'm not stupid! You're stupid."

She picked up a small rock and flung it at him. "You're a stupid Rodok."

The rock bounced off his chassis harmlessly but one of his eyes followed its trajectory. The other still had its gaze fixed on Saída.

"I *am* not *stupid*. I *am* fitted *with* an *Advanced* Intelligence *system* and *am* thus *capable* of *higher* thought, *reasoning*, and *critical* analysis."

Saída's face contorted in an expression of bewilderment. "What?"

Rodok turned around and went back to working at the illuminite.

Saída stood next to him, watching him work. The longer his drill was active, the brighter the ore glowed, but Rodok would periodically shut down the drill and let the illuminite cool and dim before he began anew.

"Stand *back*, stupid *child*," he said, as the sparks from the drill began flying again.

"I'm not stupid," she said, taking a step back. "And my name is Saída."

"It *is* nice *to* meet *you*, stupid *Saída*," he buzzed with unmistakable glee.

Saída bristled at the continued taunts. This Rodok's voice was starting to get annoying.

"You're stupid. I'm going home."

Saída walked away, going back the way she came. She didn't notice the sound of the drilling had stopped. When she reached her harness, still dangling in the air, she tried to reach for it, but couldn't. It was too high. She grunted and tried to jump as high as she could, but to no avail. The most she could do was touch the harness with her fingers.

Then she felt metallic hands pick her up and raise her towards the harness. Saída clasped the harness around her waist and pulled on the cable to make sure it was still strong. Rodok left her and she began to climb back up, occasionally looking back down at him.

"Do *not* return, *stupid* Saída," he said. It sounded more like advice than a warning.

"I *will*," Saída shot back, her eye fixed on Rodok's.

Rodok buzzed a monotone laugh.

"*As* you *wish*."

CHAPTER TWELVE

Sektor 15

Gardener fiddled with different energy settings on her forge, pushing, turning and pulling various buttons, dials and levers which let steam pour out of the top exhaust ports. The illuminite was finally done melting and was collected into a round container inside the forge. Saída could see the machine working under a pane of special glass, the golden illuminite burned bright like a liquid star. Saída had never seen it in this form.

"How many times have you worked with illuminite?" she asked.

Gardener wiped sweat from her forehead, continuing to work at a strange block of metal at one of the piston-hammers, near the forge.

"Just a few times," said Gardener. "It's a pretty rare metal. Most of the ones I've worked with have been stolen, just like this one."

Saída leaned back in her chair. "Nope. This one's mine."

Gardener scoffed. "Uh-huh."

Saída bristled at that. "It belongs to me. It comes from my home world."

"Sektor 47?" Gardener asked.

"It's Meraj."

Gardener nodded. "Meraj, huh? Is that what it's really called? I guess I do know your world then. My great grandmother lived there for a while, I think. That's the name she used for it too. Meraj."

Saída raised her eyebrows. "Is that how you know how to work illuminite?"

Gardener turned a dial on the forge and activated miniature cooling jets inside it, causing more steam to pour out of the machine.

"My mother taught me. Her mother taught her. But I think my something-great grandmother must have learned from your people. People used to share a lot, back in that age. Before the Grand Design. Though I don't think either of our ancestors ever expected us to be making weapons out of illuminite," Gardener said.

"They'd understand," said Saída. She felt herself withdrawing from the conversation. Thinking of Uncle Abbas and the stories he told her about the days before the Grand Design. She wondered just what the galaxy was like before it was colonised and corrupted. An Age of Cooperation. Could such a thing really have existed?

The sound of metal grinding on metal filled the room, as Gardener's machine fabricated something for her. She had a look of intense concentration, as she entered several keys into the machine and kept double-checking its settings.

Saída buried her doubts. No time for what-ifs.

"What are you working on there?" she asked.

"Quiet for a second," Gardener hissed, watching values and symbols turn and twist on the screen, which then portrayed a 3D model of a metallic slab being rotated.

Saída and Rodok exchanged a glance of amusement, but Saída remained quiet, waiting for Gardener to finish.

Eventually, Gardener turned back to face Saída and Rodok.

"Sorry," she said. "What were you saying?"

"Oh well, now that I have your permission…"

Gardener scratched her head. "Yeah… sorry about that. I—"

"You *were* just *making* sure *everything* was *in* order?" offered Rodok.

Gardener's demeanour flipped like a switch. She pointed at Rodok in agreement. "Yes. Yes, exactly, robot. Making sure everything was in order. You're welcome, Abbas."

"My *name* is *Rodok*."

"Huh?"

"Right," said Saída quickly. "What were you doing with the thing?"

She pointed to the machine near the forge, which still exhaled smoke.

Gardener had a twinkle in her eye as she began pressing some buttons on the fabricator's terminal.

"Why don't I just show you?" she said.

A tray was ejected from beneath the terminal and on it was a slab of synthmetal. Gardener held it up for Saída and Rodok to see. In it, Saída recognised the vague shape of a revolver pistol. A smile formed in the corner of her mouth.

"See this? After some adjustments, I was able to salvage some real schematics off your spec sheet. Once I calibrated the data, I fed it to my fabricator and made a mold for your Scimitar."

"That *is* why *you* told *Saída* to *shut* up," Rodok added.

Saída scowled. "She did not tell me—"

"Exactly, robot." Gardener beamed, holding the Scimitar mold like an award.

"Alright, so now what?" Saída folded her arms.

"Well, now's the easy part," said Gardener, moving to the forge and entering some keys into the terminal there. "Once I place the mold inside, the melted illuminite should pour in and the forge will do the rest. Then I'll complete the finishing touches once the mold is done and get to work on the other molds and finish—"

"Wait, so there's more to do after the mold is filled? And there's more than *one* mold? How many stages are there to this thing?"

Gardener scrunched her nose at Saída. "What, did you think this shit was magic?"

Saída put a hand on her hip and rolled her eyes. "I figured it *must* be, the way you can't seem to shut up about it."

Rodok moved closer to the forge as the other two bickered about gunsmithing. He watched the hot golden liquid pour into the mold, behind the glass pane of the forge. Different tools inside the forge worked to heat and cool and shape the molten illuminite into the mold. Rodok studied the entire process, collecting data. Then with a crackle, all the lights in the bunker died. The forge was shut down.

Gardener kicked the forge. "Damn it."

"What now?" Saída asked.

One of the men from the other room rushed in. "Aveline, the generator's been shut down."

"Is it a malfunction?" Gardener asked.

"Negative. We think it's been sabotaged. We found some of our men knocked out while we were out on patrol."

Gardener looked at Saída. There was alarm in her voice. "Abbas," she said. "If the illuminite goes cold, you lose your Scimitar. You need to get the generator back up and running."

Saída nodded, pulling out her pistol, loaded with a drum of lethal shells.

She followed the man out, with Rodok following behind her.

Saída shook her head. "Stay with Gardener, Rodok."

"*But* she *called* me *Robot.*"

"If any of those Redcloak assholes show up, I want you to do what you can to help these people. And more importantly, get my Scimitar."

Rodok rotated his head, agreeing.

Saída rushed back out into the sewers, gun in hand.

CHAPTER THIRTEEN

Sektor 47

It had become a daily occurrence for Saída to visit Rodok down in the caves. As time passed, her friends stopped coming to meet with her, because their parents were worried for them. Worried they would be caught up in Saída's bad luck with the Redcloaks. It hurt of course, but Saída couldn't blame them. Still, at least she had found a friend in Rodok.

The sound of the drill piercing the cavern wall, and the clutter of illuminite as it scattered on the floor had become a comforting sound that Saída enjoyed. She liked to see Rodok scoop up the Roshun and deposit them in piles. Then take the piles, with Saída's help, deeper into the caverns. Rodok had collected a large amount of illuminite, though Saída did not know how long he had been doing this.

"Rodok?" she said, vying for his attention.

"Yes?" the machine responded, making a new pile.

"How long have you been here?"

Rodok stared at her. It used to be unnerving, but now Saída recognised it as Rodok pausing for thought. Like actual humans. Rodok was undoubtedly a mechanical being, but he was nothing like the mining drones which were incapable of thought or speech beyond basic means. Rodok was something else entirely.

Rodok finally said, "I *do* not *have* authorisation *to* reveal *that* information *at* this *time*."

Saída frowned. Authorisation? That was a Redcloak word. She didn't even know what it meant.

"Why do you need auth... authory—" said Saída, struggling to pronounce the word. Her native accent made it hard to get a grasp on the language.

"*I* am *not* authorised *to* say," Rodok cut in.

Saída sat in silence and let Rodok gather up the illuminite. He hummed a melody as he walked. It had an odd metallic twinge to it. The echo in the caverns didn't help. She followed him to his lair, where he stored the illuminite.

It was hidden deep in the caverns, a labyrinth to anyone who wasn't Rodok and now, Saída. Rodok had amassed a great deal of illuminite in this little chamber. Varying stones and chunks of ore were piled up, and Rodok took great care in how he organised his piles. Saída could relate. She liked making piles too. He sat down, still humming, separating the Roshun.

"What are you humming, Rodok?" Saída asked.

Rodok stopped sorting the piles and looked at her.

"*It* is *my* activation *day* today. *I* do *this* every *year*."

Saída's eyes widened, and she grinned. "It's your birthday today?"

"I *suppose* you *could* call *it* that, *yes*."

"Happy birthday, stupid Rodok," said Saída, handing him a pebble of Roshun from one of his piles.

"Thank *you*, silly *Saída*." Rodok chuckled, the grinding gears in his metallic throat creating a sound that was quite familiar to Saída now.

Rodok pushed buttons on his arm and the centre of his chest released a puff of gas. He tugged at it with his mechanical fingers and pulled it open, revealing a glowing, gold cylinder inside. Rodok removed it and waved it over the new piles of illuminite they had brought.

Saída watched the golden cylinder fluctuate as it passed over another pile, then looked at Rodok.

"Is that your heart?"

"*Silly* Saída. *A* robot *cannot* have *a* heart."

"Then what is it?"

Rodok opened the top of the cylinder, a lid, which emitted a strangely sweet-smelling odour. Saída covered her nose. Rodok then took the illuminite stone that Saída had given him and dropped it into the cylinder, closing the lid. Then he connected it to his chest with a click. He closed the compartment, and it was resealed, leaving no indication that such an opening existed.

"Were you charging your battery?" Saída asked.

"I *am* evaluating *the* purity *of* the *ore*."

"Ohhh." Saída nodded, pretending to know what that meant.

She picked a couple of stones from the same pile, fiddling with them in the palm of her hand. She expected Rodok to be irritated but he didn't seem to mind.

"Do *not* eat *them*, silly *Saída*," he said.

Saída imagined a cheeky grin where his mouth should have been. "I'm not a baby, okay? I'm just looking," she said. "I had a pebble of Roshun but one of the Redcloak officers took it away."

Saída tapped the stones against each other, smiling as they glowed.

"What *are* these *Redcloaks*?" Rodok asked.

The question caught her off guard. Saída had never been on the receiving end of a difficult question from Rodok.

She grimaced. "They're bad people. They bully and hurt me and Uncle Abbas and everyone on Sektor 47."

"*Sektor* 47?"

Saída nodded. "Where we live. Here."

"*Are* we *not* on *the* planet *designated* Meraj?"

Saída gasped. No one said the name so casually. Not unless they wanted to be arrested.

"Uncle Abbas said that it used to be called... that. Before the Redcloaks came."

Rodok paused, then simply said, "I *see*."

"I thought you knew all of this, Rodok?" Saída asked.

"*It* is *strange*. I *should*. It *appears* I *am* cut *off* from *the* Network. *I* have *been* made... *obsolete*."

Saída was puzzled. "I don't know what that means."

Rodok's eyes danced playfully on his blank face.

"Come, *Saída*. I *think* it *is* time *for* you *to* return *home*."

CHAPTER FOURTEEN

Sektor 15

Saída stalked the tunnels of the sewers, each step measured and silent. She upturned her eye patch, revealing her prosthetic eye to scan the darkened tunnels for intruders. The resistance fighters patrolled the surrounding tunnels, while she made her way to the generator room. All she had to do was turn it back on and her beautiful Scimitar would finally be ready.

Saída turned a corner into a new tunnel. It was thinner than the ones she had seen so far. The odour was still foul as Saída stepped through the murky water, towards an open door at the end of the tunnel. It was the generator room, tucked away under an arch. Saída walked through the door, studying the dark room. It seemed clear. The generator sat in the centre of the room, a large machine with pistons and gears and wires that reached up towards the ceiling. Saída searched for the activation button when something caught her eye. In the corner, not too far from the generator, she spotted the corpse of a resistance fighter. Footsteps behind her. Saída rolled to the right, narrowly avoiding an incoming blade, which bounced off the generator.

She saw a man in red combat armour, Complex-Carbonweave like her spacesuit, brandishing a sword, which he pointed at Saída. She trained her gun on him in turn. He walked out of the shadows and Saída saw his face clearly. Short black hair and a goatee that only he would think was fashionable.

"Almost had you," the man said, a familiar gravelly tone to his voice.

"Kruger," muttered Saída.

"You remembered me. I'm touched, Abbas."

"Hard to forget. You tried to kill me the *first* time we met, too."

"And now you're all grown up, how about that?"

They circled each other in the generator room, Kruger making sure to stay in Saída's way, preventing access to the generator.

"I don't know if you know this, but I'm on official Guild business, Kruger," said Saída. "Here to apprehend Aveline Gardener. You're interfering."

"Oh, I heard. I couldn't believe Matthias actually let you join."

His sword was raised defensively.

"More like he begged me to join," Saída said. Her back was to the door.

"Somehow I doubt that, Abbas." Kruger lunged.

Saída jumped out of the generator room, into the open space of the tunnel, keeping her distance from the long reach of Kruger's sword. He grinned as he walked out of the door, arms outstretched, taunting her.

Out of instinct, Saída unloaded a couple of shots into his chest, but they just left mild scorch marks on his armour before fading. Blast-resistant, just like hers. Lethal shells wouldn't penetrate. Saída narrowed her eyes.

Kruger caressed his black beard, twirling his sword in the other hand and said, "Not a bad attempt, kid."

"Why the hell are you even here, Kruger? I doubt it was just for me."

Kruger grinned, resting his sword on his shoulder. "Why, Abbas. I'm here for the same reason as you. To deliver Gardener to the Cloaks. And imagine my surprise when I see you on your way to the generator room."

Saída stayed quiet, her gun still pointed at Kruger.

Kruger held a hand next to his ear, mocking Saída. "What's that? You're *helping* her? Oh, well that changes everything, doesn't it? I suppose I'll be collecting two bounties instead of one."

Saída took a shot, but Kruger had already moved for cover. The bullet hit his sword instead, and the blade glowed brighter. The impact of the bullet had begun to heat it up.

"*Roshun...*" whispered Saída, glaring at the blade in Kruger's hands.

"Still, I'm not surprised. You know what they say, after all," Kruger said, detaching a red mask from his belt and putting it on. A clunky helmet with two glowing yellow slits for eyes formed around his face and changed the pitch of his voice with a modulator, a thin yellow bar between the eyes that glowed as he spoke. "Birds of a feather, and all that."

He rushed towards Saída, the faint glow of his sword was the only thing illuminating the darkness, but Saída was able to see just fine with her prosthetic eye. She unloaded more shots, but they landed uselessly on his armour and sword, which became brighter and hotter with the impact of the shells.

Kruger got close enough to Saída and swung his sword. She jumped backwards, avoiding the blade, but the sword cut through the barrel of her pistol like butter. She continued to create distance between herself and Kruger, while his distorted laugh echoed through the tunnels. Her broken pistol was glowing molten red where Kruger had cut it. Saída grunted and tossed it away.

"Oh no, not your *pistol*," mock-whined Kruger.

"Where'd you get that sword, Kruger?"

"What, this? Like it?" he asked, stopping to admire it. "It was a gift from a Viceroy I did some work for, a few years back. I'd tell you more, but, well. I'm trying to kill you."

"Were you, Kruger? I guess I didn't notice since you're so bad at it," taunted Saída, reaching for her belt.

Kruger chuckled. "Abbas, you're one of the good ones."

He ran at Saída again, preparing to strike, but right before the blow connected, Saída withdrew her dagger from her belt, blocking the attack from Kruger.

Saída had to use both hands to keep the sword from overpowering her dagger, but Kruger just whistled in amusement.

"Now where did you get a little beauty like that, Abbas?"

Saída winced, the heat from the locked blades bearing down on her, and a kick from Kruger pushed her away.

She regained her balance and shifted the illuminite dagger in her hand, eyeing Kruger.

She was focused on getting past him and back to the generator so that Gardener could finish her Scimitar, but Kruger wasn't going to make it easy. The more time wasted here, the longer her illuminite went to waste.

Kruger tapped his sword against the wall, giggling to himself. This was just a game to him. *Tap.* Saída paid attention to his sword. *Tap.* The sword wasn't heating up as fast as illuminite normally did. Saída grinned.

Kruger noticed that and brandished his sword, which was now rapidly cooling down.

The two ran at each other again, exchanging blows. For every strike Kruger made, Saída parried with her dagger. Her blade glowed hotter, but Kruger's seemed to dull much faster.

"Your sword," Saída said. "I hope that's not all you got for that job, cos the Viceroy ripped you off."

"What?" spat Kruger, inspecting his sword.

Saída ran at him, trailing her dagger along the wall. The illuminite dagger began to glow white-hot. Sparks flew off the walls. Kruger brought up his sword to block high, but Saída feinted and ducked at the last second. She slashed his midriff, cutting through his armour and piercing flesh, unleashing a cloud of red mist.

Kruger clutched his side and yelled, slashing at Saída. She deflected, hitting the base of Kruger's blade, and severed it from the hilt. It bounced off the wall with a clang, dropping into the water. Defeated, Kruger fell to his knees.

"Oh relax, Kruger. It won't kill you," said Saída with a shrug. Kruger cried out in pain.

Saída placed a hand on Kruger's helmet, deactivating it and pulled off his mask. She slammed the pommel of her dagger against his neck and Kruger fell face-first into the murky water. Her dagger went dull, from a blazing white, to a cool black. The word *Daiyu* was engraved into the blade. It brought up unpleasant memories. She sheathed the dagger and focused on searching Kruger's pockets for anything important. She found Kruger's Guild badge, which she eagerly appropriated.

"Good luck piloting your ship without this, asshat," she said.

Heading back into the generator room, Saída slammed the big red button and the generator hummed to life. The lights in the room turned back on. She took a breath and pulled down her eye patch, covering her prosthetic eye. Outside, the tunnels were bright once more, lighting the way back to Gardener's hideout. One of Gardener's men met her outside the generator room.

"You find anyone?" he asked.

Saída nodded. "Bounty hunter named Kruger Vex. He's probably still passed out down that tunnel," she said. "You didn't see him?"

The man shook his head.

Saída ground her teeth. Bastard was like a cockroach.

"Did you find anyone else in the tunnels?" she asked, walking back down the tunnel. A glint in the water caught her attention.

"No one. Seems like the guy you fought off was the only one down here."

"He got one of your men. I'm sorry."

"So am I."

Saída nodded, her fingers finding the broken blade in the shallow, murky water. With Kruger still out there, she had to be on high alert. The Redcloaks on the surface, Watchers in the air and now bounty hunters like Kruger too. Something was off here. But Saída couldn't put her finger on it just yet. The pieces had barely begun to form in her mind.

"Let's head back," said Saída.

The situation was spiralling out of control. She and Rodok needed to retrieve her Scimitar and get the hell off Sektor 15 before it was too late.

CHAPTER FIFTEEN

Sektor 47

Saída ate a spoonful of daal, as she sat in the corner of the bar, watching Uncle Abbas clean the counter and prepare it for business. Redcloaks had slowly begun to return, and Uncle Abbas warned Saída to stay in the back when they came around. Usually, Saída would just visit Rodok. All Uncle Abbas knew was that she liked to play in the burned manor at the old plot. It was close enough to his bar that he didn't get too worried. Saída scratched at the wrappings on the left side of her face. She still wasn't used to the loss of her eye. Sometimes it still hurt. Like a stabbing pain, even though her left eye was no longer there. She didn't understand it.

"Saída, beti. Don't scratch. I'll change your wrappings soon. Something more comfortable."

"Sorry Uncle," she murmured, going back to her meal.

Uncle Abbas replaced a bottle on the top shelf.

"God, forgive me," he muttered under his breath. He didn't actually say 'God' but rather one of the many names in Meraji which meant the same thing. But those weren't names they said often, and especially not in the presence of Redcloaks. The names were special, private and of spiritual importance to each Meraji. It was not something they would give up willingly.

Uncle Abbas said it every day, quietly, ritualistically. It was his only form of meditation, of connection, to their religion. The way of their ancestors, which had been lost to them.

"Uncle, who are the Liberation League?" Saída asked, bringing an end to the silence.

He turned suddenly, his eyes were piercing, but there was sadness in them. She thought it was anger at first, but it wasn't. It was a profound emptiness.

"Where did you hear that name?" he asked her softly.

Saída put her plate down and hugged her knees. "I heard you and some of the miners talking about it."

Uncle Abbas leaned over the counter and gestured for Saída to come and take a seat. She did so, and Uncle Abbas patted her on the head.

"Well, Saída. They're a group of people, like us. Forty-Sevens, but they live elsewhere. Cities in the eastern hemisphere, in the north. They formed a group so they could ask the Grand Design to grant us independence from their rule."

"Isn't that good?"

"It is," said Uncle Abbas. Saída looked into his sad eyes.

"Then why were you angry with them?"

Uncle Abbas closed his eyes, the muscles on his

95

forehead contracted. Like he was trying to force his eyes shut forever.

"I was not angry with them. I was afraid. For you. And that came out like anger. It was a mistake to react like that, but in the end, beti, we are all human. Sometimes it is hard to remain calm. Especially when the ones you love are hurting."

Saída wrapped her bony arms around his face and hugged him. He grinned and hugged her back. She always felt safe in his arms and hoped that maybe he felt the same way.

"Come now, beti. No more talk of the League. We have enough to worry about. Let's get you something more comfortable," he said, picking her up and taking her into the other room. He removed her wrappings and replaced them with a soft white eye patch, which barely covered the scars above her left eye socket.

Saída kept her eye shut, because she didn't want to see Uncle Abbas's reactions to the injury. He tried to hide his despair, but his eyes always gave it away. He felt it just as she did.

CHAPTER SIXTEEN

Sektor 15

Back at Gardener's forge, Saída saw that she was hard at work, clicking away at the forge terminal, setting commands for the forge to begin the next steps for the molten illuminite and the Scimitar's mold. Next to her stood Rodok, completely motionless and an arm outstretched, holding a rag. Gardener reached out for it, wiped her face, and hung it back over Rodok's arm.

"Did I make it in time?" asked Saída.

"You almost didn't. I was about to come after you myself," snapped Gardener, busy at another terminal.

"So, we made it just in time then," said Saída, falling into a chair and relaxing a bit.

Gardener grumbled a bit but continued to work away at her terminals.

"Believe me, Gardener. I would've been just as upset as you if that illuminite had gone to waste," said Saída.

"Maybe, but I wish you'd gotten it done sooner anyway.

Illuminite is so rare, just the thought of *any* of it going to waste is a nightmare."

"I ran into some trouble. Bounty hunter named Kruger," said Saída.

Rodok turned his head, coming to life.

"Ah. *Matthias's* favourite *dog*," he buzzed.

Gardener looked apprehensive but didn't comment. She opened the glass pane of the forge, and a tray with the mold was lifted out, cooled in liquid nitrogen. She grabbed it with a pair of tongs and moved it to her fabricator, which swallowed the mold. Sounds of ticking and beeping spewed from the machine, as Gardener set to work on the next steps of creating Saída's new weapon.

Saída dared not speak as Gardener went to work. She masterfully shaped and modelled the weapon on the screen, from the grip to the hammer, all the way down the barrel. It was beautiful. Then at last came the finishing touch, the engraving of the Meraji word, 'Scimitar'.

Gardener picked up the fabricator pen so she could write it on the screen but then she turned to Saída.

"Abbas, it's better if you're the one to write it. It's your language after all," said Gardener.

Saída gulped and went forward, hesitant to hold the pen.

"Just write it over the image of the weapon on the screen. The fabricator will do the physical engraving itself," said Gardener.

Saída held her breath, moving the pen across the barrel of the gun on-screen. In the way that Uncle Abbas had taught her. Not just as writing, but as calligraphy. This weapon would be her connection to him. To Meraj.

CHAPTER SEVENTEEN

Sektor 47

Saída sat in the cavern, biting at an old ration, while Rodok performed his daily tasks, mining, collecting and depositing illuminite. Every so often, he would stop and sit down with Saída, either to taunt her or to tell her to go home. She never listened.

She pulled the wrapper of her ration down further, taking a hungry chomp. Rodok just stared like he usually did, but it wasn't as strange as when people did it. With Rodok, it always looked like he was thinking about something.

"What are you thinking?" Saída asked.

There was an ever so slight twist of his head, as Rodok answered.

"I *am* considering *my* purpose."

Saída looked at her half-eaten ration.

"What is your purpose right now? What do you collect the Roshun for?"

"*That* is *classified*."

Saída nodded. She had understood that to mean he couldn't, or didn't want to tell her.

"Why is it class-a-fied?"

"That *is* also *classified*."

"Do *you* know why it's class-a-fied?" Saída asked.

Rodok paused.

"*Of* course," he snapped, getting back up and returning to an ore deposit.

Saída grinned. "Wow. Stupid Rodok doesn't even know why he collects rocks."

Rodok swivelled his cylindrical head to face Saída. "*I* am *not* stupid, *and* I *do* know *why*."

Saída finished her ration and tossed the wrapper into one of Rodok's piles. Rodok stopped what he was doing.

"Pick *it* up, *stupid* Saída."

"You pick it up, stupid Rodok," she said, mimicking him.

Rodok reached out to grab Saída, but she ran off, giggling. She could hear Rodok lumbering after her, but she kept rushing in and out of tiny openings, avoiding the reach of the mechanical giant.

"Saída, *stop* running. *You* will *hurt* yourself," Rodok called out. There was a shift in the pitch of his voice. He was clearly annoyed, but Saída was enjoying this game of cat and mouse. It reminded her of playing with her friends.

Rodok cornered her and lifted her up with his metal arms. Saída beamed at him, and Rodok's voice returned to its normal pitch.

"Silly *child*," he said.

"You're silly," Saída mimicked, holding back a giggle.

"*And* you *were* right," said Rodok, heading back to the cavern, to Saída's way out.

"Rodok, I don't want to go home just yet," whined Saída.

"*I* am *busy* now. *I* have *much* to *consider.*"

"About your purpose?"

Rodok set her down, near the harness.

"Indeed," he said.

"Why do you have to think about it so much?"

"*Because* I *do.*"

"Rodok…"

Saída looked at him. His imposing figure looked different today. He was slouching. His eyes remained fixed, unmoving, his hands by his side. She felt bad. Had she made him sad? Could a Rodok be sad?

"Are you sad, Rodok?" said Saída.

Rodok's voice was monotone. "Do *not* be *ridiculous.*"

"Still," insisted Saída. "Uncle Abbas told me I should apologise if I make a friend sad."

Rodok's eyes were still for a moment and then began to spin wildly around the contours of his pointed face.

"*Thank* you, *Saída.*"

Saída felt suddenly overwhelmed. The vulnerability which Rodok had just shown was not something she was used to. She stared at her feet and replied in a small voice.

"It's fine."

Rodok chuckled and lifted Saída, who began protesting immediately, helping her into the harness so she could climb back up to the top.

"I *will* think *on* my *purpose*, until *next* we *meet,*" said Rodok, watching Saída climb up.

"Your purpose is being stupid," Saída called down.

What followed was a monotone buzz of laughter that echoed throughout the caves.

CHAPTER EIGHTEEN

Sektor 15

Gardener's fabricator unleashed a hellish amount of steam as the tray was ejected, revealing the Scimitar in its glorious black sheen. Gardener picked up the gun and held it in the light, admiring her handiwork. A long-barrelled revolver with two rotating cylinders which served as bullet chambers, complete with a touch-activated hammer and a comfortable grip. Engraved onto the length of the barrel, in Saída's own handwriting, was the word 'Scimitar' in Meraji calligraphy. For how poorly drawn up her schematics had been, Saída had designed a good weapon, which Gardener turned into a masterpiece.

Saída held out her hand for Gardener to give her the Scimitar, but Gardener pulled it back, spinning the gun by the trigger guard.

"First we discuss the matter of my payment," she said.

"Name your price, Gardener."

"Take us with you," said Gardener, her eyes fixed on Saída's. "Me and my people. Take us off-world."

"I can't do that, Gardener."

"Why the hell not? I did what you asked. Now you owe me."

"The *Lancer* isn't big enough to take all of you, and even if it was, are you really okay with just abandoning your Sektor? What about the rest of the people here?"

Gardener scoffed. "Don't pretend you care about them."

Saída bristled. "You're right. I don't care about them, but I thought you *did*."

Gardener said, "It's not that simple, scavvit. It's better for them if we leave."

Rodok's mechanical body creaked as he shifted upright. "*What* are *you* not *telling* us?"

"I've told you everything you need to know," Gardener insisted.

Rodok got up and walked toward her, causing Gardener to take a defensive stance and aim the Scimitar at Rodok.

"Who *are* you?" Rodok asked, undeterred by the weapon pointed at his face.

"I made your damn gun," Gardener yelled. "Now hold up your end of the bargain, or I swear I'll melt this weapon down to slag."

Saída settled into her seat and folded her arms.

"Why the hell do you want off this rock so bad anyway?"

Gardener looked at her incredulously. "You notice the Redcloaks on your way in?"

Saída shook her head slowly. "Don't give me that shit. There are ruined cities and Redcloaks on damn near every Sektor. There's something else."

Rodok took a step towards Gardener. "*They* are *here* for *her*."

"Don't be ridiculous, Rodok. Just cos she's got a bounty on her head, doesn't mean they'd blockade an entire Sektor for her."

Gardener remained silent.

"Unless…" Saída got out of her chair. "Unless that's exactly why they did that."

"Abbas," said Gardener, aiming the Scimitar at Saída. "Please. Get us off this Sektor and I'll tell you everything."

Saída opened her mouth to respond but was interrupted when one of Gardener's men rushed in, panting.

"Flares," he panted. "Golden flares above the spaceport."

Saída's eyes widened in horror. She looked at Gardener and then at Rodok.

Gardener lowered the Scimitar.

"Looks like none of us are getting off this Sektor."

CHAPTER NINETEEN

Sektor 47

Rodok clawed at a half-depleted ore deposit, unleashing the drill from his hand, piercing through the rock of the cavern wall and reaching into the illuminite further.

Saída sat close by as she usually did, waiting for the opportune moment to speak. It was always after Rodok used the drill, when he had to stop momentarily in order to let the illuminite ore cool down.

"Your hand drill isn't as good as the pickaxes the miners use," she said.

"Yes, *it* is," snapped Rodok.

"No, really," Saída insisted. "Uncle Abbas said that they made those pickaxes with cold Roshun, so they don't have to wait for the Roshun to cool down like you do."

"I *believe* that *my* drill *is* more *than* capable *of* the *task*, Saída."

Saída studied the drill protruding through the palm of Rodok's hand. It was smooth and sharp at the point, but the end of the drill curved upwards. Its shape seemed so familiar to Saída, something from the stories Uncle Abbas would tell her.

"Is your drill a scimitar, Rodok?"

"It *is* not. *It* is *clearly* a *drill.*"

"It reminds me of a scimitar. Do you know what a scimitar is, Rodok?"

Rodok took a break from drilling and let the ore cool down.

"*Yes*, Saída. *I* know *what* a *scimitar* is."

"You know, Uncle Abbas told me—"

"*This* Uncle *Abbas* tells *you* a *lot* of *things.*"

"Do you want to let me finish, stupid Rodok?" Saída snapped.

The gears in Rodok's throat grated. "Please," he gestured with his hand. "*Tell* me *about* what *Uncle* Abbas *told* you."

Saída folded her arms and pouted, turning away from Rodok.

Rodok withdrew his drill from the ore, and it slipped back into the palm of his mechanical hand. He walked over to the rock where Saída was sitting, crouching next to her. His long arms dangled uselessly to his side, strewn across the ground, as he sat on his knees, facing Saída at near eye level.

"Please *tell* me. *I* promise *I* will *listen.*" Rodok's voice was a grinding whisper. He did not often lower his voice, but Saída recognised why he did it. Even after all this time, the machine-man still puzzled her.

"I was just thinking that your drill looks like a scimitar talwar. Like the one Yasín had."

"Who *was* Yasín?" Rodok asked.

Saída's eyes lit up. She loved this story.

"She was the bravest warrior of Sekt— of Meraj. She fought back against the Redcloaks when they first came to our home. She and her friends fought hard. They protected us," Saída said. Her hands moved about in erratic motions as she told the tale that Uncle Abbas had recounted many times.

"She had a scimitar talwar made of pure Roshun, Rodok. It could cut through the armour of any Redcloak. Any who invaded our home. Uncle Abbas said that we call her Nur-al-Meraj. The Light of Meraj," Saída said.

"*What* happ—" Rodok began but stopped himself.

Saída rested her chin on her knees.

"Uncle Abbas said that she died a martyr. Trying to save our people. It all happened a really, really long time ago."

"I *am* sorry, *Saída*."

"It's fine," she said. "Uncle Abbas said that we should be happy that she tried. That we come from strong people. Even if it doesn't feel like it anymore."

"*Well*, I *think* you *Meraji* people *are* quite *strong*," buzzed Rodok.

"But you've only met me."

"*And* that *was* enough."

Saída beamed. Alright. Maybe Rodok wasn't *that* stupid. She hugged him.

They walked back to the harness and Saída prepared to return to the surface, when Rodok stopped her. He splayed the palm of his hand, and a curved drill came out. He disconnected it and handed it over to Saída.

"*Here*, Saída. *Now* you *have* a *scimitar* as *well.*"

Saída held the drill in her hand, and looked from it to Rodok, then back again.

"But Rodok… What about you? Your work?"

"Saída, *do* not *worry.* I *have* found *my* purpose. *I* no *longer* require *the* drill."

Saída threw her arms around Rodok's legs, hugging him tight. They stood there like that for a while. Saída did not let go. Rodok hesitantly placed a heavy hand on her mop of short black hair.

Eventually, Saída relented and let him go. He helped her into the harness, and she began to climb back up.

"Saída," called out Rodok from below.

She looked down to see what he had to say.

"*Always* wait *until* you *can* aim *it* right *here,*" said Rodok, tapping his neck.

Saída giggled and continued her climb upwards. She didn't think he was serious.

She thought about his words that night, and many nights since. Imagining being capable of such violence scared her. She would watch Uncle Abbas in the bar and think about the Redcloaks. What would she do if they attacked again? Saída clutched the scimitar drill tightly in her hands. She would remember Rodok's words.

CHAPTER TWENTY

Sektor 15

Saída ducked in and out of alleyways, avoiding the ruined streets of the city. Isiah was dead. Another lead on Digby gone cold and now they were trapped on a hostile planet, smuggling resistance fighters off-world. Saída wanted to slam her head against a wall. They never should have come here.

Gardener followed close behind as they ducked into another alley. They took care to watch out for Redcloak drones patrolling the darkening skies. Sticking to the alleys and smaller roads had kept them hidden so far. Saída held out her hand, cautioning Gardener to stop, as a pair of Redcloaks passed the alley. Then they continued onwards, climbing up the fire escape of the ruined yellow apartment complex in front of them. They climbed to the second-highest floor and snuck into an apartment through the window.

The inside of the apartment was charred. Bits of broken furniture could still be made out. The door leading out into the rest of the complex was still intact, but in the apartment itself, there looked to have been an explosion that left half of it completely destroyed. It was like the complex had a chunk bitten out of it. Saída and Gardener looked out onto the ruined street below, considering their next move.

"What's the situation?" Gardener said, bringing her SETRA close to her lips.

A crackle and a gravelly voice responded soon after. "So far so good. The robot is pretty smart. We've managed to avoid patrols, but it's taking more time because we've got wounded."

Gardener bit her lip. "Alright, keep me updated."

Saída was crouched behind a flipped table, peering out onto the street, watching a drone fly dangerously close.

"We're on a timer, so anyone who can't get to the *Lancer* on time gets left behind, Gardener. That includes us."

Gardener pinched the bridge of her nose. "You're not getting your gun until we all make it off this rock. That was the deal."

"No way in hell did I agree to that. You saw your chance and you sure took it."

"Like you weren't doing the same thing, Abbas. I've got a bounty on my head. You were just gonna collect the gun and turn me in," snapped Gardener.

Saída rose to her feet and snarled, "Maybe you just helped make that an easy decision, Gardener."

They glared at each other, but the distinct *tik-tik-tik beep* of an approaching drone grew louder. The two of them dove for the table and shut their mouths, as a Watcher floated into the apartment through the open wall.

It was close, but just behind the table. Its eerie song filled the air and fear gripped Saída's heart. *Hmm-hm-hum. La-lalaa-la.* A distorted echo, a tainted lullaby. Gardener reached for her gun, but Saída put her hand on Gardener's. She shook her head slowly and brought a finger to her lips. The Watcher floated off, still humming its spine-chilling tune. It hadn't noticed them. Saída and Gardener breathed with relief. Saída recalled the drones on Meraj. She would never forget the sounds they made. Their song. The song of death.

Saída shook it off and got up from the table, heading for the exit.

"We've still got a ways to go before we get to the spaceport."

Gardener responded with a stiff nod. The Watcher had disturbed her too.

The two of them exited the apartment and made their way down to the stairwell of the dilapidated apartment complex, passing through what would have once been a genuinely nice place to live. Before the Redcloaks bombed the place to hell, Saída could see that this had been a decent building with a degree of comfort significantly better than what she was accustomed to. Saída walked to a window looking out towards the distant outpost. She could see the flares from it, still flying and exploding high in the sky. A tightening sensation gripped her throat. The golden flares were an event reserved for Redcloak celebrations. For the people of every Sektor though, it just meant things were about to get worse. A lot worse.

"We need to move," Gardener said, heading down another flight of stairs to the first floor. Saída followed, dagger at the ready, hoping they wouldn't encounter any hostiles. Her breath caught in her throat when she saw a pair of charred corpses attached to a half-opened apartment door on the first floor. There must have been many victims who didn't even know what the Redcloaks were about to do. There was nothing she could do for them, they had to keep moving. And yet, it felt wrong to Saída. It felt wrong to abandon them like that. But she had to.

Once on the ground floor, Saída motioned for Gardener to follow her out the back door of the apartment complex. Was this really all because the Redcloaks wanted Gardener? So much destruction just for her? Saída felt a pit in her stomach, and it was only growing worse.

"After we're off this Sektor, I'll drop you off wherever the hell you want, but for now, shut up and do what I say."

Gardener scowled but agreed with a jerk of her head and followed Saída out of the alley and across another razed street. They were getting close to the spaceport. Now Saída just had to come up with a way for her to sneak in and get to the *Lancer* without alerting the Redcloaks. They were almost out.

The howl of a warning siren filled the night sky, drowning everything else out. The sound sent a shiver down the back of Saída's neck. She felt like her ears would bleed. Saída and Gardener ducked behind a dumpster as they noticed Redcloaks walking back towards the spaceport. As the siren wailed, Saída's SETRA beeped, and she activated it. Its screen lit up with a trimensional, greyscale image of Rodok that seemed to float off the screen. Some of Gardener's men were behind him. Saída pulled out the SETRA's antenna and pointed it at the alley wall, projecting and tethering the screen onto the wall, turning the image flat. The projection flickered every now and then, but she could clearly see Rodok and the others, albeit under the cover of darkness. She returned the SETRA to her belt.

"Saída," buzzed Rodok. He was worried. "The *Lancelot* just *landed* in *the* spaceport."

They were stunned into silence, and left stewing in trepidation at the news until the siren finally ceased. Gardener looked at Saída, waiting for a reaction, but Saída just stared through her.

"I'm going to need a gun," Saída whispered.

Gardener nodded slowly. "You can have mine then, but this doesn't change anything. You get the Scimitar after we escape."

She handed Saída her pistol. It was nothing special, just a standard issue, probably taken off of some Redcloak. Saída tested the weight of the pistol in her hand, inspected the barrel and the ammunition in the magazine. Lethal shells. Then she pushed Gardener against the wall, arm against her neck, aiming the pistol at her gut.

"Who the *hell* are you, that the Grand Design sent a damn *Knight* to find you?"

Saída felt the barrel of a gun, the Scimitar, aimed at her in turn, and Gardener replied, "We don't exactly have the time to be worrying about that right now, Abbas. So, either pull the trigger and we both get put out of our misery or fulfil your end of the deal and get us the hell off this Sektor."

"If *you* ladies *are* quite *finished*," said Rodok. "I *think* I *may* have *an* idea."

"What'd you have in mind, robot?" asked Gardener, her eyes not leaving Saída's.

"If *we* can *sneak* into *the* spaceport *undetected*, I *can* unlock *the* landing *pads* and *all* the *Redcloak* ships *on* them. *But* we *will* need *a* substantial *distraction*."

Saída reluctantly withdrew the pistol from Gardener's gut and holstered it.

"Fine," she said, glaring at Gardener.

"How are you gonna get in, robot?" Gardener asked him.

"*I* will *jump*."

"You'll… jump?"

"*Yes*. I *can* carry *three* people *at* once. *We* will *require* multiple *jumps*."

"Hence the substantial distraction," Gardener said.

"*Precisely*," Rodok whirred.

Saída turned away from Gardener and the trimensional projection of Rodok and walked deeper into the alley. Fear had her lungs in a vice, and it was getting hard to breathe. At least it seemed that way to her. She closed her eyes and thought back to Uncle Abbas. The bar. Their home.

"Abbas?" called Gardener.

Saída pulled Kruger's mask from her belt, a dour expression on her face. "I think I've got something."

Gardener clicked her tongue in annoyance. "I have a feeling I'm not gonna like this, am I?"

"Nope," said Saída, putting Kruger's mask on her face and activating the helmet. The voice modulator that altered Kruger's voice now worked to her advantage, distorting her voice, and changing it to the same pitch as his had been.

Saída pulled out a pair of electrocuffs and slapped them onto Gardener's hands and she groaned. "I hate you."

"The feeling's mutual, Fifteen," responded Saída, altering her accent. "What do you think of that? Pretty good Kruger impression, right?"

Gardener squinted. "I've never even *met* the guy."

"*Try* making *your* voice *gruffer*," suggested Rodok.

"Alright, how about now?" asked Saída. The voice modulator was doing the heavy lifting, masking her real voice.

"*As* close *as* I *think* you *will* get," said Rodok. "*Are* you *sure* this *will* work?"

"Hell no. But it's all we've got. Our distraction might buy you guys enough time to get to the hangars," said Saída, producing Kruger's Guild badge from her coat. "Kruger has one of those Guild ships, so the badge should serve as the key too. We'll get out on that. They're not letting us get out alive, which is why you need to open up the spaceport and give *us* a distraction too."

"Very *well*."

"Keep an eye in the sky, Rodok. Follow my lead and get those ships ready. Have Gardener's people board as many as possible. Then get to the *Lancer*."

Rodok rotated his head and his miniature drone popped out of his shoulder, then his projection faded and it was just Saída and Gardener once again.

"Keep the Scimitar well hidden, Gardener. All this better be worth something in the end."

Gardener nodded. "Let's get this over with, *Kruger*."

Saída put a hand on Gardener's shoulder, and with the other on her pistol she walked out of the alley, occasionally pushing Gardener to really sell the ruse. They walked towards the entrance of the Redcloak outpost.

It was a small entrance, shielded by tinted glass, but even in the darkness, Saída could make out the Redcloak inside. The barrier would need to be lifted before they could enter the spaceport. She made a silent prayer that Rodok and the others would be able to find their way in.

The Redcloak guard stationed at the entrance raised his gun at them.

"Identify yourselves," he cried.

Saída raised a hand and gave Gardener a shove. "Kruger Vex, Guild bounty hunter. I've got Aveline Gardener in my custody."

Gardener remained quiet, glaring at the Redcloak.

"Gardener? You actually caught her?"

"Of course I did. Didn't take too long either."

Gardener rolled her eyes.

"Now, be a good Cloak and let me through. I've got a ship to get to." Saída was on guard but lowered her hand.

The Redcloak stammered, "I'm sorry, but the spaceport is on lockdown. Orders from up high. We have orders to transfer any prisoners directly to Sir Gideon and his squad."

Saída ground her teeth. "Well maybe I can change his mind. Where is he?"

The Redcloak lifted the barrier with the push of a button and motioned for them to enter.

"In the main yard, near Hangar Seven."

Saída pushed Gardener through the entrance, and they walked into the Redcloak-infested spaceport. The spaceport was still just as bleak as it had been when Saída had arrived, but floodlights now illuminated the place. She glanced at the anti-air mag-lock cannons littered across the walls and noticed that the flares had just begun to die out. The machine was sitting, deactivated, near one of the cannons. Saída noticed that all the hangars were locked down too. Many of the Redcloaks who had been out patrolling the city had been recalled. Saída felt like she and Gardener were sheep in wolves' clothing. One wrong move and every single gun in the spaceport would be trained on them.

Up above she spotted Rodok's drone flying in the air. Good. He was watching them. Hopefully, he would have found his way in. The walls were high, but not as high as the ones in the spaceport back home. He could make it. She had faith in Rodok. He must have already scouted out a place with less activity, where he and Gardener's people could safely infiltrate from.

At the end of the yard, near Hangar Seven, Saída spotted a squad of elite Redcloaks. They wore silver armour and the cloaks that they wore had the insignia of the Grand Design, but unlike regular Redcloaks, theirs were branded in silver. The helmets they wore were silver, with black V-shaped visors obscuring their eyes. At their centre was a man with long golden hair, and armour to match. The symbol of the Grand Design proudly emblazoned on the breastplate in bright red, with intricate markings carved into the golden armour. Every part of his body was covered except for his head. Attached to his belt was a golden mask with a red, X-shaped visor. Saída scowled. A helmet equally as opulent as the rest of his armour. Every muscle in her body itched for her to start shooting, or to turn back and run.

The man in the golden armour smiled at them as they walked closer. He started to clap, the sound of metal-on-metal bit into the silence in the outpost. Saída noticed how his gauntlets glowed brighter, with each clap.

"Illuminite," she whispered.

Gardener grimaced.

"Well done, soldier. Well done," the Knight said.

He was decked out in illuminite armour. This wasn't like the blast-resistant armour that Saída and Kruger wore. This armour was impenetrable.

Saída remained silent.

Several Redcloaks stood on either side of them, around the spaceport walls. Several metres ahead, the Knight and his squad. Saída kept her hand on Gardener's shoulder.

"Oh. Pardon my manners," he said. There was something else there. Underneath the smile. It made Saída's skin crawl. "I am Sir Gideon Welbridge of the Knights of the Grand Design. In service of his Holy Eminence, the Kaiser, and his Archbishops. Now your identification, soldier?"

Gideon stood tall, the smile never left his face. Even from this distance, his blue eyes pierced Saída.

"Oh of course, Your Lordship. Right away," Saída grumbled, slowly reaching for her coat pocket and drawing out Kruger's badge. She noticed some of the Redcloaks going for their weapons, but Gideon and his elite Redcloaks remained calm, watching with amusement.

Saída held out Kruger's badge and waited. Gardener took a sharp breath. Beads of sweat dripped from Saída's forehead into her eye, under the helmet. It was hot, and her eye began to itch.

One of the silver Redcloaks pulled out a scanner and aimed it at the Guild badge in Saída's hand. The exchange was silent.

"Kruger Vex, a bounty hunter employed by the Guild. Checks out, Sir," the silver Redcloak said to Gideon.

"Well, now that that's all cleared up," Saída said, raising her voice, "I'd kindly request you let me get onto my ship and deliver the girl to the Guild."

"I commend you on your capture of this dangerous fugitive, but I'll be taking over from here, Kruger. I'm sure you understand. The Grand Design sees farther than you, after all."

Saída exhaled, a silent wisp of breath that betrayed her apprehension to Gardener, who clenched her fists.

"I've got a lot of respect for the Grand Design, truly, I do. But the Grand Design won't put food on the table, so I'd like to take her to the Guild all the same. After that, she'll be transferred over to you, I'm sure," said Saída, raising her voice again.

Gideon didn't drop the damn smile. "Money is no object. Hand her over to me, you'll still be paid top shard. You wouldn't question a Knight's honour, would you?"

Saída was running out of options. She pocketed Kruger's badge and her fingers hovered over the pistol where it was holstered.

"You're sick, twisted! You vile sack of shit," yelled Gardener, surprising Saída and the Redcloaks both.

"Hm?" Gideon craned his neck.

"Orisa was just beginning to heal and then you dropped bombs on us. You killed our people. You couldn't handle the fact that w—" Gardener yelled.

"It's *Sektor 15*," interrupted Gideon. "And why do you think that is, Aveline?"

Saída frowned under her helmet. What the hell? There was a strange familiarity to the way he said her name.

"Look," Saída hollered. "I think we've all tired ourselves out. Just let me get onto my ship and we'll forget this all happened, how about that?"

Gideon regained his composure.

"Take off your helmet."

"What?"

"Take off your helmet. If you're really Kruger Vex. Take. Off. Your. Helmet," he said.

Scav. She knew this moment was coming. She couldn't keep stalling. How much longer did Rodok need? She was about to reach for her pistol when the elite Redcloaks aimed their weapons at her.

"I've grown tired of this charade," muttered Gideon. He raised his arm.

"He won't risk hurting me, point the gun at me *now*," Gardener hissed.

Saída pulled the pistol out of its holster and brought it to Gardener's neck and yelled, "I wouldn't do that if I were you, Gideon."

Gideon hesitated but lowered his arm.

Saída dared not breathe. It actually worked.

"This is getting a little sad, Saída." Gideon chuckled. The way his cheeks stretched to give way to his teeth, the crow's feet around the dead stare of his cold blue eyes. The fact that he called her by her name.

Saída's eye twitched, but she kept silent, the barrel of the gun digging into Gardener's neck.

"It is Saída isn't it? You're the only other Guild employee here aside from Kruger," Gideon continued, taking a SETRA from one of the elite Redcloaks. He tapped the clunky buttons on the handheld device as he went through the data.

"Saída Abbas, working for the Guild as an official employee. Quite a step up from a contractor, no?"

He looked up from the SETRA and flashed his pearly whites at her.

"Unlock the roof—" Saída began.

"Don't interrupt me," he snapped. "If she speaks again, kill her," Gideon said, turning to one of his subordinates.

Saída took a step back, Gardener in tow, the pistol never leaving her neck. She wasn't sure it was a bluff, but the only thing keeping her alive right now was Gardener.

"There's no way. He won't risk it," muttered Gardener.

"Shut up." Saída's eyes were focused on Gideon, and the silver Redcloaks who had their weapons aimed at her.

"You don't have any legitimate identity records, no doubt a false origin point. You covered your tracks well. Unfortunately, that means you're an illegal. You have no right to be working for the Guild."

Saída eyed the Redcloaks around the outpost. All eyes were on her and Gardener. She noticed the Redcloaks grip their weapons tighter, how they shifted their stances, eagerly awaiting the order to fire. The elite Redcloaks in comparison were calm. Still. They moved only when their master commanded and not a moment sooner. There was silence. Saída looked up to the sky. Rodok's drone. He was still watching. She looked around the spaceport, the roof was still locked down. She was starting to panic.

"Nothing to say, Saída? Oh, that's right." He turned to his subordinates. "She can speak again."

Saída was boiling. If she was quick enough, one well-placed shot to the head. Before he could go for his helmet. But then every Redcloak would fire at her and Gardener.

"Alright Gideon," said Saída. "You've convinced me."

"Oh?"

"I'll let you have Gardener."

Gideon raised an eyebrow. "Will you now?"

"Sure. You said you'd pay me, right? Top shard you said. Screw the Guild then. Take her. I don't care where my money comes from."

"What are you *doing*?" hissed Gardener.

"Splendid," Gideon said. "Hand her over then."

"Hey, I'm not stupid, Gideon. I'll just take a walk over towards the spaceport now. Hand her over to you once I'm safely on my ship."

"I don't think—" Gideon began, but the sound of massive metallic shutters being spread apart filled the outpost.

The roof of the spaceport was being opened. The hangars were opening up. Rodok had done it. Saída grinned under her helmet. She was going to hug the shit out of him if they made it out of this.

"Who authorised that?" Gideon yelled. "Lock them down!"

The roar of engines filled the air and several Redcloak ships floated out of the top of the hangar roofs. Some flew out into the atmosphere, but others circled around and fired on the spaceport. Heavy shelling bombarded the Redcloaks on the edges of the spaceport, sending massive clouds of dust into the air. Redcloaks scrambled around the outpost trying to avoid getting hit, and Saída and Gardener took advantage of the chaos and ran towards the hangars.

The elite Redcloaks fired on them as they ran, but Gideon pushed the gun away from them, yelling at his subordinates, "No, you fools! You'll hit Aveline!"

Saída disengaged the electrocuffs on Gardener, and the two of them rushed through the dust clouds, tackling a Redcloak out of the way. Saída fired a pistol at pursuing Redcloaks. Gardener picked up a rifle from a fallen Redcloak and fired on the ground, creating more dust to hide them from view. The ships had stopped firing on the spaceport. They began circling around it. Gardener's men had done well.

"Fire mag-locks," screeched Gideon from within the storm of dust.

"While the bastard's distracted," Saída said to Gardener, pointing to Hangar Nine, where the *Lancer* was docked.

Redcloaks began to fire on the ships from the anti-air cannons, unleashing magnetically charged shells. Gardener's men returned fire from their ships, but one of them was brought down by a magnetic shell that pierced its hull. It came crashing down onto the city, falling through a wrecked building, shattering it completely. The shockwave that followed threw everyone in the outpost off their feet. Dust rose up in the air once more.

Saída put two shots into a Redcloak who had fallen near her then got to her feet, shambling on ahead. Gardener followed. They slammed through the doors of Hangar Nine, and the dark and dusty chaos of battle outside gave way to the pristine hangar that hosted various landing pads inside. Outside, they could still hear the skirmish between Gardener's men and the Redcloaks' mag-lock cannons.

There were only a few ships remaining on the landing pads in the hangar inside. Most of them were Redcloak ships. At the very end, taking up three landing pads' worth of space, was the *Lancelot*, Gideon's ship. It was a Dreadnought-class monstrosity. Mag-lock cannons built into its hull, turrets across both ends, an entire bridge of its own, just like the big capital ships from Sektor Prime. Encountering this ship out in space meant only one thing.

Saída's thoughts wandered to Rodok, as she spotted the *Lancer*. She wondered why he hadn't already left. She raised Kruger's badge in the air and his ship hummed to life, an Enforcer model Guild-issue ship with a deep-blue sheen. Saída had seen tackier ships, she had to admit.

"Gardener, get to the cockpit and start the engines," Saída ordered, as they made their way onto the ramp. Gardener nodded.

Saída contacted Rodok, through her helmet.

"Rodok, why haven't y—" she began.

A shrill chirp echoed in the hangar. A brilliant white light hit Saída in the face. Her helmet shattered apart. Heat seared her left cheek. Saída crumpled to the floor from the blast.

"I don't recall giving you permission to leave," said a helmeted Gideon, walking towards the ship.

"*Shit*," Gardener yelled, and went for her rifle. Half of her shots missed, and Gideon laughed as the ones that didn't, bounced off effortlessly, the impact of the shells only increasing the gold sheen of his armour to a bright glow.

Gideon thumbed the hammer of his pistol and aimed at Gardener. A bolt of blue electricity hit her in the chest, and she doubled over in pain. Gideon walked up the ramp and crouched over Gardener, who writhed on the floor. He waved his gun in the air.

"Don't worry, Aveline. I wouldn't have come unprepared. Hope the voltage isn't too high."

He grabbed Gardener by the collar and leaned in close. She stared at the expressionless red visor of his helmet in horror.

"You've had more than enough time hiding. This experiment is over. It's time to—"

The sound of heavy, mechanical footsteps caused Gideon to turn around. Rodok threw a right hook. The clang resounded in the hangar. Gideon slammed into the side of the ramp. His helmet began to glow.

"*GO.*" Rodok uttered a mechanical screech. He lifted Gideon by his cloak and tossed him back out onto the landing pad.

Saída clutched her face and turned on the floor. The illuminite bolt had just scraped her cheek, but even then the pain flashed white-hot across her face. She was going to pass out. She slammed her fist against the floor and got to her knees. Gardener was recovering from the electric shock, and Saída helped her up.

"Come on," said Saída, holding Kruger's badge in her hand. "We have to get out of here."

They helped each other up, using the atrium walls as support and limped towards the cockpit. Saída could see

Rodok battling Gideon in the hangar through the window of the cockpit. Gardener placed the badge into the key-slot and began to punch in coordinates.

Gideon ran at Rodok, dodging another punch and trading blows with the metal giant. He landed three strikes to Rodok's chassis. No effect. Gideon's gauntlets glowed with heat. Rodok hit Gideon's helmet. The gold shimmered like light. Gideon yelled, increasing the ferocity of his punches. Rodok kneed him, but Gideon was ready. He clamped his glowing left hand onto Rodok's shoulder and squeezed, crumpling it like paper. Rodok's red eye shifted to his wrecked shoulder, then he swatted Gideon away with a smack of his metallic arm. Gideon fell with a loud thud. Rodok grabbed Gideon's leg, lifted him up and swung him through the hangar doors, which shattered on impact. Rodok turned around and stared at Saída through the window. He pointed upwards and then zoomed towards the *Lancer*.

"G-Gardener…" Saída groaned. She was barely conscious, the burning sensation on her cheek was intense, she couldn't hold onto consciousness. She heard Gardener's voice.

"Hold on, Abbas," she yelled. "We're almost there. We're almost there."

Gardener closed the ramp of the ship and lifted off, shooting out towards the sky, the *Lancer* following close behind. Some of the ships piloted by Gardener's men followed, but another was shot down as they made their escape. Gardener grunted and increased the speed of Kruger's ship, rocketing out towards space. They were greeted by the sight of the Redcloak blockade, several satellites that orbited the world armed with destabilisation fields, guarded by a single Dreadnought-class ship.

Gardener gritted her teeth, tightening her grip on the controls.

Saída was barely holding on. "We prepared for this, Gardener."

The satellites were still. Saída watched. The blockade had been taken by surprise. They weren't expecting so many sudden departures in Redcloak ships. That wouldn't last. Gideon would be dispatching his orders any moment.

The Dreadnought's cannons began to glow.

"They wouldn't fire on their own ships, would they?" Gardener cried.

"Use the flares!" Saída yelled.

Gardener pushed a button. The next moments passed in agonising slowness.

The Dreadnought fired. Kruger's ship emitted a wide arc of red flares that sent bursts of light around them, away from them. The Dreadnought's mag-lock shells hit the flares. Gardener pumped her fist in triumph. Then the Redcloak ships of Gardener's men followed, and were shot down, one by one. Gardener screamed as she saw her people being slaughtered by the Dreadnought's cannons. Saída couldn't hear her own voice under the excessive sounds of explosions and blasts around them, but she yelled. Gardener deployed more flares, those of her people, what few ships remained of them, followed her lead. The Dreadnought's cannons began glowing again. The satellites pulsed and a wave of electricity in net-like streaks of blue sprang out from them.

The *Lancer* jumped in front of Kruger's ship and shot out a pulsewave of its own. She and Rodok had used that trick plenty of times to escape similar situations, a counter-pulsewave that rendered portions of the destabilisation net inactive. The *Lancer* opened a space for them within the net, then rocketed away towards the right. Some of Gardener's men were caught in the net and their ships sputtered to a halt, lying dead in the void. Gardener slammed her fist against the dashboard. The Dreadnought's cannons were at maximum charge. It aimed at them.

"Gardener," Saída cried.

Then the Dreadnought cannons stopped.

"What the...?" Saída began, but Gardener wasted no time.

She hit the boosters and Kruger's ship jumped into a nearby Ring. What remained of Gardener's people were scattered, fleeing in different directions. Kruger's ship entered the Ringway and the space around them inverted and expanded, leaving Sektor 15, Orisa, a tiny speck in a matter of seconds.

The deep cut across Saída's left cheek was the mark of the deadly bite of an illuminite bolt. It had come from an illuminite bullet. Saída had been lucky. The wound was created and cauterised in one move, but she would bear this scar forever.

"Abbas, can you hear me?" asked Gardener, but there was no response. Saída had passed out from the pain.

CHAPTER TWENTY-ONE

Sektor 47

In a few days, Saída and Uncle Abbas would celebrate her eleventh birthday. Saída was busy working on readjusting what little furniture they had at the back of the bar, while Uncle Abbas cleaned the front and got ready for customers. Saída puffed her cheeks as she moved a large wooden table towards the window, the legs of the table scraped against the wooden floor of the back room. Saída admired the way the height of the table symmetrically lined up with the windowsill. She set to work moving her and Uncle's bedrolls towards the other end of the room, where the table used to be.

Uncle Abbas walked into the back room carrying a flagon and flashed a grin at Saída as her tiny frame carried three pillows and their blankets all at once.

"Slowly, beti. One at a time," he said. "We still have plenty of time."

"But I want to make sure we've redecorated in time, Uncle," said Saída behind the mountainous blankets.

Uncle Abbas set the flagon on the table and walked over to Saída, taking the blankets from her. Saída frowned.

"I could have done it."

"Yes beti, I know. You are *very* strong. But even the strong need help sometimes."

He and Saída set their bedrolls and pillows down, then put the blankets over them. Saída matted them until she was satisfied there were no crimps in them, while Uncle Abbas made sure the pillows were set properly. They sat together in front of the bedrolls and Saída leaned on Uncle Abbas, resting on his arm.

"Do you think my friends will come this year, Uncle?"

Uncle Abbas frowned. His moustache quivered a bit as he thought of what to say. Saída inched closer to him, and he wrapped his arm around her.

"Beti, I think, even if they don't, you and I will still have a lot of fun. Our decorations are nice, I've managed to get some Chai and there is no daal." The last bit prompted a mischievous twitch in his moustache, which made Saída giggle.

They sat in silence for a few moments then Uncle Abbas whispered, "Are you angry with them?"

Saída lay down, putting her head on Uncle Abbas's leg.

"No. I'm just a little sad. I know why they can't come to see me anymore."

"It's because our birthday decorations are just relocating the furniture," he joked.

"And because you always make daal."

"Everybody loves daal, Saída," he said in mock hurt.

They laughed together and sat for a while. Uncle Abbas stroked her hair and recited a prayer for safety, as

Saída drifted off to sleep. She had been working all day, moving the furniture, and cleaning the back room. Uncle Abbas smiled as she fell asleep.

"Let our prayers give you pleasant dreams, beti."

*

When Saída awoke, night had fallen. She could hear the rowdy shouts of Redcloak patrons from the front of the bar. She was under the covers of her blanket, but the calm she had felt earlier in the day was now replaced with anxiety. She gently pressed against her cotton eye patch. It stung her socket like a needle. She wanted water.

Saída got up and walked over to the flagon left on the table by Uncle Abbas. She raised the nozzle to her lips and drank. The water was tepid and did little to soothe her dry throat. She poured some in her hand and pressed it against her eye patch, hoping the liquid would ease the pain, but it just grew damp and itchy. Saída ripped it off with a grunt of frustration.

"That's off-limits," she heard Uncle Abbas's voice echo from the other room.

A voice drawled in response from behind the door. "Come on, mate. Only looking for the toilet." He laughed. A cold, dry laugh. Like nails scratching on sandpaper. Saída put the flagon down and walked closer to the door, tiptoeing, and holding her breath.

"There's one outside," Uncle Abbas said. His voice was raised. A hint of panic. Saída realised he was trying not to let the situation escalate into violence, but he must have thought she was still asleep.

"Maybe I'll just use the one you got in here though," the voice retorted. The sound of laughter drowned out Uncle Abbas's protests and the doorknob began rattling violently.

"Damn f... Bloody thing's locked," muttered the Redcloak. Saída was so close she could have heard him breathe.

"Hand over the key," another Redcloak slurred.

"Why don't I give you all another drink?" Uncle Abbas suggested. "Free of charge."

Saída heard a bit of shuffling and ran for the window. The sound of raised voices in argument, and then the Redcloak at the door spoke again.

"Next time just give us the bloody key."

Saída climbed onto the table and in her haste, knocked over the flagon. The water inside spilled onto the wooden table, a dark stream flowed off the corner. She saw the key turning and slipped out of the window. Her back was glued to the wall and her feet planted firmly on the edge of the cliff as she stared down into the chasm. She could just about see some of the larger mining equipment far below. The cold wind bit at her damp eye socket and Saída gritted her teeth and shut her left eyelid.

The door opened and she heard some footsteps.

"What the hell you got in here?" the Redcloak jeered.

Some more footsteps. Another voice, closer to the window.

"Oi. Take a look at this. Spilled flagon."

Uncle Abbas interjected. "I'll clean that up later. As you can see—"

"Abbas, I heard you had a kid. Where is she?"

"I don't know what you're talking about."

The other Redcloak cut in. "A friend of ours told us you had a kid. Where is she?"

Uncle Abbas stammered. "Sirs, there are quite a lot of children around here. Sometimes I babysit. That is all."

"Abbas, you're not lying, are you? Our mates were quite hurt regarding how you treated them last time they were here. You sure you don't want your regulars back?"

Saída clenched her fists. She wanted to scream at them, to call them names and curse them. But she stayed silent.

Uncle Abbas swallowed. "They're welcome back anytime."

The Redcloaks sniggered.

"Well, we'll make sure to tell 'em you miss 'em. Now come on, Abbas. You said on the house, right?"

"Those were his words," said the other Redcloak.

"I believe he said 'free of charge'," said another Redcloak, mocking Uncle's accent which elicited another round of raucous laughter from the others.

Saída waited until the door slammed shut, then inched around the cliffside, towards the side of the bar. Uncle Abbas must have been relieved she wasn't in the room when the Redcloaks barged in, but he would no doubt be worried about her.

"I'll signal him from the window," Saída whispered to herself. Then she would go see Rodok for a while. At least until the early hours of the morning, when all the Redcloaks would be gone.

Saída turned the corner of the bar, making for the window, when she came face to face with another Redcloak. The Redcloak was smoking a cigarette and she stared blankly into Saída's eye.

Saída froze.

"I take it you're the child they were so excited about in there," she said. She had a familiar accent.

"You're Meraji," Saída gasped.

The Redcloak looked away and leaned against the wall. She tapped her cigarette and bits of ash fell to the ground.

"You shouldn't say that word, girl."

Saída looked at the woman's attire; cheap armour and a thin red scarf that went down to her hips. Not really a cloak.

"You're a Redcloak," Saída whispered. Even stating the obvious, she couldn't believe her own words.

"I am," the woman said, taking another drag of her cigarette.

Saída's hands balled into fists and her one-eyed glare pierced the Redcloak.

The woman laughed in response to Saída's budding anger.

"I get enough money to feed my family. Once a week. Every week. So long as I do my job."

Saída took a step back.

"What's your name? I'm Aqsa," said the woman, taking another puff of her cigarette.

"I'm not telling you."

Aqsa smirked. "Do you hate me?"

The question threw Saída off guard. She lowered her eyes and thought about it. Her first reaction had been shock at seeing another Meraji so close to the bar, especially this late at night. Her second was anger at seeing Aqsa's red colours. Saída looked Aqsa in the eye.

"Yes."

Aqsa smiled, but Saída noticed a flicker of sadness in her brown eyes. And then it was gone. Replaced with tired apathy.

"You should consider joining when you're older. They'll still treat you like shit, but at least your uncle won't go hungry. Or maybe you'll just take over his bar, once he's old?"

"Uncle Abbas won't get old," Saída snapped.

Aqsa laughed again. Her voice was scratchy. Husky. She leaned over and pinched Saída's cheek. It hurt.

"You're so cute." She grinned. Her eyes were expressionless.

Saída slapped her hand away.

She was about to give Aqsa a piece of her mind, when the Redcloaks inside the bar yelled out. Saída took a step back, away from the window.

"Sandskin, get in here and pour us some more drinks," called the Redcloak from inside.

"Yes, sir," Aqsa responded, her voice loud and clear. Gone was the scratchy, low tone. She responded like a soldier called to attention.

Aqsa tutted and dropped her smoke to the ground, rubbing it in with her boot.

"Run off, bachay. Before they see you."

With that Aqsa walked into the bar, and Saída heard one of the Redcloaks berate her for coming too late. Saída looked at the ground and frowned. She never knew that Meraji people could become Redcloaks too. Why? It made no sense. She and Uncle Abbas had a hard life, but they still managed without joining the Redcloaks. Saída shook her head. She could think about it later.

She made sure that she was out of sight of the bar window as she made her way towards the abandoned plot of land, the pathway to her secret meetings with Rodok. Signalling Uncle Abbas would have been too risky. She would just have to trust that he would know she was okay.

In the moonlight, the red dirt seemed too dark, almost black. Flecks of ashen residue from the smog glittered across the ground. The remains of the illuminite that was used up in the factories. Saída felt like she was walking on space. Her thoughts went back to Aqsa and her tired eyes.

"What was her problem?" Saída muttered.

She crossed the old, broken stone walls that surrounded the abandoned plot, and walked past the stone piles that she liked to collect there. She missed playing with her friends here. Her thoughts wandered to her birthday and then for a moment, she felt a tinge of excitement. Her friends wouldn't be able to come, but maybe Rodok would. Or at least, she could come visit him on her birthday.

Saída walked into the ruins of the derelict manor, sliding her palm over the charred walls, and glancing at the ceiling where bits of the ancient chandelier mount were still visible. The fireplace used to have a painting above it. Though long burned away, pieces of the frame and canvas remained affixed to the wall. Paintings were something done by artists to capture memories forever. Uncle Abbas told it to her, like his father had told it to him. It was not dissimilar to how Saída and her friends used to make funny pictures in the dirt.

A loud buzzing noise snapped Saída out of her trance. She looked to the door leading downstairs into the basement. The noise had come from there. Saída looked to make sure no one was around and then she descended. The buzzing started again but stopped by the time she reached the basement.

"Rodok, I said to be careful. I could hear the buzzing from upstairs."

Rodok looked up at Saída from the mining equipment he was working on. The basement was very different compared to how Saída had originally found it. It was much cleaner and most of the old equipment and machinery had been moved to the side of the room, thanks to Rodok.

"You *said* it *was* okay *to* work *at* night," Rodok protested.

"Late night, Rodok. I said at *late* night. There are still Redcloaks at the bar."

Rodok ceased what he was doing, withdrawing an appendage jutting out of his forearm, which had been emitting a small but intense blue flame.

"Fine," said Rodok. "*I* will *continue* welding *later.*"

Saída went to the end of the basement, towards the tunnel that she used to use to spelunk down into the caverns to meet Rodok. Where it had once been a small hole that she squeezed through, now it was completely drilled through, leaving an opening large enough for Rodok to climb into.

"I *told* you I could *do* it," said Rodok, coming up behind Saída. Despite the few inches she had grown, Rodok still towered over her, like a great metal pillar.

"It still took you a year to do it." Saída smirked.

"*Eight* months," Rodok retorted.

Saída and Rodok walked back near the old machine he was working on and sat down next to it. Saída sat cross-legged, while Rodok simply squatted. Saída remembered how she and Uncle Abbas had been so happy just that morning, excited for her birthday. How fast that had turned into fear and… whatever she felt after meeting Aqsa.

Saída frowned.

"*Would* you *like* to *talk* about *it*, silly *Saída*," Rodok asked with a subtle shift of his head.

"I met a Redcloak woman today." Saída shifted uncomfortably. The basement floor was much more comfortable to sit on than the cavern floor was, but today she just couldn't sit still. She got up and started pacing. "She was Meraji. Like me and Uncle."

"*And* you *have* never *seen* a *Meraji* Redcloak?"

Saída shook her head. Her left eyelid was still closed, but the stinging pain she had felt in the cold had finally subsided.

"She didn't tell the others I was there. She let me go even though she knew that the other Redcloaks were looking for me."

"*Did* she *see* you *coming* here?"

Saída shook her head again.

"I don't know what I'm feeling right now, Rodok. It's making my stomach feel weird."

Saída sat down directly in front of Rodok, looking up at his crimson eyes as they swam around the contours of his head.

"Hm. *Perhaps* it *is* because *you* have *not* eaten?"

"That's not why, Rodok," she said, shutting her eye.

"It *feels* wrong *to* see *someone* like *you* fight *for* those *who* delight *in* your *suffering*."

Saída's head flooded with images of the various Redcloaks she had met throughout her short life. The worst ones. The not-so-bad ones. At the centre, she saw Aqsa. Meraji. And a Redcloak. Her stomach growled.

"*Also*, I *think* it *is* because *you* have *not* eaten," Rodok buzzed.

"You're right," said Saída finally.

"*I* never *get* tired *of* hearing *that*."

Saída flashed him a look of annoyance. "Shut up, stupid Rodok."

"*No*," he said, and the two grinned at each other. Well, Saída imagined he was grinning anyway.

"She said she did it so she could feed her family. And the Redcloaks were still treating her badly," Saída said, clutching her stomach. At this point, the only thing she could do was wait to return home after the Redcloaks had left.

"*So*, she *did* it *for* her *family*?"

"Still…"

"*Is* it *not* the *same* for *Uncle* Abbas?"

"No, it's not," Saída snapped, slapping the ground.

"*Why* not?" asked Rodok, unfazed by Saída's outburst.

"Because. Because it's not. Uncle Abbas *had* to give them drinks. Even his father had to."

"*I* agree *that* it *is* not *the* exact *same* situation, *but* at *the* end *of* the *day*, both *serve* the *Redcloaks* because *they* have *little* choice."

"No," said Saída, glaring.

Rodok rose to his feet, the shifting of his legs from their haunches sounded like the sliding of a sheet of metal.

"*I understand* that *this* was *an* unsatisfactory *response*. Sorry."

Saída scratched her head and frowned.

"I'm sorry for getting angry with you," she said, unable to look him in the eyes. She hated this feeling. It felt so wrong. And there was no way Uncle Abbas's situation was like Aqsa's. Just no way.

A little piece of metal, no bigger than a pen, floated into the basement from the stairs and landed in Rodok's shoulder with a clink.

"Saída, *the* drone *has* returned. *The* Redcloaks *have* left *the* bar. *It* is *safe* to *go* home."

Saída's stomach growled right on cue.

"Rodok, it's my birthday in two days. I'll try to come back here then. I'll bring some birthday bread."

"*I* do *not* consume *food*, Saída," he said.

Saída raised her eyebrows. "I meant for me, stupid Rodok."

"*Now* I *will* take *it*."

Saída stuck her tongue out. "No, you *won't*."

She ran up the stairs, leaving Rodok buzzing in the basement. She could just about make out the sound of welding again as she left the old manor. Saída ran past the stone walls and towards Uncle's bar. She could see it in the distance. The night sky intermingled with streaks of light as dawn approached. Saída hoped she could still get some food and a good night's sleep before the day came.

Uncle Abbas came out of the bar and spotted Saída running towards him. He did the same, arms outstretched, and she jumped into his arms. Uncle Abbas lifted her up and held her tightly, whispering a prayer in her ear and kissing her on the cheek.

"When I heard the Redcloaks coming I went out the

window," Saída said, as Uncle Abbas carried her into the bar.

"You did good, beti. Very, very good."

She sat on the stool as Uncle Abbas brought her some food. It was cold, but Saída wolfed it down all the same. Her stomach had really begun to hurt.

"Uncle, did you see that Meraji Redcloak?" Saída asked, finishing her plate, and wiping her mouth.

Uncle Abbas set to cleaning the dishes that had piled up, including Saída's plate.

"I did, beti. What of it?"

"She saw me."

Uncle Abbas paused what he was doing. He didn't turn to look at Saída.

"But she didn't do anything. She didn't tell anyone. She let me go," Saída mumbled.

Uncle Abbas shut his eyes for a moment, then continued washing the dishes.

"She is Meraji, after all," he said.

"Why would a Meraji join the Redcloaks, Uncle? Why would she help them?"

Uncle Abbas put a few dishes away.

"Saída, I don't like it either, but sometimes that's the only way for people like us to survive here."

"People like us? We're nothing like her," Saída snapped.

"Saída, beti. What is the difference between her doing this for her survival and me doing it for ours? In the end, we are both serving the Redcloaks."

He looked sad, but Saída could tell he was trying to get her to soften her anger for Aqsa.

"Why are you less angry with her than the Liberation

142

League, Uncle? She's doing so much worse things to us," Saída yelled.

"Saída," he replied. He was calm, but stern. Saída looked away.

"Sorry, Uncle."

Uncle Abbas returned to his dishes and there was silence for a while. Saída felt bad about raising her voice at him. Aqsa stood against everything Saída had come to know. How could one of their own people join the ones who hurt them every single day? It was so unfair.

"Saída," Uncle Abbas began. "The issue with the League is entirely different from Meraji people joining the Redcloaks. Neither are good, both have their ups and downs, but ultimately, we all just have to try and survive."

Saída listened intently, her eyes fixed on Uncle Abbas's back.

"It just means that we are all good and bad in different ways and are trying to do what is best for us, and our children," he said, turning around and caressing Saída's cheek. His hands were still wet from washing the dishes. "The only thing I care about is you, and making sure that you have a decent life. As best as I can provide for you."

Saída stifled the urge to cry. Uncle Abbas leaned over the counter and hugged her.

"Relax, beti. Don't worry. I'm here. I'll always be here."

Uncle Abbas had taken care of her since she was a baby. He had protected her, clothed her, fed her. He was the only reason why she was still here. Saída thought of Aqsa and what she said. Joining the Redcloaks seemed so *wrong* after everything they had done, everything they were doing. She touched the covering on her missing eye, digging her fingers in, letting herself feel the hollowness of her eye socket. Could she do it too? Join the Redcloaks to protect Uncle Abbas? Or was Aqsa wrong after all. Saída watched Uncle Abbas tend to the remainder of the dishes. There was no question that Uncle Abbas would always protect her. But now, thanks to Aqsa, Saída was faced with a question she never really considered.

How far would she go to save Uncle Abbas?

CHAPTER TWENTY-TWO

Sektor 72

Saída's eyes opened, and she found herself sitting in a chair beside Gardener. They were in the cockpit of Kruger's ship, in front of the dashboard. "Rodok?"

"What?" said Gardener, placing a hand on Saída's shoulder. "Don't worry, Abbas. Robot got out. I saw your ship leave."

Saída exhaled. Her eyes hurt. The mechanical one too. She felt like needles were poking them out from the inside. Her cheek burned, but the pain was dulled and a small medpatch was covering it. Gardener must have done that.

"Where are we, Gardener?" Saída asked, her throat felt cracked and dry.

"Right now, nowhere. Empty space. Far out of reach of any nearby Sektor or patrols."

"We're not close to the Deadzone, are we?"

Gardener shook her head. "No, no. Don't worry about that. I'm not stupid."

Saída noticed that Gardener was clutching her stomach.

"You okay? Still feeling the effects of the electric discharge?"

Gardener nodded. "Hurts like a bitch."

"It sure does," said Saída, recounting her own experiences.

Saída turned to the dashboard and leaned over to make a call, but Gardener stopped her.

"If you wanna get in touch with Robot, he contacted me earlier. He said he'll give us some coordinates and that's where we'll meet up with him."

Saída leaned back into her chair. Silence.

"You know, it was really touch and go for a—" Gardener began.

"Cut the shit, Gardener," Saída snapped. "He let us go. Those cannons had us dead to rights, but Gideon let us go. Who are you?"

Gardener drew circles on the dashboard with her fingers, not meeting Saída's eyes. Saída noticed she had been disarmed. Both the Scimitar and the pistol Gardener had loaned to her were with Gardener.

"I'm Archbishop Samson's daughter," said Gardener.

"And there it is." Saída glared at Gardener.

"My father used to be the Viceroy of Sektor 15, of Orisa. When his brother, my uncle, died, my father replaced him as an Archbishop."

"So why did he want you back so bad, that he'd send a Knight for you?"

"Not just any Knight. Gideon is my cousin," said Gardener, sidestepping the question.

Saída stared, wide-eyed. "That's… gross."

Gardener finally looked at Saída. "He honestly wasn't this bad when we were younger."

"They're *all* bad, Gardener."

Gardener frowned but didn't respond.

"So, the blockade," Saída muttered. "It *was* because of you. Not taxes. Rodok was right."

Gardener shook her head. "Not exactly. My father allowed for a bit of independent rule during his governance and then when he became Archbishop, he let a native of Sektor 15 become the new Viceroy."

"How generous. That's got nothing to do with the blockade," Saída said.

"Let me finish. This new governor did her best to strike a balance between what the Grand Design demanded of her, and what the people of Sektor 15 wanted. She tried to keep the colonisers happy while raising the standard of living for her people. But then…"

Gardener's voice broke and she stopped.

"She was your mother," Saída guessed.

Gardener looked hurt. "Yes. She was assassinated. And people were convinced it was a plot by the Archbishops and his *Holy Eminence*." She spat out the last words like they were poison.

"These last few years must have been hard. I know how it feels."

"Yeah," Gardener said bitterly.

"And so, the Grand Design baited your people into retaliation and used that as an excuse to bring you back under their control?"

Gardener sniffed and looked out to the empty void of space. "Hence the blockade," she said.

"And your dear old father sent his nephew to come bring you to safety. He really *does* care," Saída continued.

"Shut up, Abbas."

"And what are you going to do now that your resistance efforts are scattered, and your people are left to fend for themselves?"

"There are other resistance cells all over the Sektor. They'll keep up the fight. I'll regroup with mine and then we'll return."

Saída laughed.

"And what the hell are you doing to help your people?" Gardener snapped.

"Absolutely nothing," said Saída. Gardener was about to respond, but Saída didn't let her. "Because there is nothing I *can* do, Gardener. There is nothing any of us can do. We resist, we die. We rise up, we get squashed. We demand independence, we get dismissed and slaughtered as rebels."

There was a bitter tinge in her mouth as she spoke. Gardener had her turn. Now it was Saída's.

"There is only one thing I care about now, Gardener, and that's finding Digby Hickston. And you jeopardised that by putting my life in danger. I don't even know if I can return to the Guild anymore, and I don't know if I'm going to see my face plastered all over the hyperwaves, with a bounty on my head. So, thanks a lot for that."

Neither looked at the other. Saída instead focused on the distant stars in the darkness of space. How cold and quiet everything was, in the little pocket of emptiness where Kruger's ship floated. Saída brushed her fingers against her cheek. All that risk had been so she would have a real lead on Digby and the emblem of the medallion, but now because of it, she was at risk of losing the only real job she had. Possibly her freedom too. She furrowed her eyebrows. It didn't matter. So long as she completed the medallion, so long as she could make her way back home to Uncle Abbas. That was the only thing that mattered right now.

"Here," Gardener said. Saída turned to look at Gardener, who held out the Scimitar in one hand. Saída took it.

She admired the way the gun felt, smooth in the way that illuminite was, pure black, and designed exactly how Saída had wanted. Better even. The bullet chamber was large, divided in two sections that seamlessly connected to form rings. There were eight slots for shells, and eight slots for illuminite rounds. Sixteen in total. It was admittedly less than the average revolver or handgun could hold, but the output of the Scimitar would make up for in power what it lacked in ammunition capacity. Saída brushed her thumb over the long barrel of the gun, over the word *Scimitar*, written in Meraji calligraphy, in her own handwriting. Finally, on the hammer of the gun, there was a groove on which Saída's thumb would rest.

"Once you place your thumb on the hammer, it'll remember you. Then no one will ever be able to use the gun but you. That's a Gardener specialty," said Gardener.

Saída placed her right thumb on the hammer of the Scimitar. It emitted a light whistling noise, and parts of the gun lit up, along the barrel and the grip. Saída clicked to switch loadouts, prompting the whirring, and rotating of the bullet chamber. Now all Saída needed was illuminite bullets.

"It's a masterpiece," Saída breathed. "The Scimitar is… better than I imagined."

Gardener smirked. "I told you. Legendary."

"So," Saída said, taking a pause. She was unsure of how to ask the question after the tense argument they had just had.

"How did I get this good?"

Saída nodded.

"My mother was a gunsmith too. And her mother before her. Our Sektor used to thrive on metalwork in general, but our family started to make the really special stuff. So that we could fight back."

Saída waited.

"I said before that generations ago, one of the women from my family travelled the galaxy to learn. She said Meraj was the greatest of the galaxy's treasures. That story, and the working of illuminite has been passed down to me," Gardener said. She was enjoying telling the story. "Though I've got to admit, I didn't know Meraj was a planet. Least of all Sektor 47. The Grand Design has taken too much from all of us, Abbas."

Saída leaned forward. "Did you hear any more details? Like what Meraj was like before the Redcloaks?"

Gardener looked apologetic. "Sorry, no. I think parts of the story got watered down over the generations too. My mother barely remembered the word Meraj. I think all that remained was the skill to work illuminite. Though, if I'm honest, even I can't really bring out its true potential. I'd always hoped to learn though."

Saída nodded. "My uncle told me about the days of Meraj before it became Sektor 47. Stories he'd heard from his own father and grandfather. It was supposed to be beautiful. A place of peace and community. Those stories almost didn't feel real."

"They *were* real, Abbas. Orisa was the same way before these bastards colonised it and destroyed it. Before they—" Gardener tapped her fist against the dashboard. She took a deep breath and relaxed her hand.

"But that was a long time ago," Gardener said. "Well before my time."

"So. You were telling me your life story?" Saída said, changing the subject.

Gardener chuckled. "Well. My father met my mother because he wanted her to make weapons for the Redcloaks."

Saída snorted. "And then they fell in love and got married, right? Is that how it's supposed to go?"

"They didn't get married. And sometimes I really don't know if it was love or not. He softened over time, I think because of my mother. Started treating the people a little better."

"That's why he appointed her as Viceroy after he left?"

Gardener nodded.

"How long has all this been going on?"

"A few years. He left, my mother was Viceroy for about two years and then she was killed. We've been fighting back ever since."

"Is that why he sent Gideon after you? Because he actually wants to keep you safe?"

Gardener frowned. "I don't know. I think that might be part of it. I'm his only child. But I'm sure he'd just get me to make weapons for the Redcloaks, just like my mother."

"No room for you in the inheritance?"

"Please. A woman? And a black woman at that? No. If anything, Gideon's going to be the one who inherits my father's wealth and titles. Not that I want anything to do with stolen wealth anyway."

Saída shuddered. The idea of someone like Gideon becoming Archbishop, having that kind of power over the galaxy. It was sickening.

Saída looked at the Scimitar in her hands and then back to Gardener. "Not surprising, to be honest."

"Yeah." Gardener leaned back into her chair and closed her eyes.

The blue-grey insides of Kruger's ship reminded Saída of the Needle, how it was all one boring colour on the inside. At least there were no bright lights in here.

"Ugh," muttered Gardener. She was looking at Kruger's Guild badge. "Look at this, Abbas."

She showed Saída the name registered on the badge. *Kruger Vex.* Just below it, the name of the ship.

"The *Mistress*? Seriously?" Saída said.

"This Kruger guy must be actual slime," Gardener said, putting the badge to the side.

"Oh yeah," Saída said. "He tried to kill me the first time we ever met."

"Really? What happened?"

"Er, pretty much what you'd expect. I was thirteen, I pickpocketed his shardcounter, he tried to shoot me in the face, Rodok broke his arm."

"Well, you *did* steal his shardcounter."

"Would you shoot a kid who stole your shardcounter, Gardener?" Saída asked smugly.

"Touché."

"But *Mistress*, though?"

"I guess Kruger loves his ship a little too much."

Saída and Gardener laughed together.

The sound of beeping filled the room, and the two women turned their heads towards the dashboard.

"And that'd be Robot," said Gardener.

"Alright, look, I wasn't going to say anything but that's really been bothering me," said Saída, folding her arms.

"What has?"

"You. Calling him Robot. Is that on purpose or what?"

"Abbas, is this really important?"

"Look, just call him *Rodok*, okay? You're hurting his feelings."

"Okay, fine. Whatever. Now let's answer the call, please."

Saída pressed the glowing comms button, bringing up a greyscale, trimensional view of Rodok which flickered and emitted static.

"Saída," Rodok buzzed. "*I* am *glad* you *are* safe."

"We got lucky, Rodok. Real lucky."

"*I* *fear* that *we* will *not* have *as* much *luck* going *forward*."

"Rodok, did you hear anything from my people? After we got scattered?" Gardener asked.

Rodok stared at her blankly.

"*I* *have* not. *I* assumed *you* would *know* how *to* get *in* touch *with* them."

Gardener took a seat by the dashboard and looked out the window at the distant stars. She covered her mouth.

"Saída, *I* have *sent* you *coordinates* for *where* we *shall* meet."

Saída nodded. "See you soon, Rodok."

The projection faded and Saída checked the coordinates Rodok sent, and punched their destination into the nav terminal.

The *Mistress* began to move again, its engines roared to life and flew off, towards a nearby Ring. Saída sat at the controls, making sure the ship remained steady as they entered the Ringway, and the darkness of space turned to a ghostly white.

"Keep an eye on the radar," Gardener said.

"I'm sure you'll find them, Gardener."

"It's going to take time. Too much time."

"Well, lucky for you, that's pretty much the only thing you've got."

The *Mistress* crossed over into Augustine Territory, and Saída was quick to flip a switch on the dashboard. An invisible pulse sent a shockwave through the Ringway, hitting the *Mistress*. The ship remained unharmed, but Saída and Gardener felt the vibration in their bones.

"Alright," said Saída. "I don't think we got pinged."

"You sure?" Gardener looked out into the empty white void, pocked with black stars.

"They work fast. Don't think I recognise this checkpoint," said Saída.

"They're already searching for the *Mistress* then."

"Well, Gideon knows for a fact that this is the ship we escaped on. We need to ditch it as soon as we can."

Saída guided the *Mistress* out of the Ringway and back into regular space. The galaxy returned to its comfortable, familiar darkness. The *Mistress* dropped into a gradual descent and maintained a steady pace. In the distance, a speck of grey had become visible.

"Which one is that?" Gardener asked, peering at the enlarging grey orb.

"The Ghost Moon? It's Sektor 72. We've never been there before, but according to Rodok, it's another abandoned Sektor."

"How many abandoned Sektors are there?"

Saída shook her head. "Couldn't say. How many of these worlds have they drained of resources and discarded? This is just another one on the pile."

As they came into the Ghost Moon's orbit, Saída could see how the grey world was actually a mishmash of white and obsidian. The planet gave Saída an eerie feeling. Nothing like Sektor 23, with its abyssal green gases, but it looked just as empty and lifeless.

The *Mistress* was hit with a barrage of harsh winds as it entered the atmosphere of the world. A sheet of white began to form at the edges of the cockpit window.

"Should've brought a thicker coat," joked Gardener.

Up ahead, Saída spotted the *Lancer*, near the edge of a cliff. Rodok stood outside, watching as they landed the *Mistress*.

Saída lowered the ramp of the ship and walked out with Gardener. The intense winds of Sektor 72 chilled her to the bone, and she clutched her sides instinctively, trying to keep herself warm.

"*Saída*," said Rodok.

"Why'd you pick this place, Rodok? It's so ffff... cold." Saída shuddered.

"*I* did *not* think *it* would *be* this *bad* for *you* two," Rodok buzzed.

"Oh b-bullshit," stammered Gardener, rubbing her hands together. "You knew exactly what you were doing."

"I *chose* Sektor *72* because *it* was *abandoned*. And *the* communications *relay* the *Grand* Design *built* here *will* mask *our* presence."

Saída noticed Rodok's shoulder. She had seen Gideon crush it.

"Your shoulder…" she murmured, gingerly pressing her fingers into the indents left by Gideon's own. Rodok's shoulder was hurt in a way Saída didn't think was even possible.

Rodok looked at his shoulder, then back to Saída. "*Yes.* Unfortunate."

"The drone—" began Saída, but she was cut off.

"*Destroyed.*"

Rodok didn't want to talk about it. Saída nodded.

Gardener peered over the edge of the cliff where the *Lancer* was docked. There was nothing but darkness beneath the grey crags of the Ghost Moon. She shuddered.

"Where's the relay s-station?"

"*Far* down *below.*" Rodok lowered the ramp of the *Lancer* and gestured for them to come inside. "Come. *We* must *go.*"

Saída made her way to the *Lancer's* ramp but stopped when she saw that Gardener hadn't moved. Another gust of wind hit them and Saída felt like it had bitten off her ears.

"Gardener?" she called out.

"I'm going to take the *Mistress*, Abbas. I need to find my people."

"Don't be stupid. The *Mistress* is going to get tagged by the Redcloaks. If that happens you won't be able to use the Ringways anymore. You've got a better chance of finding your people if you come with us. We'll drop you off somewhere safer."

Gardener shook her head. "I know it's risky, but I can't wait any longer. I'll ditch the *Mistress* when I get the chance, but for now I need to go."

"Fine."

She reached into her belt pouches and fished out a tiny metal cartridge.

"What're you doing, Abbas?" Gardener asked, and Saída tossed her the cartridge.

"That'll mask your ship ID for a couple pings. It's what Rodok and I use in the Ringways." Then Saída added, "Ditch the *Mistress* fast."

Gardener offered her hand and Saída shook it.

"I do hope you find your people, Gardener," Saída said.

"Thank you, Abbas."

As Gardener walked back towards the *Mistress*, Saída called out to her, "Hey, just so you know, this doesn't make us friends."

Gardener turned to look at Saída and smirked in response. "Believe me, feeling's mutual."

As Saída and Rodok watched the *Mistress* take off, he turned to Saída.

"*We* have *something*."

Saída's eyes widened. "Digby?"

Rodok rotated his head in confirmation. A surge of excitement filled Saída. She grinned. *Finally.*

The burning sting of failure seemed a distant memory to Saída now as she strode towards her ship, feeling empowered and energised to get back to the hunt. She would find Digby and the Hickston emblem. She *would* save Uncle Abbas.

The *Lancer* roared to life and began to lift off. An instant later it was shooting out beyond the cold, windy skies of the Ghost Moon, Sektor 72 and back into the emptiness of space.

"You *have* a *message*," Rodok's voice buzzed through the *Lancer's* systems.

Saída pushed a button on the dashboard and a small trimensional projection came up. A scruffy-looking man with dark circles under his eyes and a perpetual stubble. Saída scowled at Rodok's unmoving body. She didn't appreciate the ambush.

"Saída. Hello. It's been too long." It was strange seeing Colton after so long. *"I know you're still looking for Digby Hickston."* Colton scratched his stubble. His eyes shifted left to right, as if he were wary of eavesdroppers. *"I finally have something. But there's a catch. You're going to have to come back. I'm sorry. I wish there was another way. I really do. I'll be at the Twelve Dead Men. See you soon."*

The projection faded and Saída settled into her chair at the dashboard. She felt the weight of Colton's words sink in. Her skin felt numb as she dredged up memories of her time in Silwanapur. The very thought of returning to that twisted city had her guts in a knot. Why did she need to go back? Colton knew as well as she did what the risk would be. And yet, Colton of all people wouldn't have asked her to return unless the information he had was solid. The possibility that Digby could even be hiding on Sektor 12 crossed her mind and she felt a sudden wave of elation. She had been waiting for this. A real lead. After their failure on

Orisa, they needed a win. Hopefully, Colton's info would take her one step closer to catching up to Digby, and the emblem of the medallion.

With a deep breath and a solemn prayer, Saída gave the order.

Rodok whirred in the affirmative, setting course for Sektor 12 and the island city of Silwanapur. It was her home once and to be returning to it now, four years later, it made her uneasy. She was worried about Daiyu. Saída looked at the Scimitar in her hands, once again admiring the beauty of the craftsmanship. She thumbed over the Meraji calligraphy, thinking of Uncle Abbas.

Some things were more important than fear.

CHAPTER TWENTY-THREE

Sektor 47

Saída bit off a big piece of her roti and scarfed it down. Uncle Abbas did the same, scooping up some daal with his.

"Thank you for not making me eat daal today, Uncle," said Saída.

"Beti, why do you say that like eating daal is a punishment?"

Saída giggled and pinched some white rice and dropped it into her mouth. The taste was bland, but the soft texture of rice was what she enjoyed. Rice was a rare delicacy for them. At least, it was again. Saída remembered when she lost her eye to the hulking Redcloak. That year Uncle Abbas had managed to get some special food like rice for her. The good food had helped her recover faster, along with medicine and the care that he had provided.

"Uncle," said Saída, moving the roti around on her plate. They sat together at the table, next to the window.

The sun was especially vibrant today, and along with the light, came excessive heat.

"Saída, stop playing with your food," said Uncle Abbas, taking a sip of water while chewing.

"Then you stop doing *that*." Saída pouted, folding her arms in mock disapproval.

"What? This?" asked Uncle Abbas, taking another sip of his water while chewing. Saída recoiled.

"Sorry beti, I suppose I have some bad habits too." He grinned.

Saída looked out of the window again, feeling the heat on her face. Beads of sweat had formed on her forehead and gently trickled down her face. She wiped her forehead and took a sip of water. In the heat, her eye socket always felt itchy. So itchy.

"Uncle, can I ask you a question?" Saída brushed the knuckle of her thumb against her eye patch.

"Of course, beti."

"When I got injured, how did you get all that food and medicine, Uncle?"

Uncle Abbas froze. His moustache twitched and he stammered. "Uh, well. Beti. You see…"

Saída looked at him expectantly, her eye fixed on Uncle Abbas, as he was taken aback by the sudden question. He looked her in the eye and his expression changed, from one of surprise to something softer. He looked at Saída with affection. There was no sadness in his eyes, like Saída had so often seen. Right now, there was only one thing he was feeling, and Saída could feel it too.

"Beti. Saída. All you need to know is that no price is too steep to pay for your safety and well-being. I want you

161

to know that no matter what happens, that will forever remain the case."

"Uncle—" Saída began, but Uncle Abbas cleared his throat and pinched Saída's nose playfully.

"Come now, beti. I have a surprise for you."

He led her to the other room, into the bar, and showed Saída something wrapped in brown cloth, sitting on the counter.

"Happy birthday, Saída," he said.

Saída unwrapped the cloth, beaming as she uncovered a piece of fluffy brown bread inside.

"Meetha toast," she said proudly.

Saída threw herself at Uncle Abbas's belly, giving him a big hug. He laughed and patted her on the head.

"Alright, beti. Now I'm going to set up the bar. Why don't you go and enjoy your toast?"

Saída wrapped up the bread in the brown cloth again and held it in both hands.

"Actually, Uncle. Can I go outside? I'll come back once the Redcloaks are gone."

"Saída, you know what I said after last time."

"Please, Uncle. It's in the old house. I never go farther than that. Please?"

Uncle Abbas tried to look disapproving, but he couldn't hide his joy. "Fine," he said. "But be careful."

"Yes! Thank you, Uncle. Love you," said Saída, rushing out the door of the bar.

"Love you too, beti," he said, and then called out as Saída ran, "And don't forget to come back on time. You need to practice your calligraphy."

Saída ran towards the old plot with the burned house,

excited to show off her Meetha toast and make Rodok jealous. She ran downstairs into the basement and found Rodok staring at a wall in the corner.

"Uh, what are you doing?"

Rodok's eyes moved from the front of his head to the back, and he spotted Saída. Then his body rotated one-eighty degrees.

"I *was* sleeping."

"You said that you can't sleep, you liar."

"*How* do *you* know *I* was *not* lying *before*?"

"Are all Rodoks this bad at lying?" Saída asked, coming into the room, and sitting next to one of the mining drills that Rodok had been disassembling.

"*Silly* Saída. *There* are *no* other *Rodoks*." He squatted next to Saída, watching her place the brown cloth onto the floor. "What *have* you *got* there?"

Saída unwrapped the cloth, revealing her birthday gift. "Meetha toast." She beamed.

"*Meetha*?"

"Yes. Meetha. Like… umm… sweet. Sweet toast," she said.

"*Is* this *your* birthday *bread*?" Rodok asked.

"No. Well, actually it is. But the birthday bread I thought I would get is just normal. This is Meetha."

"I *will* steal *it*," said Rodok, a mischievous tone in his mechanical voice.

"No," Saída cried, placing a protective hand on her toast.

"Ha. *Ha*. Ha," buzzed Rodok.

Saída picked up her Meetha toast and took a bite of it, making sure not to take too much. She wanted to savour it. The sweet, sugary flavour danced along her tongue and the fluffy texture of the bread made her heart sing. Saída closed her eyes and munched on it quietly.

"*What* does *it* taste *like*?" Rodok asked.

Saída gave it some thought. "Like… like fluffy sugar," said Saída.

"*And* what *does* sugar *taste* like?"

"Um. Like sugar?"

"*Ah*. That *makes* sense."

They sat for a while, as Saída finished off her Meetha toast. She made sure to save the fluffiest part for the last bite. Saída rested her head against the drill machine and stretched her legs out, swinging her feet left to right. Rodok sat next to her and did the same. His feet were reminiscent of human feet, but he had no toes. Saída leaned her head against Rodok's arm and stared at his weird feet.

"Where are your toes?"

"*What*?"

"Your toes, stupid Rodok. Where are they?"

"*This* again? *I* do *not* require *toes*."

"Why?"

"*Because—*"

As Rodok prepared to explain, a sound coming from above alerted the two of them.

"Saída?" called the voice from above.

Saída gasped. "Uncle? Why is he here?"

She got up to run upstairs, and Rodok moved to follow her.

"No, Rodok. You have to stay here. If Uncle sees you then I don't know if he'll let me come back here."

Rodok took a step back and rotated his head in understanding. Saída ran towards the stairs, but an invisible force gripped her heart tight as she saw Uncle Abbas descend the stairs into the basement.

"Saída, there you are, beti. The Redcloaks left early today so I came to bring you... home." He tapered off as he saw Rodok. A lanky, mechanical creature that stood seven feet tall. Uncle Abbas's eyes widened.

"Saída," he whispered. "Come here *now*."

Saída complied and Uncle Abbas came between her and Rodok, shielding her from the metal man. Saída whimpered but stayed silent. She looked from Rodok to Uncle Abbas and noticed the look of fear in Uncle Abbas's eyes.

"Begone, Redcloak machine," Uncle Abbas yelled.

Rodok twisted his head, but his eyes remained affixed on Uncle Abbas.

"*You* are *Uncle* Abbas?" he buzzed.

Uncle Abbas sputtered, "You can talk?"

"I *can*."

"Th-then tell your masters that I am doing everything they have demanded. They should leave the child out of this. She has done nothing."

Rodok took a step forward, his metal foot clunked against the stone floor of the basement. Uncle Abbas raised his fists to fight.

"I'm warning you, machine."

Saída finally found her voice, murmuring, "Uncle, wait—" but Uncle Abbas gestured for her to get behind him. "Saída. When I say run, then I want you to run. Get back home. I will follow."

Uncle Abbas's eyes never left Rodok's crimson glare.

"*There* is *no* need *to* worry, *Uncle* Abbas. *I* am *no* Redcloak *machine*."

Uncle Abbas didn't lower his fists. "Saída, now. *Run*."

Uncle Abbas rushed forward and threw himself at Rodok, trying to tackle him, but fell uselessly against the android, who was immovable.

"Uncle, wait," Saída said.

"Saída, I told you to go," yelled Uncle Abbas.

"Uncle, he's not a Redcloak. He's my friend."

Uncle Abbas stopped trying to push Rodok and took a step back. "What?"

"*It* is *as* she *says*, Uncle. *I* am *her* friend," whirred Rodok.

Uncle Abbas took a few steps back, sizing up Rodok, who remained motionless, at the same spot. His red eyes danced around his face.

"Beti, what's the meaning of this?" Uncle Abbas asked. He didn't look away from Rodok, still wary of the mechanical stranger.

"Uncle, he saved my life. When I was trapped in the caves below. He saved me. He helped me get out."

"Is this where you've been coming every time you leave the house?"

Saída gripped her arm and looked down in shame. "Yes, Uncle."

"Saída... Do you have any idea how dangerous this thing could be?" He did not raise his voice, but Saída could tell that Uncle Abbas was livid.

"He's not a thing, Uncle. His name is Rodok and he's my friend. Mera Dost."

Uncle Abbas shook his head. "Beti, you don't even know what it *is*."

"I *am* an *android*," Rodok interjected.

"He's Rodok," said Saída.

"Come on, Saída. We're going. Now," ordered Uncle Abbas.

Then he turned to Rodok. "And you. I don't know what you are, but you stay here. And stay away from us."

Rodok studied Uncle Abbas closely. "As *you* wish."

"Rodok, no," Saída whimpered, but Uncle Abbas led her by the hand and back up the stairs.

The walk back home was silent and Saída felt the pain that clutched her heart had made its way up to her throat. She felt the urge to sob, but it was stuck there in her throat, refusing to move. It was agonising.

When they returned to the bar, it was still late at night.

"Saída," began Uncle Abbas, but she ran into their room without another word. She didn't want to hear what he had to say. Saída dove under the covers of her mattress and turned away from Uncle Abbas's side. She closed her eyes and thought of Rodok. She was angry. Tears flowed from her right eye as she tried to sleep. Angry that he had accepted what Uncle had said so easily. And she was angry at Uncle too. He hadn't even thought to listen to her. The pain that gnawed at her throat dulled as the tears streamed down her cheek, and she wondered if she would ever see her friend again.

CHAPTER TWENTY-FOUR

Sektor 12

"**W**e *are* here," buzzed Rodok, the lights of the *Lancer* dimmed, and he transferred his consciousness back to his body.

Saída watched the vast, clear blue oceans of Sektor 12 from the sky as the *Lancer* closed in on a massive island in the southern hemisphere. There were many island cities on Sektor 12, the biggest was the Capital, in the north. Where the Viceroy lived. But that wasn't the true power in Sektor 12.

That honour belonged to Silwanapur, the run-down, dirty metropolis that sat on a thimble-shaped landmass. The once pristine city had lost its golden-black lustre and was now replaced with dead buildings of faded yellow and brown, stains of age across the skyline and ruined roads that had once been smooth asphalt and steel. Rodok brought the *Lancer* into the central spaceport of Silwanapur, situated in the heart of Hightown. The spaceport itself was quite different to the one on Orisa, or even the one on Sektor 47. No dome-covering and no hangars. Instead, individual landing pads were scattered around the port, on multiple levels, some accessed by stairways, while others were way out on platforms built out onto the coast. They landed on Landing Pad G-13, on the far-eastern side of the spaceport.

Saída idly rotated her chair as she sat, mulling over her next steps.

She walked out of the cockpit and into the *Lancer's* armoury. There sat her armour, spacesuit and what remained of Kruger's helmet. Her own mask had been damaged too, on the gas world of Sektor 23. She unholstered her Scimitar and loaded a chamber with lethal shells.

"If *everything* goes *according* to *plan*, we *should* be *in* and *out* in *a* few *hours*," whirred Rodok, taking Kruger's severed blade out from one of the lockers. He balanced the blade between two fingers and studied it carefully.

Saída holstered the Scimitar and took the blade from Rodok's hands.

She opened a glass compartment on the fabrication machine that sat in the corner of the armoury and placed the blade inside. A series of beeps led to a menu popping up on the terminal that showcased the make-up of the blade.

46% Illuminite. 54% Tetrasteel.

"Just forty-six? Shit," said Saída, and input a new command into the machine. The blade was lowered into another compartment and disappeared from view. The sound of churning and flames shooting out of blow-torches came from the machine.

"With any luck the fabricator should be able to come up with at least two or three illuminite bullets," Saída said, walking out of the armoury.

Rodok followed.

"*We* will *need* to *get* our *hands* on *more*."

"That we will, Rodok," said Saída, putting on her eye patch.

The two walked down the ramp of the *Lancer* and into the city. The familiar musty smell of Silwanapur did little to ease Saída's worries. The chatter of arrivals and departures in the spaceport mingled with the distant noises of hover-cars and grav-bikes, of dogs barking and the yelling of the beggars who dotted the filthy streets of the city. And Saída held her breath.

Rodok placed a hand on Saída's shoulder. "*She* does *not* know *you* are *here*."

Saída shook her head slowly. She was watching everybody, everything, every face in the crowds.

"She always knows," Saída whispered.

Saída hated the black market. The slumrats who peddled their goods here were as likely to cut one's throat as they were to rip them off. Still a fair price by black market standards though. She passed by a couple of gawking mercenaries. Even now, her dark skin tone elicited such reactions. She glared at them, and they turned away. Up ahead, Saída spotted a lone food stall selling different ethnic foods. Most catered to the immigrants who came here from Sektor 7, some from Sektor 13, mostly local favourites like fish cooked in rice cakes and grilled squid, but she was pleasantly surprised to see some of the rice was being cooked with a unique blend of spices, surprisingly similar to how it was sometimes prepared on Sektor 47, if they were ever lucky enough to get their hands on the requisite ingredients. The rich and spicy fragrance created a pang of hunger and nostalgia. She paused, taking in the smell of home, but it didn't take long for that nostalgia to be overtaken by darker memories. The vendor noticed her and gave her a friendly wave, gesturing to a bowl of the rice, but Saída shook her head with a polite smile. The interaction reminded her of her first days in Silwanapur. She and Rodok had spent hours searching for food. It was a kind old man running a grilled fish stall who had offered her some. She had gone to his stall every day for years until his death. He was a good man.

A group of men in white monk robes, turned a corner, blending in with the crowds in the street. Missionary Scholars, no doubt on another *peaceful* mission for the Grand Design, thought Saída. They were crooks as far as she was concerned. A bunch of old men who used their status as supposed holy men to get what they wanted. She bumped shoulders with one of them, passing their group, but the scholars immediately offered a bow and apologised profusely, in keeping with their image of being good-natured monks. She ignored them. They'd prefer it that way. The less attention drawn to such *esteemed* gentlemen at a black market of all places, the better it would be for them. Saída recalled bitterly a time when one of these so-called peaceful scholars had attacked her. Rodok put him through the wall behind the rice vendor. It was still broken. Saída noticed the scholars theatrically bow to another passer-by. They were really putting on a show today. She scoffed. Let them retain their reputation of harmless old men who served a greater cause. They'd get what was coming to them.

A tingling sensation on the back of her neck had her feeling on edge. She had called this city home for several years. She knew it like the back of her hand. There was something in the air today. It wasn't anything she was unfamiliar with. Growing up in this city, Saída had gotten used to cops conducting surprise raids, swooping in to demand cuts of the black market profits or to extort locals. Gang wars were also common. Quiet one moment and the next, streets ablaze with gunfire and blood. It was a day just like today when her friend, Lin, had been shot. A victim of a stray bullet. The sensation at her neck grew worse. There was something coming. She had to get to Colton fast. Saída had her hand on her Scimitar pistol. A place like this, bustling with all kinds of brazen criminal activity, she had to be on guard. Now was no time to reminisce.

Leaving behind the sunny street and the foul odour of sweaty stall-workers and thugs, Saída made her way to the Twelve Dead Men, a bar at the end of the street. The broken authenticator buzzed as the doors to the entrance clanged open. It was a dingy little bar, with wooden tables and stools littered about. There was a music station in the corner, which had been given an old-timey makeover, playing soft tunes that didn't overpower the ruckus of the patrons. The fluorescent lighting buzzed and fluctuated, despite the amount of solar energy that was being funnelled into the place. The bar was going for a vintage aesthetic, but Saída knew that the disrepair was not an intentional part of the atmosphere. The chatter of the bar's patrons filled the air. They talked freely, unrestricted due to the lack of cops in the bar. Saída was no stranger to what went on during these discussions. It was when the worst got to stake their claim on just how bad they were. Just how scary they could be. Everyone had to pretend to be impressed or had to one-up the story with a tale of their own exploits. Saída smirked, recalling the days when she had to take part in these rituals, so that she could fit in. So that she could survive.

At the end of the bar counter, a rotating belt moved drinks around to various patrons. Saída spotted her informant, Colton, pick one up and chug it down. The bartender was busy getting another bottle ready for him.

"Hey Hanzo," Saída called out to him. "Still alive?"

Upon seeing Saída, his old face crinkled in joy.

"Little Saída! How time flies," he said. Even after all this time, the old man still considered her a customer.

"Not that little anymore." Saída smiled.

Hanzo poured Saída a glass of water. "Ah, you'll always be Little Saída to me. Missed you, kid."

Saída raised her glass to him. "I missed you too, old man."

She turned to Colton. "What've you got for me?"

Colton finished his drink and waited for Hanzo to pour him another one. Beggar's Tap.

"Nice to see you too, Saída. Where's Rodok?"

"He had something to do. Now. What've you got?" Saída was still angry with him.

Colton shook his glass, wiped the sweat from his face and sniffed. He always looked miserable. He grunted as he picked up a file from the stool beside him and placed it on the counter. It slid over to Saída as the belt rotated. She raised an eyebrow as she picked it up.

"Paper?"

"You can read, can't you?"

Saída opened the file, sorting through the pages and examining the photos carefully. She furrowed her eyebrows as she picked up a document, as if it were a precious jewel. Her eyes flicked from the photo to Colton and then back to the document.

"Is this real?"

"Honest truth," said Colton, nodding his head. "Viceroy Hickston disowned him privately, so that the media wouldn't make a big deal out of it. Of course, he only did that because somebody leaked the info on Digby on the hyperwaves. GDNN had a field day."

The Grand Design News Network was the only newscast on the hyperwaves. They were owned by the Grand Design and only ever spouted their lies. Saída never tuned in.

"So it's finally public knowledge then. Since when?" Saída studied the photo.

Colton nodded. "Very recently. Ever since the Voidstriders started making more of a name for themselves."

"And that's why Hickston cut him loose," Saída surmised. "He finally got too infamous."

"A few years back, when you asked me for info on Digby, the Voidstriders were just a small-time gang. He could get away with a lot more. Now that isn't the case. The Voidstriders are a lot higher profile. If the Church found out about Digby's piracy, the Hickstons stood to lose a lot more than reputation," Colton said, watching his reflection in the brown liquid Hanzo poured into his glass.

Saída grinned. "Disowned by his own father. Well, that makes things easier for me. Means he won't be able to run back home." Saída bristled at her choice of words. *My home.* She cleared her throat, unable to believe what she was about to say. "Your file said he's here? In Silwanapur?"

Colton offered a weak smile. "That's why I called you back. He should be headed to Landing Pad H-12 later today, in fact. I think he's gonna take his dad's money and find some place cushy to lay low. You gonna hand him over to the Guild?"

Saída stiffened. If there wasn't a bounty on *her* head yet.

"Yeah. Of course."

And Saída would complete the medallion.

Colton signalled for a refill on his drink and Hanzo deflated.

"There's… something else," muttered Colton, without looking at Saída.

"Oh, you son of a bitch," she muttered, leaning back into her seat. A look of disbelief was plastered across her face. "Who else have you told?"

"Takamura family…"

Saída rose from her seat, and Colton did too, trying to back away.

"Saída, it wasn't my fault, they threatened t—"

She grabbed him by the collar with both hands and hissed, "You *asshole*. You gave my mark to *Takamura*?"

"Oh boy," sighed Hanzo.

"How long ago was this?" demanded Saída as she let go of Colton, letting him slink back into his chair.

"An hour before you showed up."

Saída glared at him.

"I didn't give them the file. I told them where he'd be… just told them it would be later than it is. You can still make it, Saída."

"You better hope you're right, Colton." Saída motioned with the Scimitar, waving it at him.

Colton grunted. "Look. I got you the info, alright? You've got time. Get to him before they mess it up. That was my last favour. We're done now."

Saída glared at Colton again. He lowered his eyes, trying to avoid her gaze, instead looking into his glass of Beggar's Tap.

"If I lose Digby because of you, then we are *far* from done, Colton."

Colton said nothing. Saída nodded to Hanzo, who looked relieved, then she picked up the file and walked out of the bar.

Back in the scorching heat, Saída noticed the market was cleared out. The stall-keepers had closed for the day and there weren't too many people left. She was ready. She stared at the file in her hand and started sorting through it again. It was full of information on Digby. Scans, history, crimes and now his whereabouts. Landing Pad H-12. Now that Digby had been disowned by his father, Saída could even bring him into the Guild after she had got the emblem. Would bring in a nice number of shards. Assuming she was still counted as part of the Guild.

The sun was beginning to set, and a cool wind had just rolled in. It was almost a nice day. Then a cry rang out through the empty street.

"Oi!"

Two rowdy men in suits walked towards Saída with a swagger that only the men of the Takamura family were overconfident enough to pull off. It was her old friends, Kengo and Akio.

"Shit," muttered Saída under her breath.

"Yo, Saída," said Kengo. "Boss wants a word. Wants the file."

"Tell Takamura to back off. This mark's mine." Saída shut the file and looked at the two men, red suit and blue.

Kengo, in the red suit, laughed.

"Don't make me kick your ass again, Kengo," threatened Saída.

"Don't get cocky. You only won, cos I held back. Didn't want the boss to see me beat up a lady, is all."

Saída raised an eyebrow and put a hand on her hip. "Right."

"And the boss isn't here right now," Kengo said, cracking his knuckles.

He threw a punch. Saída dodged and clocked him in the throat, causing him to fall to his knees, gasping for air.

Akio, in the blue suit, ran at her, yelling, but was stopped short by a mechanical hand. Rodok grabbed his arm and pulled it at an unnatural angle, standing an imposing seven feet tall. His chassis was freshly painted black chrome and shone in the sunlight. His eye darted around his head, scanning for other attackers.

"What the hell—" Akio managed, but yelped as Rodok twisted his arm further.

"I had that," said Saída, going back to her file.

"I *know*," chimed Rodok.

Saída gestured to the file. "According to Colton, Digby

is here on this Sektor. We might finally have some luck on our side, Rodok."

"And *how* is *Colton*?" asked Rodok.

"What? Rodok, focus."

"I *am* just *asking*. We *have* not *seen* him *in* a *while*."

"Look, important thing is, we know where Digby is, and we need to go. *Now*."

She emphasised the last word, so Rodok knew it was time to let go. He tightened his grip on Akio's arm, who slammed his foot into Rodok's mechanical legs and yelled in pain. Rodok let go and Akio crumpled to the ground, next to Kengo.

"We need to be careful. Just because he's been disowned by Hickston doesn't mean he won't still have some kind of backup. He's still a Voidstrider," warned Saída as she and Rodok walked out of the black market district and back towards the spaceport.

They crossed through the merchants' district of Hightown. It wasn't all too different from the black market. Only difference was that here it was the law-abiding, so-called legitimate businessmen and women who fleeced you. Saída sneered at the bourgeois families who saw fit to haggle the prices of cheap clothes that would cost them nothing, and the indecisive people who held up the lines at insta-food places. Standing next to an inactive police drone were two cops drinking coffee, staring long and hard at every obvious immigrant who passed them by. Saída instinctively turned away from the direction of the cops and took an alternate route towards the spaceport. She didn't want to risk getting the cops on their tail so early.

"Saída," whirred Rodok.

She could hear voices in a foreign language up ahead, near Landing Pad H-12. It was one of the Sevens, one of many native languages of Sektor 7.

"Takamura and his people are already here," Saída said. "Can't exactly go in guns blazing. Digby might get shot. Or worse, the cops might show up."

"Or *worst*, you *and* I *may* get *shot*. I *just* got *my* chassis *repainted*."

"We've got no choice. We need to get past those guys or else we're gonna lose Digby again."

She walked towards the Takamura family, who had congregated right below the landing pad. Saída looked at the stairs leading up to where she assumed Digby's ship would be, but there was nothing there. *Scav*. Takamura had already gotten to him.

Saída strode onto the platform and the Takamura family aimed their pistols at her and opened fire. Rodok was a split second faster and leapt in front of Saída, shielding her from the onslaught. Saída stopped and waited for the barrage to end. Rodok's chassis was too strong to be penetrated by lethal shells. His new paint job, however, was ruined. The impact of the shells revealed just how old and rusted Rodok's black chassis had become.

The rain of bullets stopped, but the ringing in her ears didn't. Saída called out, "Nice to see you too, assholes."

"Saída Abbas," declared Takamura, swaggering in his well-tailored white suit, making a show in front of his lackeys. "I thought I told you what would happen if I ever saw you again."

"Shit, Takamura, it's been four years. I thought you'd have forgotten by now."

"You still owe me for *Ironside*."

"Last I checked you got yourself a pretty sweet Hammer-class ship out of that deal, Takamura."

"You know damn well that it ain't about that, Saída," cried Takamura. "I don't give a shit about the shards or the ships. I give a shit about the *principle*."

Rodok, still protecting Saída, rotated his head, fixing his red gaze on Takamura.

"I *did* not *take* you *for* a *romantic*, Takamura."

Takamura responded with an enraged yell and fired at Rodok again. Strands of his perfectly slicked-back hair came loose.

Rodok buzzed a monotone, "*Ha*. Ha. *Ha*."

"Alright, Tak, listen," said Saída. "Now that we've all got that outta the way…"

"Where's the damn file, Saída?" demanded Takamura.

"Hey, I'll give you the file and Digby too if you want, I just want whatever he's got on him, alright? I'm willing to let the rest go."

Takamura holstered his gun and swept back his hair.

"The file. Now."

"Fine." She tossed it from behind Rodok. One of Takamura's lackeys picked it up and brought it to their boss. Takamura flipped through the pages and studied the file.

"Dammit. This gives us nothing."

"What the hell do you mean, nothing?" asked Saída. "He's supposed to be up there on the landing pad. Or he *was* unless you morons let him get away."

Takamura shook his head and handed away the file.

"No way. We've been casing this place for hours. Digby never landed."

"Landed?"

"Yeah. He was supposed to land here."

"I was told he was gonna leave from Landing Pad H-12. That he was already here."

"Wait," began Takamura. "You don't think…"

"Yeah," Saída said grimly. "Colton Haynes screwed us."

"Son of a… I'm gonna kill him," growled Takamura.

"Get in line."

A siren blaring in the distance caught their attention, Saída saw police drones beginning to make their way to the landing pad. Takamura sneered.

"Temporary truce?" Saída asked.

"Go to hell, Abbas. If I see you again…"

"Yeah, yeah."

The Takamura family rushed to their vehicles, some fled in hover-cars, others on grav-bikes. Takamura himself escaped in a stylish white luxury jeep which sped off, gliding across the derelict roads.

Saída and Rodok made a mad dash for the side alleys outside the spaceport. The open-air layout of the spaceport allowed them an easy way out. They were able to duck into an alley behind the landing-pad stairway and onto a street outside the spaceport in no time. In the distance the sirens grew louder and Saída surmised that the cops had already made it to Landing Pad H-12. She put a hand against the wall and took a moment to breathe. The thought of possibly losing Digby had her stomach in knots. They had to find Colton. She and Rodok headed for the building complex that housed Colton's office, ducking in and out of alleys and streets, passing by various stores in the merchants' district and crossing over into the eastern end of Hightown, avoiding cops and Takamura family enforcers alike.

They arrived at an old building in what was one of the seedier districts in Silwanapur. The surrounding buildings were either trading hubs for contraband or stages for delinquents to party the night away. The outside was worn-out synthetic metal. Poorly reinforced. The more modern districts boasted buildings that were made from far more durable materials. The buildings in front of them looked like they were about ready to collapse at any moment. No wonder Colton called this place home.

Saída looked at the second-storey window, to the left side of the building, and gestured to Rodok to climb it. He rotated his head in agreement.

Saída raced into the building, crossed the filthy lobby, and ran up the stairs. The sounds of people arguing, children crying, and other sounds of daily living dimmed and rose around her. She kicked open the door to the Haynes Agency office. A young woman, his secretary, tried to speak, but Saída pushed her aside and entered Colton's office, just in time to see him trying to jump out the window. Rodok was already there, pushing Colton back and climbing into the room. The window strained and shattered against Rodok's frame in the process.

"Colton. *Colton.* Colton," tsked Rodok, rotating his head with every mention of the name.

Colton straightened his tie, avoiding eye contact. He was full of booze all the time, and the dark circles under his eyes never seemed to fade. Rodok's imposing figure forced him to sit back down at his desk.

"I didn't make you for a rat, Colton. Maybe I should have," said Saída.

"Screw you, Saída," he responded.

Saída slammed his desk and yelled. "You *know* how long I've been after this guy. How much I've sacrificed."

"And what about what I've sacrificed? You think it's easy doing this shitty job, trying to help people when all everyone wants is dirt on everyone else? You know better than anyone else how horrible Silwanapur is."

Saída boiled. That was rich coming from him.

"You chose that, Colton. You never showed up. We waited. It was *your* decision to stay."

Colton looked helpless. "You don't know the whole story, Saída," he whispered.

Saída noticed that. She could see that there was something, some deeper reason. She knew he wouldn't just do what he did. Not after everything they lived through in Silwanapur. But at that moment she didn't care. She couldn't. Uncle Abbas was on the line. And she was out of patience.

"You know what I think, Haynes? I think I do know the whole story. I think you're just like everybody else in this city. I think you drew me back in to pay off your debt to the Triad. You used me."

Colton jumped off his seat, pointing his finger at Saída, but Rodok forced him back into the chair. Colton shook off Rodok's arm but remained seated.

"After all this time, is that what you really think?"

Saída opened her mouth to speak, but Colton pulled

183

something out from under his desk and slapped it onto Rodok's chassis. A burst of electricity immobilised the android where he stood. Colton ran for the door, but Saída tackled him, pinning him against the wall.

"You shouldn't have done that. I needed to get to Digby. I've got someone counting on me and Digby was the only way I was getting back to him," she snarled. "And now you've taken that away from me."

Saída pulled back her fist to strike, but Colton seized the moment and headbutted her. She fell to the floor, disoriented.

Colton clenched his fists.

"Digby left yesterday. He wanted info. I told him I had nothing for him. Didn't want to get involved with the Voidstriders. I'd suggest you didn't either, Saída, but I know you better than that. Digby kept mentioning a name. Belgrave. I don't know if that'll help. Now I'm done. With all this," said Colton.

Saída closed her eyes. "Daiyu will never let you leave this city, Colton."

Colton looked away. "Not this time, Saída. This time she won't catch either of us," he said and walked out.

*

The city was oddly calming at night. With the daily rat race momentarily paused, the people of the city were able to regain some sense of themselves, of time they had lost during the day, grinding away at their lives to please someone else, or to achieve some hollow sense of self-satisfaction. There weren't many notable sights to see on

184

Sektor 12, but the Silwanapur lake was certainly one of them. The lights of the city were reflected in the water, swaying and rippling, creating a magical aura. The colours of all the night-time restaurants, hotels, and pubs were a mix of blue, white, yellow, pink, and red that splashed onto the water, creating a surreal kind of art on the dark canvas of the lake. Saída lit a cigarette, snapping off the tip and igniting it. She stared at the water in silence. Rodok stood next to her, motionless, his single red eye was still. Saída had been leaning against the wall, then slowly, slid down and rested her arms on her knees. She exhaled and the smoke was so light it blended in with the night air.

"That *could* have *gone* better," said Rodok, still unmoving.

"Shut up, Rodok."

Saída took another puff of her cigarette and pulled out the Scimitar from its holster. It was cold in her hand, the metal familiar. Studying it up close, she paid special attention to the grooves inside the barrel of the gun. Imagined the way it would alter the shells it would fire. How much extra power would be behind those shots, compared to the regular pistols that she had used before? She holstered the Scimitar and took another drag of her smoke.

"Cops still around?"

"*Their* presence *seems* to *have* lessened, *but* yes, *there* are *still* plenty *lurking* about," replied Rodok.

Saída stood up, swatting away the dirt from her clothes.

"Let's head back to the *Lancer*, I wanna get out of here."

"*Would* you *like* to *catch* a *synthshake*, as *you* say?"

"I'm not in the mood," grumbled Saída, chewing on the cigarette and putting her hands in her coat pockets.

"*You* are *upset*."

"You're damn right I'm upset. We've been on the trail for years, and we still can't find Hickston's *bastard* kid, who—"

"*Actually*, records *indicate* that *Digby* was *a* legitimate *heir* to *the* Hickston *fortune* up *until* his *disownment*—"

"—keeps finding ways to slip out of our grasp like he's a damn snake. That's why I'm upset, Rodok. Cos of four years of failed plans and cold leads."

"*Ah*."

"That's all you got?"

"I *simply* thought *you* were *more* upset *about* your *friend*."

Saída scoffed. "Haynes? I don't give a shit about Haynes, Rodok."

Rodok gave her the look, a subtle twist of his head, something most wouldn't notice, but Saída had been on the receiving end enough times to know exactly what it meant.

"He wasn't my *friend*, alright? He was my informant. I'm only pissed I couldn't sock him in the jaw before he got the drop on us."

Rodok put his hand on his mechanical hip and twisted his head further, readjusting his eye to stay focused on Saída.

"*Right.*"

Saída looked away, embarrassed.

"Quit it already. That's not how I do it."

She took a final puff of her cigarette and flicked it away, watching tiny sparks fly as it disintegrated in the air, leaving no traces.

"I'm not mad at the guy anymore. He did what he had to. I did what I had to. No hard feelings. That's just how this shit goes in our line of work."

"*Then* stop *moping* and *let's* get *back* to *the* ship."

Saída scowled and gestured for Rodok to lead the way and the two started walking.

"Excuse me, ma'am, sir. I need to see your IDs," said a man with a low drawl.

Saída and Rodok turned. A cop with a police drone hovering next to him stood close by. The moment he spotted Saída, his hand immediately hovered over his holster. Saída rolled her eyes.

"Ma'am, I need you to hand me some identification right now."

He turned to say the same to Rodok but did a double take when he saw he was a machine.

"*Take* a *walk*, little *man*," threatened Rodok.

"You have a bipedal drone?" he asked incredulously.

"*What* did *he* just *call* me?" Rodok asked Saída.

"Listen," said Saída. "We're busy, and we're leaving. Run off back to the farm."

It took a moment for the cop to register the insult, but he withdrew his pistol and took aim.

"You will comply. Hands in the air," yelled the cop, a vein popping on his ashy forehead.

Saída revealed her prosthetic eye and scanned the drone as it levitated next to the cop. Police drones were nowhere near as deadly as Redcloak Watchers. They were simply companion pieces to police units in cities. Silent, docile floating orbs skewered with antennas. It was processing something. Saída's crimson eye dug into the drone's processing systems and uncovered the source. It was calling for backup. Saída pulled out her Scimitar and shot the drone. The sound of a tiny explosion followed. The shell pierced through the armour of the drone, disabling it. The drone emitted a screeching noise, hitting the railing and falling into the lake. She felt the entire Scimitar vibrate in her hand at the moment of the shot. The power of the Scimitar was exhilarating. Saída trained her gun on the cop before he could react.

"Tell you what, why don't *you* put the gun down and maybe I'll let you walk away?"

"I'll shoot, I swear I will," yelled the cop. Rodok, faster than the cop could react, grabbed the gun from the cop's hands and crushed it between his metallic fingers.

"I know your type," muttered Saída. "Never enough immigrants or refugees to fill up your quotas. I just took your drone out so you've got no backup coming. You're all alone now."

The cop faltered. Saída grabbed him by the collar and shoved the Scimitar in his face. His eyes widened in horror.

"Wanna see what a shell does to a human skull up close?" Saída growled.

"*We* do *not* have *the* luxury *of* dealing *with* another *body*, Saída," said Rodok, putting a hand on her shoulder.

"Just one of these days, I'd like to show these assholes what it's like," growled Saída.

"*You* and *I* both *know*, you *never* can."

The cop was crying, Scimitar still in his mouth. Saída was close to pulling the trigger.

"I want to do it, Rodok," she spat.

The sound of a distant explosion echoed through the city.

Saída was distracted. And Rodok had heard enough. He pulled Saída away from the cop with one hand and with the other, he lifted the cop and threw him, screaming, into the lake.

Saída yelled in frustration, but Rodok maintained his hold on her, not allowing her to break free.

"The *politics* of *humans* bore *me*, Saída. *These* are *the* antics *of* a *child*. We *are* returning *to* the *Lancer*."

Saída glared at him.

"Let me go, Rodok. *Now*."

His crimson eye was locked with hers. The gears in each of their mechanical eyes turned and shifted, like they were communicating.

"*I* will *not*."

They glared at each other. Minutes passed. Then Saída yelled. And she relented.

"Fine, asshole. You win."

"Indeed," said Rodok, releasing her arm.

Saída pocketed her hands and started walking back towards the ship, but Rodok stopped her.

"*Saída*."

"What?"

"*Make* no *mistake*. I *would* help *you* eliminate *every* person *that* draws *breath* in *this* city, *on* this *entire* Sektor, *if* you *wanted*. But *I* will *not* let *you* jeopardise *yourself* like *a* fool. *We* have *come* too *far* for *that*."

There was silence, and the two of them looked at each other long and hard. Saída nodded. She understood. She agreed.

She followed Rodok back to the *Lancer*, but her mind wandered to the explosion. Just what had Colton done?

CHAPTER TWENTY-FIVE

Sektor 47

Saída sat in the back room sulking and staring out the window. The night air was stale and carried an uncomfortable, wet heat. Saída wiped sweat from her forehead and rubbed her eye patch. Uncle Abbas was in the front dealing with Redcloak patrons again. She hadn't talked to him in the last few days. Not since he forbade her to go see Rodok.

The sounds of clinking glasses and rowdy yelling never really registered to Saída as it had just become a part of life, but today it disturbed her. Today it made her angry. A sudden cheer and smack prompted Saída to get to her feet and glare at the door. She wanted to rush out and scream at all the Redcloaks that were there. She clenched her fists and exhaled sharply, letting the rage out in a silent scream.

Enough was enough. Saída didn't care anymore. She was going to go see Rodok. She climbed onto the table and slipped out of the window, planting her feet carefully on the ledge outside. Since she had grown, the ledge had become smaller. It was harder for her to shimmy across the side, but she persisted and made it to the other end. To the side of the bar, Saída snuck carefully, checking the corner. She half expected to see Aqsa again, smoking and acting high and mighty. There was nothing. No one stood outside the bar. Instead, Saída made out the muffled noises from inside and took a quick peek through the window. Uncle Abbas was busy pouring drinks and cleaning glasses, making sure he didn't get any of the orders wrong. By now the Redcloaks didn't bother too much with tormenting Uncle Abbas at every turn. They came for their drinks and left. They had gotten bored, but every so often, they'd feel the need to put Uncle Abbas in his place. To make him feel small in his own home. Saída clenched her jaw. On his own world.

She ripped herself away from the window and ran towards the old plot, and into the derelict house. She ran down the steps to the basement and called out for Rodok, but there was no response. The lights in the basement were shut off and there was no sign of her mechanical friend anywhere.

"Have you gone back into the caves?" Saída wondered aloud.

Saída set to finding the old mining equipment that she used to use to rappel down the caves, before Rodok had made his way up towards the basement and made things easier for her. She tightened the belt around her waist and set to tether the equipment to the drilling machine that she used to use as an anchor but realised that it lay disassembled in the corner of the room. Rodok had been working on it for months, neither of them had realised she would eventually need it again. Saída rubbed the back of her hand. She was growing anxious. She searched the room for anything she could use as an anchor point and spied a beam that held up the roof of the basement. She tied the cable around it. Three times she wrapped the cable around it and pulled, testing its strength. She huffed in satisfaction. That would be good enough. Saída released more of the cable from her belt and walked into the mining tunnel, into the little cave where she once used to squeeze through. Now it was an open hole into the dark caverns below. Where she hoped Rodok might be.

Saída was about to turn and climb down when she spotted something familiar in the air. The size of a pen, but it flew in front of her, and the surprise caused Saída to take a few steps back. It was Rodok's drone. He was watching her.

"Rodok, why did you leave?" she asked, gesturing with the palm of her hand. She was irritated.

There was no response from the drone, but it whizzed around the air and returned to its original position.

"I don't know what that means, stupid."

The drone came closer to Saída's face and gently brushed against her nose, then it went back down, descending into the darkness of the caverns.

Saída's face fell. "This isn't fair…"

Saída reluctantly unfastened the mining belt from her waist and unwrapped the cable from the beam in the basement. As she did, she noticed the beam was rotting from the side. It might not have been able to support her weight, had Saída taken the risk and gone down. She closed her eyes and resisted the urge to cry, palming the rotting, wooden beam.

Even if she couldn't hear him, she understood what Rodok was telling her through the drone. She hated that he was right. He was stupid.

Saída moped on the way back to the bar, it was nearing dawn and the Redcloaks had no doubt left by now. Uncle Abbas would be furious with her. She had done all this for nothing. She hadn't even gotten to see Rodok again.

Saída entered through the front of the bar, the lights were turned off and the counter was clean. All the dishes were washed. Uncle Abbas was definitely awake. Saída put her hand on the door-handle and stopped. She exhaled. Her heart was in her throat. She felt nauseous. On the other side of the door, Saída would have to face Uncle Abbas, and his disappointment would be justified. She had disobeyed the one thing he asked her not to do. And yet, Rodok was the only friend she had. He was important to her. Uncle had to see that. Saída had to have faith that he would. He was Uncle Abbas.

Saída opened the door and walked into the back room. The lights were turned off and Uncle Abbas sat by the table with a glass of water, looking out at the moon.

Saída was quiet but took a seat at the opposite end of the table. Uncle Abbas had already set a glass of water for her too. They sat in silence for a while, taking in the calm of dawn. Uncle Abbas rotated the glass in his hands and pursed his lips. Saída couldn't look at him.

Then, in Meraji, Uncle Abbas spoke.

"You know, when I was a boy, not much older than you are now… When I was a boy, Abu told me something that I never forgot. He said that no matter what happens, no matter what humiliations we face, or how much our lives are squeezed… The one thing we must never lose is our freedom. If not our home, then our bodies. If not our bodies, then our minds. We must never lose that freedom, even if its final haven is in our minds, Saída."

Saída looked up and Uncle Abbas looked her in the eye. As if a gentle breeze had replaced the humidity, Saída felt calm. Uncle Abbas looked at her and in the moonlight, his brown eyes shone with a brilliant splendour. Like the patterns of stars painted on the ceilings of a Masjid.

"You embody that freedom, Saída. No matter what you have suffered, you have never lost that freedom. And I would be a fool to try and take that away from you."

Saída was confused, tears welling in her eye. "Uncle… what are you saying?"

"I'm saying that I should have listened to you and given you a chance to tell me what you wanted to say," said Uncle Abbas, shifting to the middle of the table, closer to Saída. He put his hand on her cheek and wiped away her tears.

"Tomorrow, we will go to the old house together and meet with the machine. I will speak with him and listen to what you have to say and then I will decide." Uncle Abbas paused. "However, if I decide that it is still too dangerous and that it cannot be trusted, then you have to promise me that you will stay away from it. Okay?"

Saída looked down, hesitant to agree. She didn't want to say goodbye to Rodok if Uncle Abbas still decided against it in the end.

"He's my only friend, Uncle. His name is Rodok," sniffled Saída.

"Beti, I know. I know how hard this must be for you. But your safety will always be the most important thing for me. So please. Understand what I am trying to do."

Uncle Abbas's eyes were half closed, and Saída understood. She knew how hard this was for him. The risk behind it. If he couldn't guarantee that Rodok would not be a threat then it would be safer to keep Saída closer to him. Saída dried her eye.

"Okay, Uncle. I promise that you'll see that Rodok is good. You'll see that he really is my friend. We won't let you down, Uncle. Promise."

CHAPTER TWENTY-SIX

The *Lancer*

Rodok plugged into the main terminal of the *Lancer* and transferred his consciousness to the ship, activating it. His mechanical body deactivated, and the ship's interior was illuminated with a faint blue glow as Rodok took over its internal systems. The engines roared to life and the *Lancer* lifted off the landing pad and jumped into the stratosphere, towards the emptiness of space and the giant Ring that hovered nearby. They left the overcrowded, blue-grey world of Sektor 12 and the city of Silwanapur behind them. Saída was relieved to see it go. Colton had been right. Daiyu hadn't made a move. But *why?*

She sat at a table in the atrium of the *Lancer*, while Rodok hummed the tune of 'The Red Children', an old song by an artist who really loved their collection of weapons. The lighting of the ship flickered to the rhythm of his voice, growing brighter and dimmer with its cadence. Saída was focused on cleaning and maintaining the Scimitar. It had performed far beyond her expectations. With the kind of power it displayed, Saída hoped an illuminite bullet would really let it do some damage.

"Rodok, did you notice them?"

"I *did*."

"We were being watched. Since the lake. Three of them."

"*Daiyu's* men."

"She let us go. Why?" Saída put the Scimitar down.

"*In* truth, *I* cannot *say*. But *there* is *no* point *in* worrying *about* her *now*. We *are* off-*world*. Safe."

Saída took a deep breath, trying to let all the tension she had built up out with a sigh. Rodok was right. She had to let go of her fears. She picked up the Scimitar again.

"Any hits on Belgrave?" Saída asked, wiping down the barrel of the Scimitar.

"*Nothing*," buzzed Rodok.

"Isiah is dead, and Colton shared what he knew already. I don't know where we go from here, Rodok."

"*The* Voidstriders *are* dangerous *but* tightly *knit*. Small. *There* is *a* reason, *so* few *people* knew *that* Digby *Hickston* was *their* leader. *At* least *until* recently."

"You think Belgrave could be another Voidstrider? I thought it was a code for Digby's hideaway."

"It *could* be *either* one *or* neither."

"I guess we could always try to find another Voidstrider, but who knows how long that might take. We already got lucky once with—" began Saída.

The sound of steam whistling came from the armoury. The bullets were ready. Saída set the Scimitar down and went to the armoury to check the fabricator. Rodok went back to humming his song.

The process was complete. Kruger's blade had been melted down and the illuminite was separated from the Tetrasteel. Saída pushed a button on the control panel and the fabricator ejected a tray from one of its many panels. Sitting in the tray was a single black bullet.

Saída picked it up and sulked. All that metal just amounted to a single bullet of illuminite.

"*How* many *bullets*, Saída?" buzzed Rodok through the intercom of the *Lancer*.

"Just one. Kruger really got screwed by that Viceroy."

"*Well* make *sure* you *do* not *waste* it."

Saída returned to the atrium, to the table with the Scimitar. She snapped the gun back into place and separated the chamber in two, loading one with lethal shells and the other, with the single black illuminite bullet. The chambers snapped together and locked back into the Scimitar. Saída thumbed the hammer and double-tapped it, switching the chambers with a whirr.

"Two loadouts," said Saída, holstering the gun.

"I *think* you *mean*—" began Rodok, preparing to make a snide comment, but his tone changed. "*Saída*, the *news*."

Saída frowned. News?

Saída circled the atrium and went into her bedroom, the tiny room huddled between the bath and the cockpit. She ignored her unmade bed and grabbed her SETRA off the bedside shelf and walked back out. Saída dug her thumb into the ID scanner of the SETRA, activating it. She pulled out the antenna and projected the image from her tiny screen onto the wall. She twisted a dial on the side and the trimensional projection activated, showing a number of options to choose from: Communication. Hyperwave. Data.

"*Switch* to *the* news, *Saída*," buzzed Rodok.

Saída flicked her thumb and found the Grand Design News Network channel under 'Hyperwave' and 'Newscast'. A silhouetted woman was speaking.

"*...took control of the Bounty Hunters Guild station, more commonly referred to as 'The Needle'. With the Guild no longer working independently from the Grand Design, Crusaders will begin staffing the Needle as soon as...*"

Saída scoffed. "*Crusaders.* Just call them Redcloaks. Everybody else does."

"*...bring you word from the honourable Knight Benedictus, Sir Gideon Welbridge.*"

Saída touched the medpatch on her cheek as the image of Gideon appeared on the projection. He was grinning, blond hair swept back and the same dead blue eyes he had on Orisa.

"*Hail citizens of the Grand Design. By order of his Holy Eminence, Kaiser Willem Ulius Albert Edward V, my Crusaders have occupied the headquarters of the Bounty Hunters Guild. All prisoner transfers have been put on hold as the Guild transitions into an arm of the military. All bounty hunters employed by the Guild are required by order of the Kaiser himself, to return to the Guild and hand in your badges, regardless of your status as employees or contractors. You will be reinstated as Crusaders or Officers dependent on your devotion to the Grand Design.*"

Then it was as if his cold, dead eyes looked directly into Saída's.

"*Any who fail to do so will be deemed outlaws and in opposition to the Kaiser himself. You will be hunted down, and you will be executed.*"

Saída felt a lump in her throat and swallowed. The silhouette of the woman returned, spouting more flowery words for the glory of the Grand Design and the strength of the Kaiser, but Saída retracted the SETRA antenna, deactivating the projection. Saída placed it on the table where she had been cleaning the Scimitar.

She sat down and pondered their next move.

"It *seems* that *we* are *soon* to *be* unemployed," said Rodok. The lights in the atrium dimmed.

"Or…" said Saída.

"Or?"

"You heard Gideon didn't you? Prisoner transfers have been put on hold."

"*Saída*, what *does* that *have* to *do* with *anything*?"

"Think about it, Rodok. We need intel from a Voidstrider, and we've got one sitting pretty in the Needle. Digby's guy at that."

"*Mac*? What *guarantees* that *he* will *have* information *on* this *Belgrave*?"

"There's no guarantee, Rodok. But there aren't exactly any other options."

"Saída, *we* already *interrogated* him. *I* am *sure* he *does* not *know* where *Digby* is."

"Probably not, Rodok. But we didn't know about this Belgrave intel before. For all we know he kept it close to his chest. If we'd known back then we could have pressed him on it."

There was a pause. The *Lancer's* lights flickered.

"I *do* not *know*, Saída. *If* he *did* not *reveal* this *information* on *threat* of *death* then *he* does *not* know *or* will *not* share."

"We didn't ask him about Belgrave," repeated Saída. She clasped her hands together and stared at her feet. "It's all we've got. All other leads have dried up."

"*You* are *putting* far *too* much *on* the *line* based *on* information *from* a *man* who *has* betrayed *us.*"

Saída buried her face in her palms. She nodded. "But he's never been wrong before."

"Saída… *If* we *do* this, *it* will *mean* breaking *Mac* out *of* the *Needle.*"

Saída shrugged. "Either way, we're criminals. This way at least we have a chance at saving Uncle Abbas."

"*Very* well," said Rodok. "*How* do *you* want *to* do *this*?"

CHAPTER TWENTY-SEVEN

Sektor 47

As Saída heard the last of the Redcloak patrons leave the bar, she felt sick. She took a seat at the table, waiting for Uncle Abbas. The moment of truth was approaching. The door-handle turned.

"Saída, it is time," Uncle Abbas said. His voice was solemn. No hints of wit or playfulness like usual. He knew how much this meant to her. And Saída knew he did not want to give her false hope.

She nodded. Her stomach turned. This was their only chance. Rodok had to convince Uncle Abbas. There was a crescent moon in the sky, barely visible behind the thick layers of smog in the air. Saída and Uncle Abbas trudged along the dry, cracked earth, towards the old house. Saída checked the sky for any sign of Rodok's drone. Perhaps it was keeping watch. She hoped he would see.

Arriving at the house, Saída looked up at Uncle Abbas and murmured, "Uncle, wait here. I'll go get Rodok."

"Beti, I think it's better if we go down together. It will be less risky downstairs anyway."

Saída nodded and made for the stairs. She had been hoping to prep Rodok for this before Uncle Abbas was finally able to talk to him.

Among the stony walls of the basement and the disassembled, rusted mining machinery, Uncle Abbas took a seat at the foot of the stairs. Saída went to the opening that led down to the caverns and peered over the edge, into the darkness below.

"Uh. Rodok?" she whispered.

"Beti, I think you'll need to be a little louder," said Uncle Abbas.

Saída scratched her head. Of course. Yes. Louder. Her face turned red, and she looked away from Uncle Abbas, back to the caverns below.

"Rodok?" she called out. "Can you hear me? Please come up."

Silence.

"Rodok, can you hear me?" she called out again.

Nothing.

Saída sat down and bit her thumb.

"Perhaps he did not hear?" Uncle Abbas clasped his hands together.

"Or maybe he's gone," mumbled Saída, allowing her chin to rest on her knees.

"Beti, I'm sure that's not the case," said Uncle Abbas. His attempt to reassure her was a little half-hearted. As much as he had chosen to trust Saída, she could tell that he preferred to never have to see or risk meeting Rodok again.

Saída felt a pang of anger but swallowed it. Her throat

hurt and her eyes burned. Her eye burned. As did the eye, that wasn't there. Uncle Abbas was the only parent she had. He loved her. He wanted what was best for her. But why did he scare Rodok away? Why did he do that to her? Saída yelled out, tears welling in her eyes and red, itchy pain swelling in her throat.

"*Rodok!*"

Saída curled into a ball and leaned against the wall, trying to hold back her sobs. Uncle Abbas walked over to her. Hesitant. Softly, he wrapped his arms around her. He felt resistance, Saída pushing away from him, but he didn't let go.

"Beti… I'm so, *so* sorry. I didn't realise… I *should* have realised."

Saída stopped trying to get away and instead covered her face. She didn't want Uncle to see the tears.

A distant metallic clamping caused Saída to open her eye, through a gap in her fingers. She looked on as a rusted black, metallic hand clawed onto the edge, and then the other followed. Rodok lifted himself up onto the edge of the floor and climbed into the basement, crimson eyes fixed on Saída.

"I *came* as *soon* as *I* heard *you*, Saída," he said, placing a gentle, heavy hand on her head. "*I* am *sorry* for *leaving.*"

Saída looked at Rodok, then at Uncle Abbas, and realised she had stopped crying. Then she started wailing again. The floodgates were open and now Saída felt the need to unleash all the anger and sadness that she had been keeping bottled up.

"Both of you are *stupid,*" yelled Saída, covering her face again.

Uncle Abbas exchanged a quizzical look with Rodok then looked back at Saída.

"I know, beti," he whispered, giving her another hug. "I know."

*

Saída opened her eyes, squinting at the bright lights of the basement. She noticed she was under a blanket, lying near the stairs of the basement. She must have fallen asleep. She spotted Uncle Abbas and Rodok in another corner of the room. They were sitting across from each other, chatting.

"And you've just been talking with Saída? Whenever she would come to meet you in the caves below?" asked Uncle Abbas.

"Yes, *Uncle*. We *spoke* on *a* wide *variety* of *topics* over *the* last *few* years. *I* remember *every* single *conversation*. Would *you* like *to* hear *a* recording?"

Uncle Abbas looked at Rodok sceptically, but then he relaxed. "No. No, I believe you."

"Well, *it* is *good* you *did* not *ask* for *proof*, because *I* lied. *Ha*. Ha. *Ha*."

Saída giggled.

"So, you don't actually have recordings?" Uncle Abbas asked.

"*I* do. *But* not *of* Saída. *Though*, I *do* remember *every* conversation *we* have *ever* had."

Uncle Abbas shifted around, settling into a cross-legged position.

"So, tell me then, Rodok. What exactly are you?" Uncle Abbas asked.

"I *am* an *android*. Designation *1-1-2-1-3-4-7*, Priority *target:* Confidential. *Serial:* Unlisted. *Manufacturer:* Redacted," buzzed Rodok, puffing his mechanical chest in… pride?

"So, you are a robot? Like a Redcloak drone? But one that can walk and speak like people?"

Saída stifled a laugh at the way Rodok swivelled his head. He looked offended.

"Uncle *Abbas*, I *am* a *being*, fitted *with* the *highest* quality *Advanced* Intelligence. *I* am *capable* of *higher* thought, *logic*, and *analysis*. I *am* far *superior* to *any* technology *that* you *or* these *Redcloaks* could *possibly* have *seen* or *developed*. In *fact* the *laboratory* I *was* built *in* is *the* galactic *hub* for *scientific* innovation."

"Was none of that information confidential?" Uncle Abbas asked in genuine curiosity.

Rodok faltered. "I… *hmm*."

"So does that mean that you can choose to disclose information if you wish?"

"I *cannot*."

"But through conversational loopholes…" Uncle Abbas left the thought hanging in the air.

"*Well* played, *Uncle* Abbas," buzzed Rodok.

"Thank you, Rodok."

Saída couldn't hold it in anymore and let out a giggle. Uncle Abbas and Rodok looked her way and Uncle Abbas flashed a grin.

"Look who's awake," he said, coming to sit by her side. Rodok did the same.

"It *is* good *to* see *you* again, *silly* Saída." Even though his face was featureless, Saída could tell that Rodok was smiling.

Uncle Abbas patted her head. "I'm so sorry about everything you've had to go through, beti. I was so focused on your safety that I forgot about everything else. You are a child. You deserve friends."

Saída looked at Uncle Abbas, how the lines around his face creased in that half sad, half happy smile that he did for her, whenever he wanted to reassure her. When he wanted to let her know that even if things were bad, they would get better. She hugged him.

"I love you, Uncle," Saída whispered.

"I love you too, beti. That will never change."

"You too, Rodok. Join the hug." Saída beamed.

"If *you* insist, *Saída*."

Rodok crouched and wrapped his arms clunkily around Saída and Uncle Abbas.

Saída and Uncle Abbas chuckled at how Rodok tried to emulate their hug, but the three of them remained as they were for some time. Together, in their arms, Saída felt safe for the first time in a long time. She was with her family, her home. Things were finally normal again. Something she was not expecting to ever have again.

"*Dawn* is *fast* approaching," buzzed Rodok.

"Then I suppose it is time for us to be off," said Uncle Abbas, putting a hand on Rodok's shoulder. "I am glad I met you, Rodok. I apologise for the way I treated you when we first met."

Rodok's eyes whizzed around his face. "*Apology* accepted, *Uncle*. Thank *you* for *giving* me *a* chance."

"Oh, you don't have to keep calling me Uncle," said Uncle Abbas.

Saída frowned. "Yes, he does. Everyone does."

"I *must* agree," buzzed Rodok. "*After* hearing *everything* Saída *has* to *say* about *you*, no *other* name *would* suit *you*."

"She has been saying only good things, I hope," said Uncle Abbas.

Rodok said nothing. Uncle Abbas raised his eyebrows.

"Rodok, stop lying," hissed Saída, kicking him in the shin.

"*Nothing* but *good* things," buzzed Rodok mischievously.

"Well, regardless," said Uncle Abbas, "Uncle isn't really a name, Rodok."

"Still," said Rodok and Saída in unison.

Uncle Abbas sighed and his moustache twitched. "Very well."

Uncle Abbas took Saída by the hand and they waved to Rodok as they climbed the stairs out of the basement. The sun had just begun to rise as they walked back to the bar in silence. There was a light breeze in the air and the pink hue of the horizon brought a feeling of calm to Saída. She looked up at Uncle as they walked, and he squeezed her hand, smiling back at her. Today was okay. Actually, today, Saída was better than okay. She was happy.

CHAPTER TWENTY-EIGHT

The Needle

Saída glared at the dashboard interface.

"Present your Guild badge for verification," the voice buzzed through the comms panel. The voice was different from the one she was used to. Gideon worked fast. The entire station was most likely full of Redcloaks who had replaced Matthias's staffers.

Saída fished out her badge from her coat and placed it on the scanning board. The badge floated in suspension on the board as a full scan was taken and sent over to the Redcloak.

After a few minutes, the Redcloak spoke again.

"Guild badge verified. You're clear to dock."

Saída put the badge back in her coat pocket and switched off the comms panel.

"Alright, Rodok. You know what to do."

The lights in the cockpit flickered, and Rodok brought the *Lancer* in closer to the Needle.

The rings around the Needle rotated constantly, funnelling the station with artificial gravity, keeping the station locked in place.

Rodok brought the *Lancer* into the landing pad inside the Needle and Saída immediately felt the effects of the faux atmosphere that the Needle maintained, creating an invisible wall between the vacuum of space and the inside of the station.

"Be *careful*, Saída," buzzed Rodok as he landed the *Lancer* next to a slew of other ships inside the Needle. Saída had half expected to see the *Mistress* among the ships but remembered that it now belonged to Gardener.

Saída exited the *Lancer* and crossed into the depressurisation chamber. Once she saw the indication that she was safe to proceed, she walked out to the main lobby of the Needle. Various other bounty hunters had returned as commanded by Gideon. Some she recognised, some she had never seen before.

"Remember to wait for my signal, Rodok," muttered Saída, touching her silver earring, a more discreet, close-range form of communication than her SETRA.

Groups of bounty hunters stood around the lobby, talking to each other. Many spoke in Prime, but a few spoke languages from their Sektors. Technically illegal, but the bounty hunters never much cared for such trivialities, what with their profession being in the legal grey area anyway. Most ignored Saída as she walked past them, but a few sneers and mutterings didn't go unnoticed. It was the same every time she met any of her 'colleagues'. A sandskin woman had no place being a bounty hunter, least of all one employed by the Guild officially. Not like it would matter soon enough.

Saída stepped into one of the lines at the end of the hangar, where bounty hunters were handing in their badges and picking up new registration cartridges from the Redcloak at the end. Saída spied one of Gideon's elite Redcloaks standing nearby. Instinctively, she hunched, trying to stay hidden behind the line. None of them had seen her face on Sektor 15, but she wanted to avoid them all the same.

The line moved and Saída felt a shove from behind. She turned and some bounty hunter with a scarred forehead was looking at her.

"Didn't know they let sandskins into the Needle."

Saída bit her tongue. Normally this would be a great time to break some bones, but the last thing she needed was a fight. Saída ignored him and put her focus back on the line ahead. The Redcloak at the end was taking badges and handing out cartridges.

Forehead pushed her again.

"I weren't done talking to ya," he coughed.

"Yeah, well I was," snapped Saída.

"*Yeah, well I was,*" mimicked the bounty hunter, mocking Saída's accent.

Saída clenched her fists and wound up her arm to elbow the man, when she noticed something poking out of the jacket pocket of the bounty hunter in front of her. It was his Guild badge. Saída eyed the hangar to see if any Redcloaks were watching. Then she slipped her fingers into the bounty hunter's jacket and grabbed his badge.

"What the hell you doing, sand—" began Forehead, but Saída placed the stolen badge in his hand.

Before Forehead had a chance to respond, Saída tapped the man in front of her.

"He's got your badge," she said.

"What?" replied the bounty hunter, scratching his black hair mindlessly. He looked at Saída, nose scrunched in annoyance.

"Guild badge. He's got your Guild badge," muttered Saída, pointing to Forehead.

"Wait, hold on a damn minute," sputtered Forehead.

The black-haired bounty hunter's eyes widened, and he patted his jacket pockets, searching for his badge. He glared, grabbing Forehead's collar.

Saída stepped out of the line, slinking away from the growing altercation.

The black-haired bounty hunter shouted something about integrity and Forehead tried his best to defuse the situation. Saída watched on in amusement.

The black-haired bounty hunter threw a punch. His Guild badge fell to the ground and there was a yell from across the hangar.

One of the elite Redcloaks walked up to the ensuing fight, and forcefully separated the two bounty hunters.

"You dogs need to keep yourselves under control or you'll be going home in jars."

The elite Redcloak smacked the butt of his rifle into Forehead's gut, causing the man to crumple.

"Hold on a minute, he stole my badge," yelled the black-haired bounty hunter, but it didn't matter. The elite smacked him upside the head. Then followed up with a boot to the face. The bounty hunter recoiled on the floor.

"Then pick it up and stop whining," commanded the elite, through gritted teeth.

Saída took the opportunity to slip further into the line while everyone was distracted watching the elite handle the two rowdy bounty hunters. She suppressed a smirk as the elite beat the two men down.

"Back in line, ingrates," yelled the elite Redcloak. His silver helmet hid his face from view, but Saída imagined a vein popping in his forehead. "Anyone steps out of line again and I'll have your guts."

Saída bowed her head, looking away from the elite as he walked by her, back to the edge of the hangar. He was standing near the elevator. She watched as bounty hunters who handed in their badges took their cartridges into a hallway to the right of the elevator, where Saída presumed the rest of their application would be filled out and their eligibility to become Redcloaks would be judged.

She eyed the elite, who stood motionless beside the elevator, holding up his rifle like a bayonet. Watching the line. His helmet turned ever so slightly as he scanned the entire lobby, watching for any sign of disturbance. Perhaps even hoping for it. Saída grimaced.

"*Saída.* I *am* making *my* way *down* into *the* lower *levels*," buzzed Rodok in her ear. Saída tapped her ear with the palm of her hand, brushing against the silver earring. "*Are* you *in* the *elevator* yet?"

Saída coughed twice.

"*Understood.* I *will* check *again* soon."

Saída stepped forward as the line grew shorter. Almost there. The elite Redcloak was still watching them all. When it would be her turn to hand in her badge, he would see her clearly. The moment of truth. One more bounty hunter left the queue.

"Guild badge here," muttered the Redcloak at the desk. He had a thin moustache and no hair. He looked up at Saída and whistled. "A sandskin woman, eh?"

Saída ignored him and handed over her Guild badge. It was a good thing the *Lancer* wasn't a Guild ship, or she and Rodok would have been in trouble once they had to escape.

"Well, I guess you people don't really like that word," the Redcloak muttered, looking over her Guild badge. He tapped a glowing symbol on the badge and scanned it by swiping it on a slot in the terminal on his desk.

"Saída Abbas, you have an impressive number of bounties captured. Three years working as a contractor, and only just became officially employed? Shame it has to end so soon."

The elite Redcloak fixed his gaze on Saída. She averted her eyes.

"Where are you from?" continued the bald Redcloak. "Your Origin Point is listed as Sektor 12, but your accent is different."

Saída felt her skin grow cold. "Uh… 6. Sektor… Sektor 6," she lied, eyes darting between the elite beside the elevator and the smiling Redcloak at the desk.

"Wow, Sektor 6. I wouldn't have guessed. Your parents must have been servants for some noblemen then?"

Saída's eyes stared at the bald Redcloak, unblinking. "Yes. Yeah, exactly that," she mumbled. "My mother was a servant on Sektor 6."

The elite Redcloak started moving towards the line. Saída felt beads of sweat forming on her forehead.

"Why didn't you stay? Surely being a servant is a much

easier job than being a bounty hunter? You're quite a beauty. You could even have caught the eye of a nobleman had you remained," he said.

Saída was no longer looking at the Redcloak at the desk. Her eyes were fixed on the elite who was getting closer. His gaze was still fixed on her. The dark V-shaped visor around the helmet obscured the elite's eyes from view. The Redcloak droned on and on, but his voice was drowned out by Saída's thoughts. She felt her heartbeat rising. How could she get out of this situation? How many of these Redcloaks and bounty hunters could she take out before she was gunned down? She could feel the blood rush to her ears. She felt numb.

Saída's arms dropped to her sides. Her hand was close to the Scimitar, concealed under her coat.

"…thought about becoming a Crusader? I'm sure there would be a place for you in the infantry division. Lower class of course, but—"

The elite Redcloak walked over to the desk. Saída began to reach for the Scimitar, when the elite stopped looking at Saída and grabbed the bald Redcloak's shoulder, squeezing tight.

The bald Redcloak yelped, dropping the Guild badge on the desk.

"Keep. It. *Moving*," growled the elite, shoving the Redcloak. He grasped his rifle with both hands again and continued moving down the line.

The bald Redcloak placed Saída's badge into a pile with several others, a decommissioning box which deactivated the badges permanently. Saída felt a pang of regret watching her badge go. The end of an era.

The bald Redcloak grabbed a cartridge from another box, unloading it with a clink and handing it to Saída.

"Fill out the registration form. Submit your blood for testing... and make your way to the hall. To... to the right of the elevator," he said with a whimper, avoiding Saída's eyes.

The elevator was clear. The elite was patrolling the ever-increasing line of bounty hunters. Saída gulped.

She walked towards the hall where she was pointed. As she got close to the elevator, she changed her trajectory and made a dash for it. The doors slid open as they sensed her movement and she slipped inside. A couple of the bounty hunters in the line noticed her. She slammed the button for the elevator to take her to the top of the Needle and the elevator sprung to life, jetting upwards.

She checked the blinking lights of the elevator controls panel; the light illuminated the button corresponding to the floor she was on. The middle of the Needle, where the lobby was, was around the fortieth floor. Now she was up in the eighties, where the admin offices were. Matthias's office, however, was on the top floor. The ninetieth.

Saída appreciated the brief moment of calm. Then the elevator ground to a halt and the force of the sudden stop slammed Saída against the elevator doors. The lights dimmed and the elevator grew dark. The elevator was stuck. Saída punched the doors.

"*Saída*," buzzed Rodok in her earpiece again. "Status?"

"Well, Rodok. I'm in the elevator," groaned Saída, getting back up to her feet.

"*That* is *good*."

"Bad news is the elevator just got shut down. They are definitely sending a squad my way."

Saída opened the Scimitar's dual chambers, counting down her bullets. One chamber full of lethal shells and the other housed the single illuminite bullet she had managed to recycle out of Kruger's blade.

"*That* is *most* regrettable," buzzed Rodok. "*Did* you *make* it *to* the *top*?"

"Almost," said Saída, holstering the Scimitar, surveying the cramped deathtrap she now found herself in. "I'm between eighty-seven and eighty-eight. I'm going to have to find some way out of here. How close are you to the holding cells?"

"*Quite* close, *Saída*. I *have* discovered *Mac's* cell *number*. I *am* making *my* way *down* there *now*."

"Alright, Rodok. With any luck, I'll be able to get to Matthias's terminal soon."

There was yelling from the other side of the elevator doors. Redcloaks were coming.

"*Good* luck, *Saída*. Do *not* take *any* chances."

Rodok's monotone voice fizzled out of the earpiece and Saída took a sharp breath, pulling out her illuminite dagger from its sheath. Even in the darkness, the Black Jade insignia glistened beautifully.

"When do I ever take chances, Rodok? When do I ever?" she whispered to herself, anxiety taking hold of her.

She thumbed around in the dark for the elevator's emergency button, finding it on a panel at the edge of the back wall. She pushed the button. Nothing happened.

"Disabled," Saída spat. She looked up at the emergency hatch on the ceiling. Without the emergency button, she wouldn't be able to pull it down.

The sound of sparks flying alerted Saída to the elevator

doors. She saw the top of the elevator doors glowing yellow, turning to red, increasing in heat. The Redcloaks were going to force the door open. She had to hurry. Saída upturned her eye patch, revealing her crimson eye and scanned the emergency hatch. Thanks to the eye, she could see wires connecting to a hidden panel behind the elevator walls. It was connected to the emergency button.

Saída brandished her illuminite dagger and held it up to the elevator doors, where the heat was greatest. The pure black dagger began to glow a dark red, then orange. Finally a brilliant white as it reached maximum heat. As the Redcloaks were halfway through the elevator doors, Saída sliced through the metal panel like soft butter, making a rectangular cut. The metal slipped off with a heavy thunk.

Saída ripped the wires out of the panel in one fluid motion. Electricity sparked and the emergency hatch came loose. The Redcloaks were almost upon her.

Saída gripped her dagger backwards, jumped up and grabbed the handle of the emergency hatch. She climbed out and pulled the hatch shut after her. The mechanisms clicked and the hatch was locked once more. Now that she had reset it manually, there was no way for the Redcloaks to get to her from down there. She heard the doors burst open and the unloading of lethal shells into the elevator. She shuddered. A minute too late and that would've been the end of her.

She was on the eighty-eighth floor. Two floors below her destination. Saída plunged her still-burning dagger into the steel doors and pushed it in a horizontal line. The echo of her illuminite dagger cutting through steel reverberated throughout the hollow elevator shaft. She heard muffled yelling from the elevator below. Saída ground her teeth and pushed harder. The Redcloaks would probably be sending patrols to the eighty-sixth and eighty-eighth floors now. She just needed enough space to slip through.

Saída managed to cut open a hole big enough for her to squeeze through. She kicked the melted steel open, revealing a hallway that led to the admin offices on the floor. Taking care to avoid the still shimmering gold edges of the door, Saída crawled into the hallway and sprinted towards the other end. The Redcloaks would be bringing up the elevator from the opposite end of the Needle, which meant it would still be active. That was Saída's chance to get to the top. Just two more floors.

Saída dashed into the offices, pushing past men and women in suits, kicking aside a desk to reach the other hallway. It led to the only other working elevator of the eighty-eighth floor. The doors slid open and a squad of four Redcloaks rushed forward, firing lethal shells. Saída dodged to the right, taking cover in a doorway. The office workers screamed in terror and ran for cover. The bullets flew, blowing up furniture and monitors alike. A man fell. People screamed.

Saída waited out the Redcloaks' firing spree, Scimitar in hand and blind-fired two shots from cover. The firing began again.

When the firing petered out, Saída heard the familiar click of ammo being reloaded. She fired off three shots. Two Redcloaks went down screaming. Saída slipped back behind cover just as the remaining two Redcloaks opened fire on her again.

That was it. One last push.

Saída grabbed a small vase that had fallen near her feet and tossed it into the hallway. The Redcloaks opened fire in that direction and Saída dove into the hallway on the other side. Using her prosthetic eye, Saída found the optimal trajectory for the Scimitar. Her next two shots hit home. Four dead Redcloaks lay in the hallway, and the walls and floor were splattered with blood.

Saída sprinted for the elevator again, grabbing one of the pistols of the fallen Redcloaks on the way. She punched the elevator panel to get to the top floor and scavenged a few shells from the pistol, reloading her Scimitar. The doors opened on the nineteenth floor.

"Rodok, I'm at the top floor. Get ready," said Saída.

"*Affirmative. I am in front of Mac's cell.*"

"Did you have any trouble with the guards?" asked Saída as she walked through the hallway to Matthias's office. It hadn't been too long since she had been here last, but the normally nice view was now obscured by the massive hull of the *Lancelot*.

"*I did not,*" buzzed Rodok.

"Well, that makes one of us. I'm going to need one hell of an escape route because both the elevators are out."

"*When you are done unlocking Mac's cell you should be able to access the admin commands over the elevators as well.*"

"Let's hope you're right, Rodok," Saída said and walked into Matthias's office.

Matthias was standing in front of the window. He would have been watching the stars, were it not for the *Lancelot*. The ship was floating in view of the entire nineteenth floor.

"You know, I never doubted this day would come," Matthias said, without looking away from the window, his hands locked together behind his back, as he surveyed the view as if in leisure.

Saída aimed the Scimitar at him. She could see Matthias's reflection in the window. His spectacled eyes betrayed no emotion. He just watched her in the window, observing her.

"I'm not here for you, Matthias, but I have no issues killing you if I have to," threatened Saída.

"If not for me, then why exactly have you come back?" asked Matthias, finally turning around to face her. He had a black eye. "Surely you were aware the Redcloaks had taken over my Guild?"

Saída lowered the Scimitar.

"I need you to unlock your terminal. Right now."

Matthias scoffed. "I shall do no such thing," he said, walking around his desk. He stepped closer to Saída.

"Matthias…" Saída began.

"You, however, can do whatever you want," said Matthias, looking Saída in the eye.

Saída furrowed her eyebrows. "What?"

"You heard me."

Matthias walked back to the window, his gaze never leaving the *Lancelot*. Saída walked around the desk, cluttered with useless trinkets and stationery and a miniature statuette of a Spear-class ship that sat next to a terminal. Saída took a seat at Matthias's desk. The terminal was an older model, one that didn't utilise trimensional technology. It didn't even contain a SETRA antenna slot. Saída clacked away at the physical keys attached to the terminal, accessing the admin commands. A beep sounded and a green warning spread over the terminal screen.

Enter Passphrase.

Saída squinted, and focused her prosthetic on the terminal, searching for any giveaways to the code. The eye scanned the terminal's data, but there were no hints to be found.

"The passphrase can't be typed, can it?" Saída mused.

Error.

Saída noticed a tiny device connected to the side of the terminal, an audio receiver.

"What's the passphrase, Matthias?"

Matthias maintained eye contact with the *Lancelot* outside the window.

"I did my best to turn the Bounty Hunters Guild into something valuable for the galaxy, not just the Grand Design. It has been my life's work. Now, I suffer the indignity of being stripped of that command, by the same government that *lauded* my predecessors."

Saída tapped the side of the terminal in frustration.

Error.

"The passphrase, Matthias."

"After everything I have accomplished in the name of galactic safety and peace of mind for its citizens."

Saída rose from her seat. "Give it a rest, Matthias," she snapped. "I know what you're building up to, so you can stop already. But I'm not going to apologise for it."

Matthias looked at her with a quizzical expression. "Apologise? For what?"

Saída returned the look. "Because... Because I failed to bring in Gardener?"

And because she drew Gideon's attention towards the Guild.

Matthias scoffed. "Please. You think *you're* the reason these Redcloak bastards took over the Needle? Don't be absurd."

Saída raised her eyebrows. For whatever reason, it seemed like Matthias didn't know. Gideon hadn't told him. Perhaps he hadn't told anyone.

"Then why did they take over the Guild?" asked Saída.

"Who can say? Perhaps it is the *will* of the Grand Design, like that fool Knight said?" Matthias smirked; his words dripped with venom.

Saída looked at the black-blue hue of the bruise around Matthias's eye. "Gideon do that?"

"Yes. For failing to *adequately* carry out the Kaiser's will. Mark my words, this is only the beginning. The Grand Design is going to use any excuse to take control of everything they don't have their filthy hands in." Matthias placed a hand on the window and spat, "Fascists."

Saída scowled. "Oh, so *now* it's fascism? When they take *your* home?"

Matthias turned around, ready to trade barbs with Saída, but she pinned him against the window, grabbing him by the scruff of his neck.

"Give me the passphrase, Matthias or I'll blow your brains out," she growled, choking him, Scimitar digging into his skull.

"Al-alright... *Alright*," Matthias coughed, and Saída let him go. He rubbed his throat and muttered, "Looking-glass."

The terminal beeped. *Authenticated.*

The green warning vanished and Saída took a seat, navigating the old operating system, searching for the admin commands. She reactivated elevator functionality first, overriding the controls so that the only place they could be controlled was from Matthias's terminal. Next, Saída began searching for the prisoner cells. Several tabs on several levels appeared and in the corner of the screen, she noticed an emergency option to unlock every cell on the Needle.

"What are you looking for?" asked Matthias, still rubbing his throat.

"A prisoner I left here a few weeks back," said Saída, clicking onto another sub-level directory.

"Why?"

"That's none of your concern, Matthias."

Saída found the tab containing the holding cells in the lower levels of the Needle. She tapped her earpiece. "Rodok, what's the cell number?"

"Perhaps if you asked me?" Matthias said.

"Matthias, shut the hell u—"

The sound of a gunshot. Saída looked at Matthias. He clutched his stomach as blood pooled from behind his hand, a dazed look on his wrinkled face. "What?" he gurgled and fell to the ground.

Saída hit the floor immediately, knocking the stationery and the statuette off the desk in her haste. She unholstered the Scimitar and thumbed the hammer.

"Saída," whistled a cheery Gideon from behind the desk. "You hand your badge in at the *bottom*."

The tone of his voice was colder, more mechanical. He intended for this to go one way. Saída raised the Scimitar. She held her breath. She didn't hear footsteps.

Gideon was waiting for her to make the first move. Matthias lay on the floor, blood pouring from his wound. He was face down. Saída couldn't tell if he was dead or dying.

"It's a shame you had to shoot the old man," said Saída from behind cover. "I was going to do that myself."

Gideon chuckled. "Step on out from the desk, Saída. If you comply, I'll just arrest you."

Saída eyed the terminal from the floor. The screen was sitting on the search functions for the cell number. In the corner, she saw the emergency option to unlock every cell. It had to be now or never.

Saída noticed the miniature Spear-class statuette near her hand. She had an idea. Just like the vase distraction in her firefight with the Redcloaks earlier, she could distract Gideon long enough for her to hit the emergency release function. Saída tossed the statuette at the wall, then rose to slam the terminal keys, but a searing pain spread through Saída's arm before she could follow through with her plan. Gideon had shot her. She fell beside Matthias, dropping the Scimitar. Her raven hair was tinged in Matthias's blood, and she clutched her right arm in pain. Gideon laughed and walked over to her, kicking the Scimitar away. He wore his gold illuminite armour and his bright-red cloak flowed behind him. Saída looked up at his smiling face, into his hollow blue eyes.

"There's no... No way you could have seen... that coming," struggled Saída.

"Is that right?"

He stepped on her injured arm. Saída howled in agony, feeling the bones in her arm crack under the weight of

Gideon's armoured boot. She mindlessly smacked her left fist into Gideon's armoured shin, spittle spraying from her mouth as she tried to bear the pain.

Gideon grabbed Saída by the neck and lifted her up with one arm, still smiling.

He tossed Saída across the room and she hit the wall, nearest to the hallway. Saída scrambled to her feet and ducked out of the way and Gideon's fist went deep into the wall, getting caught in the cables and wires on the inside. He struggled to pull it out and Saída saw her chance. With her good arm she threw a vicious left hook at Gideon's face.

She felt her knuckles connect with his cheekbones, but Gideon showed little reaction. Saída tried again. Her third punch broke Gideon's nose. Blood dripped down to his lips, but he showed no indication of pain.

She took a step back. "What the hell?"

Gideon grabbed her neck with his free hand, holding her in place as he pulled his arm from the wall. A crackle of electricity brought forth loose cables from the hole in the wall. Gideon turned his attention back to Saída and threw her again.

Saída slammed against the wall, disoriented.

Gideon took his time walking to Saída.

"I wasn't expecting you to come back to the Needle after they broadcast my announcement. I thought I'd need to actually try hunting you and Aveline down."

Saída slumped against the wall. She tried to get back on her feet. Blood dripped from her arm to the floor. Her head was throbbing.

Gideon grabbed her face and slammed it against the wall. He squatted, keeping her in place, watching her.

He gazed over her prosthetic eye, but he paid it no mind.

"I did a little thinking, after our last meeting. A lot of you look alike, so it's easy to mix you up. I didn't really consider where you might be from, but it's Sektor 47 isn't it? The little rock that Hickston governs?"

Saída screeched at Gideon, her face still pressed against the wall. She clawed at Gideon's face, but he tightened his grip.

"My uncle has some servants from your home. I met him recently, so I got a good look at them. You're definitely from Sektor 47. Come to think of it, I believe my father owned some factories there too. Well, they're mine now of course."

Saída was desperately thinking of a way out.

Gideon frowned. "Why don't you speak?"

He released his grip on Saída's face, letting it go for a moment. Saída gasped and coughed, and Gideon slammed her face back into the wall. The shock of the blow darkened her vision. She was bleeding from her forehead now and the blood dripped down her eye like sweat. Her crimson eye remained open, watching Gideon.

He thumbed over the medpatch on Saída's cheek.

He ripped off the medpatch and studied the wound. Saída's skin crawled as Gideon brushed his thumb over her scar.

"Where is Aveline, Saída?" he asked politely, digging his thumb into the scar. Saída felt like another plasma bolt had scraped her cheek, the white-hot pain returned, but she resisted the urge to scream.

Saída spat in his face but Gideon had no reaction.

The terminal beeped, drawing their attention.

Matthias, still clutching his stomach, had slammed the keys on his monitor, initiating the emergency release of every prisoner in the holding cells.

Gideon groaned and let Saída go. She slid to the floor, watching as Gideon walked over to Matthias, behind the desk.

"Treason as well? The Kaiser is most displeased."

Gideon grabbed Matthias's head and with a twist, snapped his neck. Matthias's lifeless body fell to the bloody floor.

"Now, how the hell do I reverse this?" he muttered, studying the terminal.

Saída touched her earring. "Rodok," she wheezed. "Now."

"Saída, *what* is *wrong*? Are *you* alright?" came his panicked response.

Saída had to ignore him, she had to shake off the pain. She crawled towards the Scimitar, which was lying at the other end of the room, near the cables that had come loose. Gideon saw her, but did nothing, focusing on the terminal.

Saída clawed at the Scimitar, gripping it with her left hand, and struggled to get to her feet. The blood from her forehead dripped over her eye, forcing it shut, but Saída kept her prosthetic eye open. Her disorientation made it hard to focus. She aimed the Scimitar at Gideon.

She fired three shots, but her arm wavered. Two shells hit the window but disintegrated on impact. The third met its mark and shot a hole through the terminal. Sparks flew as the terminal was disabled and Gideon threw up his arms in frustration. His armour glowed a shade brighter, where the shell had hit him, through the terminal.

Saída spat blood, getting up on one knee. She revealed a set of bloody teeth as she grimaced. "My bad, I was aiming for your face."

Gideon walked around the desk, towards Saída. She aimed at his face and fired another shell, but Gideon brought up his armoured gauntlets in time to protect himself. A tinge of white filled his gold arms. The shells were destroyed as they came into contact with his illuminite armour.

"You'll need a little more firepower than that," he said, lowering his arms again.

She double-tapped the hammer of the Scimitar, switching to the illuminite loadout.

"I've got illuminite too, Gideon," growled Saída.

There was a moment of shock in Gideon's eyes as he covered his face in panic. Saída fired. The sound of a shrill chirp erupted from the Scimitar, following a blaze of brilliant white light. The illuminite bolt made contact with Gideon's arms and for a split second Saída thought it was over. But the illuminite bullet ricocheted off of Gideon's gauntlets and bounced off the walls of the office. Saída fell backwards and Gideon remained still. Then there was silence.

Saída stared at Gideon in horror. He lowered his arms and began to laugh. Saída's reaction only served to empower the Knight.

"Was that really your trump card?" said Gideon, holding up his still glowing arms. "Foolish girl."

Saída lowered the gun. She had one shot. It didn't work. She crawled backwards. She felt helpless. Fear began clouding her thoughts. She felt the Scimitar grow heavier in her hand. It didn't work. The illuminite bullet didn't work. She was never going to see Uncle Abbas again.

Gideon said softly. "Tell me where Aveline is, Saída. I'll make it quick."

Saída looked at Gideon, his face was expressionless. She heard a crack. The sound of glass straining against great pressure. Gideon heard it too. He followed Saída's eyes to the window. The illuminite bullet was lodged firmly in the glass. The window had begun to crack around it. The bullet was struggling to break free.

Gideon looked at Saída. For the first time, she felt like she saw something other than superiority and malice in his expression. She saw uncertainty.

She was no longer disoriented. Her prosthetic was locked on. Saída aimed the Scimitar at the window and fired a shell at the trapped illuminite bullet. On impact, another flash of white destroyed the glass around the bullet.

The lights of the Needle went out, replaced by a dim, red glow. The desk and the terminal were sucked out, followed by Matthias's corpse. The force was strong and Saída took hold of the only thing in sight, the loose cables from the hole Gideon had punched in the wall earlier. Gideon was straining against the sucking vacuum. He lurched forward, trying to grab Saída's foot, but the force of the vacuum was too great. He clawed at the floor, his gauntlets glowing brighter. Gideon let out a blood-curdling screech. He was sucked out by the void, crashing through the window.

And then he was gone.

Saída screamed as she held onto the cable. Every muscle in her arm burned, but she held on. The cable was coming loose. Electricity sparked in the wall. Saída looked out at the shattered window. The *Lancelot* was moving. No... the Needle was moving. The space station was tilting. The cable came loose and Saída felt the deadly pull of the vacuum. She fell towards the window. Then Tetrasteel shutters slid over the broken window just in time for Saída to slam into them.

Saída turned over and took a deep breath. The station slowly returned to its bright white colours as the emergency red seeped out.

It was getting hard to stay awake.

Saída gasped, "I win."

CHAPTER TWENTY-NINE

Sektor 47

"**B**eti, not so close to the fire," warned Uncle Abbas, as Saída took a seat next to Rodok.

She munched on a piece of bread as Rodok stoked the fire with a large stick. The three of them sat in the plot of the old burned house, around a bonfire that they had made. It was late at night, and there was no one in sight. They could relax and enjoy themselves. They had been doing this for a while now. Whenever Uncle Abbas would give her the signal that there would be no Redcloaks around that night, she would go and let Rodok know.

Then they would set up a bonfire and Uncle Abbas would bring food, and the three of them would sit and talk until dawn.

"I *too* feel *hungry*," said Rodok, setting aside the stick. His eyes whizzed around his head, looking at Saída and Uncle Abbas with each.

"Rodok, shut up," said Saída, rolling her eye. She took another bite of her bread.

"*Uncle*, please *give* me *a* piece *of* that," buzzed Rodok, holding his mechanical hand out. Uncle Abbas tore off a piece of his roti and handed it to Rodok, who promptly tossed it into the fire. "*That* was *delicious*. May *I* have *another*?"

Saída guffawed, mid-chew, and Uncle Abbas just shook his head at Rodok.

"No. No you may not."

Uncle Abbas picked up a small tin container and handed it to Saída. There were pieces of dried fruit in them. Saída munched on them and looked at the fire. The flames crackled and danced around, flaring up when the wind increased in intensity.

"Uncle, what is the spaceport job like?" asked Saída.

Uncle Abbas took another bite of his roti. "You don't need to worry about that, beti. It's only for teenagers."

"But Uncle, I am a teenager now," Saída muttered.

"*Not* for *another* few *months* you *are* not," chimed in Rodok.

Saída groaned.

"Why the sudden interest, beti?" asked Uncle Abbas. He opened his own tin container and began to snack on some dried fruit.

"Well, I was wondering if I could earn a few extra coins for you, Uncle. So that you could get more stuff for yourself. Maybe then you could take a day off?"

"Beti," began Uncle Abbas, "we are doing fine. You don't need to do that. Least of all not near the spaceport. Too many of those brutes around there anyway."

"*Besides*, as *you* have *said* before, *wandering* too *close* to *the* inner *city* past *curfew* can *result* in *a* fine *or* imprisonment," said Rodok.

"I guess," muttered Saída, hugging her knees.

"Thank you though, beti. I appreciate that you were thinking of me," Uncle Abbas said with a twitch of his moustache and a twinkle in his brown eyes. Saída beamed.

Rodok picked up the stick and began stoking the flames again.

Uncle Abbas eyed him, and he twirled his moustache. "Rodok."

"*Yes*, Uncle?"

"Who was your manufacturer?"

Saída suppressed a giggle. Uncle Abbas didn't know when to give up.

Rodok sighed, a miniscule puff of steam exuded from his chest.

"*Redacted*," buzzed Rodok.

Uncle Abbas scratched his chin. "Do you yourself know the answers to all of that, Rodok?"

Rodok paused. "I *cannot* say."

"For what purpose were you mining the Roshun?"

"I *cannot* say."

"What is Advanced Intelligence?"

"*Redacted.*"

Uncle Abbas sighed.

"*I* am *sorry*," muttered Rodok. Saída patted him on the back.

Uncle Abbas offered Rodok a sympathetic smile.

"It's quite alright, Rodok. I know you would tell us if you could. I am just wondering how we might get answers without you breaking protocol."

Saída idly munched on her dried fruit. It was a dull green. Shrivelled and small. She imagined trees were the same, just a lot bigger. She wished she could see one. A real one. Not like the small ones near the inner city.

"Have you ever seen trees, Rodok?"

"*What*?" Rodok asked.

"Trees, stupid Rodok. Have you ever seen one?"

"I… *yes*. I *have*."

Uncle Abbas raised his eyebrows. "Can you describe them?"

Rodok stopped stoking the fire. "*They* are *not* like *the* little *ones* you *have* here. *They* are *massive*, the *wood* is *red* and *brown*. The *leaves* are *a* bright *green*. Sometimes *golden*. Sometimes *red*."

"The trees we have here are closer to the inner city," said Saída, taking another bite of her snack. "Near where all the Redcloaks live."

"Yes, Saída, but those are still quite small and weak. May as well be synthetic. The ones Rodok speaks of… I don't think we have ever had them in this hemisphere," Uncle Abbas mused.

"The *trees* here *were* few, *but* their *leaves* were *a* bright *green*. Thin, *tall* trees. *Too* few *remain*," said Rodok.

Uncle Abbas nodded. "Most were cut down around the time my grandfather was a young man."

"That means you've been here a really long time, Rodok," Saída gasped.

"I *do* not *know*."

"Have you ever been to the eastern hemisphere of Sektor 47?" asked Uncle Abbas. The flames reflected in his brown eyes gave off a magnificent glow.

Saída inched closer to Rodok, looking up at him. Waiting with bated breath.

235

"*I* have *not,*" he said.

Saída clicked her tongue.

"Still, I am a little surprised. The trees you described. I don't think their kind grew on this side of Sektor 47. And if you've never been to the eastern side..." said Uncle Abbas.

Saída's eyes widened.

"Rodok, which Sektor are you from?" she yelled excitedly.

"Saída, beti! Not so loud," hushed Uncle Abbas.

Saída murmured an apology.

"Rodok, can you describe what you remember near the trees? The ones that you described?" asked Uncle Abbas. His eyes were fixed on Rodok's red eyeballs which flitted around his head.

Rodok paused, contemplating. Maybe he was checking to see if he was even allowed to speak further. Saída hoped he could. She was so intrigued.

"*I remember...* golden... *shimmering* flowers. *Near* a *forest* of *trees.* Large *trees.* Red. *Gold.* Green *leaves.* The *flowers* were... *Redacted.* A *lake.* Across *the* Glass *City...* Redacted. *Redacted.* Redacted." Rodok's head began twisting left and right, going one-eighty, then three-sixty degrees, alternating in half and full rotations. His voice buzzed louder. His eyes darted around his face in a wild panic. "*Redacted.* Redacted. *Redacted.* Redacted. *Redacted,*" he whirred.

"Uncle, what's wrong with him?" cried Saída, grabbing onto Rodok's arm and pulling. "Rodok, wake up, please," she wailed.

A sharp whistle cut through the cold night air. The sound of approaching footsteps.

Saída and Uncle Abbas turned to see a group of Redcloaks brandishing batons, circling their little camp in the old plot.

"Well, well, well. What do we have here?" jeered one of them, eyeing Saída.

Another Redcloak spoke. "A group of nasty sandskins breaking curfew."

The third Redcloak grinned, smacking the baton against the palm of his hand. "Methinks we should teach them what happens when you break the Viceroy's laws."

"We were just leaving, there is no need for this," said Uncle Abbas. He tried getting up but one of the Redcloaks forced him back onto his knees. "I'll give you free drinks tomorrow," yelled Uncle Abbas.

"We don't need shit from you, Abbas," said the ringleader. "Boys," he ordered.

One of the Redcloaks walked behind Saída, ready to hit her with the baton, but stopped at the sight of Rodok. "What the hell...?"

The other Redcloaks moved closer to get a better look at him.

"What the hell is this thing?"

"It looks like a person," said the second Redcloak.

"It's clearly mechanical. Some kind of drone? Is it one of ours?" asked the third.

"Leave us alone," muttered Saída, inching around the bonfire, closer to Uncle Abbas.

The ringleader turned, his eyes fixed on Saída's eye patch. "I think I heard about a one-eyed freak living around these parts," he sneered.

"Let her go," said Uncle Abbas, still trying to reason

with them. "I'll give you whatever you want. Just let the child go."

The Redcloaks all turned their attention back to Uncle Abbas, leaving Rodok, who sat in silence, as if he were deactivated.

"I don't think so, sandskin," said the ringleader, smacking Uncle Abbas across the face with his baton.

Blood spilled from Uncle Abbas's bottom lip, but he jumped over Saída, shielding her from an attack.

The Redcloak kicked Uncle Abbas and yelled, "You think you can just ignore the Viceroy's laws and do whatever the hell you want, sandskin? There's a curfew for a reason."

He smacked Uncle Abbas again. Saída started crying. "Stop it," she yelled. She picked up a rock and flung it at one of the Redcloaks who sidestepped it with ease. He laughed.

"Stupid leech," he smirked, readying his baton for a strike.

A mechanical black hand wrapped around his head from behind, and twisted it, snapping the Redcloak's neck. He crumpled to the ground.

The other Redcloaks turned to face Rodok, who towered over them. His crimson eyes locked onto theirs.

Before anyone had the chance to speak, Rodok slammed his metal fist into the throat of the ringleader, whose eyes went blank at the moment of contact. Another corpse for the pile.

"Wait, please," cried the final Redcloak, but Rodok grabbed his throat and squeezed, mechanical fingers pressing against the soft flesh of the man's neck.

Saída and Uncle Abbas watched in horror as Rodok squeezed the life out of the Redcloak.

Rodok tossed him to the side like a rag doll. His eyes zeroed in on Uncle Abbas and Saída. He crouched, getting closer to them.

Saída hid behind Uncle Abbas, whimpering.

"*Saída.* You *do* not *need* to *be* afraid. *I* would *never* hurt *you,*" Rodok said softly.

Uncle Abbas placed his hands on Saída's shoulders. "He's right, beti. He saved us."

"I *am* sorry *you* had *to* see *that,*" said Rodok.

Saída shook her head. "No, it's... it's fine." Her tiny heart thumped with such intensity, Saída felt it would burst out of her chest. "I was just... I didn't think you could do all that."

Saída looked into Rodok's expressionless eyes. Bright-red orbs with no irises. Tiny gears moved within an ocean of red. Rodok had saved them. He was her dost. Saída threw her arms around Rodok and hugged him. "Thank you, Rodok."

Rodok gently placed a hand on Saída's head, patting it.

A cry rang out in the air and Uncle Abbas rose to his feet. Saída and Rodok turned their attention beyond the stone walls of the ruined manor. A Redcloak had spotted them. Before they could react, the man took off running.

He was too far away. Rodok moved to intercept him.

"Leave it, Rodok," said Uncle Abbas. His voice was low. He was afraid. "It's too late. He will get to the barracks before you can stop him."

Saída looked at Uncle Abbas.

"Uncle, what do we do? He's seen us near dead Redcloaks."

Uncle Abbas stood there a moment, as if turned to stone. Then he spoke in a strange, calm voice. A voice she had never heard.

"We have to get to the bar. Quickly. Now. Rodok, you as well."

Rodok lifted Saída off the ground and followed Uncle Abbas, leaving the corpses and the bonfire behind.

CHAPTER THIRTY

The Needle

A voice buzzed in Saída's ear.

"*Saída?*"

Saída had been staring at the ceiling for what seemed like hours, barely moving. She was half lying on the Tetrasteel shutter that now covered the shattered window, half on the floor. She scanned her surroundings with her prosthetic eye, noticing the slanted office around her. The Needle had tilted over at an odd angle.

"*Saída, can you hear me? This is Rodok. Please tell me that you are alright.*"

Rodok. He was okay.

It hurt to speak. She gritted her teeth. Her throat was too dry. She swallowed.

"Would you miss me if I wasn't?" she croaked.

"*Just a little,*" replied Rodok. "*Saída, I have Mac. He is subdued. There was some trouble, but I was able to get him out. We are close to the hangar. The Redcloaks are still fighting the prisoners in the lower levels.*"

Saída exhaled through her teeth and sat up. Her arm was a broken, bloody mess.

"Are you outside the main lobby?"

"*No. We are inside. But well hidden. There are not too many Redcloaks in here. Most of the fighting is taking place in the lower levels. You need to get down here now.*"

"Why don't you take them out? Get to the *Lancer*?" asked Saída, getting to her feet. She made sure the Scimitar was safely holstered. Just three shells left.

"*I cannot risk Mac being shot. There is an elite here.*"

"I've got a bit of a problem, Rodok. I have a broken arm. It hurts like a bitch. And I shot out the window of the Needle. It got tilted."

"*The Needle seems mostly fine down here. The Ring did go wild for a moment, but things seem to be back to normal regarding the station's functions. Can you get to the elevators?*"

Saída looked down the hall. It was an upward slope now. It would be hard to climb up with a broken arm.

"I can try," said Saída.

Her right arm dangling uselessly, Saída activated the magfield on her boots and began climbing up the slope, sliding her feet upwards, as the magfield locked onto the metallic floors of the slanted office. She used her good arm to keep herself steady, leaning against the hallway window. On either side of her, the hallway windows showed her the vastness of space. Saída could still see the *Lancelot* floating in space. Even with Gideon dead, the ominous stare of his ship caused a chill down her spine.

At the top of the hallway, it split into two paths. Both led to elevators that would take her down. Saída deactivated her magnet boots and prayed for safety. She slid down towards the elevator on the right.

Her feet hit the metal doors and she pressed the sole of her boot against the elevator button. With a ding the doors opened. She noticed scorch marks at her feet, where the Redcloaks had fired earlier. Near her feet lay the wall panel she had cut open during the blackout.

Saída's head spun trying to make sense of the changed layout of the Needle. She found the control panel above her and pushed the button to take her to the lobby.

The elevator descended to the lower floors of the Needle. Saída took a moment to breathe. She had survived. Against all odds, she had made it. She *was* going to save Uncle Abbas too. Nothing would stop her now.

The elevator reached the lobby and Saída readied the Scimitar.

The elevator door slid open and Saída peered out. A shell scorched the elevator doors and Saída took cover.

"Rodok, I made it, but I'm down to three shells," whispered Saída into her earring.

"*Understood. See if you can draw their fire, long enough for me to get Mac into a more secure position.*"

She felt pain in every muscle. "Alright, Rodok," she grunted.

Saída fired blindly into the lobby. A few shots were returned. Saída waited, then fired again. The shots came back quicker this time. They were closing in on her. The bruises on her face were swollen. They felt heavy.

Saída got ready to fire again, but a Redcloak dashed into the elevator, pushing past her. It was the bald Redcloak from earlier. He hesitated for a moment, a stunned

243

expression on his face. Saída didn't take the chance. A shot to the chest took him out and he slumped against the now bloody elevator wall.

"Rodok," yelled Saída through gritted teeth. She was beginning to lose feeling in her legs. "*Come on.*"

Saída was out of shells.

She spied the gun dropped by the Redcloak. She reached for it, but a silver boot stepped on her hand as her fingers touched the weapon. Saída grunted in pain and looked up into the barrel of the elite Redcloak's rifle.

She couldn't see his eyes through his black visor, but she could hear the satisfaction in the elite's voice.

"Mongrel," breathed the elite. Saída refused to close her eyes. She gritted her teeth and braced for the end.

Rodok's arm came into view. He smashed the elite's head against the wall. Rodok stepped into the elevator, holding the elite in place. The blow disoriented the elite, who loosened his grip on the rifle. Then Rodok pulled the elite's head back and smashed it again. And again. And again. The clash of illuminite on metal echoed inside the elevator, as the helmet of the elite became brighter. From silver to a blinding white.

The elite screamed, "Stop! *Stop!*" but Rodok kept slamming. Saída was on the floor, barely conscious. She could barely make out the sound of muffled clanging. She felt the blood in her own ears. She looked up. The illuminite helmet was burning the elite alive.

When the elite's lifeless hands dropped the rifle, Rodok let him go. The elite's body fell onto the corpse of the bald Redcloak. Rodok peeled his mechanical hand off the elite's head and Saída noticed that he had left part of his fingers and palm grafted onto the still-glowing helmet.

"Rodok," wheezed Saída, looking at his hand. It no longer resembled a metallic human hand but looked like a skeletal claw.

"*Can* you *walk*?" asked Rodok, offering his uninjured hand.

Saída nodded and took it. Rodok helped her to her feet, and Saída holstered the Scimitar, making sure to grab the elite's rifle.

She leaned on Rodok as they walked through the lobby unopposed.

Saída saw corpses of bounty hunters and Redcloaks littered across the lobby.

"*When* the *lights* went *out*, the *elite* and *the* Redcloaks *fired* on *the* bounty *hunters. Some managed* to *escape* to *the* hangar. *I* am *unsure* of *their* fate."

Saída nodded.

The two of them made it to the end of the lobby, by the depressurisation chamber. Rodok let her go and Saída steadied herself against the wall. Rodok walked into a supply closet close by and opened it, pulling Mac out of the tiny space. Aside from a few scrapes and bruises, Mac seemed to be unharmed, just unconscious. He had been given an ugly yellow jumpsuit, same as all the prisoners of the Needle. His hair had been cut short and he had grown a bit of a beard since she had last seen him.

Saída walked into the depressurisation chamber, while Rodok carried Mac. They crossed into the hangar. They made their way back onto the *Lancer*. Saída noticed that half the ships were missing, but plenty had been left behind, their owners having perished on the Needle. Part of her wanted to stick around and salvage what they could, but she didn't want to risk staying on the Needle any longer.

Back on the *Lancer*, Rodok tossed Mac's unconscious body on a couch in the atrium, and returned to the cockpit, transferring his consciousness into the *Lancer*. Saída took her seat at the dashboard and strapped herself in.

The engines roared to life and the *Lancer* flew out of the Needle and towards freedom. Saída lay her head back on her seat and closed her eyes when a sharp collision with the hull of the *Lancer* caused it to go out of control. A maglock cannon shell barely missed the ship, nicking the hull. The *Lancer* spun wildly out of control.

Saída gripped her safety harness and checked the dashboard for a damage report.

"No. No, no, no," she gasped.

"It *is* the *Lancelot*," said Rodok. "The *ship* is *firing* at us."

Saída activated the radar, seeing the blips on the terminal representing the *Lancelot*. She could see how big the *Lancelot* was in comparison to the *Lancer*. Outside the window, the *Lancelot* readied its hull cannons for another shelling. Near the *Lancelot*, floating in space, were the remains of different ships, completely torn apart. The *Lancelot* must have been picking apart any who tried to escape.

"I *will* take *evasive* manoeuvres," said Rodok.

Another shot came at the *Lancer*, but Rodok was ready, manoeuvring into a barrel roll and expertly dodging the maglock shell.

The *Lancelot* readied another shot, this time closer from the bridge.

"Rodok, cut power to the guns and throw everything into the thrusters. We can't fight the *Lancelot* head on. We need to get the hell out of here."

"*Agreed*," buzzed Rodok. The interior lights of the *Lancer* flickered as Rodok diverted power around the ship's systems.

"Get ready to dodge, Rodok," said Saída, watching the *Lancelot's* bridge cannons charging another shot.

Then it fired. Saída expected another maglock, but instead the *Lancer* was hit with a pulse wave that shot out from the *Lancelot*, enclosing around everything in the vicinity like an invisible hand. The lights of the *Lancer* went dim, the systems began shutting down and Rodok grew silent. Saída felt them being pulled towards the *Lancelot*.

Saída tried hitting various buttons on the dashboard, but nothing worked.

"*Scav*," she growled, unstrapping her harness.

She limped through the atrium, towards the engine room. The door slid open, and Saída found the small room with the engine coolants. Glowing tanks full of water around the engine kept it cool, but they also generated electricity in case of emergency. Emergencies like now. Saída flipped open the panel and pulled the lever.

Electricity coursed through the tanks as the interior of the *Lancer* hummed back to life. The moment the ship was revived, Saída yelled out of the engine room, "Rodok, we're being pulled in. Hit the thrusters and show these assholes why we call it the *Lancer*."

The *Lancer* picked up speed. Saída struggled back to the cockpit and strapped herself in.

The *Lancer* used the pull of the *Lancelot* and the power of its own thrusters to propel itself forward with great velocity. The nose of the *Lancer* peeled open like a metallic flower and a powerful Tetrasteel battering ram emerged from it, the *Lancer's* secret weapon.

Saída braced for impact. The *Lancer* rammed into the hull of the *Lancelot*. The impact resulted in a shockwave blast that bored a massive dent into the *Lancelot*, pushing it backwards, and out of their way. Saída felt disoriented by the shockwave. The scene was a blur. The resulting force had completely shattered the *Lancer's* spear, leaving it embedded in the hull of the *Lancelot*.

"Rodok, go!" yelled Saída, and the *Lancer's* engines roared once more, it turned its angle and sped off, shooting into the nearby Ringway and far into the stars, leaving the *Lancelot* and the Needle far behind.

Saída fell back into her chair, grinning. She could barely hear what Rodok was saying anymore, but it didn't matter. Without its captain, and a severely damaged hull, the *Lancelot* wouldn't be going anywhere for a while. They had done it. Mac was free, Gideon was dead and soon they would have their lead on Belgrave.

CHAPTER THIRTY-ONE

Sektor 47

Uncle Abbas frantically grabbed clothes and shoved them into a small backpack, along with a tin of food and a flask of water. He scanned the back room for anything that he could add to it.

"Uncle, what are you doing?" asked Saída.

Uncle Abbas went back to the front of the bar and peered out of the window, then turned back to Saída and Rodok. He gave Rodok the backpack and knelt beside Saída. He gingerly held her hands and looked her in the eye.

"Beti…"

"No. Uncle. No," whimpered Saída, tears welling in her eyes.

Uncle Abbas put a hand on Saída's cheek and wiped away her tears.

"Beti, I know. I know what you are feeling. But there is no time for that now. You and Rodok must go."

"Why can't you come with us? You *have* to come with us, Uncle. We can live in the caves. We'll be hidden from all these Redcloaks," she protested. Her vision blurred with tears. The vague shape of Uncle Abbas's pocked brown skin, his bushy black moustache were burned into her mind. She couldn't just leave. She would not.

"Listen to me, beti. Listen," said Uncle Abbas. "You and Rodok must go down into the mining pit, find another way back up and around. Away from the bar."

Rodok slung the backpack on and crouched next to Uncle Abbas.

"*Are* you *sure* you *cannot* come *with* us?"

Uncle Abbas looked at Rodok, sadness and surprise mingled in his eyes.

"Rodok… you know that someone has to buy time."

"*Then* let *it* be *me*. You *and* Saída *hide*, I *will* kill *those* who *come* here. *Then* it *will* be *fine*," said Rodok.

Uncle Abbas put a hand on Rodok's face. "Listen to me. This is not like before, where they let us get away with what they consider insolence. There are dead Redcloaks on our hands now. They will not take that lying down. They will not stop. There is nowhere for us to go."

"Uncle, there has to be something we can do? Please?" Saída began. Then in Meraji, she said, "I will not go. I will *never* leave."

Uncle Abbas grabbed Saída in a bear hug, squeezing tightly. Tears streamed down his cheek, and he sniffed. "Yes you will. And that is final, beti. I love you so much. More than there are grains of sand in the deserts of Meraj. More than the flowers that once bloomed plentifully. I love you more than Meraj itself. And that is why you *will go*."

Saída shut her eye tight, swallowing the pain that built up in her throat, holding back the urge to scream in sorrow, in rage. At the unfairness of their existence.

Rodok placed a hand on Saída's shoulder.

"Rodok, you will take Saída to the spaceport in the outskirts of the city. You will find a ship, you will steal it and you two will escape," said Uncle Abbas, turning to Rodok.

He took a chit from his pocket and handed it to Rodok. "This is the rough layout of the spaceport. Find the Redcloak ships. You can fly them, yes?"

Rodok twisted his head, his version of a nod.

"Good. Then you need to go. Take Saída now. With any luck, the roof of the spaceport will still be open, and you will have no issues getting out."

Saída looked at Uncle Abbas. She said nothing. He smiled, but she didn't return it. She couldn't.

"Beti... we talked about this."

"Then promise me," said Saída. She looked him in the eyes.

"Promise you what, Saída?" asked Uncle Abbas.

"Promise... that you will be okay. I'll only go if you promise that you're going to be okay."

Uncle Abbas stole a glance at Rodok.

"I'll be okay, Saída," he said. He kissed her on the forehead, caressing her cheek. "Now you go. Find a place out there that is not as bad as here. Live your life. And be safe."

"You have to promise, Uncle. You have to," cried Saída.

"Beti... I *promise* that I will be okay. I would not lie to you."

Saída nodded, taking a deep breath.

"*Let* us *go*, Saída," said Rodok.

Uncle Abbas stood and looked at Rodok. "Take care of her, Rodok. No matter what, you take care of her and make sure she lives a good life."

Rodok stared at Uncle Abbas. "*Uncle. I promise* that *I* will *never* leave *her* side."

Then Uncle Abbas looked her in the eye. It seemed to Saída, like all fear, all panic had left his body. And that worried her even more.

The sounds of distant shouting caused Uncle Abbas to peer out of the window once more.

"Go now," he said. "I will deal with them."

"*Wear* this, *Saída*," said Rodok, handing her the backpack. "Then *climb* onto *me*."

Saída slung it over her shoulders and climbed onto Rodok who walked to the back room.

"I love you, Uncle," Saída called. Uncle Abbas was looking out the window. He turned and smiled at her.

"I love *you*, beti," he said, and then he was gone.

Rodok climbed out of the window in the back room, and slowly downwards into the mining pit below. Saída recoiled as she saw how far the drop was and shut her eye, clinging tightly to Rodok, as he made his way down the cliffside.

By the time they reached the bottom, dawn was fast approaching.

"*Stay* on *my* back, *Saída*. We *will* return *to* the *caverns*."

Saída nodded, her thoughts wandering to Uncle Abbas. He promised. So, she didn't have to worry. She choked back a sob. Her heart hurt. She felt like she was abandoning

Uncle. She felt like she was being abandoned. It wasn't fair to Uncle Abbas, but she couldn't help it. Tears fell from her eye, her throat burned, but Saída tried not to cry.

Rodok took a running start towards the old cave, where Saída had found him years ago. Where he had made an opening and thrown her out. The memory made her feel better, but it wasn't long before the dread returned. Rodok barrelled through the cave, running deeper into the caverns, until the paths became more slippery. He slowed down, the deeper in they got.

Saída spotted the twinkling lights of illuminite embedded all around the cave walls and ceiling. She recognised they were close to what used to be their old hideout. In front of the basement of the old manor.

Rodok knelt and Saída climbed off. All she could think about was Uncle Abbas. What was happening at the bar. What the Redcloaks would do. How Uncle would fight back. Whether he would be able to. Her face crinkled and she wailed. The sound of her cries echoed throughout the caverns. She ran. Back to the exit. Back to Uncle Abbas. She wasn't going to leave him. She was going to save him, and they would be safe and all live in the caves together. They would be safe from the Redcloaks.

"*Saída* wait!" Rodok called after her in a panic.

Saída couldn't see where she was going. It was dark now. She had passed the caverns that were full of light, deeper into the darkness. She tripped and fell. Her eye was useless in the dark. She felt her leg catch on something and she screamed.

"*Uncle!*" she wailed, her voice went raw. Her heart was ready to burst. She couldn't leave Uncle. She wouldn't. She got up and forced herself apart from the rocks, tearing away at part of her trouser legs. Saída felt her body tiring. The burst of energy she had had was fading, but still she ran. Deeper into the caverns, looking for the way out. So she could run back up the mountain, and find Uncle Abbas.

Saída looked around in a panic. She screamed for Uncle Abbas. She felt her way around the stony walls, finding that the passages were getting thinner, more claustrophobic. She was lost. In her desire to return to Uncle, she had been separated from Rodok as well. Now she was alone. Truly alone.

"Uncle!" she cried. She heard nothing but the shrill echo of her weary voice return.

"Rodok," she called. Nothing but the echo.

Saída curled up in a ball and closed her eye. She felt her tears stop flowing. She was afraid. She had been stupid. She should have listened to Uncle Abbas. She should have stayed with Rodok. But how long would that have lasted? How long would it be before Rodok would also go? Something would happen. And without them, she was alone. Saída was alone.

"Uncle... Rodok." Saída sniffled, cradling her head with her hands as she lay in darkness. "I'm sorry," she whispered. She was crying again. "I love you, Uncle. I'm sorry. I'm sorry."

Saída prayed. Prayed for safety like Uncle Abbas had taught her. She sobbed into the stony surface of the darkness, thinking she was alone.

She was alerted to the thudding sounds of metal feet. She looked up. Was it Rodok? She heard the metallic sound again. She called out. A trembling whisper. She swallowed and called out again.

"Rodok, is that you?"

And then there he was. She ran to him.

Mechanical arms wrapped around her in an embrace. It was Rodok. She turned and found herself staring into his crimson eyes. Through the tears and the screaming, she had not made out the sound of the android looking for her in the caverns. But he had found her.

Saída felt relief wash over her. She buried her face in Rodok's metal chest.

"I'm sorry, Rodok, I'm sorry. I wanted to find Uncle Abbas and then I got lost and I didn't… I didn't know… where," Saída wailed.

"I *know* Saída. *I* understand. *I* know *it* is *hard.*"

Saída sniffed. "I'm scared, Rodok."

"I *know.*" Rodok put a hand on her head, patting it softly.

Saída got closer. The next words were a whisper. She was afraid to even say the words.

"Rodok…" said Saída. "What if they kill Uncle Abbas?"

Saída felt her stomach drop.

"*Saída*, Uncle *Abbas* made *a* promise *to* you. *And* he *has* kept *it.*"

"What do you mean? How do you know?"

"I *have* seen *it.* He *has* been *arrested.* They *will* take *him* to *jail.* He *will* be *punished.* But *he* will *live.*"

"Then Rodok, we have to help him," Saída said, and already she felt her fear evaporating. This was normal for them. Uncle Abbas had been arrested before. He really would be okay.

255

"*Saída*, you *made* Uncle *Abbas* a *promise*. So *did* I. *We* must *honour* that."

"But Rodok—"

Rodok looked at her expectantly. Saída had expected him to interrupt.

"We have to save him, Rodok. If we don't then I'll…" Saída felt the urge to cry again.

"*You'll* what, *Saída*?"

"I'll be alone…"

"*What* about *me*?"

"What if you go too?" Saída said. Tears welling in her eye. "What if I have nobody?"

Rodok brought a finger to her cheek, wiping away her tears.

"*Saída*. I *am* not *going* anywhere."

Saída got up in a rush. "But that's what Uncle Abbas said as well. And now he's kidnapped. What if something happens to you? Or to me, and you can't find me? It's not fair, Rodok. None of this is fair!" Saída yelled.

Rodok crouched next to Saída and placed a hand on her little shoulder.

"*Uncle* Abbas *made* you *a* promise, *did* he *not*? Please *trust* him, *like* he *has* trusted *you*."

Saída looked away, but Rodok's crimson eyes were fixed on Saída.

"And *as* for *me*," began Rodok, "I *can* assure *you* that *we* will *never* be *separated*. Or *at* least, *I* can *make* it *so* that *we* never *are*."

"How?" Saída asked. "There's no way that you can know that, Rodok."

"*There* is *one* way, *Saída*. If *you* are *willing*."

Saída nodded slowly. Rodok let out a whiff of steam.

She watched Rodok dig his mechanical fingers into one of his eye sockets, grasping an eyeball and pulling firmly. It plopped out with a squelch, and golden fluid dripped from the eye, which surprised Saída. The empty eye socket in Rodok's head closed up and blended with the rest of his metallic face, like it had always been that way. Like he had always just had the one eye. Saída stared in awe. Rodok held the eyeball in his fingers, and then Saída noticed something. A wriggling, shimmering mass of tiny, almost invisible wires at the back of the eyeball. They moved like they were alive.

"What are you doing?" asked Saída, recoiling.

Rodok was silent. Saída got a better look at the crimson eye. The wriggling tentacle-like wires at the back of it, still moving, writhing.

"*Would* you *like* your *sight* back, *Saída*?"

"What are you talking about? How? With your eye? Will… will that even work?"

"It *will*."

"How do you know?" asked Saída.

Rodok's single crimson eye flitted and rotated in place, staring at her.

"*It* is *designed* to."

"And… and what does this even have to do with your promise?"

Rodok turned the eyeball in his fingers, giving Saída a better look at the wires that squirmed at the back of the eye. There were more than she could count. The wires she could see were made of even smaller ones. Like countless semi-translucent coils bundled together. The way they moved and shimmered under the light of the illuminite was the only way Saída could make them out. The illuminite that glittered in the cave helped reveal the secret behind Rodok's eye.

"*These* are *artificial* nerve-*endings*. They *will* reconnect *to* the *back* of *your* eye *socket*, your *optic* nerve, *and* restore *any* damaged *nerves*. You *will* be *able* to *see* again. *Better* than *before*."

Saída stared agape at Rodok. Her gaze shifted from the eye in his hand, to the one in his face.

"*With* this, *I* will *always* be *by* your *side*. Whether *I* am *physically* with *you* or *not*. And *you* will *have* access *to* sight *like* never *before*."

Saída gulped. "Will this actually work? You're a machine and I'm… I'm human. How?"

"I *said* it *once* before, *Saída*. You *could* not *dream* of *the* technology *that* created *me*."

Saída looked Rodok in the eye. Her brown eye staring into his red.

"What about you?"

"*What* about *me*, Saída?"

"Won't you miss your other eye?"

"*So* long *as* we *are* together, *I* do *not* think *so*, no."

She imagined Rodok was smiling. His voice sounded happy. For a moment, the horror of the day vanished.

Saída nodded. She took a deep breath. "Thank you, Rodok."

Rodok placed a gentle hand on her head. "*You* are *most* welcome, *Saída*."

Saída lay back down and removed her eye patch. She closed her eye as Rodok placed a mechanical hand on the side of her head, preparing for the procedure.

"Wait, don't you have to clean it first?" Saída asked, opening her eye.

"*It* is *self*-cleaning, *Saída*. Do *not* worry."

Saída shut her eye again.

"Will it hurt, Rodok?" she whispered.

"*I am* sorry, *Saída*. Yes. *It* will."

Saída felt something soft, yet metallic push through her eye socket. She felt a wet wriggling on the inside. It felt itchy. She wanted to scratch the inside of her eye socket. The wriggling grew more intense. Then pain. Dull at first. Slow. In the back of her head. Leading towards her eye socket. Like a trail of oil suddenly lit on fire. Her eye burned. Her head hurt. She screamed. Rodok held her down, as she thrashed around on the surface of the rock, screaming into the caverns. The pain grew. It felt like she had been punched in the eye again by the giant Redcloak. With his spiked gauntlet. Straight in the eye. Piercing through the socket. Saída imagined blood dripping out of her eye socket again, but she felt nothing but her own sweat dripping down her face as she screamed.

Once again, she was in the dirt, blood dripping from her eye socket as the two Redcloaks watched her. Within the pain, Saída felt rage boiling. She clutched her necklace, the scimitar drill that Rodok had given to her years ago and felt it pierce her skin. She felt the warmth of her own blood and let the fire in her eye engulf her.

CHAPTER THIRTY-TWO

The Java Blues

Saída took a seat opposite Mac, who was handcuffed to a chair in the atrium. Saída's broken arm was in a sling, and in the other, she held the Scimitar, aimed at Mac.

Mac's eyes were fixed on the Scimitar.

Rodok stood beside Saída, treating the wounds on her arm. Saída's face was lacerated and bruised. She had used medpatches to accelerate her recovery, but it would be a while before she was fully healed.

Rodok dabbed at a cut with antiseptic and Saída winced, gripping the Scimitar tighter. Her crimson eye made Mac look away.

"What the hell happened to you?" he asked.

"Had a bit of a scuffle with the Knight Benedictus, Mac. Thanks for asking," Saída said. Her right eye was shut, the wounds from her fight with Gideon made it hard for her to stay awake. All she wanted to do was sleep.

"You survived," Mac said incredulously.

"And he's dead," said Saída matter-of-factly.

Mac stared, wide-eyed and mouth agape.

"You *killed...*" he stammered.

"Here's what's going to happen, Mac," said Saída, settling into her chair. She shifted uncomfortably, making sure to let her broken arm rest easy. "I'm going to ask you a question. You don't answer. You lose your foot. You beat around the bush, I kneecap you. You waste my time... Get me?"

Mac nodded slowly.

"Good," said Saída. "Now, you remember our last conversation don't you? When you gave me the location for this?"

Saída set the Scimitar aside and pulled out Digby's medallion which she had retrieved on the gas-infested world of Sektor 23. She held it between her fingers, eyeing the etchings on the rim of the medallion as she showed it off to Mac.

"You found it?" Mac asked incredulously.

"Were you expecting the gas to get rid of us? Or that we'd give up once we noticed it? Yes, Mac. We found it."

Saída set the medallion down and picked up the Scimitar again.

"Digby has the other part of the medallion. The emblem that goes in the middle. Where is it? Where is he?"

Mac hesitated. "Look, I didn't know anything about an emblem or nothing. I already told you all I knew."

Saída managed a smile. It stung.

"Not everything, Mac. Tell me about Belgrave."

A look of desperation broke on his face. The creases

under his eyes wrinkled as he squinted. The name meant something to him.

"Who, or what, is Belgrave, Mac?"

Mac gulped.

Saída double-tapped the hammer of the Scimitar and the gun whirred.

"Wait, wait, wait," sputtered Mac in fear.

"Mac, you worked for Digby. He clearly valued you enough to give you the medallion to hide. So, tell me. Where would he be now? Is Belgrave a code for something? His hideout?"

Mac was sweating. He looked to his left. His right. To Rodok, to Saída, all around the atrium.

"There's no way out, Mac. We're alone in the void," said Saída.

"Listen, the situation is a little more complicated than you're making it out to be, alright? Digby is a strange guy, I don't really know where he coulda gone, we didn't really, uh," stammered Mac.

Saída pointed the Scimitar at Mac's knees.

Her finger was on the trigger when Mac squealed.

"Wait! Wait, please, I don't work for Digby alright! There. I said it. I don't work for the guy. Never really did."

Saída frowned and took her finger off the trigger. "Bullshit. Your profile said you were a Voidstrider."

Mac flinched. "I was, I joined a while back, a low-level grunt at best. Thought I'd rake in the shards but then shit started getting too hot, so I bailed. Honest."

Saída continued to pile on the pressure.

"We had good intel that you received a package with Digby's insignia on it, you pointed us to it and then we found the medallion. You wouldn't have something so valuable if you were just low-level. You're lying to me, Mac."

"I swear to you I'm not," cried Mac. "Yeah, I did have the package, but it weren't Digby who gave it to me, alright?"

Saída shoved the gun under Mac's chin, getting out of her chair.

"Then *who*?"

Her crimson glare pierced Mac, and he broke.

"Freddy Belgrave," whimpered Mac, shutting his eyes. "H-he's the one calling the shots. He and Digby were the founders of the Voidstriders. Freddy was second in command."

Saída settled back into her seat, Scimitar still aimed at Mac.

Mac refused to look at Saída, but continued his story. "They had a falling out of sorts. I don't know the details. Freddy launched a coup. Rounded up a bunch of men and attacked Digby."

Saída leaned forward. "Were you part of the attack?"

"Yeah. Digby was holding the package when we ambushed him. When the fighting began, all hell broke loose. I saw the package and my shot for some money and I took it."

"You took the box and ran?" Saída muttered. "Then what?"

"Well, I knew if Freddy survived he'd wanna find me. So I tried to lay low while I could find a buyer. I hid the medallion and tried to earn some quick cash and stay hidden. Until you found me," Mac added sourly.

Saída glared at Mac. "And this Belgrave? What's he like?"

Mac gulped. "He's dangerous. To be honest, he creeped me out more than Digby did."

"And you really don't have any idea where Digby could be?"

Mac shook his head.

Saída pointed the Scimitar at his knees again.

"B-but Belgrave might," he yelped. "He was close with Digby, before they fought. Real close."

Saída was out of options. Desperation was setting in.

"Where is he?"

"I can't really be sure, he's got a lotta haunts."

"Mac," warned Saída.

Mac looked at her and nodded. "My guess would be he's at the Java Blues. He likes that place a lot. But if he ain't there, then I don't know."

Saída exhaled. "Java Blues? That old satellite they turned into a club over in Samson Territory?"

"That's the one."

"Shit," Saída said.

"*Is* something *the* matter, *Saída*?" asked Rodok.

"Well, I'm not exactly at my best right now," she replied, gesturing to her broken arm. "Still. Can't say no to the only lead we've got."

"So, are we done here?" asked Mac. "If you could just drop me off on any of the Sektors on the way there, I'd appreciate it," he said.

Saída got up off her chair and looked down at Mac. "And have you miss out on your old pals giving you a big hug? No," and she walked off to the cockpit.

*

The Java Blues club orbited around Sektor 19, a luxury resort Sektor where most of the aristocracy and the nouveau riche from Sektor Prime and surrounding worlds often came to vacation. The Java Blues itself was a run-down old shell that floated above the golden-green atmosphere of Sektor 19. If it weren't for the brilliant neon signs affixed to the large satellite itself, it would have been easy to miss. Rodok brought the *Lancer* in close to the designated landing strip that jutted out of the base of the satellite.

The *Lancer* settled onto the strip and a rotating belt moved it inside the hangar of the neon club. Once inside, the opening to the strip outside was shut and oxygen filled the hangar. Saída, Rodok and Mac walked out of the *Lancer*, and into the hangar area, where they saw all manner of ships parked on the inside. Saída noticed that some of them were luxury models from the higher end manufacturers of Sektor Prime, all of which were subsidised, and owned in part, by the Grand Design. From the hangar, they walked into the main lobby of the club, where they were greeted by an employee.

"I'm sorry, ma'am, er... sirs." He looked at Rodok. "You'll have to leave any weapons on your ship. Club policy."

Saída wore an eye patch over her prosthetic eye and her coat draped over her shoulders. She looked the employee up and down, noting the overly neat red vested attire he wore. The complete opposite impression from the state of the satellite on the outside, no different from a floating pile of junk with neon plastered all over it.

"Already done," said Saída.

"I'm sorry, but the scan indicates you still have something on your person," said the employee, gesturing with a palm-sized scanner.

Saída pointed to her eye patch. "I have a false eye. That's probably what you're picking up. And this," she said, pointing to Rodok, "is my servant."

"A drone modelled to look like a person? I've never seen anything like it," said the employee.

"Yes, it's a new model. Not on the market yet," said Saída. "Anyway, if there are no more issues, we'd like to find our seats."

The expression of the employee changed to one of respect. He must have thought that Saída was extremely wealthy to afford something like Rodok. She suppressed a smirk.

"Is this your first time here, ma'am? I'm afraid that the third floor is off-limits except for members, so I'll have to ask you to remain on the first two."

"That's fine," said Saída. "We're just here to meet with a guy named Belgrave, he's a regular here."

The employee's face went pale. "And you're a, uh, friend of Mr Belgrave then?"

"Yeah, now tell us where he's seated. I've got a report for him," interjected Mac.

The employee gulped. "Second floor, please don't mention me to him."

"*Perhaps*, if *you* had *not* wasted *so* much *of* our *time*," threatened Rodok.

Saída and the others walked past the employee and made for the stairs to the second floor. They ignored a large man who stood in front of the stairs to the third floor, a bouncer for the members only section, and walked into the second-floor lounge.

In the lounge, melancholic tunes filled the air, the music played in a sombre rhythm. Red velvet adorned the walls, and the railing on the second floor was made of gold. Down on the first floor, a band played on stage. Various affluent patrons chatted and drank as they enjoyed the music. The song in particular pulled at the heart. The band sang about loneliness and despair in a home turned hostile. Something Saída understood too well. In the corner, at a table, a man in a white suit and a group of thugs drank together and whistled at the performance below.

"That's him," said Mac.

"Alright. Then introduce us," said Saída, giving Mac a push.

Saída and Rodok followed Mac up to the party. Mac sheepishly waved and butted into the merriment. The man in white, Freddy Belgrave, had a pencil-thin moustache and black back-swept hair. His eyes turned cold the moment he saw Mac and Saída behind him, but he offered them a warm smile.

He pointed at Mac, grinning. "This *guy*. We was lookin' for ya, Mac."

His retinue of thugs seemed to find humour in that, and Mac offered a nervous laugh.

"Yeah, boss. I'm glad to be back. I got, uh, held up."

"Woah, hey relax, pal." Belgrave grinned. "We all know why you ran. No shame."

"Sorry," whispered Mac, looking down. Saída pushed him aside.

"Let's drop the act, Belgrave. I've got the medallion. You've got information I want."

Belgrave's thugs didn't like that. One of them got up to intimidate Saída. She didn't acknowledge him.

Belgrave looked at Saída's broken arm and then her face, still covered in medpatches. He took a sip from his martini glass and set it down. A dark liquid, with a light-brown foam resting at the top of the glass, capped with three coffee beans. Saída had never seen a drink like that.

"Why should I listen to anything you've got to say?" said Belgrave. "Me and my boys were having a nice evening before some sandskin bounty hunter showed up to disturb us."

"Boss, it's about… I think you should hear her out," said Mac.

Belgrave looked to his men. "Boys, give us a moment would ya?"

His thugs murmured and shuffled off to another table nearby. Saída took a seat, while Mac and Rodok remained standing. Belgrave's eyes wandered to Rodok. He whistled.

"Tell you what. I'll give you whatever you want in exchange for that sweet drone of yours."

"Not for sale," Saída said.

"Shame. Then you'll have to prove you ain't wastin' my time."

A swanky guitar riff floated up to the second floor, drawing Belgrave's eyes to the performance below.

"You know Digby?"

Belgrave turned back to Saída. "That all you wanna know?"

"You know it's not, Belgrave."

"Please, call me Freddy, Ms…?"

"Abbas."

"Well, Ms Abbas, I think you already know that I'm a Voidstrider, so the connection's obvious.

Saída raised an eyebrow.

Belgrave pulled out a cigar, lit it and began smoking.

"Digby was, is, the boss. I'm his second. But you see, me and the boss were havin' a bit of a spat. You could say we had different ideas for where to take the Voidstriders. He was attractin' too much heat from all over, givin' us too much trouble. So, I tried to take control of the Voidstriders."

"And you failed."

"Half. Failed. Pretty sure I nailed the bastard in the shoulder, but he got away. Coward ran off. And then of course, your boy Mac here went and stole Digby's box."

Belgrave gave Mac a sideways grin as he addressed Saída.

"Sounds like you didn't have a whole lot of love for your boss," said Saída, eye fixed on Belgrave's hands. So long as both hands remained on the table, that meant he couldn't shoot her.

"Well see, he's weak. That's the difference between me and him. He grew up with a silver spoon in his mouth and got the boot from his dear dad. My family got dissolved when I was born. He's a coward, I ain't. I got vision, he don't. There's no question I'm the right choice to lead the Voidstriders. No one knows the pain these degenerates feel better than a degenerate like me."

"Do you know where Digby is now?" asked Saída.

Belgrave raised a hand as the performance below hit a crescendo. The singer's raspy voice sang of the lonely road away from home. A home he could never return to. Saída frowned. The song ended in uncertainty.

"The end is always my favourite part," said Belgrave, returning his attention to Saída. "The way it builds up and then just... nothing." He closed his eyes, as if to emphasise the last word. Saída wondered if a man like him could really understand.

"So, Digby?" asked Saída, returning to the point.

"Right, right. So, after the coup, I got to thinking about Digby and where he might've run off to. I had a tip-off that he was on Sektor 12 a few days ago, but I couldn't act on that without getting involved in the Daiyu-Takamura turf war."

"He was already long gone by the time I got there," said Saída.

Belgrave took a sip of his drink and nodded.

"Yeah, so I got to raidin' the rest of Digby's hideouts. You'd be surprised at the things he left behind in his haste to find a hole to crawl into. Drug recipes, trade routes, contact info for some *surprisingly* high-ranking officials in the Grand Design. And of course, I found a lot of plans he'd made. All paper. Untraceable."

"Get to the point," said Saída.

Belgrave took another sip of his dark martini. "Calm down, sweetheart. I'm gettin' there."

Excited whispers and murmurs coming from downstairs indicated to Saída that a new song was beginning. Belgrave looked at the stage expectantly.

"Each one of Digby's hideouts had somethin' new to show me. Sektor 9, Sektor 13, Sektor 60, Sektor 72. The rat had a buncha hidey-holes all over the galaxy. Well, we found 'em all."

Sektor 72. Saída remembered the harsh cold winds and the stony cliffs on the Ghost Moon where she and Gardener had parted ways.

"Digby's a coward and a piece of shit, but he's smart. Thing is…" He leaned in.

The singer's raspy voice filled the air once again.

"We didn't find him on any one of 'em," Belgrave said.

Saída couldn't help but raise an eyebrow.

"Interestin' right? It's like he disappeared off the edge of the galaxy."

Belgrave pulled out a tiny cartridge from inside his suit pocket, then said, "I wasn't able to get Digby. Wasn't able to get the medallion either. But I did get this. Digby dropped it while he ran."

The tempo of the music increased. The singer had started getting into the song. Pouring out his frustrations into the mic.

Belgrave continued. "Fit this baby into a SETRA and you'll find scans on scans of symbols and numbers. So many they'd make your eyes bleed. My guess? It's a cipher of some kind."

"Did you manage to solve it?" asked Saída.

Belgrave grinned and took another little sip of his drink. "Nope."

"Then it's worthless and you've wasted my time," she lied.

Belgrave wagged his finger at Saída. "Don't expect me to buy that shit. You're clearly just as desperate to get to Digby as I am. You wouldn't be here if you weren't. Think of solving the problem as its own little reward."

"Fine. Hand it over, Belgrave," said Saída.

271

"Not so fast, Ms Abbas. Now comes the discussion of my price, and what you're willing to pay for my cipher."

"Name your price then." Saída shook her head. "I'm telling you right now that I'm not a rich woman. And I sure as hell won't pay top shard for a half-assed cipher."

Belgrave looked towards the stage where the band played their blues. The singer sang his soul out about the cruelties he'd faced, ending the song on a sombre, melodic note. One last note of rebellion. The crowd clapped and whistled. They didn't realise he was singing about them. Belgrave sneered.

"You believe this shit?" he said, gesturing at the band. "We give 'em every possible opportunity and they still keep finding ways to complain."

"Name your price, Belgrave."

"*Damn* good music though. And I'll tell you when I'm good and ready, sandskin. Don't rush me."

Rodok stepped forward, but Saída raised her hand to stop him. Belgrave laughed.

"Here's my price, Abbas. I'll give you the cipher, you decode it and find Digby. He has something on him, an Icon. Bring that to me. Digby too. I want him alive. You do that, and we call it a done deal. A win-win."

"His Icon?"

"That's right. The mark of leadership for the Voidstriders. You bring me that and we're square. Just make sure you don't kill his coward ass."

"And how do you know I'll hold up my end? Good faith?" asked Saída with a smirk.

Belgrave chuckled. "Good faith. That's funny. Very cute…"

He slid the cipher over to Saída and she pocketed the little cartridge.

"You got a week. Bring me Digby and the Icon back by then. If you don't, I promise you, there is nowhere you'll be able to hide. Not Sektor Prime, not Sektor 12, not whatever shithole you crawled out of. Don't screw with the Voidstriders."

Saída got up. "Heard you loud and clear."

"That's what I like to hear. Boys," he ordered, summoning his thugs once more. "Escort the lady back to the hangar."

"We're fine without the entourage," said Saída, and walked away. Rodok and Mac followed. Belgrave's thugs trailed after them.

Saída could hear the band as she walked away. A new song was just starting up. The strumming of the instruments jammed and created the sound of a twang that lingered far too long. The song was ruined.

CHAPTER THIRTY-THREE

Sektor 47

Saída sat in darkness, panicking. She scrambled around to find the familiar softness of her bedroll, to hear the sound of Uncle Abbas's loud snores. There was nothing but the hard, cold surface of the cavern floor and total darkness. Saída grabbed at her face, feeling cloth wrapped around her eyes. She pulled it off and blinked, and immediately, the darkness was overtaken by light and the caverns in which she had gotten lost were illuminated as if by Roshun. The way out was near. But Rodok was gone. Her head, her eyes, hurt. A dull throbbing persisted, even after the procedure was over. Then Saída realised she could see. Truly see. It was strange. After so much time with just one eye, she had gotten accustomed to the constant clumsiness, to not being able to judge distance or keep track of movement properly. Now she could see. She could really *see*.

"*Saída*. You *are* awake," said Rodok. Saída turned to see Rodok shimmy out of a small opening within the cavern walls. He was carrying the backpack that Uncle Abbas had given them.

"I *hope* you *were* not *alarmed* when *you* did *not* see *me*. I *expected* you *would* still *be* asleep *for* a *while*," said Rodok, setting down the backpack and walking over to Saída.

"I did feel a little worried at first… but you said it already, Rodok. You said we'll be together so long as I have this." Saída pointed to her new mechanical eye. "Besides, I would have come looking for you anyway."

Rodok chortled, emitting a cold droning sound from his throat.

"*And* how *are* you *finding* your *new*-found *sight*?" asked Rodok. It was strange seeing Rodok with just one eye, but it danced around the contours of his sharp face all the same.

"Well… I thought I would see half of everything in red," admitted Saída.

"*Because* the *eye* is *red*?"

"It was a normal thing to think, alright?"

Rodok twisted his head in agreement.

"What were you doing? Where did you go?" Saída asked.

"*Do* you *remember* where *I* stashed *the* illuminite *I* used *to* drill? *I* went *back* there *and* grabbed *as* much *as* I *could* fit *in* the *pack*. It *will* be *useful* to *us*. We *can* sell *it*."

"I'm not sure how I feel about selling our Roshun, Rodok." Saída scowled. "Especially not to anyone who works for the Redcloaks."

"*Be* that *as* it *may*, Saída. *We* need *to* prioritise *your* survival *above* all *else*."

"Our."

Rodok twisted his head. "*What*?"

"Our survival," said Saída. "We stick together. And we do what we have to so that both of us can survive. Promise?"

"You *and* your *promises*, silly *Saída*..."

Saída crossed her arms. "Promise. You have to."

"I *promise*."

Saída nodded. "Good. Now. When do we go?"

Rodok pointed to his shoulder and Saída noticed the drone was missing.

"*See* for *yourself*, Saída."

"What do you mean? How?"

"My *drone*. It *is* out *there*, above *ground*. Scanning. *I* want *you* to *tap* into *it*."

Saída looked confused. "Uhm... I... don't know how to do that. Are you sure I even can?"

"It *will* be *challenging* at *first*. But *yes*, you *can*. Close *your* eyes, *focus* your *processors*."

"My what?"

"*Your* eyes *are* connected *to* your *brain*, Saída. *That* means *my* eye *is* connected *to* your *brain* as *well*. Use *it*."

Saída nodded and closed her eyes. She tried to focus on imagining the outside. The old plot. The mining pit. The bar. She felt a wave of pain in her prosthetic eye. She pressed her palm against it and gritted her teeth.

"*Try* again, *Saída*."

"I tried to imagine it, but I didn't see anything."

"I *do* not *know* what *imagination* is, *Saída*. Do *not* imagine. *See*. The *drone* is *out* there. *Connect* to *it* and *open* your *eyes*."

Saída sighed in frustration and tried again. She closed her eyes. Focused on the drone. Picturing the drone.

276

Imagining it. *No. Don't imagine. See.* She felt a sharp pain in her head. She felt the drone. She opened her eyes and for a split second, she saw the outside of the old plot, from a bird's eye view. Then the image was gone. Saída clutched her eye in pain.

"I saw it," gasped Saída. "Just for a moment…"

Rodok placed a hand on her shoulder. "*Good*, Saída. *Try* again *after* a *little* while."

Saída shook her head. "No. I almost had it."

"*Saída… do not* force *yourself.* Take *it* step *by* step."

Saída closed her eyes again. She searched for the same feeling, the same trigger that she felt earlier. Rodok's drone. Pain shot through her brain, to the back of her prosthetic eye. She opened it, but only it.

The scene was clear. Night had fallen. The bodies of the Redcloaks that Rodok had killed last night were covered in tarps. There was no one else around. Saída wanted to check the bar. The drone began to move. Then the pain in her eye became too great. Saída fell to her knees, tears fell from her organic eye. Behind her prosthetic eye she felt a scraping, sweltering sensation. Rodok knelt beside her and placed a hand on her back.

"*Saída*? What *happened*?"

"Rodok… I can see. I can do it… but it hurts."

"Your *brain* is *not* used *to* the *level* of *complicated* functions *your* prosthetic *can* accomplish. *Give* it *time*, Saída. *But* never *force* yourself *like* that *again*."

"But Rodok—"

Saída looked into Rodok's eye. He crouched so that they were face to face and gently put both hands on her shoulders.

"*Promise* me."

"I promise," said Saída.

"*Thank* you."

"What is this thing, Rodok?" Saída asked. The vision she had just seen didn't seem real.

"It *is* a *holofeed*, Saída. *It* will *allow* you *to* see *the* galaxy *as* I *do*. Now, *you* saw *it*, correct? *The* old *plot*?"

Saída nodded. "There don't seem to be any Redcloaks there. Is that where we're going to escape from?"

"*It* is. *We* waited *until* nightfall *so* that *there* would *be* less *Redcloaks*. From *the* old *manor*, we *will* make *our* way *to* the *inner* city *and* the *spaceport* at *the* edge. *There* will *be* patrols, *but* we *will* do *what* we *can* to *avoid* them."

Rodok gave Saída the backpack to wear. She clambered onto his shoulders and Rodok began to climb. The backpack was heavy with illuminite and the food and clothes that Uncle Abbas had packed for her. She missed him so much. She wanted to see him again. Saída shook those thoughts away. She clutched Rodok's thin, metallic neck tightly, watching as he climbed up the caves.

The rock gave way to his metal fingers with ease, and before long, they had made their way to the top. Rodok climbed into the basement of the manor and Saída looked at it with a mixture of anguish and nostalgia. How quickly things changed. Just a few days ago this place was a safe haven for her and Uncle Abbas and Rodok. And now...

"*We* will *keep* moving, *Saída*. Hold *tight*."

They walked out and Rodok lowered Saída off his back.

He pulled off the tarp from the corpses.

The dead Redcloaks had begun to bloat. Flies buzzed

around the corpses. Saída looked away. She felt sick. Rodok covered the body with the tarp again and turned to Saída. He was wearing the cloak of a dead Redcloak. It was dirt-ridden and smelled awful. Saída gagged.

"*Come* on, *Saída*. We *do* not *have* time *for* your *human* sickness."

Saída covered her nose and nodded.

Rodok pulled up the hood and Saída climbed back on. She took one last look at the old manor, then as Rodok sprinted towards the inner city, she looked towards the bar, far in the distance. It looked normal from what she could tell. She wished she could see inside it. See Uncle Abbas's smile one more time. Saída shut her eyes and remembered Uncle Abbas's promise. He would be okay. And some day, she would come back to find him.

*

The inner city was a bleak place. It was a slum. Little hovels, cramped homes made of brick and mortar, separated by narrow alleys that led out to the bigger streets and dirt roads, built on the foundations of the homes that once rested in the city. Homes built to last, to house generations of Meraji citizens, until the Redcloaks demolished them and replaced them with what Saída now saw before them. They were no longer homes, but the resthouses for the miners and the servants of the Redcloaks, lowly subjects of the Grand Design.

Rodok slipped into an alley between two dirt-red hovels, carefully sneaking across. His metallic foot splashed in a puddle. He stopped. Saída tapped into the drone, accessing a bird's eye view of their area. She clenched her teeth in pain.

"No Redcloaks," she whispered, and shut her eyes, letting the pain subside.

Rodok moved out of the alley, onto the dirt road.

Lamp-posts dotted the street. There were little resthouses all around. Saída noticed white lights emanating from the lamps, the wisps of heat that came out of them. The moths that lingered too close. Saída scanned both sides of the streets. Completely empty.

"Where are all the patrols, Rodok?"

"It *does* not *matter*," buzzed Rodok, shifting his head left and right. "We *have* a *chance*, and *we* will *take* it."

Saída frowned. It did matter. She thought about Uncle Abbas, a sinking feeling plagued the pit of her stomach. She missed him so much it felt like a punch in the gut every time she thought of him. And yet she could not stop. She would not.

Rodok moved along the right side of the street, passing the lamp-posts. Any Redcloaks who were around would spot them. Saída gripped Rodok tighter.

"We should get out of the light," she whispered.

Rodok buzzed in agreement.

He slipped into another alley, crossing over to the next street. More puddles. Rodok's feet splashed in them as they ran. Still no sign of any Redcloaks. Saída was worried. They were in the city section closest to Uncle's bar. Still a ways to go before the spaceport.

Rodok jumped and Saída grabbed onto his cloak, nearly falling off as Rodok climbed onto the side of one of the resthouses. On the roof, Saída took a moment to sit down and catch a breath. Rodok stood, the red cloak he'd stolen flapped in the wind. Saída shivered. The nights were getting colder.

The sound of snoring caught Saída off guard, and she yelped, turning to the centre of the roof to see an old man sleeping on a charpai. He was missing a leg and wore an aged brown kurta. Saída felt a pang of sadness as she watched the old man turn in his sleep.

"Do you think he's a miner?"

"I *doubt* he *could* mine *in* his *condition*."

Saída frowned. Rodok was right. The old man probably worked as a servant for the Redcloaks' families. Saída turned around and joined Rodok in looking out at the city ahead. The full moon was out today, and Saída couldn't help but feel an overbearing sense of pressure. The moon was huge, visible from anywhere in the city. The size of a small world in its own right. The moonlight was enough to guide anyone through the pitch-black nights of Sektor 47.

"Meraj *truly* does *have* a *beautiful* moon," said Rodok.

Saída nodded. "It does."

They sat a while longer. The old man remained asleep, peacefully, Saída hoped.

Rodok pointed towards a large building in the distance, at the edge of the city. Saída could see where the retractable silver dome of the spaceport rested at its edges. It was always left open, but Saída knew all it took was the push of a button and the dome would cover the entire spaceport, leaving no room for escape.

"That's the spaceport," said Saída. "I've only seen it once before. But I remember its silver dome."

Rodok unfurled the piece of paper that Uncle Abbas had given him and checked it.

"How will we get in?" asked Saída.

Rodok crumpled the piece of paper and hid it back inside a compartment in his body.

"*Quietly*, if *possible*. If *all* else *fails*, I *will* cut *open* one *of* the *walls*."

"You can do that?" Saída asked, incredulous. "Will your drill work on them?"

"*Provided* the *walls* are *not* made *of* pure *illuminite*, yes."

Saída got up and Rodok knelt, so she could climb onto his back again.

"We still have a ways to go before we reach the spaceport," Saída said.

"*Indeed*. I *have* directed *my* drone *to* keep *following* us *from* the *air*. Tap *into* it *only* when *necessary*. Conserve *your* energy."

The moon watched over them as they continued sneaking through alleys and side paths, avoiding the streets wherever possible. They were in the commercial district of the city now. Rows upon rows of resthouse-turned-stores littered the street. Shops selling cheap clothes, approved food rations and medical pharmacies.

Then she heard it. *Hmm-hmmm-hm. La-laa-la.*

Saída hid behind Rodok. *Watchers.*

Saída spotted two of the drones floating towards the far-right end of the street. Their distorted humming caused Saída to panic. Her breathing became ragged. Rodok put a hand on her shoulder. She remembered the stories. She knew the devastation they could cause. She imagined the entire city in flames as the multi-eyed mechanical abominations hummed their twisted lullaby in glee. She whimpered in fear. Then the drones rounded the end of the street and disappeared from sight.

"*They* are *gone*. I *will* protect *you*, Saída," said Rodok.

Saída nodded and hugged his shoulders.

Rodok continued onwards. Towards the spaceport. They crossed through another street, passing from an alley between two carpentry stores. They hid behind resthouses and old shops whenever a patrol passed by. The closer they got to the spaceport, the more Redcloaks seemed to be patrolling.

"We *will* have *to* be *more* careful *now*," said Rodok as they avoided a patrolling Redcloak. They ducked behind a garbage dump as they waited for the patrol to pass.

"There's still a lot less than I would have expected, Rodok. I'm worried about Uncle Abbas."

Rodok snuck a peek at the street. The coast was clear.

"*Saída*, he *can* handle *himself*. Have *faith*."

Saída shut her eyes. *Have faith.* Alright. She could do that. She would.

Rodok hopped over a grav-bike and made his way past a closed drugstore, heading into another back street sandwiched between a butcher shop and a café, both shut down.

Saída tapped into the drone again. She saw the city from above. The moon shone over the land brilliantly, over the dirt roads and the alleys and the streets, which all coalesced to form interconnected pathways that led into and out of the inner city. The spaceport was very close now. A few more streets and she and Rodok would be at the outer wall of the spaceport.

"Hey!" called a grouchy woman, her voice coarse, like sandpaper. Saída shut her eyes and regained her regular vision. She turned to see the Redcloak who had spotted them, standing next to the butcher shop. Rodok gently let Saída down. He remained facing away from the Redcloak.

The Redcloak's expression lightened. "Oh. Why aren't you on patrol, soldier?" she asked.

Saída heard the gears churning in Rodok's throat.

"I found this kid wandering out past curfew. I'm taking her to a holding cell."

Saída watched in stunned silence. Rodok had perfectly emulated the voice of one of the Redcloaks that he had killed last night. Saída looked to the Redcloak and back to Rodok.

The Redcloak raised her eyebrow. "At the spaceport?"

"Yeah. Found her wandering around here so I'm gonna drop her off at the closest place I know." Rodok continued to mimic the dead Redcloak.

"But isn't the closest... What's your ID, soldier?" she said, unholstering her gun and walking into the alley.

"7-2-2-1," said Rodok. He had seen the ID on the dead Redcloak.

Saída waited as the Redcloak checked the ID against her SETRA. Her eyes widened.

"That number's been out of commission since last night—" she began, trying to aim her pistol.

Saída clung to the wall, watching Rodok move as a blur, clasping his hand around the Redcloak's pistol. It crumpled like a piece of paper in his metallic hand. The Redcloak opened her mouth to call for help but Rodok grabbed it and slammed her face into the wall with extreme force. She dropped to the ground, bleeding from her head. She was dead.

Saída clutched her stomach and took a sharp breath. Rodok put a hand on her head and ushered for her to follow.

"Rodok," she whimpered.

"I *am* sorry *you* had *to* see *that*, but *there* was *no* choice. *It* had *to* be *done*."

Saída steeled herself. She nodded. "I… I know. I know."

*

The rest of the way was quiet. They crossed in and out of alleys onto streets, avoiding Redcloak patrols. The presence of the patrols was fluctuating. Saída tapped into the drone again. A patrol seemed to be nearing the alley where they had left the Redcloak's corpse behind, tucked out of sight. It would only be a matter of time before the body was discovered. Saída swallowed, trying to shake out the image of the bleeding Redcloak from her head.

"I didn't know you could do that," whispered Saída as they walked through the alley.

"*Do* what?"

"Copy voices."

"I *can* mimic *any* voice *I* hear," buzzed Rodok as he helped Saída climb over a fence which blocked their way.

"Can you mimic mine?" asked Saída. She climbed down from the chain fence on the other side. Rodok crouched low and in one fluid motion, jumped over the fence.

"I *can*. But *I* will *not*."

"Oh." Saída frowned, trying not to sound disappointed. Rodok offered Saída his hand and she took it.

"*Perhaps* when *we* are *safe*."

Saída looked up at him and grinned.

The next street over was clear. Saída spied that one of the lamp-posts was busted, but that didn't matter. The moonlight was enough. There were no Redcloaks nearby. Up ahead, through a narrow street, stood the great metal wall of the spaceport.

"We're here," Saída gasped.

"*Yes*. We *will* take *one* of *the* side *walls*. Going *through* the *gate* will *be* an *assured* way *to* get *caught*."

The sound of distant yelling alerted them. Saída looked at Rodok, fear in her eyes.

"*They* found *the* body. *We* need *to* hurry."

Saída nodded. She gawked at the spaceport wall, craning her neck to keep the top in sight. The walls of the spaceport must have been around fifteen metres tall. Rodok led her around the wall, somewhere more secluded, with fewer openings for them to be seen. They found a spot close to a thin passage which led out to the main street.

"Are we going to climb the wall?" asked Saída.

Rodok brushed his mechanical palm over the Tetrasteel wall.

"I *will* not *be* able *to* gain *enough* purchase *for* that. *The* wall *is* too *smooth*."

"Then maybe we can jump?" suggested Saída, occasionally looking back through the alley for any sign of patrols.

"*No*. The *wall* is *too* high. *We* will *stick* to *the* original *plan*. I *will* cut *an* opening *into* the *wall*."

Rodok gestured for Saída to take a step back and crouched. She did as she was told, while Rodok began tracing a rectangular outline at the wall.

Saída hesitated. "That will create a lot of noise, Rodok."

"*Yes*," said Rodok, readying his drill. "It *will*."

The screech of Tetrasteel being scraped and pierced echoed in the night. There was shouting in the distance. A patrol must have noticed the sound. The drill cut against the thick Tetrasteel wall, and Rodok was able to tear through.

Sparks flew as Rodok's drill cut into the Tetrasteel wall with ease.

The sound of the drill seemed to get louder. Saída could feel her heart beating out of her own chest.

One more vertical cut. It was enough. More cries from the streets. The Redcloaks were getting closer. Rodok slipped his fingers under the large tears the drill had made in the wall. He pulled it downwards, bending the steel enough to create an opening. The sound of footsteps was getting closer.

"*Saída*," buzzed Rodok as he peeled apart a portion of the Tetrasteel wall with both hands. "When *the* opening *is* big *enough*, crawl *through*."

Back on the streets outside, Saída heard orders being yelled out. Redcloaks were searching for them.

"Rodok, what about you?" Saída whispered, panic in her voice. "What about *you*?"

"I *will* find *you*," buzzed Rodok. Ripping open part of the wall, like a hole in a fence, he created an opening for Saída. "Go *now*. Find *Hangar* Three. *Go*."

Saída lay on her belly and crawled through the opening,

out the other end, inside the spaceport. Saída found herself behind a large building, a hangar. No Redcloaks in her immediate line of sight. She turned around just in time to see Rodok force the torn Tetrasteel back together like poor patchwork.

Saída heard the sound of Rodok's metal feet as he bounded off, fleeing the Redcloaks who had reached the wall. Saída could hear them on the other side. Yelling about someone in a red cloak fleeing towards the western wall. Saída got up, taking shaky breaths. Hangar Three. She looked at the large building. There were two others next to it. Along the sides of the walls, Saída noticed large cannons. The sound of approaching Redcloaks frightened her. She could hear them trying to pull at the torn steel, but it didn't budge. More orders being yelled. She took a step backwards, looking around in every direction. She had to go.

Saída ran towards the hangar ahead and away from the direction of the Redcloaks behind the wall. She ran towards what she hoped was Hangar Three.

Alone.

CHAPTER THIRTY-FOUR

The *Lancer*

Leaving the Java Blues a speck in the *Lancer's* rear-view cameras, they barrelled off into space. Rodok hummed the song they'd heard at the club, and Saída inserted the cartridge into her SETRA. The screen came to life with a blur of static and Saída studied the scans in the cipher. Digby's medallion sat beside her on a table in the atrium. She looked at the distinct etchings around the rim of the medallion, at the hollow opening in the centre, where the Hickston family emblem would go. Something Digby would no doubt have kept close.

Saída frowned as she studied a scan and spotted the exact same symbols as an earlier scan, now with different numbers. They made her head spin. Times like these she realised lacking a proper education was a huge downside.

"Did ya make any progress, sandskin?" asked Mac, placing a hand on Saída's chair.

She didn't take her eyes off the cipher.

"Mac, what the hell are you still doing on my ship?"

"Well, uh, if I stayed then Freddy would've probably definitely killed me."

"Mac, *I* could probably definitely kill you," snapped Saída, tapping onto another scan and comparing the etchings to the medallion.

Mac uttered a half-hearted laugh.

"Mac, have you ever seen a human being compressed into a recycler tube and fired off into space?"

Mac took his hand off the chair. "Er... no?"

"Sure? Rodok could show you. You'd be surprised. In fact, hold on. Rodok," she called.

"Now hold on, that's not really necessary—" Mac said, raising his arms.

"*What*?" buzzed Rodok's voice from the ship intercom. The brightness of the atrium lights suddenly spiked. Rodok didn't appreciate his song being interrupted.

"Show Mac the recycler tube trick, he's bothering me," said Saída.

"*I* am *busy*."

"Just suspend flight and do it."

"*No*."

Saída glowered, put her SETRA down and pulled out a pair of electrocuffs from her coat. She handed them to Mac.

"What do I do with—"

"Cuff yourself. Preferably somewhere far away from here," snapped Saída, turning back to the cipher.

Mac wordlessly took the cuffs and wandered off.

Saída checked another scan. Digby had made far too many symbols. The medallion only had six etchings on it. Six symbols. So that was six symbols that Saída had to decipher. Only problem was that in the cipher, much like Belgrave had told her, the numbers weren't consistent under the same symbols.

Saída threw her head back and groaned. Her arm was killing her. Her injuries were taking too long to heal, and this cipher was annoying as hell.

"*Have* you *made* any *progress* on *the* cipher?" Rodok asked through the ship.

Saída closed her eyes and inhaled. "Well. I've narrowed it down to the numbers which match the etchings on the medallion. But that was the easy part."

"I *see.* And *what* is *the* problem?"

"The problem, Rodok, is that I never went to school, so I have no idea if this is actually really difficult or if I'm just too dumb to decipher it."

"*Belgrave* assuredly *had* a *school,* and *he* could *not* decipher *it* either."

Saída frowned. "Belgrave didn't have the medallion."

"*Saída,* I *think* we *both* know *that* would *not* have *mattered.*"

"Where are we now, Rodok? Any patrols?" Saída asked. She didn't want to think about the cipher.

"No *patrols* so *far.* We *are* nearing *the* Central *Zone.*"

Saída nodded.

"*Do* you *require* assistance *now,* Saída? *Perhaps* I *can* take *a* look *at* the *cipher.*"

Saída nodded. "Yeah, I could use a break. Suspend the *Lancer* and come see."

The lights of the *Lancer* interiors reset to normal and the engine ground to a halt. Saída made a mental note to make repairs and refuel the engine when they got the chance next. The damage it sustained after their escape from the Needle still hadn't been taken care of.

The ship stopped moving, becoming locked to one point in space. Suspension was successful.

Rodok came into the atrium from the cockpit and patted Saída's shoulder. She handed him the cipher.

"All yours, stupid Rodok."

Rodok's eye followed her, darting around his head mischievously. "I *have* not *heard* that *in* a *long* time, *silly* Saída."

Saída rested her head against Rodok's body. He placed a hand on her head.

"We're closer now than we've ever been," whispered Saída. "Closer to home. To Uncle Abbas. I don't... I don't want to fail again, Rodok."

"*We* will *not* fail, *Saída*. We *will* find *Digby*, and *the* missing *emblem*."

Saída grinned. "Can you imagine what Uncle Abbas will have to say about all we've done?"

"I *cannot* imagine *he* will *be* too *pleased* at *our* choice *in* profession."

"Oh yeah," said Saída. "I didn't think about that. We shouldn't mention Silwanapur."

"*Agreed. The less* said *about* the *Black* Jade *Triad*, the *better.*"

Saída thought back to those dark days of her youth. Uncle Abbas would be so disappointed in her. The thought made her want to curl up and shut the galaxy away.

"*Saída*, hand *me* the *medallion.*"

Saída looked up. Rodok was tapping through the scans

in the cipher. She grabbed the medallion off the desk and put it into his mechanical palm. Rodok scanned it with his eye. A dark-red web emitted from the glow of Rodok's eye and he gazed over the symbols on the medallion. Then he handed it back to Saída. He turned his attention back to the cipher and kept reading.

"Find anything?" Saída asked, stowing the medallion.

"*Saída*, when *you* were *checking* through *these* numbers, *how* high *did* they *go*?"

Saída furrowed her brows. "No higher than triple digits. Most were just double digits though. Why?"

Rodok turned the cipher over to Saída. "*Hm*. It *does* not *matter*. Perhaps *you* are *thinking* of *this* in *the* wrong *way*?"

"Then what do you suggest, Rodok?"

"I *do* not *know*," admitted Rodok. "I *detected* no *signs* of *encodata* in *the* scans. *I* cannot *discern* the *pattern* without *more* information. *Perhaps* you *should* take *a* break. *Some* perspective *would* do *us* good."

Saída nodded, then she turned the medallion over in her hand. Some perspective. Her eyes lit up. She had an idea.

She reactivated her SETRA and pulled out its antenna. She switched over to the cipher and, using the antenna, projected the first scan onto the table and tethered it.

Rodok shifted in place. "*What* are *you* doing, *Saída*?" he asked, puzzled.

"Rodok, it's what you said. It gave me an idea. I think you were right when you said I've been looking at it the wrong way."

Saída switched over to the next scan, and projected it onto the table, over the previous trimensional projection.

She matched the symbols from the first scan, onto the second. Some didn't fit and were a strange visual jumble, but others fit snugly, and the image was becoming clearer.

"*Ah. I see it now*, Saída." Rodok twisted his head in glee.

Saída switched to the third scan and repeated the process, tethering its projection onto the table, in line with the others. The numbers were beginning to reveal themselves.

Rodok studied the table as Saída projected the final scan. Multiple tethers of the same trimensional view, layering the symbols on top of one another, all at different angles, finally revealed the truth.

Rodok held out the medallion and Saída let out a half-giggle. Her eye watered as a wave of elation washed over her. Uncle Abbas weighed heavy on her mind. They were so close now.

"*See*? If *Belgrave* were *smarter* than *you*, he *would* have *discovered* this *first.*"

"I seem to remember you weren't able to figure it out either, Rodok," said Saída.

"Well, *Saída*," said Rodok, putting a hand on her head. "I *am* not *as* smart *as* you."

Saída giggled, shaking off Rodok's heavy hand as the android buzzed happily.

"Come on, Rodok. Let's get to the nav terminal," said Saída. The medallion's secret was finally revealed.

Pocketing the medallion and her SETRA, she followed Rodok to the cockpit.

Rodok clicked on the dashboard and switched to the navigation terminal where a map of the known galaxy popped up. They were at the centre, between all Territories, the invisible Central Zone.

"*Will* you *do* the *honours*, Saída?" asked Rodok.

Saída held her breath as she entered the numbers, the coordinates, into the terminal.

The screen flickered as the numbers appeared.

"*Galactic* coordinates *set*," buzzed Rodok.

The nav terminal screen pulled out of the Central Zone and began moving outward, towards the far end of Samson Territory. All the way to the edge. Saída's face fell.

Rodok stared at the screen blankly. Saída placed her hands on the dash and shut her eyes.

"*Saída*, I *am* sorry. *It* seems *we* were *wrong…*"

Saída shook her head and looked at the nav terminal again. The coordinates pointed somewhere she thought impossible.

"No, Rodok," said Saída, staring at the destination prompt set by the coordinates. The very edge of the Deadzone. "I don't think we were."

CHAPTER THIRTY-FIVE

Sektor 47

Saída sneaked along the back of the large building. Hangar Three, Rodok had said. Saída just had to make her way there. Then everything would fall into place. She peeked out from behind the building, surveying the rest of the spaceport. It was a large fort-like outpost. A few Redcloak guards absentmindedly patrolled the spaceport. Saída noticed there was only one close to the building she was hiding behind, while another was closer to the cannons and the barracks, on the far side of the run-down spaceport.

Saída took a chance and tapped into Rodok's drone. It flew high above the inner city. Saída had a bird's eye view of the place. The wall where Rodok had drilled an opening had a few Redcloaks inspecting it from the outside. Saída watched as patrols out in the city had begun to frantically search for a murderer. They would no doubt make the link soon and bring the whole spaceport under lockdown. Saída and Rodok had to escape fast.

Her drone flew over the spaceport and Saída took note of the layout. It seemed that the Redcloaks weren't used to disturbances here, especially at night, so they were quite lax. After all, who would be foolish enough to try and escape? An attempt like that hadn't been made in a long time. The Redcloak near her building walked off towards the barracks. Saída spotted herself behind the building. Pain shot through her eye, and she ended the link with Rodok's drone.

She clutched her mechanical, crimson eye in pain. It was strange having seen herself like that. The realisation that she was watching herself like a bird, it made her lose concentration. Her eye burned. Saída whimpered. While her palm was pressed against her mechanical eye, Saída used her good eye to look around. She followed along the opposite end of the hangar towards another. A small gap between the two buildings made her wary. She had to be careful. Any disturbance would have the Redcloaks raise the alarm. Her mind wandered to the Redcloaks in the inner city. Assuming they weren't already on their way to lock down the entire spaceport.

Saída peered out from the alley. The Redcloak that had walked off earlier was smoking a cigarette there. Saída retreated behind the corner. She felt tears coming but shook them away.

"I have faith," she whispered to herself in Meraji.

She clutched her necklace, where she had tied her little scimitar to the drill that Rodok had given her. She ripped it off and held it in her hand like a little dagger.

She looked again. The Redcloak idly tossed his cigarette and put it out under his boot, and walked out of the alley. Saída moved out from behind the wall and darted across, taking cover behind the next hangar. She looked around. The coast was clear.

Again, Saída tapped into the drone. This time she would be more careful. The drone flew over the spaceport, spying the buildings below. The Redcloak had gone back to the first hangar, loitering in front of it. Between the second and third hangars, there was no Redcloak guard. It seemed that the only guard for the three buildings was the lone Redcloak. Saída remained linked to the drone. It floated downwards and across the open field. Away from her and towards the hangars closer to the barracks.

Saída was behind Hangar Five. The three buildings close to the barracks came into view and Saída felt her resolve crumbling.

Right next to the barracks. Hangar Three. Her destination. There was another Redcloak patrolling near Hangar Three. The pain was returning and Saída delinked from the drone, clutching her prosthetic eye. She slid to the ground. Without Rodok, this seemed impossible. She didn't know how to avoid being seen by the two Redcloaks patrolling the spaceport. Any kind of noise would attract the attention of the Redcloaks.

Saída thought back to when the Redcloak took a break to smoke. She got up and moved towards Hangar Six. The alley between was empty. No Redcloaks. She slipped in and made her way down, finding herself near the entrances of the two hangars. They were shut down. All the hangars were. Saída spotted the Redcloak leaning against the shutters of Hangar Four.

The moment she saw the Redcloak walk into the alley,

Saída ran. Saída closed the gap between hangars steadily, panting, trying not to make any noise. No sign of the other Redcloak. Saída felt her blood pumping. She noticed the lights in Hangar Three were on. She felt a rush of hope. *Rodok.*

She was only a few metres away now. She would hide and find a way inside. Then a searing pain hit her, spreading through her entire body. She dropped to the ground. She writhed in agony, screaming as the burning sensation of electricity trickled from her eyes to her toes.

The loitering Redcloak grinned. He holstered his pistol and crouched near Saída as she squirmed. The Redcloak had hit her with a non-lethal shell.

"And what have we got here? A little sandskin so far from home?" said the Redcloak.

Saída's body felt numb. The Redcloak mocked her as she cried in pain, mimicking her wails of agony.

"Imagine my surprise when I go take a smoke and I see you running off towards these hangars," he said. "And here I thought the graveyard shift would be boring like usual."

The Redcloak got up and gave Saída a swift kick in the belly. Saída coughed, reeling from the blow. She could feel herself beginning to pass out. Tears fell from her eye as the Redcloak prepared another strike. He was intending to take his time and torture Saída.

Then suddenly, relief filled her body as the electricity subsided. She was limp, but began to regain feeling in her arms, in her legs. She saw the Redcloak rip off her backpack and dump its contents onto the ground.

He stepped on the clothes that Uncle Abbas had packed for her. He sorted through the food that Uncle Abbas had packed in the tin container for her. The Redcloak took out a piece of roti and bit into it. Saída looked into his eyes, and he grinned at her, spitting the food out. Then he took another bite and spat it out again. He did the same thing again.

He picked up a chunk of illuminite that had fallen out of the backpack and jeered, "Oh hell, it's my lucky day isn't it?"

He pocketed the illuminite and took another bite of Saída's roti.

Saída's spare clothes lay in the dirt, under the feet of the Redcloak. The food Uncle Abbas had cooked with his own hands, the money he had tirelessly worked for, the food that had been packed with such hope and love for her, chewed and spat out, wasted. Saída burned with rage. Her body surged with adrenaline. She clutched the scimitar drill in her hand. The Redcloak jeered as Saída rolled over.

"No use trying to run now, sandskin." He spat out another piece of half-chewed roti.

Saída was shaking in pain, in fury as she clutched the scimitar drill, and she used all her willpower to plunge the makeshift dagger into the Redcloak's thigh. He yelped and staggered.

Saída felt the adrenaline leaving her body. The Redcloak yelled in rage and pulled out the scimitar drill, tossing it onto the ground. He kicked Saída in the face. She was disoriented, bleeding from her nose. She saw a pair of boots walking towards her. Next to the Redcloak who was kicking Saída.

The Redcloak yelled orders. Something about a sandskin. He called the other Redcloak a sandskin.

"What the hell do you think you're doing, sandskin b—" yelled the Redcloak.

Saída's eyes wandered up just as the second Redcloak plunged a dagger into the belly of the first. He sputtered and grabbed onto the woman's cloak, but she withdrew the dagger and stabbed him again. The Redcloak fell to the ground, coughing, bleeding out.

The woman turned, kneeling beside Saída.

"Hey, bachay. Look at me. Look at me," she said. Saída recognised her husky voice.

"A-Aqsa?" managed Saída.

She helped Saída up and began to collect her things, returning them to the backpack.

Saída was in a daze and brought her fingers to her nose. Not broken, but it hurt a lot and blood dripped out of it. Aqsa took a clean rag from her pocket and dabbed at Saída's nose with it.

"You can't seem to stay out of trouble, bachay," said Aqsa.

Saída wondered why Aqsa didn't pry further. Saída expected questions about why she left the bar. What she was doing all the way here. It didn't matter. None of that mattered now. Saída was safe. Assuming Aqsa wouldn't turn her in.

Aqsa paused and Saída looked into her brown eyes. The same sadness she had seen years ago. Aqsa was the same woman Saída had encountered outside Uncle's bar years ago. Though now she had a scar over her lip.

"I see you've got yourself a fancy new eye," said Aqsa, changing the subject. She finished cleaning the blood off Saída. "Really fancy."

"Saída. My name is Saída," she said, a little embarrassed.

Aqsa smirked. She pinched Saída's cheek lightly.

"Cute." She smirked.

Saída batted Aqsa's hand away and shot her a look of annoyance. She hated Aqsa's condescending tone.

"Are you leaving, Saída?" asked Aqsa, point-blank. She handed Saída her backpack.

"I am." Saída slung her backpack over her shoulders. Aqsa had put Saída's belongings back in. Except the illuminite. Saída rummaged around in the dead Redcloak's pockets until she found it and placed it back in her backpack. A little way off, she found her scimitar drill lying in the dirt. She wiped it off on the dead Redcloak's clothes and pocketed it.

"Alone?" Aqsa raised her eyebrows.

"No. Not alone. I have someone with me. He said to meet me in Hangar Three."

"Trustworthy?" Aqsa raised an eyebrow.

"More than you," Saída muttered.

Aqsa let out a raspy chuckle. She looked at Hangar Three, the lights were on inside.

"Is he inside?"

"I think so." Saída nodded. "Can you help me?"

The sound of yelling interrupted them. They looked in the direction of the spaceport gate. The row of cannons along the wall hid most of it from them, but they peered past the cannons and checked the gate in the distance. A Redcloak patrol was on its way in.

Saída's expression contorted in horror. It was too late. They were coming to lock down the spaceport. She looked at Aqsa.

Aqsa pulled out her handgun from her holster and cocked it. Saída took a step back.

"Are you going to arrest me?" Saída gulped.

"Stupid girl," sighed Aqsa. "Get inside and find your friend."

"But what about the dome?" asked Saída. "They'll raise it if they lock down the spaceport."

"I'll make sure that doesn't happen. Now go."

Saída felt bad.

"Wait, Aqsa, why don't you come with us?" Saída blurted.

Aqsa gave Saída a kind of half smile. The kind of condescending smile that made Saída feel stupid. She knew Aqsa couldn't leave. She had her reasons for staying.

"Goodbye, Saída."

Aqsa fired three shots in the air and ran off towards the Redcloaks at the gate. She yelled about intruders in Hangar Five. Saída took one last look at Aqsa as she joined the Redcloak patrol. Her ploy seemed to have worked. Now it was up to Saída. She had to find a way inside Hangar Three.

CHAPTER THIRTY-SIX

The Deadzone

The *Lancer* set course for the Deadzone. Saída's arm still hurt. Medical analysis said it would take another few weeks to heal completely. She rotated her seat in the cockpit as Rodok's lifeless body stood next to her. The *Lancer's* lights remained dim as Rodok transferred power from the artillery and broadside turrets to the engine and the propulsion systems. The *Lancer* was picking up speed, blazing through the galaxy through the milky whiteness of the lightspeed Ringways, towards the Deadzone.

Saída tapped the screen of the nav terminal, watching as a grid popped up. It showed her the distance between the *Lancer*, surrounding planets and the edge of the Deadzone, where Digby's hideout was. Saída muttered a quick prayer that they would actually find Digby there. Or else they'd risk being pulled into the Deadzone for nothing. Saída felt uneasy. A tightness in her chest. They were so close. One final step.

She got up off her seat and moved out to the atrium. Mac was sitting at the central table with a can of synthshake. Her synthshake. She couldn't help but notice he wasn't cuffed to anything.

"So, I'm guessing you figured out the cipher? Gotta say that's pretty impressive for a san— I mean for a person like you."

"Cuff yourself. Now."

Mac groaned and pulled out the electro-cuffs from his pocket. He placed one on his hand and the other to the table.

"It's not really necessary," he complained.

"Well, I don't like racists on my ship, so we can't all have what we want, Mac," said Saída and headed into the armoury.

"I'm not racist though," said Mac, puzzled.

Staring into the mirror, Saída peeled off the medpatches from her face. She tossed them into the recycler tube in the corner and opened one of the lockers. She fished out her damaged mask and put it under her arm. Then she grabbed a repair kit and walked back out.

She took a seat at the table near Mac and placed the mask and repair kit down, flicking it open and revealing an array of tools.

"I guess the broken arm makes it harder to carry everything, huh?"

Saída pulled out a recalibrator from the kit. "Shut up, Mac."

She set to work trying to fit the nozzle of the recalibrator into the damaged circuits of the mask.

"I'm just trying to make small talk," Mac muttered.

The nozzle scraped against the mask, pushing it away. Saída gritted her teeth and pulled the mask closer and tried again.

"So…" Mac was staring at her face. "Gideon really did a number on you, huh?"

The nozzle slipped again. Saída clenched her fist around the recalibrator.

"Shut the hell up, Mac," she muttered, and repeated the process, trying to set the nozzle into the circuits and repair them.

The nozzle slipped again, pushing the mask away. She couldn't do it with just one hand. She slammed the butt of the recalibrator onto the table in frustration.

Mac fell silent. Saída's fist shook as she gripped the recalibrator. She shut her eyes and resisted the urge to yell at the top of her lungs. The damn *Deadzone* of all places. She tried to steady her breathing. It was for Uncle Abbas. Everything was for Uncle Abbas. It didn't matter what she had to do, she was finding her way back to him.

Mac slid the mask over to her, keeping his hand on the end of it. Keeping it in place.

He looked away. Saída attempted to reinsert the nozzle of the recalibrator into the circuits. This time it worked. The nozzle locked in place and began rotating, following along the circuits, running diagnostics on the faceplate, and repairing the damage.

The nozzle returned to the recalibrator and Saída heard the click which indicated that it was safe to withdraw. She did so and returned the tool to the repair kit. Mac let go of the mask and went back to his drink.

Saída picked up the mask and inspected it thoroughly.

The circuits along its surface were old but repaired to a satisfactory degree. The crack on the eye slit that the mask had sustained during her time on the gas world, Sektor 23, had also been repaired. She activated the mask and a grey helmet formed around it, heavy and clunky in her hand. Saída stared into the glowing red bars of light where the eyes of the helmet were, and at the rebreather apparatus at the mouth. She smacked it against the table a few times. Sturdy and light, the way it was meant to be. Not like the gaudy helmets of the elite Redcloaks or Gideon himself.

The memory of the Knight made her shudder. Saída was glad he was dead.

Saída checked to see that she had enough oxygen tubes for the helmet. Once she was satisfied, she deactivated it, returning it to its simple mask form.

"*We* are *close*," boomed Rodok's voice from the intercoms.

Saída attached the mask to her belt and rushed to the cockpit, leaving Mac behind.

Outside the *Lancer's* window, Saída saw the Deadzone before them. They saw a vast field of asteroids floating aimlessly in the invisible vortex. Among the asteroids and the strange force, were shipwrecks that forever served as a reminder to the rest of the galaxy. Many were once some of the greatest Capital Ships created by the Grand Design for the express purpose of exploring and colonising the rest of the known galaxy. But that had ended in failure. Now the dreadnoughts of Redcloaks past mingled with the cruisers of mercenaries, vagabonds and those unlucky enough to have wandered in. The Deadzone was a graveyard dedicated to the fools who ventured too close and were pulled in by the invisible vortex. Even now, Saída felt the *Lancer* straining under the force that pulled on them from deep inside the Deadzone. It was hard not to shake off the image of an all-consuming maw that sucked in everything that drew too close. She winced at the thought of the *Lancer* being ripped apart, between the asteroids and the force of the vortex.

"*Saída*, do *you* see *it*?"

"Certain doom, yeah, Rodok, I see it."

"That *asteroid*."

Saída checked the nav terminal, hoping to spot it on the grid, but the screen shimmered with static. The terminal was getting interference. She gave it a smack, hoping to fix it but it was no good. The Deadzone was too close.

"*Saída*, that *asteroid*, it *is* just *outside* the *Deadzone*," Rodok buzzed.

Saída made an invisible trail between the biggest asteroids on the edge of the Deadzone and then she noticed the one Rodok was referring to. Massive, spinning slowly. There seemed to be a building on it. Some sort of outpost. The asteroid itself was also different. Saída zoomed in with the help of her prosthetic eye. The entire structure seemed to be man-made.

"It's like a mini space station…"

"*Made* to *look* like *an* asteroid, *yes*," finished Rodok.

Saída took a deep breath. She grinned. They'd found him. Digby. The search was over.

"Take us in, Rodok."

The lights in the cockpit grew brighter as Rodok took the *Lancer* closer towards the asteroid.

"I *will* redirect *propulsion* against *the* vortex. *I* hope *that* will *be* enough *to* keep *us* out *of* reach."

308

"Digby seems to be making it work for him. The asteroid is locked in place, just out of reach of the vortex."

"Most *likely* utilising *similar* technology *to* the *Needle*. Gear *up*, Saída."

Saída nodded and headed back to the armoury.

"Are we there? Did you find it?" asked Mac, still cuffed to the table.

Saída ignored him and headed into the armoury, shutting the door behind her. She reloaded her Scimitar and put on her spacesuit. She was careful with her broken arm, but the pain was unavoidable. Saída also grabbed the rifle that she had taken from the elite Redcloak on the Needle, swinging it around her shoulder.

The *Lancer* shuddered and Saída steadied herself as the floor shook under her. They were being pulled in. She headed towards the cockpit, ignoring Mac's pleas to tell him what was going on. They were getting dangerously close to one of the smaller asteroids that were floating outside the Deadzone.

She grabbed onto her seat and braced for impact as the *Lancer* hit the asteroid. The collision threw Saída to the floor, onto her broken arm and she yelled in pain. Rodok redirected thrusters against the asteroid and the *Lancer* bounced away from it, away from the Deadzone and closer towards Digby's hideout.

"I *cannot* hook *into* the *asteroid* fast *enough*. The *Deadzone's* force *is* too *strong*," buzzed Rodok.

Saída got back on her feet and checked the dashboard. The *Lancer's* hull received some damage from the collision with the asteroid but otherwise all systems were still functional.

"Rodok, the cables?" yelled Saída.

The lights in the cockpit flickered.

"*Tetrasteel* cables *are* still *functional*, but *we* are *out* of *range*. We *will* need *to* push *closer*."

Saída looked out the window as the *Lancer* headed closer to another asteroid.

"Rodok, redirect all power to the engine," said Saída. The asteroid was getting closer. Digby's hideout was close, but not enough. They were being pulled in too fast. "Have all thrusters aimed at the asteroid. Then boost."

"*Saída*, if *we* do *that* then *we* will *run* out *of* fuel. *The* Lancer *will* be *dead* in *the* void."

"Then we better hope Digby's got fuel. Now *do* it," commanded Saída.

The lights inside the *Lancer* fluctuated in a wild series of patterns. Then the lights in the cockpit went out. The nav terminal shut off. The thrusters moved around the grooves of the ship, being redirected towards the asteroid. Rodok's body came back to life, and he grabbed onto a lever on the dashboard. With a glance at Saída, he pulled the lever down.

There was a boom, and dazzling blue flames blasted the surface of the asteroid. The *Lancer* was off, leaving scorch marks. Rodok slammed a button on the dash and two Tetrasteel cables launched out of the underside of the *Lancer*. The cables pierced Digby's asteroid and dug into the rock. The *Lancer's* thrusters propelled the ship forward into the asteroid and Saída and Rodok strapped themselves into their seats, bracing for impact.

The *Lancer* landed on Digby's asteroid with a loud crash as the underside of the ship scraped against the rock.

Saída could tell the ship was now in dire need of repairs. The *Lancer* completely shut down and a dim red glow seeped out from the interiors. The emergency lights were on. Saída activated her helmet.

"Rodok," Saída croaked, the helmet distorting the sound of her voice. "You okay?"

Rodok swivelled his seat to face her.

"*Yes.*"

Saída unstrapped herself from the seat and motioned Rodok to follow her.

"We're going to be losing the oxygen in here soon," she said.

Mac groaned as he lay on the floor of the atrium, still cuffed to the table. Saída slipped off the electro-cuffs, releasing him.

"What the hell...?" Mac groaned again.

Rodok walked out of the armoury and handed Mac a spare mask and a spacesuit.

"*Put* these *on*, Mac," ordered Rodok. "*I* believe *this* should *be* sufficient," he said, handing Mac a single oxygen tube.

Saída activated her own spacesuit, and the baggy suit tightened around her body, sending waves of pain into her broken arm. She stifled a cry. Saída placed two oxygen tubes into the helmet rebreather. That would keep her sorted for the next few hours. Rodok helped her put her arm back in a sling.

"We have two goals," said Saída. "Number one, we capture Digby. Number two, we get fuel for the *Lancer*. We split up and signal once we see Digby or the fuel. Got it?"

Mac activated his helmet and spacesuit. "Yikes, that's

tight," he said, pulling on the back of his spacesuit. "Yeah, why do I have to go along with this exactly?"

"*Because* you *want* to *live* and *we* want *to* keep *an* eye *on* you," buzzed Rodok.

"Can I at least get a gun, then? Who knows how many people Digby's got here?"

"*Ha*. Ha. *Ha*," buzzed Rodok.

"Look at where we are. I doubt someone as paranoid as Digby has any lackeys with him," muttered Saída.

She walked into the depressurisation chamber and Rodok and Mac followed suit. The *Lancer's* ramp opened up and they walked outside. Immediately their bodies felt lighter as they stepped out onto the rocky surface of the asteroid. High above them, Saída saw countless asteroids and shipwrecks inside the Deadzone. It was all above them from her perspective. The gravity on the asteroid felt weird to Saída. Lighter. This was a special space station. Even walking on it felt different to spacewalks Saída had undertaken in the past.

"See that," she said, pointing to the chromatic, whitish outpost in the distance. "That's where he'll be."

"*Digby* may *have* other *supplies* as *well*. Food, *water*, spare parts," said Rodok as they walked towards the outpost.

"Then we'll take what we can carry," said Saída. As they walked, the asteroid spun slowly. A result of the artificial gravity that kept it locked in place. They watched the Deadzone above them disappear from view, then reappear shortly after. Saída focused on the ground in front of her. The rotation of the asteroid gave her serious vertigo.

"Come on, sand— uh... why don't you just gimme the rifle at least?" protested Mac.

Saída tightened her grip on the rifle strap. "Rodok, if the need arises, make sure you use Mac as a meat shield."

"Of *course*," buzzed Rodok.

"Fine," grumbled Mac, but slowed his pace so that he was behind Rodok.

A large outcropping of rock stood between them and the white building of Digby's outpost. Saída felt eyes on them. She activated her prosthetic eye and scanned the horizon. Cameras. Digby was onto them.

"Take cover!" she yelled through the distorted modulator on her helmet and bounded towards the outcropping. Mac and Rodok followed, but reduced gravity made them slower.

Machine guns slid out from the outpost building and opened fire on them. Rodok pushed Mac behind cover and took the brunt of a full clip on his chassis. He lifted his arm, blocking most of the shells like they were tiny pellets.

"What the hell are you made of?" grunted Mac.

"Rodok, if you can tank those bullets, see what you can do about disabling the guns closer to the outpost," ordered Saída.

"Wait *here*," buzzed Rodok.

Saída unholstered the Scimitar. "I'll draw their fire."

"And I'll just watch, I guess," yelled Mac under the hail of shellfire.

Rodok ran out from behind the outcropping and sprinted for the outpost, while Saída provided suppressing fire. A hail of bullets caused her to withdraw her arm and wait.

"Your drone's making quick work of those things," said Mac, peering from the corner of the outcropping. Saída snuck a look too.

Rodok ripped off two of the machine-gun turrets and used them in each hand, firing on the others. Rodok shredded the turrets to pieces under a hail of machine-gun shell-fire, leaving them crushed and broken beyond repair. Then he crushed and discarded the two guns he was holding, signalling for Saída and Mac to join him.

They ran into the outpost and met up with Rodok in front of the chromatic building. The building reflected the darkness of space. Saída wondered if that was an intentional part of the design, whether to keep people off Digby's trail or just an example of obscene expense.

"It's a shame we don't have your drone anymore. We could've scoped the whole place before setting one foot in," said Saída.

"*We* will *just* have *to* make *do*. Mac *and* I *will* take *the* western *entrance*. That *part* of *the* compound *is* larger. *Perhaps* we *will* find *the* supplies *there*, if *not* Digby *himself.*"

"Sounds good. I'll take the east entrance. Keep your comms up. Signal if there's any trouble."

"Sure you don't need me to come with you, instead of going with the drone?" Mac asked, gesturing to Saída's arm.

"Get real, Mac. I don't need help from a third-rate pirate."

Mac shrugged and followed Rodok towards the western side of the compound. Saída turned and headed for the east.

She blasted open the control panel at the eastern

entrance and the door slid open, leading into a depressurisation chamber.

The inside of the compound was full of bleached white walls, full of all sorts of paintings, sculptures, and calligraphy. This white reminded her of gaudy model homes in advertisements catering to the upper middle classes of Sektors in Augustine Territory. *Affordable* luxuries for those who weren't part of the aristocracy, but still very wealthy. Saída's eyes narrowed as she noticed a framed parchment with Meraji calligraphy beautifully painted on it.

The word *'Bahadur'* rang out like a gong in Saída's head. She clenched her fists and turned away. She moved further down the hallway, into a living room. Saída noticed the sound of opera singing coming off a phonograph.

In the living room, Saída spotted red and white furniture, couches, chairs, and a table. A fireplace in the wall. The phonograph lay on the table, the horn was playing an opera song that Saída recognised. A classic aria performed by some famous singer. Svetlana, or maybe it was Stanislava. Saída couldn't remember. At the base of the phonograph, a collection of cartridges were slotted in a row. The song ended and one cartridge was ejected at the back and a new one was slotted in from the front. A new song began.

The phonograph was set to auto-play. Had Digby been enjoying an evening of music, or was this a distraction? Saída held the Scimitar at the ready.

She walked out of the living room and continued down the hallway. Digby's bedroom was up ahead, but before that came another room. Its door was ajar. Saída double-tapped the hammer of the Scimitar and placed a hand on the door, gently, so as not to move it. She focused her breathing.

Saída slammed the door open and checked the corners. Nothing. The room was dark, lights turned off, but Saída could see clear as day thanks to her prosthetic. It was an office of some kind. Saída saw a terminal with multiple screens. Camera feeds from all over the compound. Including outside. She saw Rodok and Mac skulking through a large storage room. Mac seemed to be the lookout while Rodok searched through boxes and containers looking for fuel.

In the corner of the screens, Saída saw movement. Somebody just left the hallway. Digby must have slipped from out of his bedroom into another room. Saída clicked the Scimitar and turned to leave but noticed something peculiar. The camera feeds to the outside of the compound were disabled. She didn't remember Rodok destroying any cameras. She would have to ask him once it was safe.

Saída snuck back out to the hallway and continued onwards. Art of various landscapes from different Sektors adorned the hallway. Green fields, barren deserts, ice-covered valleys, urban metropolises under nightfall. Saída felt the medallion grow heavy under her spacesuit. She was so close.

The sound of a shuffle alerted Saída to an attack from behind. She dodged out of the way and turned. A frail-looking man with brown hair and a green jacket stared at her. His eyes were puffy and red. He waved around a golf club, trying to keep her away.

"Digby Hickston, I presume?" Saída asked.

"How did you find me? Father said no one would find me here. Old man's never right about a damn thing," Digby cried and took another swing. Saída dodged and backed up along the hallway. Digby's voice was nasally, like a petulant boy with the body of a man. Quite different from Gideon's. Yet it grated against her ears all the same.

"So, your father's the one who hid you? Guess Colton had the right idea. Your excommunication was just for show," said Saída. She eyed Digby's movements carefully. The man was erratic. Twitching. He was definitely high on something. Firedust, she guessed.

"Colton? Colton Haynes?" Digby yelled. "*Damn* that piece of... I knew I shouldn't have gone to the bastard."

"Why? You should be happy. He's the one that helped you escape."

Digby swung again, smashing into a canvas on the wall.

"He didn't do shite, he told me he wanted nothing to do with me. Even after I showed off..." Digby trailed off. He sniffed. His eyes were darting all over the place.

"Showed off what, Digby?"

He focused on her. "What's it to you, sandskin?"

"Everything."

Digby swung again but Saída anticipated it. She ducked and smacked the butt of the Scimitar against Digby's kneecap. There was a crack as the blow connected. Digby howled in pain. Saída followed with a kick that sent Digby barrelling backwards into the hallway. She kicked the golf club away, following Digby, who crawled backwards, yelling slurs at Saída.

She aimed the Scimitar at him.

317

"Give me the emblem for your medallion, Digby. Then give me the Icon of the Voidstriders. You don't have to die today."

They were near the living room now. The phonograph was still playing a beautiful song.

Digby stared at Saída, cradling his bloody mouth. He broke out into laughter.

"That's it? That's all you wanted? Of all the things that are worth millions of shards in here, you want a scavvin' hunk of metal?"

Saída glared at him. "Where are they?" She raised the Scimitar.

Digby showed off his bloody teeth. His puffy red eyes stared into Saída's. He reached into his jacket and produced a small half-sphere. Gold. The emblem on it belonged to the Hickston family.

"You came all the way to the edge of the Deadzone for this? Take it. I don't even want it. I'm done with your shite planet, done with Father, done with the damn Grand Design. Screw you all."

He tossed the emblem at Saída's feet. She kept her eyes on him.

"Where's the Icon, Hickston?"

"Don't call me that, sandskin," he snarled.

Saída shot his kneecap. Digby screamed. Blood pooled on the floor. Digby grabbed at his knee, trying to stop the bleeding. He screeched at her.

Saída was taken aback. It felt so natural. Just a simple pull of the trigger. So much pain. All she wanted was the Icon. Digby deserved it anyway. It was fine.

"The Icon, Hickston. Or I'll take the other one too."

"I already *gave* you the Icon, bitch," yelled Digby, tears dripping from his eyes as he yelled his throat hoarse.

"What? This?" asked Saída, sliding the emblem out of Digby's blood with her foot.

Digby wailed. She assumed he meant yes. Saída holstered the Scimitar and crouched, picking the emblem up between her gloved fingers. The emblem was stained with Digby's blood, but Saída could see through her prosthetic that there was circuitry inside it. It was legit. With this, the medallion was finally complete. She could get home safe. Find Uncle Abbas.

"Shit," muttered Saída. "This is the Icon too. Why? Why the hell would you do that, Digby?"

"Please," whimpered Digby. "In… In my office. Med supplies. Please."

The colour was draining from his face.

Saída pocketed the Icon and grabbed Digby's face.

"Hey. *Hey.* Look at me, Digby. Why turn the emblem into the Icon? What does that mean?"

Digby's eyes bugged out. Tears and sweat and blood mingled on his face.

"It… It was all I had. I used it as the backup."

"Back up for what, dammit?"

"Please… I'll die…"

Saída scowled. She got up and headed for the office to get meds for Digby when she heard footsteps. She slipped into the office and peered out. Three men in spacesuits. They came out of the depressurisation chamber at the far end of the hallway. Digby was slumped over the doorway of the living room. The phonograph still played. The singer wailed without end. One of the men stood over Digby.

"Digby, buddy. How you been?"

Freddy Belgrave. Saída made sure the emblem, the Icon, was secured safely. She held the Scimitar at the ready. The rifle was still slung over her shoulder. She had to be careful.

Digby looked up at Belgrave.

"F-Freddy? You found me?" he sputtered.

Belgrave smirked. "Well, I wasn't gonna take the credit, but yeah let's just say I'm the one who found ya."

Belgrave knelt beside Digby and patted him on the cheek. "The Icon, you leech. Where is it?"

Digby's eyes darted all over. He still clasped onto his knee. He was so pale now. The veins in his neck were visible. He shook his head. Slowly. One of Belgrave's grunts walked into the living room.

"Did you give it to the sandskin?" asked Belgrave.

Digby spat in his face. Belgrave almost scowled and wiped the bloody spittle off.

"Leech?" coughed Digby. "You're the leech. Riding on the coat-tails of your betters."

Belgrave sighed.

He gripped Digby's throat with one hand and squeezed. Saída held her breath. Belgrave nearly popped a vein, straining to squeeze the life out of Digby, who helplessly pawed at Belgrave's face. Belgrave didn't look away. He stared directly into Digby's eyes. He watched the light dim and expire as Digby took his last breath. The sound of a crash caused him to peer into the living room. The phonograph had fallen off the table. The song stalled, stuck on an agonising note.

"Hey," said Belgrave. "I was enjoying that."

"Sorry, boss," came a voice.

"Well, whatever," said Belgrave, wiping his hand off on Digby's shirt. "Bag the phonograph too."

He got up and pulled out a pistol. A solid gold pistol. Saída turned her nose in disgust.

He walked along the edge of the hallway, leaving bloody footprints as he did.

She'd left footprints too. *Scav.* He knew she was there. Saída backed away, deeper into the office. She gripped the Scimitar tighter, and closed her organic eye. She saw through the complete darkness, and she was ready to fire.

Nothing.

Saída peered over at the camera systems. The disabled cameras on the outside. Now some on the inside were disabled too. Of course. Belgrave must have put a tracker on the *Lancer.* He never intended to give her a week. Bastard was always going to swoop in for the kill.

The camera in the storage chamber, where Rodok and Mac were, had been disabled too. Saída took a chance. She brought her gauntlet close to her lips and whispered, "Rodok, status? Belgrave's here."

No response. She pursed her lips.

Then the door swung open, and a grunt ran in screaming, firing blindly into the darkness. Saída was already crouched low. One well-placed shot put him down. Then the other ran in. Saída panicked. She missed one shot, but the second found its mark in the man's chest. Then another in the head. Saída checked the Scimitar. Three shells left.

"Abbas," called out Belgrave. "I know you're in there.

Hand over the Icon and we all walk out alive. Well, aside from the guys you just killed." He chuckled to himself.

Saída checked the grunts for ammo. One bullet. She scowled. Where was Belgrave? Either behind the door, or at the end of the hallway with that tacky golden pistol.

Saída tried to contact Rodok again. No response. There were probably more pirates with Belgrave here. Probably keeping Rodok busy. Saída took another look at Digby's monitor. The door was shut, Belgrave wasn't going to attack her head-on. Saída wasn't going to get baited.

She combed through the security systems on Digby's monitor. All the cameras were disabled now. No way of resetting them. Thanks to Rodok, all the machine-gun turrets were out too. Saída spotted an option to cut the lights to the entire compound. A momentary distraction, to cause mass confusion. Saída held her breath and pushed the button.

She readied the Scimitar, then threw open the door and waited for Belgrave to fire. Three shots rang out from the left. Saída returned fire and Belgrave dived into the living room. That was her chance.

Saída took a right from the hallway and ran into a larger chamber at the end, Digby's bedroom. She noticed a bunch of Voidstriders in the darkness, trying to make sense of what was happening. She took out two of the closest pirates and ran for the door that led into the storage chamber. The remaining pirates jumped for cover, allowing Saída to get past them. She slammed the door behind her, wincing at the sound of shots being fired at the door after her.

The storage chamber was a massive room with hundreds of boxes, containers, and hygiene units. She tried to spot Rodok or even Mac, but all she could see were Belgrave's Voidstriders shambling about in the dark. The Voidstriders started activating their helmets. She had to escape, and the only way out was the same entrance that Rodok and Mac had taken, which was at the other end of the chamber.

Saída prayed that Rodok was okay.

"Over here," yelled a Voidstrider. She heard firing in the distance. She took cover behind a storage unit, listening. The sounds of screams, struggling. Bodies hitting the walls. A pirate walked up close to Saída. She took aim with the Scimitar at the ground near the pirate. She pulled the trigger. The pirate turned to look and Saída popped out of cover and capped him in the head. No ammo left. Saída holstered the Scimitar and ran towards the sound of fighting. She vaulted over another storage unit and drop-kicked an unsuspecting pirate in the way.

Rodok grabbed a pirate and tossed him into a metal shelf full of boxes, causing it to fall over. Saída ran towards him.

"*Saída*," buzzed Rodok. He ran at her, and she understood. Saída ducked and Rodok jumped in front of her, shielding her from a hail of bullets.

"Abbas!" yelled Belgrave from the other end of the chamber. "Give up the Icon."

Saída grabbed the rifle from her shoulder, held it by the stock and Rodok loaded the gun for her.

"Get down, Rodok," said Saída.

Rodok knelt and Saída placed the barrel of the rifle on his shoulder, steadying it, and squeezed the trigger. A rain of illuminite bolts burst out of the rifle, peppering the Voidstriders with brilliant streaks of white light. Saída hit four pirates with the bolts, leaving them corpses with searing holes.

"This bitch has illuminite," yelled a Voidstrider.

The rest scrambled to take cover, Belgrave included, who dove behind a storage unit.

Saída kept firing, taking out a few more pirates, but the muzzle of the rifle began to overheat.

"Rodok, the fuel?"

"*Mac* had *it*."

"And where is he?"

They looked around the storage chamber.

"Scav it, we need to go," yelled Saída.

Rodok ran towards the exit, shoulder-tackling the door. It burst open and Rodok disappeared from view. The remaining Voidstriders were beginning to recover but Saída didn't want to stick around for that. She took off, running after Rodok.

*

Outside, Saída noticed that there were two other ships in the distance, both with their ramps still down, but they were floating upwards, their Tetrasteel cables having been severed. Had that been Mac's doing? She looked around. No sign of any Voidstriders. The *Lancer* was still there too, still tethered to the asteroid. Saída made a quick prayer of thanks. Rodok was bounding off towards it. Saída did the same. She spotted a dead pirate on the ground, near the outcropping and stopped to pick up his gun. Saída salvaged what shells she could and loaded them into the Scimitar.

"Status, Rodok?" Saída spoke into her gauntlet as she ran.

"*We* are *all* clear, *I* have *taken*—"

Rodok's voice faded, and the UI of her helmet went wonky as Saída felt a sharp pain to the back of her head. She fell to the ground. The illuminite rifle was knocked from her shoulder. She gritted her teeth and rolled over, grabbing the Scimitar out of her holster.

"Shoulda just handed me the Icon like I'd asked, sweetheart," gloated Belgrave.

She turned to face Belgrave as he aimed to strike her with Digby's golf club, but Saída was a split-second quicker. A tear opened in his spacesuit and blood dripped from his midriff, where the shell had struck.

Saída lay on her back, the barrel of the Scimitar smoking. The Deadzone loomed far above them. In that moment she felt like they would all fall into it.

Belgrave grabbed his side and staggered backwards.

Saída scrambled to her feet and ran, shaking off the pain, working off sheer adrenaline. There was no time to retrieve the rifle. Saída had to go.

She reached the ramp of the *Lancer*, then felt a searing pain hit her leg. She fell onto the ramp. An illuminite bolt had scraped it, causing a tear in the spacesuit.

Saída aimed the Scimitar in the direction of the shot and saw Belgrave lying in the dirt, aiming the rifle at her.

Saída analysed the distance through her prosthetic, copied the suggested angle of the shot and fired.

Before Belgrave could pull the trigger again, the Scimitar's shell collided with his hand, knocking the rifle from him, and turned his fingers into a bloody mess.

"Rodok, get us out of here!" yelled Saída as she tried to crawl up the ramp.

She saw Mac rush out of the depressurisation chamber and come down the ramp. He helped her up.

"Come on, I got you, sand— I got you," he said, helping Saída limp through the depressurisation chamber. The ramp retracted into the *Lancer* and Saída felt the ship lift off. The cables were retracted and immediately, the *Lancer* felt the pull of the Deadzone.

The lights of the newly refuelled *Lancer* shone bright and Rodok set the thrusters to full power, shooting away from Digby's asteroid, away from Belgrave and the Voidstriders and out of the Deadzone's reach.

Saída collapsed onto the floor and pulled off her helmet. Her throat was aching, her head was throbbing. Her ears were ringing, and her leg was burning. But she had the emblem.

She had the emblem and the medallion both.

"Shit, you got hit pretty bad there," said Mac, wincing at the burn on Saída's leg.

"Armoury. Medkit. Now," said Saída through gritted teeth.

"U-uh, right. Right," said Mac and ran off.

Saída checked the tear in the spacesuit. No repairing that. She'd have to toss it into the fabricator for spare parts.

Illuminite bullets were powerful. She hated that she lost the rifle. But it didn't matter.

She finally had it. The emblem. The medallion. The way home was now open to her.

"Uncle," she whispered. Tears welled in her eye. "I'm coming home."

CHAPTER THIRTY-SEVEN

Sektor 47

Saída ran around the back of Hangar Three, praying that Aqsa would be true to her word. The spaceport alarms had been activated and Redcloak presence was beginning to increase. Saída watched through the drone as more patrols spilled into the spaceport. She wasn't sure where Aqsa was, but the dome of the spaceport was still inactive. There was still time.

Saída walked along the back wall of Hangar Three and searched for a way in. Along the middle of the wall was a thin door. Saída tried opening it, but it didn't budge. It felt too rigid. Like it was frozen shut. She tried again, shaking the door-knob, applying more force. Nothing. She kicked at the door in frustration. Still nothing. The sirens continued to scream into the night. The sound filled her heart with dread. It was the sound of danger. Saída had to believe Rodok was inside the warehouse.

Saída tried the door again, slamming into it with

her shoulder. Then again, if Rodok was inside, this door would be wide open. Saída stopped. She clasped a hand over her organic eye and focused on the drone. A bird's eye view of the spaceport appeared before her once more. The dome was still peeled back. So far, Aqsa had managed to keep her word. Somehow. Redcloaks patrolled all over the spaceport. Some checked around the cannons, some around the hangars. A few were getting close to Hangar One. There was still no sign of Rodok.

The Redcloak patrol was inspecting Hangar One. They were too close for comfort. Saída unlinked from the drone and took a moment to collect herself. She had to believe Rodok would make it. Until he did, she had to find a way inside the hangar before she was spotted by the Redcloaks. Saída looked at the door-knob again. She concentrated on it with her prosthetic, gasping when she could see the tumblers inside displayed in bright red. The key slot of the door-knob was old. Something small enough could fit. Saída looked at the scimitar drill in her hand. She hooked the curved edge of the drill inside the key slot of the door-knob. Had this been one of the fancier new doors closer to the Redcloak residential district in the city, it would have required a keycard. The drill slid into the slot and Saída began fiddling with it, trying to find an opening between the tumblers. The blaring alarms masked the sound of her attempt at picking the lock. The Redcloaks were probably on to Hangar Two now. Saída felt beads of sweat forming at her forehead. The drill hooked into one of the tumblers. Saída gently lifted the edge of the drill on the inside. She felt the tip push the tumbler upwards and she felt it click.

Saída took a sharp breath and pushed the drill further in. It was working. Saída looked around, keeping an eye out for any Redcloaks. So far, so good. She resisted the urge to tap into the drone again, instead focusing on the second tumbler. She pushed upwards on the scimitar drill again. Carefully. The tumbler moved up and Saída felt another click. Good. One more would do it. She pushed the drill all the way to the end, until her fingers touched the key slot. She found the third tumbler and pushed against it. Saída struggled to manoeuvre with such little grip, but she managed it, pushing the tumbler upwards with a final, satisfying click. The door was unlocked.

Saída took another look around her. A Redcloak turned the corner of the alley. Saída froze. The alarm deafened whatever the Redcloak tried to call out. He ran at her. Without thinking, Saída withdrew the little scimitar drill from the key slot of the door and plunged it into the Redcloak's gut as he made to grab her. He staggered. Saída stabbed him in his side. The Redcloak's blood smeared the scimitar drill. It was black in the moonlight. The Redcloak fell to his knees and gripped Saída's neck. She could feel his grip weakening. At that moment, Saída remembered something Rodok had told her long ago.

Always wait until you can aim it right here, he had said. Pointing towards his neck.

Saída swung the drill into his neck. His skin tore open as she withdrew the drill and plunged it in again. And again. And again. Blood splattered onto Saída's face, and she fell backwards. The Redcloak clawed helplessly at his throat, choking in a pool of his own blood.

Saída was suddenly grateful for the siren. She didn't

have to hear the sounds of the dying man in front of her. Saída curled up into a ball, dropping the bloody drill on the ground. She had just killed someone. The Redcloak grew still. Saída's body shook uncontrollably. She stared at the blood on her hands. Black-red. She had just killed a human being. Saída remembered the looks on the faces of the Redcloaks that Rodok slaughtered. The ones that had attacked their campfire. The reason they had had to leave Uncle Abbas behind. She remembered how effortlessly he had killed them. Then Saída remembered the Redcloak woman who had grown too suspicious of Rodok. Snuffed out in a moment. The Redcloak Aqsa had stabbed when Saída was writhing in pain on the ground.

Saída clenched her fists trying to control the shaking. She picked up the scimitar drill. She had just killed a Redcloak.

She got up and headed for the door. She turned the door-knob and peered in. It was some kind of storage unit. There was a window ahead and a desk. Maybe it was an office. Saída spied shelves of boxes and other miscellaneous objects strewn around the room. This was a good enough place to hide. Saída looked back at the dead Redcloak. She could feel the blood slick in her short, messy hair. There was no time to get it out.

She grabbed the Redcloak's feet and pulled, straining to drag the corpse into the storage unit-office. It was heavy, but she managed to drag it inside. She didn't want the body found. It would lead the Redcloaks to her faster. Saída used the corpse's cloak to mop up as much blood as she could. She shut the door and activated the lock from the inside, then sat down to take a breath.

331

The room she found herself in seemed to be where the Redcloaks kept goods, storage, and shipping manifestos. Saída saw documents sitting on the desk by a large window that looked out towards the rest of the hangar. There were muffled voices coming from the other side of the glass. Saída crawled towards it, making sure she stayed out of sight.

She could just about make out what the voices were saying.

"—eally finding this shit grating now. The alarms haven't stopped for a second." A gruff, raspy voice boomed. There was something familiar about it. Saída couldn't be sure.

"Calm down, Alistair. They just started a few minutes ago," said another voice. Less gruff. Sounded more tired. Like he wanted to go home. Too familiar.

Saída snuck a peek through the glass. She was looking into the hangar, spying various ships on landing pads. The shutter leading to the outside was closed, and the ships on the inside were all deactivated. Saída saw the roof of the hangar and noticed it was a similar make as the dome of the spaceport. It could be opened. Along the sides of the ceiling, she saw rows of windows. She followed the sound of the voices and her eyes widened in horror. She recognised the two Redcloaks speaking.

Saída felt a sharp pain in her prosthetic eye. Or behind it. Her eye socket. The pain felt fresh like the day she had been attacked. The hulking Redcloak with the spiked metal gauntlets stood next to a ship in the hangar, talking with the skinny Redcloak who had been with him on that day. The day that Saída had lost her eye. The day that everything had begun to change.

Saída ducked under the desk. She was shaking. She felt cold. The pain in her left eye was back. She felt it go hollow and itchy. It wasn't real. It was a phantom pain. Saída winced. But it *felt* real. Her eye burned again. Tears welled in her right eye, her organic eye. She cried. Where was Rodok? She needed him. She curled up on the cold floor, fear and adrenaline causing her small frame to shake uncontrollably.

"Shut up, Roland," said the hulking Redcloak. Alistair. Saída now had a name to his face.

"I'm just saying... You complain too much," said Roland, the skinny Redcloak.

Saída tuned out of the conversation. She couldn't concentrate on what they were saying. Her heart felt like it was being gripped by an iron hand. Like it was being pulled out by the spiked gauntlets of the huge Redcloak. Alistair.

"...Hear about some sandskin... Caught last night... Sounds fun," said Alistair.

"Not my... just trying to fix this... out of here," Roland responded.

Saída couldn't breathe. She shut her eyes and lay down. Her cheek touched the cold metallic floor. The corpse was a few feet away from her. Her whole body shook. She wanted to scream. Scream for Rodok. For Uncle Abbas. Where were they? Why was she all alone? Always alone.

Not alone.

Saída opened her eyes. It was Rodok's voice. Somewhere in the back of her mind. She heard him say that. *Not alone.* That's right. She wasn't alone. Not so long as she had his eye. He was with her.

Saída sat up. She steadied her breathing. Inhaled deeply.

"Okay. Alright," she whispered. "I'm okay."

Saída clenched her fists. She had faith.

"How long is this going to take, anyway?" asked Alistair. Saída heard him through the glass.

She snuck another look from the corner of the window. Alistair and Roland were in the middle of the hangar. Roland wore a necklace. His ship's keycard was attached to it. He slid open a compartment on the hull of his ship, doing some maintenance work using some kind of repair tool. A concentrated blue flame shot out of the tool. It looked like a dagger made of flame. Alistair leaned against the nose of the ship, watching Roland work.

"Almost done. She's good to go but I'll need to run diagnostics in a bit."

Alistair sneered. "Don't know why you had to drag us out here, this late at night. Could've easily fixed her up in the morning."

"Yeah, well, you're the one who insisted on coming with me. I told you I was fine on my own."

Alistair waved his hand dismissively. He looked in the direction of Saída's window and she ducked.

"You see that?" asked Alistair.

"See what?" said Roland.

"I think I saw something back there."

"If you've got time to gaze then you've got time to help. Hand me that Sixer," said Roland.

"Bah…" groaned Alistair.

Saída risked another look. Alistair was handing Roland another tool for the ship. Out of the corner of her eye, Saída noticed movement. She looked to one of the windows on the right wall, near the ceiling. A long, black mechanical arm lifted the window up and a sharp, black face peered in. Rodok! He was outside the building, holding onto the windowsill at the top, surveying the hangar.

Saída let out a little yelp of excitement. She couldn't help it. That drew Alistair's attention. He saw her through the window. Her breathing grew ragged. She could feel the pain in her eye again. Alistair's lips moved.

She couldn't hear him, but Saída managed to make out the words.

Sandskin.

Saída was frozen, eyes wide, as Alistair lumbered towards her. That drew Roland's attention as well. He looked between Alistair and Saída. He dropped the tool he was using and unholstered his gun. Then Rodok jumped in.

The sound of the crash echoed inside the hangar, momentarily drowning out the muffled alarm sirens outside. Alistair turned around. So did Roland. He yelled. Then Rodok's long, black arm impaled Roland, who uselessly grabbed at Rodok's shoulders. He spluttered something unintelligible as Rodok calmly snapped off the keycard necklace Roland was wearing.

Rodok's crimson gaze fixed onto Alistair. Ripping his arm from Roland's chest, Rodok marched towards Alistair. Roland's corpse fell, lifeless, to the side like a sack of meat. Alistair roared and ran at Rodok. His spiked fists scraped against Rodok's chassis, barely scratching the rusted metal. In terms of size, Alistair nearly matched up to Rodok's seven-foot height, but Rodok still swatted Alistair like a bug, sending him flying into another ship with a loud clang. He fell unconscious. Rodok looked at Saída.

She ran out of the storage unit-office door and threw herself at Rodok, hugging him tightly.

"*Saída*, we *need* to *go*, hugs *later*," buzzed Rodok.

Saída let go and nodded. She would hold him to that.

"What now, Rodok?"

Rodok raised the keycard to his eye for a moment and then crushed it in his hand. He tossed it near Roland's corpse. Saída avoided looking at Roland's dead-eyed stare or the injury in his chest.

"*In* here, *Saída*," said Rodok as he gestured to Roland's ship. Rodok placed a hand on the open compartment on the hull and slid it closed. The word *Lance* was painted across the hull in dark red.

Saída placed a hand on it, brushing her palm against the length of the word as she followed Rodok around the ship and up the ramp.

Saída followed Rodok through the depressurisation chamber, through the central area of the ship, the atrium, into the cockpit. Rodok fiddled around with some buttons on the dashboard and unlocked a small panel. He inserted his thumb into a hole in the dashboard. Saída watched as Rodok suddenly deactivated, and she screamed.

"Rodok, what happened? Rodok!" Saída grabbed Rodok and shook him, trying to bring him back to life.

Then the ship reverberated with a boom as the engines roared to life and the lights in the cockpit were activated.

"*Saída*, I *am* alright. *I* am *inside* the *ship*," Rodok's voice buzzed through the *Lance*'s intercom.

"But your body—" Saída began.

"*Do* not *worry*. It *will* be *fine.*"

"Why did you crush the keycard then? We could have used that to pilot the ship," Saída said.

"*No*. The *Redcloaks* would *deactivate* it *remotely*. I *am* running *diagnostics* right *now*. Once *they* are *complete* and *the* ship *is* fully *functional*, I *will* lock *the* Redcloaks *out.*"

Saída nodded. The lights in the ship flickered as Rodok spoke. She marvelled at the way they grew bright and dim in rhythm with Rodok's voice.

"*Saída*, I *need* you *to* do *one* last *thing.*"

Saída suddenly felt nauseous. "What?"

"*Outside* the *ship*, near *the* shutters. *There* is *a* control *panel*. I *need* you *to* deactivate *the* dome *above* the *hangar*. Once *you* do, *we* can *escape.*"

"Alright, Rodok." Saída nodded. "I can do that."

She ran out of the cockpit, through the atrium and the depressurisation chamber and down the ramp. Saída saw the shutters at the far end of the hangar. The control panel was right next to it, just as Rodok had said.

Saída ran up to it and reached for the handle on the control panel window. She threw it open and studied the buttons. There were three. One to unlock the shutters, one to activate emergency lockdown and one to unlock the dome above. Saída slammed the button to unlock the dome. The sound of metal sliding open filled the hangar as the ceiling above parted. The sound of the spaceport alarms flooded in. Saída's grin disappeared when she noticed that far above the hangar itself, the dome of the spaceport had been activated. The gigantic metal dome was slowly closing over the length of the spaceport. Saída cried out. Aqsa had failed. Saída remembered the look on Aqsa's face. No. She was being unfair. Aqsa hadn't failed. She had bought them enough time.

Saída ran back to the *Lance*, screaming at the top of her lungs, "Rodok, the dome is closing, we need to go!"

Saída hopped onto the ramp of the *Lance* and the ship lifted off the ground. Rodok completed the process. They could make it. They *would*.

Saída began to run up the ramp and into the depressurisation chamber when a cold metal hand grabbed onto her leg. She fell face first onto the hard surface of the ramp, her vision blurred, and she became disoriented. She looked behind her and realised as her vision cleared, Alistair was holding onto her leg with one hand, and onto the ramp with the other.

"You're not going *anywhere*, sub-lifer," he growled, pulling at Saída.

Saída screamed and tried to crawl away, but the Redcloak's grip was ironclad. Alistair pulled Saída closer towards himself, as he tried to climb onto the ramp. With the *Lance* gaining altitude, it was becoming harder.

Saída kicked Alistair's face, trying to throw him off but it wasn't working. Her kicks did nothing, and Alistair's scarred face contorted to form a smile as he looked at Saída clearly for the first time.

"I recognise you, sandskin. You're the one-eyed freak," he said. "Got yourself a replacement, did you?"

He squeezed on Saída's leg, and she felt her bones crack beneath the pressure. Saída screamed, she prayed aloud, tears in her eye as she screamed and kicked again, trying to break free. Alistair pulled himself up, closer onto the ramp. The *Lance* was rising up above the hangar. The spaceport dome had closed nearly halfway.

"You're going to die on this dust-ball, sandskin, but before you do, I'll make sure I take your *other* eye too," Alistair growled.

He let go of Saída's leg and raised his fist, intending to bring it down on Saída's face.

His face was so close. She could see the veins popping in his forehead, the way his teeth gnashed as he yelled, the way his eyes bugged out. Saída gritted her teeth and pulled out her scimitar drill from her pocket, driving it into Alistair's left eye. She felt the squelch of the drill piercing his flesh as she dug deeper into the eye socket. Saída yelled in fury as she tried to hook the drill deeper and deeper.

Alistair screamed in agony and clutched his eye in pain, trying to dig out the scimitar drill that Saída had left embedded in his eye. Saída turned her attention to the hand that Alistair was using to hold onto the ramp of the *Lance* and kicked with as much force as she could muster. With each kick she loosened his grip on the ramp. Alistair let go of his eye and tried to go for a punch, but it was too late. With one final kick, Alistair's hand slipped off the ramp and he screeched as he fell back down into the hangar below.

Saída crawled into the depressurisation chamber and the ramp closed up behind her. She had lost Rodok's gift to her, the little scimitar drill. But she was alive.

As she crawled into the cockpit, Rodok's voice boomed through the intercom.

"*Saída*, find *something* to *hold* onto."

Saída grabbed onto the base of one of the seats and held on tight. The dome of the spaceport was almost shut. Redcloaks had taken control of some of the cannons in the spaceport and fired on the *Lance*. Rodok took evasive manoeuvres, avoiding the brunt of the damage, though a few well-placed shots to the hull caused the ship to shake on the inside.

The *Lance* picked up speed and Saída watched as the nose of the ship peeled back, revealing a great, metal battering ram, like a spear. Saída tightened her grip onto the base of the chair and braced for impact.

The ship tore through part of the steel dome, squeezing through in the nick of time, just as the spaceport was fully locked down. Saída felt the vibration through her ribcage as she was thrown against the wall. More shots came for the ship but ended up hitting the dome of the spaceport. Saída looked through a terminal on the dashboard as they left the spaceport behind. The dome had a big *Lance*-shaped hole in the centre where it was joined together. Their ship flew off towards space and Saída watched as the city that had been her whole life shrank into nothing in mere seconds.

Saída was about to say something to Rodok as the *Lance* began to leave the atmosphere of Sektor 47, when a voice buzzed through the intercom.

"*This is Sektor 47 Monitoring Station. We have an unauthorised departure logged from the western hemisphere. State your business.*"

"Copy that, Monitor, this is designation 2-A-1-9-4-7, all permissions received via proper channels. This is an urgent matter. Dispatching codes now."

Rodok perfectly mimicked Roland's voice over the intercom. Saída climbed onto the seat in the cockpit and strapped herself in, gently massaging her injured leg.

After a pause, they spoke again.

"Codes accepted. Glory to the Kaiser. Over and out."

Rodok cut communications and the *Lance* jetted off into outer space.

Saída stared, mouth agape, at the darkness of the void. Millions of tiny stars twinkled all around them and space seemed to go on forever. This was the world above worlds. Saída could barely begin to grasp how big it was.

The *Lance* flew past a big satellite that orbited Sektor 47. The Monitoring Station, Saída assumed. Saída looked at one of the terminals on the dashboard, which showed the *Lance*'s rear-view cameras.

As they flew off into the void of space, Saída got her first true look at Sektor 47. At Meraj. The world had large parts that were dusty brown, but on the edges, Saída could see there was green and there was blue. There was white and there was red. It was beautiful. The Redcloaks hadn't completely ruined it yet. Meraj still defied them. And so would she.

Saída placed a hand on the monitor. Her thoughts wandered to Aqsa. Had she seen them escape? Had Uncle Abbas? Her heart hurt to think of him. Did he know that she and Rodok were finally safe? What was he doing at that moment? Tears fell from her eye as she sobbed quietly.

"Wait for me, Uncle. I'll come back," Saída whispered in Meraji, as she saw her home shrink into a tiny ball as they left it behind.

"I'll come back for you."

CHAPTER THIRTY-EIGHT

Sektor 47

Saída winced as she checked the injury on her leg. She sat on one of the couches in the atrium as she applied a medpatch. The illuminite bolt fired by Belgrave had left a singed cut across her calf muscle. The medpatch would heal it up but it would leave a scar.

"Damn it," Saída muttered. She seemed to be collecting them like Colton and his stupid bottlecaps.

"I think we're good to go," said Mac walking out of the armoury.

"We?" Saída raised her eyebrows. "Don't think we'll let you off that easily, Mac."

"What the hell did I do now?" he asked, shrugging.

"*You* tried *to* run, *for* one *thing*," buzzed Rodok.

"I didn't try to run, I loaded up the engine with fuel. If I'd tried to run, I'd be gone," Mac protested.

Saída scoffed. "Wrong. The only ones who can fly this ship are the ones who know the code. Me and Rodok. You'd be going nowhere."

"What about how I got rid of Belgrave's ships? That's gotta count for something, right?"

Saída put her electro-cuffs on the table and slid them over to Mac with a smug expression.

Mac fell silent and picked up the cuffs. Resigned to his fate, Mac picked a chair and cuffed himself to it, choosing to rest his head against the table.

Saída turned her attention back to her wounds.

"Rodok, did you find the tracker?" Saída touched the fading blue mark on her eye. The bruises from her fight with Gideon were healing.

"I *conducted* a *full*-body *scan* of *the* Lancer. *I* detected *a* foreign *body* inside *the* ship *vents*. It *has* been *removed* and *destroyed*. The *Voidstriders* can *no* longer *track* our *movements.*"

"Good," breathed Saída. "Then all we need to worry about now is getting back into Sektor 47."

"*We* will *be* approaching *shortly*, Saída."

Saída got up and walked to the cockpit. "Do you think those Monitor people will remember us?"

"I *do* not *think* so. *We* have *broken*, repaired *and* modified *the* Lancer *too* many *times* for *it* to *appear* as *the* same *ship* it *was* eleven *years* ago. *And* of *course*, the *ID* code *is* completely *different.*"

Saída nodded. "You're right."

"*You* are *worried.*"

"I am. Something always goes wrong. Especially when we're so close."

"*Then* we *will* deal *with* it, *like* we *deal* with *everything.*"

"Don't get cheesy on me, stupid Rodok."

"I *would* never, *silly* Saída."

Saída pulled the medallion out of her pocket and set it on her lap, then fished out the emblem, Digby's Icon, and compared it to the medallion. The slot in the medallion was a perfect fit for the Icon. Saída slotted it in and the two connected with a snap. The emblem of the Hickston family was a seagull with wings outstretched over a body of water. Saída rotated the emblem with her thumb. The medallion was finally complete. They had been on the hunt for a way back to Meraj for years. Escaping Daiyu, becoming a bounty hunter for Matthias, then on Digby's trail for the last four years. Now, in the weeks since they first booked Mac on Sektor 31-B, the moon, Little Hal, Saída finally allowed herself to feel happy. She had done it. Uncle Abbas was finally within reach. She grasped the medallion tight in her hand and looked out the window of the *Lancer*.

Sektor 47. No. Meraj. Finally, in her sights once more. After eleven years, she gazed upon the dust-brown, blue, green, white, red world once more. She noticed that there was far more dust-brown and far less colour than she remembered. Saída frowned. The Redcloaks hadn't stopped leeching off her world's resources. They hadn't stopped using her people as miners, forcing them into servitude and making profits off of their backs. Saída closed her eyes. She remembered Uncle Abbas. The way his eyebrows would crease his dark-brown skin. The way his brown eyes twinkled whenever they shared a laugh. The twitch of his bushy black moustache. She was here for Uncle Abbas. That was all. She had to let everything else go.

"Halt, cruiser. This is Sektor 47 Monitoring Station. You are approaching restricted space. State your purpose."

The voice buzzed through the intercom on the dashboard. Saída felt a pit in her stomach. It was finally time. She pressed the button to speak.

"Monitoring Station, this is Captain Abbas of the *Lancer*. My purpose is trade and transport. I have special permission from Viceroy Hickston himself. Transmitting a scan to you now."

Saída grabbed the medallion and placed it on the scanning board on the dash. The medallion was suspended in mid-air and floated as a complete scan was taken of it. Saída pushed another button, and the data scan was transmitted to the Monitoring Station.

The station orbited around Sektor 47 like Saída remembered, but it was different now. Newer. The station had definitely seen upgrades since the last time she saw it. It was possibly even completely new.

Static over the intercom.

"Transmission received and approved. Captain Abbas, you are clear to land on the eastern hemisphere. Sending over coordinates to an approved spaceport now."

Saída frowned. "Hold on. Repeat, Monitor. Eastern hemisphere? I need to get to the west. Can you provide coordinates to a designated landing zone there?"

"I'm afraid that the west is a restricted zone. Civilians are prohibited from entering. Transmitting coordinates to an approved spaceport in the east now."

"I have the Viceroy's express permission. I demand to be let into the west," Saída said, slamming her arm on the dash.

"The western hemisphere is a restricted zone. The order came from the Viceroy himself. No exceptions and

345

that includes the passport that you provided. Coordinates transmitted. Please land where directed. Even the Viceroy's guests are beholden to the law. Glory to the Kaiser."

The comms shut off with another bout of static and Saída slumped in her seat.

"I don't believe this. Why the hell is it restricted?"

"Saída. It does not matter. We are clear to land. We will find a way back home when we can," buzzed Rodok.

Saída nodded. "Take us down."

The *Lancer* flew past the Monitoring Station and towards the more colourful side of Sektor 47. Towards the green, red, white side of the world. Saída tore her eyes away from the dust-brown side of her home. The restricted zone of Sektor 47. Saída frowned. She hoped Uncle Abbas was okay down there. If anyone knew how to make the best out of a bad situation, it was him. They would see each other soon enough.

The beautiful blue skies of Meraj greeted the *Lancer* as it entered the atmosphere of the planet. Saída gasped in awe as the *Lancer* dropped further below, across a magnificent blue lake. She grinned as Rodok tipped the ship slightly, digging one of its fins into the water and splashing it across the window of the *Lancer*.

Across the lake was a spaceport and Rodok lifted the *Lancer* back into the air and in through the open roof. Saída noticed that there were no hangars inside the spaceport. It was much smaller than many she had seen, especially the one that they had escaped eleven years ago. The *Lancer* landed on one of the open pads, among other ships and Saída noticed the gates of the spaceport were open. People walked in and out like it was nothing.

"What the hell is going on…?" Saída mumbled. She unstrapped herself from the seat, grabbed the medallion and ran outside.

"*Saída* wait," buzzed Rodok but she didn't listen.

Saída ran through the depressurisation chamber, down the ramp and onto the landing pad.

She didn't see any Redcloaks. She saw people like her. Citizens of Meraj. They walked and talked and mingled like normal. No sense of fear, no looking over their shoulders. Nothing.

Saída ran towards the gates. The city welcomed her in. Proper roads leading into the spaceport. Pavements to walk on the side. She followed them, finding herself being drawn in by a storybook version of Meraj that she thought only existed in history, in her dreams. Beautiful buildings on the outside. The kinds of buildings Uncle Abbas would describe in his stories. The kinds of buildings that no longer existed on Meraj. Not since the Redcloaks came and took everything over. Large white, brown, and red buildings with pointed arches, onion domes, minarets. Saída saw rich and colourful symmetrical symbols proudly displayed across the buildings. She saw children playing in the streets with no fear of retribution from the Redcloaks. Vendors yelling about food and clothes, men and women chatting without a care in the world.

Saída felt her heart racing.

"Excuse me, you forgot to register your ship at the spaceport," said a mild-mannered woman.

Saída turned around. It was a Meraji woman. She wore a blue kurta and she flashed Saída a friendly smile.

"Oh, you're Meraji?" she asked.

Saída tensed up. She smelled the fresh, crisp air of Meraj for the first time.

What the hell was going on?

"Yes," Saída stuttered in Meraji. "Yes, I am."

Acknowledgements

My sincerest gratitude to my amazing agent, Annette Crossland, who has gone above and beyond for me. I am forever grateful to have been so lucky to have her as my agent.

I am grateful to The Book Guild for everything they have done for Sektor 47. My thanks to Daniel Burchmore, Rosie Lowe, Sophie Morgan and Ian Skewis.

Many thanks to the following people who helped me get here: the Creative Writing Faculty at Birkbeck University and my fellow writers of Cohort 2020-2021 MA creative writing. My special thanks to SJ Kim, known to us as Jodie, you are absolutely brilliant and I learned so much from you. Thank you also to the amazing talent and doyen of the creative writing program at Birkbeck, Julia Bell, without whom I would have stumbled longer.

Thank you to Jonathan Barnes for his valuable feedback, encouragement and wonderful quote.

Awais Khan, you have been a great teacher, a wonderful friend and older brother. Thank you for everything.

Thank you to my friends like brothers, Murad, Furqan, Harris, Saad and Hashim for always being there for me through thick and thin and beyond. Thank you for your wonderful friendship.

My thanks to my family for their support always.